WHISPERS
IN THE DARK

LAUREL HIGHTOWER

JOURNALSTONE
YOUR LINK TO ARTIST TALENT

JournalStone books may be ordered through booksellers or by contacting:
JournalStone
www.journalstone.com

The views expressed in this work are solely those of the authors and do not necessarily reflect the views of the publisher, and the publisher hereby disclaims any responsibility for them.

ISBN: 978-1-947654-61-7 (sc)
ISBN: 978-1-947654-62-4 (ebook)

JournalStone rev. date: December 7, 2018

Library of Congress Control Number: 2018959588

Printed in the United States of America

Cover Art & Design: Mikio Murakami
Interior Layout: Jess Landry

Edited by Scarlett R. Algee
Proofread by Sean Leonard

DEDICATION

For Sebastian, because everything I have belongs to you.

ACKNOWLEDGMENTS

Many thanks to my mother, Lynn Hightower, for reading, encouragement, and invaluable feedback. Also for being a living reminder that writing is worth it. Thanks to my agent, Matt Bialer, and Christine Herman of Sanford J. Greenburger Associates for taking the time to read a rookie author, for agreeing to take me on, and for excellent feedback to make this a better book. Thanks to the folks at JournalStone—Christopher Payne for giving me a chance, to Scarlett Algee for diligent editing and fact checking, and to Jess Landry for helping me every step of the way. Thanks to Alan Hightower and Rachel Ballard, as well as Katie Stephens and Wes Ballard, for being my family and my cheerleaders. Thanks to Scott Rodgers, former law enforcement officer, for showing me around and letting me pick your brain, then for continuing to answer my panicked emails to help me get it right. Anything I screwed up is on me. To Nikki Beaven for making the trek to Memphis with me, and to Jess Clark and Stephanie Woolery for being my go-to Halloween and horror girls. Thanks to Julia Ritchie for fitting me into your crazy schedule for photos, not just once but twice. Thanks to the crew at work (and those who have moved on, but are still my crew) for cheering me on, for good-natured ribbing, and for making mine the kind of job that gives me head space to do the other things I love.

For anyone I may have neglected to mention, please know it's almost certainly a result of sleep-deprivation, and good for one free bourbon by way of apology.

Thanks finally to Arthur Wells, for encouragement, incredible music, and being an all-around awesome guy. To my husband, David Wells, for always being game for working vacations, for being supportive, for being a sounding board, and a partner in life. I wouldn't want to do this with anyone else. And to Sebastian, for finally showing up. I can't claim you give me the time to work, but you're the reason I get it done.

DISCLAIMER

I visited Memphis in August several years ago while researching this novel. Between eating and listening to amazing music, I spent a lot of time driving around, making notes, taking pictures, and trying to get it right. I'll admit to taking some liberties with the city's geography, partly due to my own terrible sense of direction and spatial analysis. I hope Memphis residents will forgive me, and recognize in my writing a deep admiration for this southern gem. Few places keep their promises as well as Memphis—blues, barbeque, incredible architecture and southern charm.

WHISPERS
IN THE DARK

CHAPTER ONE

It wasn't much, that bare inch of scalp sticking up beyond the protective concrete wall Charlie Akers crouched behind. Wispy blond strands ruffled in the light breeze, giving away just enough of his location for me to center him in my scope. He probably wasn't aware that any part of him was visible at all, but an inch was plenty for me. One shot and I could take the cap of his skull off, scatter his brains across the bricks behind him, and end this standoff. The index finger of my right hand was light on the trigger, my shoulder braced for the recoil. I let myself picture it, indulge in the fantasy. Anything to take my mind off the way my knee had begun to cramp.

It never mattered what position I took up at the start of one of these damned things, it always got uncomfortable. Usually I can risk moving, take a moment to shift my leg and ease the screaming joint, but not now. We were in the magic hour, the decisive time at the end of a standoff that would decide who was going to walk away whole. I didn't think it would be Akers.

Three days ago, he had knocked on the door of the apartment where his estranged wife had been hiding with their two young children. When Laura Akers opened the door, he shoved his way in and pushed a gun into the soft flesh of her stomach, promising to kill the kids in front of her if she didn't come with him. Laura's mother, disabled from an old back injury, had been hiding in silence in the bathroom and called 911 as soon as it was safe. A patrol car in the area had picked up Akers' trail as he took off with Laura and the kids, and the ensuing chase had brought him here, to a split-level home on the wrong side of Union, the weed-choked yard and foreclosure sign making it a tempting hideaway. Akers had fired at officers before leading them on a high-speed chase, and my team doesn't like guys who put kids in danger. Besides, he'd painted himself into a corner. Somehow, he'd convinced himself he was going to walk away with his family in tow. I wasn't sure if that was an indication of how far off the deep end he was, or a testament to the skill of Zack Dayton and his team of negotiators. Probably a little of both.

I was listening to Zack now through my earpiece, laying out the plan for Akers in calm tones: the agreement to exchange an RV stocked with food and a full gas tank for a peaceful release of his family. Akers' responses were less audible, but I wasn't concerned with that. Ben Teeters was crouched to my right, well within my peripheral vision and monitoring a channel that gave him a clear playback of the interaction down in the field. If things went wrong and Zack needed help before Lieutenant Llewellyn was able to issue the order, Ben could easily signal me to take the shot. I knew things would have to go pretty fucking bad before Zack would ask for that signal. He believed in the inherent good of people, and the preservation of life above all things. Even the lives of wife-beating, child-endangering creeps like Charlie Akers.

I was sweating mercilessly in the Memphis summer heat, sweltering in the thin gloves and long-sleeved top I always wore. Rivulets of sweat ran between my breasts and down my back, my clothes sticking in all the wrong places. I tried not to concentrate on it, tried to move all discomforts to the back of my mind. A black S.W.A.T. ball cap kept my thick curly hair back and the sweat out of my eyes, and that was all that mattered. I could see the tip of a tiny sneaker poking out into the grass at the edge of the concrete slab where Akers crouched, and that helped me keep my focus where it should be. The sneaker was grubby and tilted sideways, a child's habit of splaying ankles outwards. From time to time it twitched or kicked a bit, and those small movements kept my heartbeat steady, my finger loose on the trigger. I wasn't sure if the shoe belonged to the boy or the girl. They were both little, separated in age by less than a year. Zack had assured me that both children were safe, but only as long as Akers maintained his sense of control. I had no choice but to believe him for now, but I had long suspected that Zack used his negotiation tactics on the sniper and assault teams as well as on the perps. There had been no sight or sound of Laura Akers for two days now, and I had already filed Charlie Akers' wife in the sunk cost category.

"*Sergeant.*" The whisper was in my right ear, cutting into the negotiation byplay. It was only one word, but I knew who it was. Irritation rose, and I made myself quash it before answering, softly, steadily, without losing sight of my target.

"What is it, Landers?"

"*You still got the shot, Sarge?*"

"Affirmative."

"*Think maybe you should go ahead and take it?*"

I made myself take two deep breaths before answering, reminding myself this wasn't the time to deal with insubordination. "I think you should shut up and pay attention, and let the Lieutenant worry about when to order the shot." The channel went silent and I tuned back in to what Zack was saying.

"Charlie, you know I can't promise you that. What did we talk about? This is a give and take situation. I can't give you something without you giving something in return." There was a garbled response I couldn't understand, but Zack's tone was strained when he spoke again. "Charlie. We've talked about this. I can't make them go away. That team is here to make sure your kids are safe. They're not going to do anything without my say so"—someone snorted to my left—"but they're not going away, either. You're just going to have to trust me."

I frowned. Things had deteriorated in the few seconds I'd been distracted by Landers. Akers had been on the verge of coming out, had already agreed to do so without exchange of gunfire so he could take possession of the promised RV and head to California. The RV was a myth. Zack's job was to gain Akers' trust, not to let him get away with his hostages in tow. Zack was great at the building trust part, and I knew it bothered him when he had to outright lie to these guys. He preferred to talk them around to a sense of reality whenever possible, give them concessions like food, water, the use of a phone. Zack called the perps who could be reasoned with honestly "Type Ones." He always preferred dealing with Type Ones, and so did I. You rarely had to pull the trigger on a Type One.

Charlie Akers was clearly a Type Two, one of the guys who clung stubbornly to the fantasy of escape, a clean break, and no jail time. A fulfillment, in fact, of the twisted reasoning that led them to kidnap their kids, an ex-girlfriend, or some innocent hostage in the first place. Although Zack could start with small concessions to a Type Two, he knew that to end the standoff, he would have to lie. I watched the back of his broad shoulders, tensed with anxiety that never surfaced in his voice, sweating through the back of his white button-up shirt. The sleeves were rolled up to his elbows, displaying thick forearms covered in dark hair and a pair of large but graceful hands. Just now, those hands were positioned in a gesture of supplication. It was hard for me to tell whether that was part of the persona, part of the reality he had to sell to Akers, or whether things had really gone south. I was keyed to any hint of motion from Ben on my right, but everything was still for now.

A crackle of radio static, then Llewellyn's sharp tones. "Snipers, steady on. Hold fire but confirm targets are locked. Who's got the shot?"

"McFarland here, target acquired," I breathed into my mic, keeping my eyes forward. Sanders and North, the other two snipers, confirmed their positions but advised they didn't have a clear shot.

Landers' voice broke in again. *"I don't like this, boss. Zack looks like he's in trouble."*

I bit down on my lower lip. I might agree with him, but Landers

12

was nowhere on the chain of command, much to his chagrin, and breaking in on the conversation was akin to answering your cell phone in church.

Llewellyn must have felt the same way. Irritation crept into his voice, betraying the exhaustion we were all feeling after two days of high tension. "Fuck off, Landers. You break into this channel one more time and I'm gonna have McFarland acquire *you*."

There was no response, but I could hear several choked-off laughs from the ranks behind me. Landers was that consistent pain in the ass that adorns every unit, and he had grown steadily worse as it became clear that I'd had beaten him out for the promotion to the soon-to-be vacant position of team leader. Right now dealing with Landers was Llewellyn's problem, but it would soon be mine, a prospect I did not relish. I pushed the thought aside. This standoff was going to end soon, and I got the feeling Zack wasn't going to be happy with the outcome.

As though my doubts had conjured disaster, everything went to hell in a matter of seconds. I heard a shot, saw Zack drop to the ground, and at the same time Ben began signaling me wildly. My finger tightened on the trigger, but Akers' head had dropped out of sight behind the concrete wall again.

"Fuck—no shot," I hissed. Sanders and North quickly reported they still had no shot from their locations either, which wasn't surprising. Mine was the best vantage point.

"Come on, asshole, show your face. Just a little." A tantalizing fluff of blond hair rose into sight just where Akers' head had been, fluttering softly. I waited for the order from Llewellyn, but command was silent.

"Take the shot, Sarge," whispered Ben from my left, a request that was repeated several times across the channels that connected us, but something stayed my hand. With every nerve crying out to end the life of the guy who'd just dropped my friend in the field, I hesitated. Something wasn't right, and a minute later it became clear what that was. A crumpled pink bow flitted into sight, inexpertly tied and sitting askew atop the blonde head of Akers' daughter, who had hair just like her father's.

"Son of a *bitch*," said Ben. "That cocksucker just tried to bait us with his own kid." Two small voices, crying in abject misery, reached our ears through the mic still connected to Zack's shoulder. The sound pierced my heart, as it always had when my own children were small.

"Okay," I breathed. Before I could think better of it, I stood, and in one motion sighted Charlie Akers, now visible from my unprotected position. He was just turning to take his shot at me when I squeezed the trigger. Instead of dropping out of view I stayed where I was, waiting to see the outcome of my gamble. Relief swept through me as Akers dropped hard, missing his daughter by inches while she sobbed beside him. I waited but he didn't move again.

"Target neutralized."

* * *

Members of the Shelby County Sheriff's S.W.A.T. team swarmed the cracked and broken driveway, pulling both kids out from behind the retaining wall that had preserved Charlie Akers' life for that long, sweltering afternoon. Zack began to move, stiff and sore from the shot that had hit him hard in the center of the vest he wore. The vests would stop most bullets from tearing into your skin, but they still left a hell of a bruise.

I sank to a crouch as my team burst into impromptu applause. Ducking my head, I squeezed my eyes shut against the dizziness that hit me with a vengeance.

The music floated by just then, tantalizingly close, the tinny sound of an old radio tuned to a faraway station, bringing goosebumps despite the heat of the day. It had followed me for years now, drifting in and out too quickly for me to identify, a phantom tune only I could hear, familiar but always just out of reach. It reminded me in some indefinable way of my long-lost older brother Andy, of the music he used to play on the cruddy old radio he'd bought secondhand and fixed himself. Andy had been dead for years now, but I liked to believe the music was him saying hello. It was an oddity, but a happy one, and it had helped me through everything from my sheriff's academy entrance exams to dealing with my divorce.

The world in front of me seemed to shimmer, waver, and I was hit with sudden vertigo. I clutched the raised lip of the roof, fighting against the feeling that I was going to pitch over the side. A moment later the music faded, along with the sense of otherworldliness it had brought. As it always had before, the musical visitation had calmed me, emptying my head of the inevitable images of what would have happened if I'd missed. I breathed easier, keeping my grip on the rough concrete while I got my equilibrium back.

I was glad I hadn't let go when a hand on my shoulder made me flinch and nearly lose my balance. I looked up to meet Ben Teeters' eyes, shining with boyish excitement.

"Way to go, Sarge," he said, grinning. "That was a hell of a shot."

I smiled, but was unable to keep my gaze from dropping to his hand, still resting on my arm. As he realized what he'd done, Ben quickly let go, then stood, his smile dimming.

I stood too, checking the safety on my rifle and allowing myself another minute to catch my breath. When I felt steady, I swung around and headed down from the roof of the adjacent house I'd been crouching on. I noticed Ben still standing awkwardly next to me and tried to smile more naturally.

"C'mon, kid, let's go check on our buddy Zack and see if he's interested in buying us some beer." This time I touched him lightly on his shoulder, and his face cleared. He followed me as I dropped neatly to the dormer below and from there swung into the open window of the house my team had commandeered for the last two days. I was sure the owners would be glad to get it back.

Bonnie Skylar from the Bureau of Professional Standards and Integrity, what used to be Internal Affairs, was waiting for me down on the ground, dark sunglasses and sharp features giving her an unfriendly look. She, or someone from B.P.S.I., would have been on scene from the beginning of the standoff in order to step in as soon as shots were fired. She held her hand out for my weapon when she saw me come through the front door. Everyone was giving her a wide berth, but I smiled and nodded as I handed over the rifle. Her pinched face relaxed slightly.

"Ready to debrief, Sergeant McFarland?"

It was protocol for B.P.S.I. to investigate any officer-involved shootings for the sheriff's department as soon as possible after they occurred. Every good cop understands the need to self-patrol, to protect ourselves from accusations of corruption or even criminal behavior, and to keep the public's faith in us. There's nothing a straight cop hates more than a bent one, but it doesn't change the apprehension you feel when you're being investigated, and it doesn't stop the knee-jerk dislike and distrust the rest of us feel around B.P.S.I.'s people.

"Almost," I answered. "Give me a few to check on Zack, get my team rounded up?"

Bonnie pursed thin lips and thought about it, finally acquiesced. "Be quick, please."

I nodded, and she turned to walk back to her vehicle, an old unmarked Crown Vic.

Ben, who had fallen silent in Bonnie's presence, quickly recovered as he jogged next to me to catch up to the rest of our team. "If you'd fired when we told you to, you'd have taken out that little girl. How did you know he'd do that?"

I shook my head. "I didn't know it, not for sure. But I'd lost visual on the kids, and you *never* take a blind shot, Ben. Remember that, no matter what anyone else tells you."

He smiled. "Even you?" Ben was training to be a sniper, would take over my spot once my promotion went through.

"Even me, kiddo." I tapped him lightly on the chest. "Your eye behind the scope, your bullet, your responsibility. Now, round up the rest of the guys and do a weapons check, please. See if patrol needs any help winding things up, then let's get out of here and get a drink."

Ben grimaced. "Aren't you stuck with the SS over there?" He nodded toward Skylar, who was waiting by the car, watching us closely.

I smiled. "It won't take too long—I'll meet y'all there."

He nodded and turned.

"Hey, do you see the Lieutenant anywhere?" I asked.

Ben gestured over his shoulder, and I turned to see Llewellyn deep in conversation with Tara Middleton, our press liaison officer. I wondered what the hell had happened down here that he had never issued an order to shoot, or even given me an update. He caught my gaze and gave me a brief, unsmiling nod. We weren't allowed to discuss the incident until we'd both been debriefed, but I was looking forward to getting an explanation.

I returned his nod, then looked around for Zack. I spotted him sitting on the curb, but before I could take a step in his direction, I felt a light touch on my shoulder.

"Sergeant McFarland?"

I turned to find a compact, athletically built stranger smiling down at me. He was four or five inches taller than my shrimpy five-two, and I guessed his age at forty, maybe forty-five. It was hard to tell exactly—his face was tanned and weathered in a way that suggested a lifetime of outdoor pursuits, his hair mostly a silver gray, cut short. He was good-looking, with that irritating knack some men have of getting better with age, so I found myself smiling back despite my annoyance at his proximity.

"That's me."

A wider smile now, revealing straight white teeth. "I'm Evan Neal. Do you have a moment?"

I frowned. "That depends on what you want. I have a lot to do to tie this scene up, Mr. Neal." I looked behind him. "How did you get past patrol? This is a crime scene."

He produced a badge and flipped it open. "Actually, it's Agent Neal, but please, call me Evan."

I studied the ID. "FBI? Why are the feds interested in a loser like Charlie Akers?"

"Sarge? Little help over here?"

It was Landers, standing twenty feet away next to a stack of gear with an impatient look on his soft, entitled face. He flung his hands up at me, and I resisted the urge to flip him the bird.

"Sergeant McFarland, I would appreciate an opportunity to—"

"Agent Neal, I'm sorry, this is a bad time. It's my Lieutenant you'll want to speak with anyway—David Llewellyn, he's over there." I gestured vaguely over my shoulder and turned away, but was brought up short when Neal grabbed my elbow.

"Sergeant McFarland, it really is important that we talk as soon as possible." His eyes were hard, his mouth set in a tight, thin line when

I turned back. "It's you I want, not your Lieutenant."

I looked down at his hand clutching my arm, then reached around with my free hand and clamped his wrist at the joint, squeezing to grind the bones against one another. He held on for as long as he could before finally releasing me with a sharp gasp.

"You don't touch me, Neal. Ever." I turned my back on him and resumed my beeline for Zack. Don't fuck with a powerlifter, asshole.

"Rose." He'd recovered his sangfroid, though he sounded a little out of breath. "I'm staying at the Ashland, room 206. I'll need to hear from you by week's end, do you understand? It's in your best interest."

I didn't slow down, and I didn't look back, but I felt his eyes on me, and it gave me the creeps. Who the hell was this guy, showing up at my scene and making demands on my time? I wished I'd thought to memorize his badge number—it might be smart to find out more about him.

Zack was still on the curb in front of the house, twisted around to stare back at it. His gaze was unfocused, his lips parted. He'd peeled off the vest and was absently prodding his ribcage, where a welt was beginning to rise.

"Nice battle scar there, Zack."

He gave me a shaky smile. "Nice shot, Rose," he said after I sat down next to him, heaving an enormous sigh as my exhaustion caught up with me.

We sat in companionable silence, getting our bearings while activity swirled around us. "Why didn't you signal earlier?" I asked after a while, and he sighed, having known I was going to ask the question, just as I knew what his answer would be.

"I gave him the benefit of the doubt, Rose. That man was disturbed, suffering from a number of delusions, and I thought there was a good chance we could lose those kids."

I nodded and said nothing else. It was an old dance between us. I studied him discreetly as he tried to shrug back into his sweat-soaked shirt. Zack was a big guy in his mid-forties, tall and thick, with dark hair beginning to thin at the top and a full beard and mustache. His pale skin and soft midsection led some of the guys to think he was soft around the edges as well, but I knew better. He was a powerful man, and almost frighteningly intelligent. Just now he looked incredibly weary, and I remembered that Zack was likely to consider this job a failure on his part, and suffer because of it.

I placed a gloved hand on his bare one. "Did they find Laura Akers?"

He nodded without looking up.

"She dead?" I asked, and he nodded again, no change in his expression. "I'm sorry, Zack. You did good out there." He said nothing and I stood slowly, my joints stiffening as the adrenaline left my system. "Meet us for a beer later?"

He shook his head. "Don't much feel like it, Rose."

I gripped his shoulder. "Call me if you need me, Zack." I turned to find my team.

"Rose." His voice was quiet, and he avoided my eyes. "Did anything seem...different to you this time?"

I frowned. "Different how?"

"Just—like there was more to it than usual. I mean, these guys are inevitably disturbed somehow, but this is the first time I've wondered whether maybe—" He looked up at me, embarrassed. "Akers was talking about things, talking *to* them, really. It was almost like there was something else in there with him."

I felt cold but kept my tone even as I knelt down again. "Some-*thing*? Not some*one*?"

Zack flushed, shrugged, opened his mouth then closed it again, forced an unconvincing laugh. "That was an odd way to put it, wasn't it? I guess it was just the way I thought of it."

"Thought of what?"

"The second night. It's crazy, but I could have sworn I heard some-thing—sorry, some*one*—answer him. Akers, I mean."

"We've cleared the house. You think someone could still be in there?"

"No, that's not what I'm saying. At least—" He stopped, his eyes troubled, finally shook his head. "Never mind. I need to go back and listen to the tapes."

As a matter of procedure, there would have been recordings made of the negotiation team's interactions with Akers over the two-day standoff. I hadn't been looped into that channel, but I wondered what the hell Zack had heard.

He saw me watching him and flapped his big hands at me. "Go, Rose. You've got things to do. And listen, thanks. You did what I couldn't today. My wife thanks you, too."

I watched him for a minute, but I knew that look. I wasn't going to get anything else out of him today; he would need to process it first. I finally nodded, stood again, gave his shoulder a final pat. "Of course. Come talk to me if you find anything on the tapes you want me to hear."

Zack smiled and turned away again, staring back at the split-level house where one more deluded perp had made his last stand. Zack hadn't reached out to touch me back, knowing well the lesson that some of my team, including Ben, forgot from time to time. I don't want to be touched, for any reason. It's not that I'm antisocial or somehow cold. I crave human interaction as much as anyone else and I would have been glad to be able to accept a congratulatory clap on the shoulder, a comforting stroke of the arm, a hug. I don't allow physical contact for the same reason I wear long sleeves and gloves even in the heat of summer: to maintain the comfort of those around me. The moment someone touches me, they're reminded of what lurks beneath my clothes, the bumped and gnarled flesh of my arms and a good portion of my chest, back, and stomach. I've tattooed over most of the angry red skin, but the texture is still obvious to the touch.

I'm lucky that most of my face escaped the fire that ravaged my childhood home eighteen years ago, killing my father and my older brother Andy and striking a death blow to my relationship with my mother, the only one of us to end that horrible night completely unscathed. It's mostly my right side that's damaged, and the scars stop below the neckline of most shirts. The exception is a slim pucker of red that snakes up my neck to my right ear, pulling the flesh of my face ever so slightly in that direction. When I'm not wearing a hat, I can easily fix my hair to hide the damage. You wouldn't necessarily notice the altered alignment of my face unless you were looking for it, or at least that's what my ex-husband tells me. He says it makes me look a little like a pirate, so I'm not sure how far to trust Sam's judgment.

To be honest, I wasn't terribly concerned with my appearance, and only hid the scars to avoid the gaps in conversation they cause. Beauty never troubled me, and that's a freeing thing, more so than most people can imagine. Burned and scarred as I am, I was able from a young age to divorce my sense of worth from my appearance. I never walked into a room and compared myself to the women in it, knowing that I'd come out last every time. I never worried about beauty making either of my husbands stray—I knew that if they chose to be with me, they must not value appearance. When I got out of rehabilitation at the age of eighteen and knew I was never going to look normal again, I'd made a decision to reinvent myself. In so doing, I severed a bond that has kept so many women—and men—from achieving their full potential. And I never had to worry about cellulite.

As I reached the top of the driveway, I glanced up again at the house. A foreclosure that had seen better days, the facade was half brick and half yellowed siding. A couple of the windows closer to ground level had been broken, but the upstairs windows were intact and dark. I shivered despite the heat, and wondered what Zack might have heard in the dead of night.

The techs had finished taking pictures of Akers' body, and the EMTs had just rolled him onto his back. No one said anything, but they stopped when I approached and eased back to let me through. I dropped to one knee beside Akers, wanting to see the face of the man whose life I'd ended, a ritual I perform after every kill shot to make sure I always remember there are people on the other end of my rifle.

I was prepared for the mess I'd made of the top of his skull, but his face froze me in place. Even with my extra layers, my flesh crawled with cold and my chest went tight. He was looking right at me, his dead eyes dark and empty, his mouth locked in a teeth-baring grin. I was struck by a horrible sense of familiarity, something I couldn't place; staring at his grotesque, frozen features, I had the unnerving sense that I knew him. As I watched, his lower jaw dropped and his head turned toward me.

"*Hello, Rose,*" he said in a voice at once impossibly familiar and completely alien.

I choked, falling backward on my ass. *Not again*, I thought, squeezing my eyes shut and willing the vision to go away. But when I opened them again, the scene hadn't changed, and years' worth of repressed and carefully forgotten terror pushed to the front of my mind.

It wasn't possible, I reminded myself. I could see his brains on the pavement behind him. He couldn't be alive, and he couldn't know my name. Those dead eyes still tracked me, and I turned to the right, gripping the arm of the EMT closest to me.

"Did you..." I managed to say before I registered the man's surprised look. A glance to my left showed the same expression on the faces of the other EMT and one of the techs, but their focus was on me, not the corpse. Turning back, I saw Charlie Akers the way he should look, his face blank and his eyes glassy, fixed on nothing. Of course, no one else had seen what I had.

"You okay?" asked the guy on my right as I let go of his arm.

"Yeah, sure." I stood, my legs shaking. I kept my eyes down as I walked away, avoiding eye contact as I headed for Bonnie Skylar. Embarrassment made my face hot, but I tamped down the despair. It wasn't happening again. The world of the dead wasn't pushing its way back into mine—I'd left all that behind years ago.

As I reached the edge of the scene and ducked under the tape, I saw Evan Neal watching me, his eyes unreadable and the faintest of smiles on his lips.

* * *

Post-shooting debriefings are never pleasant. Every move you make during an intense life-and-death struggle is scrutinized minutely by armchair quarterbacks with all the benefit of 20/20 hindsight. "Why didn't you take an earlier shot, Sergeant McFarland?" they ask with judgment in their voices, having never fired their weapons outside of the range. It's easy to get riled up and defensive, but this wasn't my first rodeo, and I didn't take things as personally as I had the first time. Skylar was her usual unsmiling self, but all things considered, my debriefing went quickly and as painlessly as possible. For once, I was even thankful for the necessity—it calmed me and dragged my focus away from the impossible thing I'd seen.

I called my ex-husband Sam from the car before entering Louie's. It was a raucous jazz bar several blocks removed from the non-stop party of Beale Street, where my team always celebrated our victories and drowned our defeats. I let Sam know I was okay, that we'd resolved the situation and both kids had come out unscathed. He accepted my abbreviated report, as he'd finally learned to do after countless fights and sleepless nights. I didn't say anything about shooting Akers or Zack getting hurt, and Sam didn't ask. After five years of marriage and six years of divorce, Sam still worried about me. He gave me a brief update on the kids and told me he'd see me in the morning.

I knew I was lucky. A lot of single mothers would be facing custody battles or attitude from their exes if they were gone as often as I am, then chose to go out with the guys instead of rushing home to make up for time with my kids that had been cut short by work. The problem was that without this period of detox, these few hours of beer and easy camaraderie, the Rose McFarland that picked those kids up wouldn't really be their mother. I needed that division between the sniper who ended a man's life and the mother who curled up with her kids and sang them to sleep. Sam knew that, and never judged me for it.

Though sparsely populated when we first arrived, Louie's was packed and rocking by the time we were on our third round. The bar's décor was an odd mix of hole in the wall dive and performance royalty—dimly lit, with grimy concrete floors and shitty neon beer signs, but the bar top was gorgeously polished oak, carved in Ireland as all good bar tops are. There was a raised stage towards the back of the bar, with red velvet curtains hanging to either side. Louie's resident blues deity, Lester Rollins, had settled in at the keyboard, tucking his two-tone saddle shoes neatly underneath to keep rhythm on the scuffed wood. As the evening wore on, he was joined by Jack Warford, his regular stand-up bassist, as well as a couple of other musicians I didn't recognize on guitar and drums. Raised on folk and gospel as a kid in rural Kentucky, and meandering through my rock and metal phases in my late teens and early twenties, it wasn't until I hit Memphis that the blues got hold of me. I couldn't tell you when one song ended and the next began, but I knew how it made me feel—relaxed and happy and somehow cooler, as though Lester's bone-deep coolness could be passed on as easily as his dark sunglasses and Panama hat.

It was at the start of the evening, as I stood at the bar waiting on my first round, that I felt someone watching me. I looked up, feeling sickly scared with an intensity that itself was frightening, in the midst of this loud and cheerful mass of humanity. I half expected to see Charlie Akers standing across the bar, grinning through broken teeth, but it was only one of my veteran teammates, Sid Angelo. He caught my eye, and I smiled as naturally as I could.

Sid didn't smile back, but after a brief hesitation he got up from his bar stool and made his way over. He sidled close enough to make himself heard over Lester's bottomless tenor and the wail of the guitar.

"Sarge."

"Sid."

The bartender brought my beer, a draft German wheat because I dig shit like that. I took a drink and waited on Sid. He wasn't much of a talker, and it didn't do a damn bit of good trying to rush him.

Finally he cleared his throat, turned to face the band. "That was a good shot, Sarge."

"Thanks, Sid."

"I'm damn glad it's over. More so than usual."

I felt those little prickles on the back of my neck that told me I wouldn't like where this was going, but I couldn't walk away, so I kept my eyes on the band too. "Any special reason?"

He took a long, slow pull from his Woodford and Coke. "Something wrong with that place. Real wrong."

I looked at him, but his usual stone-face impression was intact. Had he seen something? Or, like Zack, heard something?

"How so?" I asked.

He looked at me. "The walls. They're thin there—too thin. Could let anything in, anything at all. Couldn't you feel it?"

I swallowed, my throat dry despite the beer. Sid had been on the team long before I'd gotten there. We'd talked over the years, but he was taciturn by nature, and our conversations had never gone below surface depth. Watching his grizzled face, I had the oddest feeling that it wasn't the Sid I knew talking right now.

"How..." I began, but he cut me off, leaning in close, the bourbon sweet on his breath.

"It's changing out there, Sarge. The dark is coming, and you need to be ready when it does. He's not done with you, you hear me?"

He.

I couldn't speak as a thousand unwanted memories whispered at the nape of my neck. For a long breath I stood on the edge of an abyss that Sid's words had opened before me, wanting to squeeze my eyes shut so I wouldn't have to watch the fall. Then I heard it again, my music. Just a couple of scratchy notes and it faded, but when I looked at Sid, he was leaning back, eyes front again.

He tossed off the rest of his drink, pushed away from the bar and nodded to me.

"Sid," I managed to say before he got too far away, but he didn't turn around.

"You don't go back there, Sarge. No matter what you hear, don't you go back."

I was chilled and alone as hell in the middle of the crowded bar, watching him go and wondering what had just happened. I finished my beer and ordered another, and by the time it got to me, I had managed to fix a smile on my face and turned to find my guys. Whatever had happened on Union Avenue today, it was over.

I sat at a high-top table with Ben Teeters and two of the youngest guys, Maynard and Hooper. Maynard was twenty-six, medium height, smooth dark skin and a charming smile. Hooper was a little older, a tall, goofy-looking redhead with a Texan accent that got more outrageous as he drank. I liked them both—good guys, promising recruits—and I was glad to have them on my team. Their easy buoyancy pushed the last of my disquiet to the back of my mind, and I began to unwind. I resisted their efforts to get me to do shots with them, instead tuning into the music and nursing my beer while Ben talked to me about the Z car he was restoring.

Maynard and Hooper were both keyed up and rowdy, and they

weren't the only ones. As the night wore on and my team slowly let go of the tension of a two-day standoff, a couple of beers turned into too many and several S.W.A.T. members were poured into cabs to get them home safely. I kept an eye out for anyone getting too far out of hand, but for the most part my guys were well-behaved, the notable exception being Landers. The guy was even more obnoxious drunk than he was sober, hitting on the waitresses, picking fights with everyone and, as the night wore on, holding forth on all the reasons he should have been chosen to succeed Lieutenant Llewellyn, who had unexpectedly failed to show up. There were muttered insinuations about affirmative action and people sleeping their way to the top, but the fact of the matter was, my exam scores blew Landers' out of the water, and my record spoke for itself.

At some point, someone stuffed Landers into a cab and things got more pleasant, so I stayed a little past midnight before heading home, after getting soundly beaten in a couple of dart games with Ben as my partner. A few of the guys were still going strong when I settled my tab, but I knew there were enough relatively sober deputies from other departments around that no one would drive who shouldn't. When I stood up to leave, I had to walk a gauntlet of congratulatory slaps on the shoulder and high-fives, and I tried not to grimace at all the contact. I declined Ben's offer to walk me to my car. With my scars, weapons, and attitude, I was no one's first choice to mess with.

I flinched when someone stepped out of the shadows just beside the entrance to Louie's.

"Rose. Glad I found you here."

"Agent Neal?" I frowned, cast a glance back at the jazz club, wondering if he'd been inside or out here waiting for me. "What the hell are you doing here? How did you know where to find me?"

He took a step closer, the muggy Memphis air stirring slightly and sending a whiff of his cologne my way. "Lieutenant Llewellyn told me where to find you."

"That's obviously bullshit."

"I told you we needed to talk. I imagine you were too busy today, after the shooting and the B.P.S.I. investigation, but it's important. We have some items of mutual concern, and it's best that we deal with them soon."

I looked behind him at the empty parking lot, hoping someone I knew would come walking up, a late arrival, or the door would swing open behind me. No such luck.

I sighed. "Mutual concern? That's got to be the most nebulous statement I've ever heard, and I've been married to two lawyers, so that's saying a lot."

Neal smiled, showcasing those even white teeth. "What can I say, I'm federal. Comes with the territory. But I can be more explicit, if you prefer. I can even give you proper names and places. Like Charlie Akers, for example. And Briar Ridge. Does that help?"

Briar Ridge. The specialized facility where I'd spent the last two years of my minority. Where I'd been sent, ostensibly, to recover from the physical effects and psychological trauma of the fire, of losing my father and my brother Andy. Where I'd really been banished because Mommy dearest couldn't bear to look at me anymore, couldn't deal with such a troublesome daughter without her strong husband by her side. Not when she knew what I was: killer, ghost-seer, and all-around bad girl. Shit like that didn't fit in with her religious worldview.

I felt cold, my pleasant buzz vanishing. Neal was still watching me with that irritating smile, waiting for my reaction. My mind seemed to have frozen, and I couldn't think of anything to say. Nothing that didn't sound like something out of a cliché drama, anyway.

"You'll have to excuse me on Charlie Akers. Only thing I know about that guy is he was a dirtbag." I tried to step around him but he moved, blocking my path.

"I don't think that's true, Rose. I know you've killed a lot of people in your time, and maybe the rest of them are starting to blur together, but not Charlie. No, I think the two of you had a special bond."

Killed so many...how did Neal know about my kill record? Was that supposed to bother me, the idea that I'd rid the world of scum like Charlie Akers?

A memory rose, of Akers' black eyes turning toward me, his rictus grin spreading as he spoke my name with his brain splattered on the pavement behind him.

Neal's smile widened. "I'm right, aren't I? You know more than you're telling. And Briar Ridge...let's just say there are certain connections. None of this is an accident. It may look that way, but it's not." He took a step closer, leaned in. "So I think you can see we do need to talk. And it needs to be before the incident review board convenes on Monday. For both our sakes."

My temper flared. "I don't know who you are, Agent Neal, or why you're here, or what you think you know. But you don't, and you won't, so fuck off."

"Rose—"

When he tried to step in my way again, I shoved him, hard. I didn't wait to see what he would do, instead taking off at a brisk walk to my car. I ordered myself not to run, not to make it into the melodrama Neal wanted it to be. Shouting *you don't know me, man* and taking off at a run—it was too angsty for me.

I was parked in the back of the lot, my Charger tucked into a corner next to a blue Ford Escort that had seen better days. Though I could hear Beale Street going strong a couple of hundred yards back, the night in my immediate vicinity was quiet, the cheerful pandemonium of Louie's closed to me now. I felt deflated, the good cheer of the past several hours fading in the wake of Neal's confrontation, and I hated him for it. Looking back once, I didn't see him lurking anywhere, and felt a little better.

I stopped by the hood of my car, bathed in the sickly glow of the light buzzing overhead, fighting an irrational urge to turn around and go back in the bar. I was tired now, and didn't want anything else to drink, but I realized I didn't want to be alone.

He's not done with you...

Sid's words.

Charlie Akers looking back at me, opening those dead lips to speak in that awful voice. Neal didn't know, I told myself. He couldn't. But I didn't like the connection he'd made with Briar Ridge. I closed my eyes against the fear and bad feelings, clenched my jaw and wished, for a pathetic moment, that there would be someone waiting for me when I got home.

With my eyes closed, I sensed rather than saw the streetlight overhead blink out. Something scuttled near my feet and I jerked sideways, blind in the sudden darkness. My heart was beating fast, but I tried to slow my breathing as I reached for my car door. Just as I was pulling it open, something moved behind me, casting a long shadow over the pavement next to my own. It was moving slow, whatever it was, but it was close, and getting closer.

I should have turned around. I was a deputy, a sniper, armed and generally more dangerous than anything that lurks in the shadows in this town. Besides which, the most likely scenario was that Neal had crept back around to give me more trouble, and I felt more than capable of dealing with him—in a physical confrontation, anyway. But right now, I had the same feeling I used to get as a kid. The one where, when you get done praying on your knees before bedtime, you scramble into bed and under the covers as fast as you can, convinced that something is reaching out from underneath to grab your bare foot. I knew it was childish, knew it was illogical, but instead of turning, I threw myself into the Charger's front seat, slammed and locked the door, cranked the engine and trounced the accelerator. In the endless seconds before the engine caught, a shadow filled the driver's side window, and I finally looked up, my heart hammering hard enough to make me sick.

There was nothing but cloying darkness outside the window, and I took a long, shaky breath. Imagination, or a minor manifestation of the conflicting swell of emotions that come in the wake of taking a life. As the terror drained away, depression settled in, and I was angrier than ever at Neal. A final glance in the rearview as I pulled out of the lot made me stamp the brakes hard.

Someone was standing in the space I had just vacated. I waited, holding my breath, hoping whoever it was would step into the light and turn out to be a tourist or a stumbling drunk, or even Evan Neal, but they didn't move. They were watching me, eyes two spots of unholy silver light, and I shuddered at the realization that I hadn't imagined that presence looming over me in the deserted lot. Someone had been that close to me—close enough to reach out and touch me. I waited another long, breathless moment, but the shadowed figure still didn't move. Instead, it began to sing, in a cracked, hoarse horror show of a voice.

"What a friend we have in Jesus, all, our sins and griefs to bear..."

Nausea rose up. I caught my breath on a sudden sob, then gunned it out of the lot while that still figure watched, singing into the muggy night.

CHAPTER TWO

Paul Summers' favorite song. A hopeful, lovely hymn about the gift of faith, turned into a joyless funeral dirge by my father. The lyrics had been burned into my child's brain over years of having it sung to me, or rather at me, like a penance. A punishment. A judgment. *Jesus isn't your friend, Rose Summers. He's too busy bearing your sins, and your parents' grief.*

"Shut up," I snarled, and smacked a palm against the steering wheel.

Not again. Not again, not ever again, I thought as I pulled into my driveway.

Except I had no control over that. I had no idea how Evan Neal had known anything about Briar Ridge, or how he could have guessed what I'd seen that afternoon, but the fact was, there was a long, dark time in my life when such sights had been a constant for me.

I had no clear idea of when it had started. Things seemed to intensify when I hit puberty, but long before that, I could remember being small, huddled in the darkness of—

the cellar oh God the cellar

—my room, or maybe a closet, while something watched me. These older memories were fuzzy, hazy with the passage of time. The more recent visions were clear in my mind, indelible with the certainty brought by intense sense memory.

Sam was the only person I'd ever told about the things I saw back then: images of scenes and people, sometimes innocuous, sometimes terrifying. Most were recognizable as the shades of people; a few seemed to be mere manifestations of intense emotion—pain, grief, terrible anger, or sadness. Others bore no resemblance to anything living or dead—great lumbering horrors, or sneaking, stealthy things I prayed weren't real. Sometimes they took no notice of me, caught up in replaying their own dramas, but other times they looked right at me. Those were the worst. The eyes that would catch mine, dead and still or red and angry—it is a terrible thing to catch the gaze of a ghost.

Back then, before the fire, all of it, every haunting, every creeping nightmare was always prefaced by the Whispers. I thought of them like that, an entity with a proper name instead of just a collection of noise, because that's what they were. Something separate from the ghosts, whose arrival the Whispers heralded by their rising noise and chaos. I would wake, a small child alone in the dark, to the sound of thousands of sibilant voices, knowing that if the Whispers were there, a haunting was never far behind. They'd gone blessedly silent after the fire that ended my childhood, but the other spirits had stuck around.

I know not everyone believes in things like that. A skeptic would say I was seeing things, letting my mind whisper suggestions until my eyes saw what wasn't there. It sounds plausible, but it's wrong. I know it is. At first, doubting my own sanity, I would research the places where these visions occurred, and all too often the people and the scenes would match up eerily with former occupants of the buildings.

Once, right after I'd gotten out of the academy, I'd gone to sign a lease on an apartment. I'd been excited about it—it had been the first floor of an old five-story house in the historic district. Vaulted ceilings, hardwood floors, crown moulding and even stained glass in the front windows: it hit all my architectural high points.

I'd known something was wrong as soon as I walked in the front door. The place was freezing in summer time, hellish black voids all over the place. It was the bathroom that sealed the deal. She was still hanging from the shower curtain rod. A dark figure, swinging gently, she looked at me with hate-filled crimson eyes. I had turned and left the apartment without another word to the landlord. A five-minute Google search had brought up the news stories—Melody Rankin, a lovelorn coed, had committed suicide in the house more than twenty years before.

But it was more than historical confirmation of the things I saw; it was a certainty I carried with me from the beginning. Having had my share of nightmares, I could trust myself to tell the difference. Besides, the ability to see spirits was simply part of my identity, the bad part that made my parents ashamed. In any case, it was obvious I wasn't the only one. Judging by the current spate of supernatural reality shows—everything from psychic kids to haunted pets—there were lots of people out there who saw the same kinds of things I did, and they were all looking for answers in their own way.

I found some of my answers at Briar Ridge. The rehab facility may have been where my mother dropped me to keep me out of sight, but it had also been my salvation.

I'd been a mess after the fire, even more so than I'd been before it. The flames had started in my room but the investigators never found an accelerant or a cause—no candles burning, no matches, no faulty wiring. The point of origin had been directly under my bed, and no one else had been in the room when it started. It was always locked from the outside at night, and the windows were nailed shut to prevent me from sneaking out.

I'd woken to smoke, thinking it was morning already, mistaking the reddish glow of flames for sunrise. Momentarily pleased at the idea of a wood fire in the morning—it sounded cozy and happy. I'd started choking, coughing so hard I thought my throat would bleed. The heat from underneath the bed had grown painful, and I'd finally realized—fire.

I don't know how long I banged on my bedroom door, begging for Dad to let me out. Prying at the window, hoping I'd get some kind of adrenaline rush that would allow me to open it, but nothing like that happened. Instead I grew weaker, confused in the smoke and heat. I'd slumped to the floor, and that's when my nightshirt caught fire.

I must have blacked out, because the next thing I remember is my brother Andy scooping me up, carrying me out, walking through fire to save me. He'd come back for me, I learned later from my grieving mother. Andy had been safe out on the lawn with her; Dad had taken them both outside. My parents had forbidden him, but my brother had come back for me anyway. Dad had gone back in for Andy, cursing my name as he did, and they'd both lost their lives. I remembered Andy gasping his last beside me on the dew-soaked lawn, his lungs and trachea charred by the flames. My mother screaming beside us, asking where Dad was, why he hadn't come out with us. I'd never seen my father again. The firemen had found him trapped by part of the roof that had fallen in on him—he had burned alive.

Mom never forgave me. The scars I carried would never be punishment enough, as far as she was concerned. The fire had started in my room; it had to be my fault. She'd been left unscathed, but without the only two family members she cared for. She'd dropped me in rehab, and we hadn't spoken since. That scratchy phantom music started soon after, and became the only family I had. My brother, I wanted to believe, still looking out for me.

My time at Briar Ridge had not only brought me through the physical rehabilitation of healing from the fire, it had been essential in getting a handle on my visions of the dead. For the first time, I was out of the damning shadow of my father. I didn't know how to stop the things I saw, but I learned not to hate myself for them, not to see their presence in my life as the stain of sin my father had always said it was. I never heard the Whispers again, though whether that was because of Briar Ridge, or because I'd left them behind along with all my childhood memories at the charred husk that used to be my home, I wasn't sure.

By the time I met Sam, the ghosts had receded, occurring with less frequency and intensity. Telling him about them later, when I knew him enough to trust him, seemed to ease them further, and by the time I made the S.W.A.T. team, they were completely gone. I hadn't seen or heard anything otherworldly in years, unless you count that music, which I didn't.

Not until I'd seen the impossible animation in Charlie Akers' ruined face, heard the cold sound of that alien voice. I had wanted to believe, with an intensity that didn't let me look straight at it, that I had finally gained control. That the reason I no longer saw ghosts was that I'd managed to become master of my own mind, and willed them away from me.

Now I sat in my quiet driveway, watching the darkened windows of my home and wondering exactly how wrong I'd been.

It was past one in the morning when I shut my front door behind me. I leaned against it for a minute, my forehead pressed against the wood, my eye glued to the peephole as I searched the shadows. Finally I gave up and pushed away. I wasn't tired anymore, but I needed sleep. I'd gotten little the last two nights, rotating night watch duty with the other snipers while we waited for things to go to hell, and Sam would be here bright and early with the kids for a family breakfast.

I tossed my purse and keys on the scarred countertop of the island bar that divided the open kitchen on the left from the living room on the right. I paused at a tall cherry bookcase at the corner of the room to pull back a set of books and replace my guns in the safe hidden behind.

As I locked the safe back, I caught the scent of men's cologne and I stiffened, feeling the soft hairs rise on the back of my neck. I wasn't alone. Cocking my head, I could see my bedroom door standing open, though I always left it closed. I could barely make out something dark lying just before the threshold.

Something had followed me home.

My breath caught, my hands fumbling with nightmarish clumsiness as I struggled to reopen the gun safe.

A pair of strong arms encircled me from behind. "Welcome home, babe," whispered a voice made husky from years of exposure to cigarettes, gun smoke, and explosives.

"Luke, you fucking jackass." I turned and punched his arm, harder than I needed to. "What the *hell* are you doing?"

"Ow, damn it Rose, watch that left hook, will ya?"

"You dick, I could have put a bullet in you."

He laughed, a deep rumbling that shook his whole body. "Why do you think I waited until you put the guns up?"

"Cowardice," I said, then he shut me up by kissing me, wrapping his big arms around my waist, crushing me to him. I reached up to put my arms around his neck, one hand buried in the soft, thickly curling hair on the back of his head. I knew I'd regret this in the morning, that I'd be better off trying to rest, but I was just so damn glad not to be alone tonight.

My fears receded as we stumbled down the hallway, pulling each other's clothes off, until I tripped outside my bedroom. Remembering that I'd seen something lying in the hallway, I leaned down to touch it and came up with a handful of velvety, fragrant petals. "Rose petals? Really, Luke?"

He shrugged in the darkness. "Read it in *Cosmo*."

I threw the offending petals at him. He dodged me then ducked to throw me over his shoulder in a fireman's carry. I forgot all about rose petals, guns, and Charlie Akers.

* * *

Morning sun was filtering through the half-drawn blackout curtains that hung across both of the windows in my bedroom. I stretched my arms to the ceiling, admiring my tattoo artist's latest work running up the inside of my right arm. This one was a rendition of a painting by Aert Van der Neer, resized for the available canvas. Van der Neer was a landscape painter of the Dutch Golden Age. He had a particular gift with light on water that my equally gifted artist Renee had replicated to my satisfaction. Van der Neer's paintings had the added bonus of featuring textured landscapes of wheat fields and restless rivers, a perfect cover for the medium of my gnarled and scarred flesh. I was pleased with the result, admiring the shiny brightness that could only come with fresh ink.

I'd gotten less sleep than I needed, but after some satisfying cardio with Luke and a big man sharing my bed to chase away the shadows, I was feeling a lot better. After Luke had gone outside for his obligatory post-coital cigarette, we'd curled up together and I'd told him about the shooting. About Zack getting hit, and my bullet taking out Akers. He'd stroked my hair and listened, kissed me and told me I'd done the right thing, that he was proud of me. Luke didn't get in a twist about my work the way Sam did, mostly because he'd been on the job far longer than me. He was in his early fifties, retired from the Shelby County Sheriff's Office for the past four years, and making a comfortable living as a security consultant. He'd been my first partner when I got out of the academy and my best friend for the last thirteen years, all of which made being in bed with him now a little surreal.

Getting involved with Luke hadn't been part of my overall life plan—in fact, if you'd asked me two months ago whether it would ever happen, I'd have said no. We'd been close for years, the way partners were, and I trusted him with my life. But we'd never crossed that line, and I'd never even realized I'd wanted to. A few weeks ago I'd been over at his place, a house his dad had left him when he'd passed away earlier that year. We were having a couple beers and I was helping him paint the living room. I'd looked up at one point to find his eyes on me, an expression of longing in them I'd never seen, and before I knew it we were making out like teenagers on the drop cloth. It wasn't anything serious; I knew Luke's serial dating lifestyle, and I wasn't in the market for long-term. But it was fun being with someone I was already comfortable with, who knew about my complicated family life and could talk shop in the afterglow.

Of course, Luke's main drawback was that he snored like a rusty chainsaw. He was still out cold next to me in my queen-sized cherry four-poster, his curly dark hair shot through with strands of silver and standing up straight from his brow, hands thrown over his face. His big frame was beginning to run to fat, the way it does in athletes, but it looked good on him. I considered letting him sleep, but a glance at the digital clock on the nightstand got me moving—it was later than I'd thought. I sat up and shook his arm.

"Luke, wake up. It's late." He grumbled and rolled over. "Luke, come on." I nudged his impassive bulk with my knee before rolling out of bed to get dressed. He opened bleary brown eyes and blinked at me.

"What's the matter?" he asked.

"Get up, Luke. It's past nine."

"So?" He stretched slowly.

"So I've got the kids this weekend. Sam will be here any minute, and you need to be gone."

"Oh." Luke's voice went flat and his expression went sullen, but he finally began moving, with the speed of a sloth.

I knew it would only slow him down if I tried to hurry him so I turned away to drag a brush through my honey-blonde hair, the curls resisting all attempts to tame them until I gave up and smoothed them into a thick ponytail. Since it was only my family, I didn't bother trying to cover my burns. My kids had never known anything else, and Sam still claimed I was the most beautiful woman he'd ever met. I always answered that he needed to get out more. The slam of the bathroom door told me Luke was at least making progress, so I returned to scanning my wardrobe, trying to remember what we'd planned for today.

"Right, the zoo." I searched my dresser for a pair of shorts that might miraculously be clean. I settled for a khaki pair, rumpled from its extended stay in a laundry basket under my bed. I added a short-sleeved, form-fitting white top that could be supplemented with a cardigan and my standard gloves once we left the house. After a glance in the mirror, I was satisfied, and headed to the kitchen to make coffee. My cell phone was ringing and I hurried to catch it.

"Rose McFarland," I answered, pinning the phone between my ear and shoulder while I opened the brown paper bag of Vienna Orange dark roast and scooped three heaping spoonfuls into the filter.

"Hey, Sarge, did I catch you at a bad time?"

"Ben? What's up? Please don't tell me we've got another situation already."

"No, it's not that. I'm sorry to bug you at home on a Saturday, but

I thought it might be important. I wanted to call you last night, but figured you'd already be asleep."

I shot an irritated look at my bedroom door, which had yet to open.

"Okay, Ben, what is it?"

"Last night at Louie's, after you left? Some guy came in asking about you."

Fuck. "What guy, Ben? What was he asking?"

"He was some fed named Neal. Flashed his badge around, tried to buy some drinks. He kept asking about you, what kind of boss you were, if anyone had any problems with you. What we thought about what went down at the Akers shooting."

The Akers shooting? Was Neal just trying to undermine me with my guys out of petulance? "What the hell? Did anyone talk to him?"

"No, Sarge, you know we wouldn't. We shut him down pretty quick. Good thing Landers had already gone home, though."

"No shit. I was just thinking the same thing."

Luke came out of my bedroom, his curly hair wet and dripping on the collar of the slate-blue shirt he was buttoning. *Who's that?* he mouthed.

Ben, I mouthed back.

"So do you know this guy or something?" Ben asked.

I sighed, leaned a hip against the counter. "No, I don't, but he seems to think he knows me. So what happened, did he just leave?"

"After a while, yeah. But I got a creepy feeling from the guy, Sarge. He kept talking about your family, asking a lot of questions."

"My family? Like, my kids?"

Luke caught the sharp tone in my voice, and his eyes narrowed.

"Some, yeah. At first he was just asking stuff like how old they were, when their birthdays were, what they were into. Then he started in on their health—were they sick much, were you out with them a lot, had anything changed lately, did it seem like everything was okay at home. Nobody was giving him the time of day, and some of the guys were getting pretty pissed off. Then he was talking about your dad's family, almost like he knew them or something. The Summerses, I guess? I didn't think you had a dad."

"I don't. He's dead, and I'm damn sure he didn't know this Neal guy."

"Yeah. He mentioned a fire, I guess he was talking about the one where you, uh…"

"Yes, Ben, that one."

"Anyway, me and a couple of the other guys got rid of him after that. We didn't like him talking about your kids and all, it just seemed weird. But he said to remind you to call him. Gave me a card. I told him not to hold his breath, but he didn't seem to care—didn't react at all, just kept smiling this weird smile. I thought you should know."

I passed a hand over my face, sighed. "Thanks, Ben, you did the right thing. I'll deal with this guy."

"Do you think he's dangerous, or just nuts?"

"Probably a little of both, but nothing I can't handle."

He chuckled. "I have no doubt."

"Thanks for the call, Ben. I'll see you on Monday."

"Okay, Sarge. See ya."

I stood frowning at the phone, my heart beating fast. Luke laid a hand on my shoulder. "Rose? What's the matter? What did Ben want?"

I shook my head and turned back to the coffee pot. "Some fed showed up at the scene yesterday, tried to talk to me. Kind of threatened me. Showed up at Louie's last night when I was leaving, got in my face, then evidently went in and tried to talk to some of my guys about me. Asked around about my kids."

Luke frowned. "How in the hell did he know where to find you?"

"Said Llewellyn told him where to go."

"Horseshit." Luke knew David Llewellyn well, had partnered with him in the distant past. "David wouldn't send anyone after you like that."

"I know. Neal was lying."

"What did he want?"

I gave him a recap of our conversations, leaving out Briar Ridge, and summing up what Ben had told me. Luke's frown deepened as he listened.

"You're not going to meet with this guy, are you?"

I chewed my lip. "I don't know. I wasn't planning on it, but I'd like to find out exactly what it is he thinks he knows."

Luke shook his head. "Rose, he's threatening you."

"Thanks, Luke, I'm not quite that dim. I did catch that. What I don't know is what exactly it is he's threatening—that'll give me a better idea of how to handle him."

Luke looked ready to argue, but the coffee pot beeped behind me and I glanced at the clock. "Jesus, it's late. Come on, you've got to go." I poured him a mug to take with him and he allowed me to propel him down the hallway, but stopped at the front door.

"You know, it wouldn't kill Sam to see us together. You guys have been split for what, six years? You've been married and had another kid since then, so I'm pretty sure he knows you've moved on."

I sighed. "It's not about Sam, okay? It's the kids. They don't need to be confused like that."

"Rose, I've known both your kids since they were babies. They know who I am. And Tommy's not even Sam's."

I suppressed a flash of anger. Luke was right; Tommy was my son with my second husband, Aaron Matthews, but Aaron had died in a car accident before Tommy's first birthday. The first time Sam had come to pick Lily up after Aaron's funeral, he'd asked to take Tommy too, and that was the way it had been ever since.

"Not like this. They know you as Uncle Luke, so they don't need to see you leaving my house in the morning. Lily's getting old enough to start connecting the dots."

His tone went flat. "All right, Rose. Fine. I'll see you." He turned, seemed to struggle with himself, turned back and sighed. "This agent, what's his name?"

"Evan Neal."

"I'll see what I can find out about him, but promise me you'll be careful."

I was scanning the street behind him, on the lookout for Sam's SUV. "I will."

He nodded and left, not stopping to kiss me goodbye. I knew he was pissed, but there wasn't time to soothe his ego. This time with my family was sacred to me, and I didn't want anyone else horning in on it, no matter how much I might enjoy having Luke in my bed. I also didn't get what his deal was, why he seemed to want a confrontation with Sam I knew we'd all be better off without, but I didn't have time to get into it. Watching from my front window, I breathed a sigh of relief when Luke's pickup started up and there was still no sign of Sam and the kids.

As it turned out, they were almost an hour late, and I'd already made a platter of pancakes by the time I heard Sam's Ford Escape pull into the driveway behind my Charger. I was working on a second pan of bacon, since the first wouldn't last two minutes—my kids would devour it. Little baby bacon eaters, I called them, and Sam could put away an impressive amount himself. I'd separated the bacon into two piles: the crispy, almost charred kind preferred by Sam and Lily, and the chewy kind favored by Tommy and myself.

There was a perfunctory knock at the door I'd left unlocked before the noisy cavalcade made its way inside. Lily was leading the way, her bright blonde curls pulled into neatly parted pigtails high on either side of her head, Sam's enviable dad skills including a mastery of little girl hairstyles. She had a baseball mitt on one hand and was animatedly arguing the merits of her favorite players from this season's Memphis Redbirds lineup, her excitement still high from the game Sam had taken her to earlier in the week. I had to bite my lip when I heard her say, "The guy's a bum, Dad, plain and simple." Sam shot me an amused look and stood back as Lily threw herself at me.

"Hey, Mom! We missed you this week. Is everything okay? Did you get the bad guy? What's for breakfast?" I set down the spatula I had been wielding and turned so that my daughter was no longer at eye level with the fat-spitting bacon pan.

"Hey yourself, kiddo." I leaned down to return her fierce hug. "Everything's good, bad guy's out of commission, and it's pancakes and bacon for breakfast. Go wash your hands."

"Yes, pancakes and bacon!" She did a short victory dance and skipped off to the bathroom. As soon as she was clear, Tommy hurried forward, his arms extended. I bent and scooped him up.

My sensitive four-year-old son is the antithesis of his fair and energetic older sister. His hair is so dark as to be almost black, and as straight as his father's had been. He's a serious child, always taking the world in with great consideration. Both of my kids look like their respective fathers—Lily's light hair, blue eyes, and fair skin making her unmistakably Sam's daughter, and Tommy's darker features and bright green eyes a legacy of Aaron. As Tommy got older, he looked even more like his father, a bittersweet thing.

Just now Tommy was clinging fiercely to me, his small head tucked under my chin. "Hey, buddy, you okay?" I asked, rubbing a hand over his back and raising my eyebrows at Sam. He grimaced and shrugged. I set Tommy back down and knelt to look at him. The delicate skin under his normally bright eyes had a smudged dark color, his little face showing more exhaustion than a four-year-old should know. He looked at me solemnly, not speaking, and finally I stood. "Okay, Tommy, you go wash your hands too, and let's eat. You hungry?"

He nodded silently and took off after his sister. A minute later they could be heard squabbling over counter space in the hall bathroom, so I figured there couldn't be anything too wrong with him. Sam dropped two backpacks in the entrance hall, then came to join me in the kitchen and bent to kiss my cheek. "Your bacon's burnin' there, Emeril," he drawled in the low country accent I'd found so appealing all those years ago.

Gesturing with the spatula, I pointed him toward the coffee and went back to the stove. "That coffee would be fresher if you guys had been here on time. What's up with little bit?"

"Interestingly, the two things are related." I could hear him rummaging in the cabinet for his favorite mug, a tall blue one with a slightly fluted top. He'd bought it for me from a potter at an art fair years ago, and had resisted all my efforts to give it back to him, but it was the one he always used when he came over. We both held strong opinions on the appropriate shape and thickness of coffee mugs.

"I found him sleeping on the floor outside Lily's room early this morning. Poor kid was totally wiped out, but didn't want to sleep in his own bed, and big sis denied him solace. He could barely keep his eyes open, so I put him to bed in my room and let him sleep for a few more hours."

I looked at him, my brows raised. "Tommy? That kid sleeps like the dead. Your Mom keeps wanting to have him tested for narcolepsy." My youngest child had been a heavy sleeper since he was a baby, neither needing nor wanting to be rocked or sung to sleep at night. He could often be found passed out in the midst of daily activities—face down in a set of Legos or stretched out on the stairs, apparently so overcome with exhaustion that he couldn't finish the climb.

"I know, it's weird, but he must be going through a phase or something—seems like he hardly sleeps through the night anymore."

"What? Are we talking about the same kid here?"

Sam's eyebrows knit. "He hasn't had trouble sleeping here?"

I shook my head. "Not that I've noticed. Tends to conk out pretty quick, and I don't hear a peep until morning."

He looked troubled. "I wonder why he'd have a harder time at my place. You'd think..." He caught himself and closed his mouth.

"You'd think it'd be worse over here because it's less familiar, right? Since he's not here as much?" Sam's assumption stung, but I tried not to let it show.

He shrugged uncomfortably.

"Is there anything else that's been different lately?"

Sam thought about it. "Nothing major, I guess. He's gotten to where he won't go down to the basement anymore, even if someone goes with him, but I guess that's pretty normal for kids his age."

The cellar oh God the cellar...

"Yes," I answered mechanically, my mind filled with a nightmare image of crumbling dirt walls, a steep staircase, and a shadowed door that promised something awful. In my mind's eye, the door began to ease slowly open, and I sucked in a breath, closing my eyes and shaking my head against the sight. *They're coming.*

I looked up to see Sam watching me, his eyes narrowed. He reached out and touched my shoulder. "You still with me, Rose?" His voice sounded strangely far away.

I stared blindly at him, then nodded and turned back to the bacon, pushing the memory away. The best thing about childhood is that it's over. That had been my mantra for years now, though I'd sworn to give my children no reason to feel the same.

"Maybe he's having nightmares. If the insomnia keeps up, maybe we should talk to Tommy's pediatrician," I said when I could trust my voice to be steady.

"But you're telling me he doesn't have a problem over here."

I shrugged and scooped the remainder of the bacon from the pan. "Kids can be weird, Sam, it doesn't mean anything's wrong with your place."

"I'm sure Tommy's okay, but if it makes you feel better we can talk to Dr. Daughtry." Sam's tone told me he'd already dismissed the subject. I couldn't explain why it had me so worried, so I let it drop.

"Those shorts look awfully good on you, Rose."

I rolled my eyes and smiled. My legs had escaped the fire unscathed, and although I'm short, they're relatively long and fit from hours of training. They're my one vanity. Sam always made it a point to bring the conversation around to complimenting me, which I'd find a hell of a lot more flattering if I didn't know I was only one of many women to get the Sam McFarland charm.

I didn't look back at him, but could still feel his gaze on me. I could have drawn him from memory. His lanky frame, and the way he had of slumping, bending over himself so you wouldn't know how big a guy he was until you stood next to him. His blond hair, mostly gray now, was cut short and accentuated a pair of oversized ears that gave him a slightly goofy look, which was both a boon and a bane to him in court when he took on the occasional criminal defense case. His dark blue eyes were almost always smiling; his softly rounded nose and chin gave him a friendly, open look. His shoulders were broad and straight when he bothered to correct his posture, and his calm voice had the power of making even the most outlandish scenario seem plausible.

I'd met Sam thirteen years ago, when I'd been a rookie deputy and he was doing the night shift ride-along that the District Attorney required of all his prosecutors, before Sam abandoned law in the public arena and opened his own practice. Back then, Sam was one year out of law school, and I was six months out of the training academy. He'd been assigned to my cruiser for the benefit of learning from my partner, Luke Harris, lately departed from my bedroom. Sam had followed up the ride-along with a number of late night visits to establishments he knew were on my beat. Two years later, Luke was the best man at our wedding, and two years after that he was made Lily's godfather. He hadn't been exaggerating when he said he'd known my kids since they were babies.

Sam and I had a good marriage at first. Great, in fact, but things had gotten rough after we'd had Lily. I'd already been a deputy when Sam met me, and he'd never seemed troubled by my job or the dangers I faced each day. All that changed when I got pregnant, and although I didn't object to being loaned out to a desk job with Property Crimes for the last few months before Lily was born, I'd always planned to transfer back to Narcotics after my maternity leave. Sam had been dismayed at my choice and gotten increasingly argumentative, never more so than when I was finally accepted to S.W.A.T. Things had come to a head quickly after that until, tired of the constant fights and hardly able to remember what it felt like to be in love, I'd walked out. It had been hellishly painful at the time, but I still thought I'd done the right thing. It had taken time, but Sam and I managed to become friends again and now enjoyed an easy relationship. In a lot of ways we were better co-parents than we were romantic partners, and the speed with which Sam embarked on a series of flings after I'd left made me wonder if he'd ever been cut out for monogamy to begin with. If it wasn't entirely painless to think of him with other women, at least it was only a pang compared with how it felt when we were married.

"You okay, Rose?"

I hesitated, considering telling him about Agent Neal's disturbing phone call, then decided against it. He would only worry. "I'm fine. Are you okay?"

"I mean, after yesterday. I saw the news this morning. That guy from the standoff, he was shot. You didn't tell me that."

"Right."

"You're still on point for sniper duty, right? Was it your bullet?"

I felt my shoulders tense up. Conversations like this were exactly why we weren't married anymore. "Does it matter whose bullet it was? We had a positive resolution, so who cares?"

"Paper said Zack got shot."

"Yes, he took one to the vest. He's fine, otherwise I'd have been at a hospital bed last night instead of a bar."

"But you didn't tell me. You didn't think it was important that your friend got shot? That I wouldn't want to know you had to kill a man yesterday?"

I felt his disapproval settling over me. I glared at the bacon pan, told myself to count to ten. Pissed at myself for those first few minutes when I'd actually felt a little nostalgic for our marriage. Even more pissed at myself for feeling disappointed. I was smart enough to know better.

Smart enough or not, my control over my temper went right out the window when I thought of how good I'd been feeling five minutes ago. I coped in my own way with the psychological effects of what I did for a living. Beers with my team, a night in the sack with Luke, and seeing my kids this morning had made everything okay, and Sam had blown that away in a matter of minutes.

Feeling his hand on my shoulder, I shrugged it off and turned to face him, arms crossed tightly under my breasts.

"Go fuck yourself, Sam McFarland," I said in a low voice. "You're not my husband anymore, and my job is none of your fucking business. Keep your sanctimonious bullshit for someone who gives a damn what you think." I was shaking with the force of my fury, and he took a step back, blinking.

"Rose, listen, I'm—"

The sound of small feet at full tilt thundered down the hallway, and Sam let it drop. We both turned with smiles to face our children and get them settled in for breakfast.

CHAPTER THREE

Zack stood in the dark on the edge of the cracked asphalt driveway, just inside the sagging yellow crime scene tape. There was a moon overhead somewhere, but the cloud cover made its light muddled and indistinct, enhancing the feeling of isolation in the middle of six hundred thousand souls. He needn't have felt alone. He stood where, could he but feel it, the walls between this world and the next were indeed thin.

He was watching the darkened windows of the decrepit house on Union where Charlie Akers' life had come to an abrupt and violent end on the wrong side of Rose McFarland's rifle. Zack smiled a little, thinking of his friend, of her stolid practicality, her utter lack of bullshit.

"*Zack*," she would say, holding one of her favorite German beers and pointing a gloved finger at him. "*People make choices. Sometimes they're good, sometimes they're bad. Sometimes they're so bad they end up dealing with us. Sometimes, they keep making bad choices and they end up dead. I don't take it lightly, but I don't waste tears on them, either. Everyone has a choice."*

Everyone did have a choice; Zack knew she was right about that. He'd gotten past the point where he lost sleep over the criminals who committed suicide by cop, helped along by Rose's unshakable belief in the right of what they did. Suicide, as she pointed out, was a choice as well.

Zack was having a hard time shaking off Charlie Akers, though. Some of that had to do with Akers himself—young kids, orphaned now, and Akers so pathetic—but the state of Laura Akers' body had helped quash any sympathy he'd felt for the man. She'd been barely recognizable, her flesh abraded and torn all over, most of her face shredded, though God only knew how that had been done. She hadn't looked like a regular assault victim; more like someone had gone over her with a cheese grater. Decomp had set in, and after nearly three days in the sweltering Memphis heat, they'd had to scrape her off the linoleum.

No, Zack's fixation had more to do with what he'd heard through the mic the second night of the standoff. It wasn't just what he had told Rose, about the way Akers had seemed to talk to people, or things, that weren't there, or even that Zack had thought he'd heard something answer Akers. It was more than that, but in spite of a desperate desire to share his fear, to unburden himself, he hadn't been able to find the words to tell Rose he'd heard his dead brother speak his name through the headphones, in those dark hours before dawn of the day Charlie Akers died.

Zack had been ten when his older brother Matt succumbed to leukemia. Matt had always been an athlete, playing football in middle school and his freshman year of high school, running in the summers, swimming, biking, hiking. Zack, five years younger and a chubby child, had idolized his older brother, puffing along after him whenever he could. It wouldn't have been surprising if Matt had dismissed his little brother, excluded him, or teased him about his weight and lack of athletic ability. But Matt never had. He'd teased Zack about other things, sure—he was an older brother, not a saint, but when it came to sports, Matt helped Zack find his strengths.

Matt had fallen ill the summer before his sophomore year. That spring he'd been constantly sick, coming down with every virus that made the rounds. Zack remembered his brother being tired all the time, never wanting to leave the couch. When training began in July for the upcoming football season, Matt had been more exhausted than ever, complaining of aches all over his body. Practice was rough, and initially no one thought anything of his frequent bruising, but finally one day Matt had been taken to the hospital with seizures, vomiting, and a high fever. The coach had suspected a concussion, but blood tests and a lumbar puncture told the doctors Matt had developed acute myeloid leukemia. Though treatment was aggressive, the cancer was more so, and Matt had died in October, two days after his fifteenth birthday.

After that, Zack spent a lot of time in his brother's room, hanging out with Matt's things and trying to forget he was gone for good. One night a few weeks after the funeral, Zack had fallen asleep on his brother's bed and woken in darkness just after two a.m. At first groggy and unsure what had jarred him from sleep, he'd gradually become aware of a low voice coming from his brother's walk-in closet. He couldn't make out any words, but it sounded unhurried, conversational. His heart thumping, Zack had crept to the closet door and eased it open.

Half-hidden in shadow, but recognizable by his tall, wasted build and smoothly shaven head, Zack's brother stood pressed into a corner, eyes wide and still. Zack was frozen for several seconds, his eyes locked on his brother's. Then Matt had moved, shuffled forward, reached a hand out and tried to smile. Moonlight caught his flesh, turning it silver, and Zack could see the bones beneath.

He had run. Slammed the closet door behind him, then the bedroom door too, not stopping until he'd reached his own room. He'd crouched there on the floor, stifling sobs of fear and loss, praying not to hear anything in the hall outside his room and at the same time feeling ashamed. His brother, his beloved Matt that he professed to miss so much, had come back, had reached for him, and Zack had run away.

He didn't know how long he'd huddled there, but at some point the adrenaline had worn off and he'd fallen asleep. He'd woken shortly before dawn to the soft sound of something brushing against the other side of the door. Looking down, Zack had seen a shadow stretching into his room from the hall beyond. Filled with sharp regret, Zack had flung open the door and found himself alone. The plush carpet just outside was mashed down, and he had sunk down to the floor and cried.

He still believed, as he had that night, that Matt had sat there the whole time, waiting for Zack to gain his courage. His regret was the most poignant childhood kind, carried every day since then with the knowledge that he'd never have a chance to make it up to his brother.

But in the dark, quiet hours of Friday morning as Zack kept his vigil, hoping for a connection with Charlie Akers that would prevent any further bloodshed, Zack heard his brother's voice. It was low, barely audible, and at first he hadn't believed. Sitting forward, cranking his headphone volume to the max, he'd waited a painful few minutes before hearing it again.

Zack.

That was all. Just his name, one syllable, whispered across a connection much farther than the hundred yards that separated Zack from the house, but he had known it was Matt, coming back to give him another chance to say goodbye.

There hadn't been time for more. Akers had woken up, the negotiation had resumed, and then it was over. Zack had waited for S.W.A.T. to clear the house, then headed in and listened. He'd heard nothing out of the ordinary, felt no touch from his brother, and his hope had faded. He'd spent hours going over the recordings, but there was nothing.

Now he was here again, alone outside the empty house. No distractions, nothing to drive Matt away or overwhelm the connection between the brothers. Zack lingered, watching, waiting. Hoping.

Silence. Heavy, oppressive with the muggy heat only slowly leaching from the day. Zack tried to read something into it: a presence, the solemnity of a meaningful moment, anticipation. He couldn't tell. He was afraid now that he'd imagined the whole thing, that the house would be empty save for the detritus of Charlie Akers' last hours on earth.

Movement at an upstairs window caught Zack's attention, made his heart start thudding, his mouth going dry. He held his breath, waiting.

There it was again—a shadow, just visible over the edge of the sill. It shifted as Zack watched, his excitement growing. He tried to stay calm; it could be as simple as a curtain moving in a draft. He stepped closer, his heavy boots crunching over broken bits of asphalt. He looked up again. The darkness behind the window was still, but Zack felt watched. Whatever crouched in the decrepit little house knew he was there.

He waited as long as he could, holding himself still, but there was nothing more. That made sense. Last time Matt had come to him, had tried to make it easy on his kid brother. This time Zack wasn't a child, and it was his chance to make things right, so it was his move. He wasn't going to fuck it up this time.

A few quick steps and he was around the side of the house, at the top of a set of concrete stairs that started at ground level and descended to a cracked and leaning basement door. He paused at the top, pulled out his phone so the screen could light his way down, fought a fleeting urge to call someone, to hear a living voice. Not Anna, his wife. He loved her unequivocally, but he feared her practicality would chase away any chance of finding Matt tonight. Same with Rose, he supposed, remembering her face when he'd mentioned ghosts after the Akers shooting. The woman was unflappable—mere minutes after putting a bullet through a man's head, and she was still grounded enough to dismiss the idea of the supernatural.

Zack was on his own tonight, and told himself it was better that way. He didn't know where this would lead, but he needed to know he could do it. Needed Matt to know it, too. So he told himself it was nerves making him uneasy, and he plunged down the dark stairwell.

The door was unlocked, the way he'd left it, knowing he'd come back. The swollen wood stuck at first, but a thrust of Zack's shoulder made quick work of it. He stood just inside the empty space, feeling the grit of the unfinished floor beneath his boots, listening to the house. Total silence. Was he imagining significance in it? The impression of someone else listening, too?

He sighted the rickety wooden staircase that led to the main floor kitchen and headed towards it, but stopped when something shuffled to his left, toward the back of the house.

His heart thudding again, Zack tried to hold his breath, peering into the gloom. He didn't have to wait long. Another shuffle, something dragging against the grit. A shadow, darker than the rest of the night. It moved, swayed. Waited.

"Matt?"

No answer, but Zack thought he could hear breathing now. Labored, wheezing. The way Matt had sounded toward the end. He took a step closer, stopped. "Matt?"

"*Zack.*" A whisper. Tired, but an uptick of hope at the end.

Zack swallowed. Matt had been waiting a long time. For the first time, Zack wondered if his brother would be angry.

More dry dragging as Matt moved again. He was close now, almost close enough to touch. Zack coughed, his asthma tickled by something in the dry air down here. What was that? What did it smell like now?

"*Zack?*" A hand reaching out, slow, tentative.

Zack smiled tremulously, reached out too. Clasped the hand he'd waited thirty-seven years to feel again. Felt it pull him closer, into a shaft of moonlight coming through a broken window high on the wall. He looked up, into his brother's face. Faltered.

"Matt?"

No, Zack realized with regret as the bony clutch tightened and pulled him close. Not Matt at all.

CHAPTER FOUR

I kept an eye on Tommy throughout the day, alert for any sign that something was troubling my son, but he seemed fine, disposing of an impressive number of pancakes and a mound of bacon at breakfast. He tore around the Memphis Zoo with his sister, squealing happily when we finally reached the reptile house, his favorite. He wandered solemnly from cage to cage, greeting each snake, lizard, and turtle by name, as though meeting friends at a party. Concerned by the notable absence of his favorite pit viper, Bertha, Tommy tracked down one of the employees and was relieved to be told that the ten-foot snake was in holding while her cage was cleaned.

Aside from being a little more tired than usual, he was his normal self, and when I put him to bed at the end of the day he instantly fell asleep. Being five whole years older, as she regularly reminded us, Lily was allowed to stay up an extra hour and read in her bedroom. Sam stayed long enough to have a beer, then folded me in a hug before heading home.

"I'm sorry, Rose. About this morning."

I sighed against his chest. "Forget it. I shouldn't have lost my temper like that. It's been a rough few days."

"I know, and I shouldn't have made it worse. I know better. You're right, it's your job. You know what you're doing."

I recognized the monumental effort it must have taken Sam to say it, whether he truly believed the words or not, and I smiled, whatever anger I'd held onto melting away. It was just Sam doing what he did best, but a timely reminder that we were better off as we were now.

"Think you'll have to work anymore this weekend?" he asked, his chin resting on top of my head.

"Doubt it, but that all depends on how industrious our city's criminal element is on Sundays. Why, you got plans?" I instantly regretted asking, knowing he would think I was trying to glean information about his love life. Hell, maybe I was.

"Nothing that can't be rescheduled. Call me if you get called back in."

I frowned at his non-answer, but reminded myself it was none of my business. I didn't have the right to ask about Sam's social life, except as it concerned my kids. I pulled away and kept my tone neutral. "Okay. See you tomorrow night."

He stood on the porch, a smile in his eyes. He reached out and took my hand, squeezing it and rubbing his thumb over mine. "Hey, remember you can call me even if you don't get called back in." I might have been imagining it, but it seemed his voice was slightly husky, and I wondered if he was trying to tempt me back into his bed. It wouldn't have been the first time since I left six years ago, but it seemed like ancient history.

"I remember," I replied, as lightly as I could. Sam held my hand a second longer, nodded and ambled down the driveway to his car. I closed the door behind him, locking it and leaning against it, watching him through the side windows.

As soon as Sam's headlights pulled out of sight, I felt lonely again, and restless. Annoyed at myself for the way I still let Sam's flirting throw me off-kilter. Divorce hadn't ended our sex life, but I often thought I'd be better off if it had. We'd hooked up a few times before

I'd met Aaron, but what was just a fun pastime for him kept me in an endless spiral of self-doubt and frustration. I'd been relieved to let that part go when I'd met my second husband, and of course I'd stayed faithful to Aaron, and Sam had respected my boundaries. The last time with Sam had been shortly after Aaron died. I'd been vulnerable, lonely as hell, and Sam had invited me over so I didn't have to sleep alone in my empty house. We'd ended up in bed, and I'd been so relieved I'd had an idiotic moment the next morning, thinking we might really try again. Then his phone had rung while he was in the shower. I hadn't answered, but his machine had kicked on and I'd been treated to the saccharine tones of his latest conquest, confirming their meet up later that same day. I'd gotten dressed and gone home, feeling like the world's biggest idiot. In the three years since then I'd kept Sam at a physical distance, and I felt like I was better off for it. It still threw me for a loop sometimes when he flirted like he had tonight, which just made me more annoyed with him.

I wandered around the quiet house, peeking in at my kids, unloading the dishwasher, finally ending up on the seldom-used second floor. It was a neat space, open and full of light from the floor-to-ceiling windows on either side. I think I'd meant to use it for yoga, or to try my hand at painting, or something artsy to distract me from the holes in my life Aaron's death had left. Instead, I'd filled it with boxes I hadn't wanted to unpack and turned my back on it, rarely venturing up here. I looked at the boxes now, packed by movers from the home I'd shared with my second husband, thinking it was as good a time as any to tackle the chore I'd left undone for three years. It had been long enough; I'd moved on in every way that counted. But as always, when I folded back the first flap of cardboard, Aaron's scent hit me, and I felt his loss all over again. I slammed the box closed: not to escape it, but because I was afraid one day that scent would fade.

I went back downstairs and realized I didn't want to be alone the rest of the weekend. I thought about asking Luke over the next day, something I'd have done without hesitation before we started sleeping together, but he'd left mad this morning and I didn't want to poke the bear. I decided to get out of town instead, take the kids on a visit to see Aaron's father in Millington in the morning.

I got myself another beer and curled up in my easy chair, feet tucked underneath me, not bothering to turn on the light. In the quiet house with nothing to distract me, my thoughts drifted from Aaron Matthews to Charlie Akers. The horrifying way he had watched me, that impossible voice crooning my name. What did Evan Neal mean by saying I had reason to know Akers? I was certain I'd never met the man. And yet...there was something oddly familiar about him.

What had Zack said? That there was something different about this one—more to Akers' disturbance than the perps we were used to dealing with. Zack had even thought there might have been something in there with Akers. What had he heard on those tapes?

It was late, but not too late to call Zack; he was a night owl. I tried his cell first, but it went directly to voicemail, so I dialed his work extension, thinking he might be putting in some overtime on a Saturday night. Anna didn't like Zack bringing his work home with him.

There was the click of a connection before the line even rang once, but no one spoke.

"Hello? Zack?"

Static, and I could hear something rustling.

"Zack? It's Rose. Are you there?"

The hiss of the open line, but there was something else there. Someone was listening on the other end, I was sure of it. If it was Zack, why didn't he answer me?

"Who's there? I know someone's there."

It seemed I could hear someone, but from a great distance. Just murmurs, the rise and fall of conversation.

"Hello?" I said, as loud as I dared with two sleeping kids in the house. "Who the fuck is there?"

The distant conversation stopped, and the line was silent. Then the sound of quick, heavy footfalls getting closer to the phone.

"*Shhhhhh*," someone whispered, and the line went dead.

* * *

I called back several times but never got another answer on Zack's extension at the station. I tried his cell again, but it was off. Finally, not knowing what else to do, I left him a voicemail to call me. I wanted to drive out to Madison and see if Zack was there, make sure he was okay, but Sam had already gone home and I couldn't leave the kids alone.

Eventually I went to bed, sure my worry would keep me awake long into the night, but I was asleep within minutes. I slept badly, my dreams turned into restless nightmares by things that crept in the shadows. I was in the middle of a heated, desperate conversation with my brother Andy when a weight on the bed pulled me out of sleep.

I opened my eyes, the dream fading but leaving behind a sense of unease as I tried to remember what Andy had been telling me.

Green eyes stared down into mine, a small face only inches from my own, soft brown hair tickling my nose.

I wrapped an arm around my son, pulling him close. "Hey, weirdo. What are you doing in here?"

"Looking at you. Were you dreaming, Mommy?"

I sighed, kissed the top of his head. "Yeah, kiddo, having lots of dreams. You hungry?"

I felt him nod.

"I'm starving, Mommy."

"How about McDonald's on the way out to Grandpa Will's place? Get some hash browns and hot chocolate?"

I'd spoken softly, but the spastic squeaking of a metal twin bed, followed immediately by thudding footsteps, told me my keen-eared daughter had heard. My bedroom door banged open as Lily stumbled in, her golden curls a mass of tangles. She squinted at me, her glasses no doubt flattened beneath her pillow or fallen under the bed.

"Mom? Did you say McDonald's? Can I get cinnamon rolls?"

"Yes. Go brush your teeth and get dressed, we're going to get breakfast and then go see Grandpa William, okay? Spend the day on the farm."

"Cool," she said, giving me a crooked smile before pelting back down the hallway.

Tommy kicked his way out from under my covers and took off after her. The two of them were ready and lined up by the front door by the time I'd gotten dressed and found my keys, and I silently praised the motivating capabilities of those golden arches.

Caving to compulsion, I drove by the sheriff's station while the kids munched their breakfast. There was no sign of Zack's car, but plenty of other vehicles in the lot for the weekend shift.

"Will you guys be okay in the car for a minute while Mom runs in to check something?"

Mouths too full to answer, Lily and Tommy both nodded.

I hurried inside with a wave to the desk sergeant, and headed for the stairs that would take me down to Zack's basement desk. It was colder down here, and a little creepy with most of the lights off on a Sunday morning. Zack's desk was clean; nothing on it to suggest anyone had been here last night. I picked up his phone and got a normal dial tone, then used it to try his cell again. Straight to voicemail. I thought about calling his wife, but decided not to intrude on her weekend. I'd been making too much of what was probably a technological glitch. I hadn't completely allayed my concerns for Zack, but I decided to head out and hope to hear from him today.

Aaron's father's farm was in Millington, a rural location not far outside of Memphis. It was no longer a working farm and hadn't been for years—William Matthews had been an attorney before semi-retiring to teach the occasional law class at Ole Miss. It was still eighty acres of gorgeous, well-maintained land full of tall trees and sunlight. There was a good-sized vegetable garden in the field to the immediate right of the house that yielded plenty of corn and tomatoes each year, and the land surrounding the old farmhouse was landscaped by Will himself. He had always loved flowers, and had a talent for cultivating eye-pleasing combinations of color and height now that he finally had the time to turn his attention to the peonies, hydrangeas, azaleas, and lilies that were his passion. The farm was also where Aaron was buried, under a simple headstone in a field close by, near his mother. I'd never known Gayle Matthews; she'd died of breast cancer when Aaron was twenty.

The house had been built before the Civil War, and was of traditional design for the era. It was a wood-frame two-story with a stone chimney on either side and plenty of windows on the front and back, most with the original glass still intact. It was still early when my Charger crunched up the gravel drive, but Will was standing out front waiting for us, two mugs of coffee in hand, one of which he gave me as soon as I reached the porch. He scooped up each of the kids in turn, giving them crushing hugs before setting them loose to work off their sugar buzzes with the farm dogs, three good-natured shepherd mixes of indeterminate age. He watched them for a minute before coming to drop a kiss on the top of my head and settle in next to me on the porch swing. I sighed and sat back, curling my feet under me and feeling safer than I had all week.

With William's attention focused on the kids, I took a minute to study him. In the same way I saw Aaron so clearly in Tommy, I could easily trace him back to Will. He was an older, more exaggerated version of his son. Lean and dark, his hair an interesting mix of silver and black, his voice was deep and mellifluous, giving great weight to even his most commonplace statements.

I couldn't seem to get away from attorneys. Aaron had carried on the family business, and for a time father and son had practiced together, mostly estate and corporate law. We'd met in the courthouse, when I was waiting to testify in a criminal trial on the same day Aaron was there to argue a guardianship issue. It had been less than a year since Sam and I had divorced, and I hadn't been looking for a relationship, let alone a second marriage. But there was something about Aaron, an inner peace and calm I wished I could touch. We'd married later that same year, though I hadn't taken his last name— I'd been established in my career by then, and hadn't wanted to go through the red tape. Aaron had said he didn't mind me keeping Sam's name, but now that he was gone, sometimes I wondered. Anything to beat myself up over, I guess.

Will sold his practice after Aaron's death, and there was a time I worried whether he would ever recover. With his wife and only son dead, and no job to go to every day, I was afraid he would simply fade away, but that hadn't been the case. He had soldiered on, and so had I.

It had been more than three years since Aaron was killed in a car accident, struck on the driver's side of his Honda Civic by an SUV that ran a red light. The driver, a man in his late sixties, had claimed he had the right of way and didn't see Aaron until it was too late.

I'd never looked too closely into it, though in the bad times late at night, with nothing better to distract me, I couldn't help myself from calculating the speed the other driver must have been going to cause the damage he did. The Honda had been completely crushed on the driver's side. When I'd gone to see it at the impound lot, I had stared at it for an hour, my hands clenched around the jagged metal at the top of the door, alternately remembering Aaron's cautious driving habits and picturing his last moments. Luke had finally come to get me. He'd said little on the drive home, but asked me, when we arrived at the empty house Aaron and I had shared, if I wanted him to get the accident report for me.

I'd told him no. I didn't want to know, didn't want to give myself a chance to develop the rage and need for retribution that I knew bubbled just beneath the surface. The driver had tried to see me, wanted to explain or tell me he was sorry, but I wouldn't do it. Maybe it was petty. Maybe I should have given the guy a chance to get it off his chest, give us both some closure. Or maybe I would have broken his face.

Will's reaction to his only child's death hadn't been touched by the anger I felt. He had withdrawn into himself and spent most nights sitting out on his porch, a single thin blanket around his shoulders, staring at nothing. I think it was the kids that brought him out of it. Will adored Tommy, and cared equally for Lily. He and Sam's mother Joy were the only grandparents either kid had ever known, and the families blended seamlessly, with no question of biology or precedence. There were plenty of times I'd had to drop Lily and Tommy off at Will's at odd hours of the night, when I got called in late and Sam was unavailable. That's another way I'm lucky—Will was a godsend. I think he was relieved that I didn't cut him out of our lives after Aaron died. Not that I ever would have done so intentionally, but we both knew that sometimes it was too hard to be reminded of what we'd lost.

"Well, Rose, are you ready to issue me a clean bill of emotional health and tell me what it is that brought you running from Memphis at this unseasonable hour?"

I jerked, slopping hot coffee on my wrist. "Shit. I always forget you can read my mind, Will."

He smiled, silver-framed glasses slipping down his aquiline nose. "Mind reading isn't necessary with you, Rose McFarland. I know you have a romantic notion of yourself as enigmatic, but I have to tell you that every thought you have marches straight across your face on its way through your mind. Tell me what's bothering you."

I hesitated. Taking William into my confidence about Charlie Akers and the ghost shit that was cropping up wasn't part of my plan. I had loved and trusted Aaron, but Sam McFarland was still the only person I'd ever felt safe enough with to tell about my visions. Still, looking up into William's lean, lined face, seeing the kindness in his green eyes, I was tempted to share the burden. I couldn't expect him to believe me the way Sam did, but even if he thought I was nuts, I'd feel less alone.

An image rose unbidden—William grappling with Charlie Akers, hounded by Evan Neal, pursued by the phantoms that had haunted my childhood. To tell him was to taint him, and William didn't deserve that. He was an old man who had earned his peace. I settled for a partial truth.

I turned away to face the front yard and sipped my coffee. "Just a case. You may have read about it."

"The shooting over on Union?"

"Yeah. It's—it was my bullet."

"I see."

I could still feel his eyes on me, but didn't turn to meet them. "He had two kids—little ones. Both under three. They were there. I had to shoot their father in front of them. I knew—I *know* it was right. I had to do it. Just had a little trouble being alone in my head this weekend, that's all. Thought it would do me and the kids good to come out here. Is that okay?"

"You know it is, Rose."

And knowing it, I felt a little better.

We spent a lazy morning and afternoon in Millington, the kids wearing themselves out and napping, then getting back up to start it over again. I read mostly, out on the porch with William or curled up on the living room couch. Around five, I helped Will make a dinner of country ham, fried corn, and mashed potatoes that we ate in the comfortable rustic kitchen. The maple plank floors were original to the house, and Aaron had helped his father hang new cedar cabinets the summer after we got married. I remembered perching in a cane-bottomed chair with a cup of coffee or a glass of lemonade and watching them work. Cedar had been Aaron's favorite wood—he would spend hours carving, planing and sanding and come in at night with the smell woven in with his soap and the natural scent of his skin. The clean, wooded scent still brought him back to me, stronger than anything else. It was the smell trapped in those boxes I couldn't unpack.

Both the Matthews men were good with their hands—I had a beautiful cherry vanity in my bedroom that they'd worked on together as a Christmas gift for me. Aaron had made a big deal out of the oversized mirror he'd attached to the top, ignoring my comments about not being much to look at. Like Sam, Aaron had called me beautiful. For some reason I had a harder time believing it from him, but I had loved him for the effort.

After dinner was over and I helped Will with the dishes, we packed the kids up in the light of the setting sun. I moved slowly, stalling a little, the sense of dread that had receded once we'd arrived at the farm beginning to sneak back in. The kids would go back to Sam's tonight. Lily was out of school for the summer, and Tommy wouldn't start kindergarten until the fall, so Sam's mother Joy usually kept them during the day. I found myself dreading the solitude.

The kids were asleep as soon as they were buckled in. Will and I took a minute to watch the sunset in the cool of the early evening, and I wished I didn't have to leave.

"Oh, Rose, I nearly forgot. I have something for you." He disappeared back into the house, and came back a minute later with a beautifully carved cedar chest in his arms. "I found this while I was cleaning out the workshop a few days ago. It was Aaron's. I think he'd want you to have it."

I ran a hand over the lid and pictured Aaron doing the same thing. "What's in it?"

63

Will shook his head. "I didn't open it. It didn't seem right, some-how. Here, it's yours."

I looked up at him, strangely reluctant to take the chest. Maybe I was just avoiding the hurt that came with remembering Aaron, same as I'd done last night. "Are you sure? If he left it here, maybe it's something for you."

"I'm sure, Rose." His green eyes were intense and I wondered if maybe he *had* opened it but didn't want to discuss the contents.

I popped the Charger's trunk and helped Will get the chest set-tled, wrapping it in a blanket to keep it from knocking around while I drove. He seemed easier once it was out of sight, his shoulder close to mine while we stretched out our goodbyes.

"Did you get a chance to go see him?" he asked. I shook my head, not looking at him but out at the sky.

"Not this time." There was a certain guilt attached to the admis-sion, remembering as we both did how often I'd come to the farm in the early days after Aaron's death, just to visit his grave. I would sit next to the headstone, between the two pink rosebushes William had planted on either side of the grave. Aaron had always brought me pink roses, a play on my name, his idea of a joke. I'd talk to him as if he could hear me, tell him about my day, my job, and our son. Sometimes Will came with me, sometimes he talked too, but more often he was silent.

I felt his hand on my shoulder. "It's okay, Rose. You don't have to feel bad. It's good to be happy again. Aaron wouldn't have wanted you to wallow in this forever."

I wondered if I was happy, or if I was just getting numb to my losses. "Do you still go every day?"

"Yes, but that's different. He's right here outside my door, and for a father there's nothing to move on to. Besides, anymore it's mostly habit. The longer it becomes since a person passed, the less they seem to be at the places we go to visit them. I don't know whether it's them or us letting go, but in the end it's a good thing."

Will's words filled me with melancholy. I didn't like the idea that Aaron could drift away from my visits, though those had become rarer and, as Will said, more a matter of routine than respect. I said nothing, then after another few minutes I stood on tiptoes to give him a kiss goodbye. Watching him in the rearview filled me with an unreasonable sadness.

I was fishing my phone out of my purse to call Sam and only dropped my gaze for a second, but when I looked up again, there was a man. He was steps away from the hood of the Charger, like he'd materialized from the ether. It happened too quick to see much; just the outline of someone tall and lanky, a pale blur that could have been a face. I cursed and stomped the brakes as hard as I could, my phone dropping to the floorboards. "Jesus!"

I glanced in the back. Incredibly, both kids were still out cold, Lily's head pressed up against the car door, Tommy's chubby chin tucked into his chest. I sat still, my heart thumping, searching for any sign of the guy. At first I saw nothing, then movement to my right. I hoped that meant he was still standing, but I couldn't see clearly.

I eased my door open and stepped out onto the gravel drive.

The evening had been still only minutes before when I'd said goodbye to William, but now the wind had picked up. Sound rushed at me from all directions, the branches of the willows and dogwoods William had planted near the road whipping about, the leaves rustling frantically. They were turned to the side, their white underbellies showing, a sure sign of a coming storm.

"Hello?" I looked around, at first seeing no one. The road was deserted.

Then, out of nowhere, there he was. Twenty feet from the car, leaning against the trunk of a weeping willow in full bloom. The tree was one of William's, just behind the black horse fence that separated his land from the road.

He was facing away from me, toward the road, but it only took me a minute to recognize his profile. Tall, dark-haired and broad-shouldered, a firm chin and aquiline nose. I knew if he turned to me his eyes would be bright green, like his father's. Like my son's.

"Aaron."

He turned, just a little, so I could see his smile, dark hair hanging over one eye. I stayed where I was, looking at him. The wind, whipping my curls all over the place, didn't touch him. He seemed to exist somewhere outside the world we were in, which I supposed he did.

He moved finally, took a few steps toward the car, kept his eyes on mine. His face was intent but immobile. "Rose," he said, his voice a soft whisper, barely reaching me across the distance.

I stepped closer slowly, afraid if I moved too fast he would disappear like a startled deer. He watched me until I was only a few steps away.

"Aaron," I said, wanting to reach for him but afraid to try. "You're here. After three years...I didn't think I'd ever see you." After Aaron died, I'd wondered if he would come to me. I'd seen so many other ghosts over the years, but none of the ones I wanted to. It had seemed so damned unfair.

His green eyes were troubled. "I shouldn't be here, Rose. It's not supposed to be this way."

I shook my head, tears spilling freely now. "I know," I whispered. "It's bullshit. You should be here, with us."

His eyes became more intense. "Not that, Rose. I shouldn't be *here*, now. It isn't safe. The door—it's opened too wide, Rose. There isn't much time now." He looked down at one hand, then back at me. "They're strong now. Too strong."

"What door? Who's too strong?"

The sudden rush of a passing car broke the spell—I turned, and when I looked back, Aaron was gone. "What door, Aaron?" I asked again, but nothing answered me. I waited for a long time, but I knew he wasn't coming back. I didn't waste time telling myself he'd never been there at all, though. When I finally got back in my car, where both kids were still sleeping, it smelled of roses and cedar.

* * *

A terse voicemail from Llewellyn about the Incident Review Board scheduled for the following morning helped to put me back on solid ground, but set me to worrying about the next day. My debriefing with Bonnie Skylar had gone well, but I wondered now about Llewellyn's testimony, and whether he would back me up. I knew my shot had been justified, but with everything that had happened since—my brush with Akers' corpse, Neal hounding me, and now Aaron's appearance and warning—it was hard not to expect the worst. I knew I would spend most of my night reviewing my own testimony and case history, and organizing my team's training schedule and shift coverage for the week. Mommy time was already ticking over to work time before we were back in Memphis.

No word yet from Zack, and another call to his cell went unanswered. I told myself there was no need to call his work extension again, and tried not to feel like a coward.

I had a bad moment when I pulled into my driveway on Belvedere and the headlights splashed across a man sitting on the front porch, but as he stood, I recognized Sam's lanky frame. He was holding a thick book and was dressed in a white polo shirt and jeans, the look I always liked best on him. I didn't want to think about how glad I was to see Sam; I'd been dreading that dark house.

"Hey," he said in a low voice as I climbed out of my car, bending to give me a hand and plant a kiss on my cheek. "They out?"

"Yep." I caught the scent of unfamiliar perfume on his collar and wondered who he'd spent the day with. Sam never told me about his dates. Part of me was glad, but it always seemed to put me at a distance from him. I tried to quash my disappointment. "Should be an easy night for you—they wore themselves out on the farm today. Give me a minute and I'll bring their stuff out to you."

"All right. I'll start moving them over to my car." He stopped, cocked his head, reached a hand out to my shoulder. "Hey, Rose, you okay? Anything wrong?"

Yes—I think I'm seeing dead people again, remember how much fun that was?

I forced a smile and a light tone. "No, I'm good. Just a little tired, and I've got a night of work ahead of me."

Sam gave me the eyebrow raise and steady five-second stare that told me I was full of shit, then turned away to work on getting the kids moved to his car. I released a shaky breath and headed for my front door, eyes open for any sign of movement or lurking shadows.

It only took a few minutes for me to gather up the backpacks, clothes, toys and other detritus the kids had spread through my house but I couldn't find Lily's book. She'd been reading *A Tale of Two Cities*, an ambitious undertaking for most nine-year-olds, but the work of a few summer days for the daughter of Sam McFarland. She was about halfway through it, and I knew if I didn't send it back with her tonight there would be a frantic call tomorrow morning. I had just stepped back on the porch to ask Sam if he'd seen it when I heard him call my name, his voice tense.

Hurrying down the drive, I saw that Lily was awake and alert, peering from the open door of Sam's car at her small brother, who was sitting rigid in his car seat in the back of my Charger, his eyes wide and blank, a toneless humming issuing from his throat. Sam was trying to get to him, but as soon as Tommy was touched, the humming increased in pitch and his head began to whip back and forth.

I met Sam's wide-eyed gaze. "What's wrong with him? Is he having a seizure?"

"I don't know. I got Lily moved over, and by the time I came back for Tommy, he was like this—he won't let me touch him."

"Tommy? Tommy, can you hear me?"

There was no response, but he began drumming his heels against the seat. I reached through and grabbed his shoulders, prepared to pull him out by force, when his small hand clamped on my wrist in an impossibly strong grip.

"*Rooooose...*" he crooned, in a voice that did not belong to my little boy.

I froze and looked at him. His little body had stilled, and he was watching me from eyes that had darkened to black. His rictus grin matched the look I'd seen on Charlie Akers, but it was so much worse twisting my son's sweet face.

"*The door's open. He's ours now, little Rosebud, and so are you.*"

I felt like I'd been slapped. Rosebud. No one had called me that in more than eighteen years, not since my father had died. I choked, frozen but fighting an appalling urge to shake that horrible grin off Tommy's face.

His fingers loosened on my wrist, and his face slowly relaxed. He blinked and was once again watching me through sleepy green eyes. "Mommy?"

I let go of my breath, gripping the car door to keep myself steady. Hating myself for that moment of terror, for even thinking of shaking my son.

"What the *hell* was that?"

I turned to find Sam standing close behind me. "You heard that?"

"Of course I fucking heard it. Was that Tommy? It sounded like... actually, I have no idea what the hell it sounded like."

I felt a rush of relief that Sam had heard anything at all.

"Mommy, is it bedtime? Can I wear my bug pajamas?" Tommy's face was clear, untroubled. He had no memory of what had just happened.

"Sure, kiddo," I answered mechanically. Keeping a hand on his chubby leg, I turned back to Sam. "Do you have the number for the on-call pediatrician?"

He nodded. "I'll call them. Do you think we should take him somewhere? The ER or something?"

I looked back at Tommy, wondering what the hell we would tell the doctor. "Let's see what they say when we call. I'll get him out of the car."

I heard Sam talking in low murmurs while I gathered Tommy's blankets and toys from the back seat, and fought against the paralyzing fear that my son's episode might have something to do with Charlie Akers. Sam came over at one point and gently thumbed up Tommy's eyelids, peering intently at his sleepy green eyes, told the doctor that Tommy's pupils were even. He walked away again and turned his back. I was working on releasing the obnoxious puzzle-piece buckle on the car seat when Sam ended the call and came over.

"One second, Tommy." I stood and moved aside with Sam. "What'd they say?"

"Keep an eye on him tonight, bring him in tomorrow."

"They don't think it's an emergency?"

He shook his head. "Evidently not. They said something about febrile seizures—supposed to be pretty common if they're running a temperature." He put the back of his hand to Tommy's forehead, then his cheek, frowning. "He feels a little warm, but I don't know. I'll put him to bed with me tonight so I can keep an eye on him. If it happens again, I'll take him in to the ER tonight."

"Call me if you do, okay?"

Sam nodded. "He's got an appointment at 10 with Dr. Daughtry. Do you want me to take him?"

I scrubbed a hand across my eyes. "I guess. I've got the review board first thing in the morning, but maybe I can cut out in time to meet you guys. I'd like to be there."

He pursed his lips, looked ready to say something, and I glared at him. Didn't he know I felt guilty enough when my job interfered with my kids? I didn't need Sam's judgment on top of my own.

"I'll make every effort, Sam," I said sharply, and he closed his mouth.

"Mom?" It was Lily from Sam's car. "Are we still going to Dad's tonight? I left my jersey there and I want to wear it tomorrow."

"Yes, Lily, in just a minute." I knelt again and reached in to unbuckle Tommy's seatbelt. "Come on, little bit, climb out."

"No!"

I frowned. "What? Tommy, what's wrong?"

He had turned around and was clutching his car seat, all four limbs wrapped securely around it. Before I could react, he burst into tears.

Sam dropped to his knees beside me and raised his eyebrows.

I raised my hands, palms out. "No idea."

Sam leaned in over me. "Tommy, kiddo, what's wrong? What's the problem, bud? Don't you want to come home to Dad's?"

"No," came Tommy's watery reply. "Don't want to go to Dad's tonight. Want to stay at Mom's, okay?"

"Tommy, you know you're supposed to go to Grandmommy's house tomorrow morning. You have a nice comfy bed over at Daddy's, and it's already past your bedtime. Don't you just want to go home with Dad and Sis, and you can see me later?"

He buried his face in the seat again and shook his head. "Don't want to go. Rather stay in this bed."

I looked over at Sam, his face wooden.

He shrugged and avoided meeting my eye. "If he wants to stay here, maybe he should stay. I can come by and pick him up in the morning before work." *He's not really my son, after all.* He didn't speak the words, but they lay between us anyway.

I shook my head. This was about more than Tommy's whim. My son was afraid of something, and I was damned sure it wasn't Sam. Charlie Akers? Or had he somehow seen or heard what had just happened to him—that horrible voice?

"Kiddo, why don't you tell us what's wrong? If there's something you're worried about, maybe something you're scared of, you can tell us. There's nothing so bad that Dad and I can't handle it." Tommy turned and looked up at us hopefully. When Dad's over six feet and Mom totes a rifle, the idea that your parents can take on the world is a lot easier to buy, especially if you're four. He studied us closely, in the solemn way that was so uniquely his, then nodded slightly.

"The whispers, Mom."

Sam frowned. "Why do you have to whisper it, honey?"

"No, it's the *whispers*. They're scary."

"What whispers, buddy? You mean like the television, if it's on after you go to bed?"

"No, Dad. It's the people whispers. The whispers in the dark."

* * *

Tommy's words made my stomach clench. A memory of the cellar from my childhood again, of crouching at the bottom of a set of stairs in a subterranean nightmare, watching the last of the light disappear as a door slammed overhead. A much younger me, a little girl, sinking to my knees in the darkness, pleading for Daddy to open the door, to let me back upstairs, not to leave me alone with them. That shaking disbelief that he was really going to do this to me, followed hard by despair when sound began to rise around me and the cellar grew cold.

I looked over at Sam, focused on Tommy, concern furrowing his brow. The music was there again for a bare few seconds, gone almost before I realized I'd heard it, a quick, reassuring touch. I was surprised when Tommy looked up at a point somewhere over my left shoulder. That was where I always heard it, too.

"What whispers are you talking about, Tommy?" Sam was asking.

"The ones at night. They come in the dark. I don't know what they say, but I don't like it."

Neither did I. That shaky little-girl fear was immediately banished by fury that these things had dared to touch my son.

"Does it sound like Daddy, Tommy? Like maybe when I'm on the phone after you go to bed, or watching television?"

"Sam." I touched his arm, but he didn't look back at me, just raised his hand and shook it a little. *Gimme a minute.*

Tommy shook his head firmly. "No. Not like that. The whispers..." He paused and thought. "They come from someone else. Somewhere else. But they're in my room. They talk to me." He looked past Sam to me, his small face solemn. "Mommy knows what they sound like. They talk to her, too."

The Whispers in the dark. The voices that had started when I was only four years old, that heralded the arrival of things that went bump in the night. The most constant part of my hauntings—how could Tommy know about them, unless they really were back?

Sam looked back at me, frowning. I opened my mouth, but closed it again when I realized I had no idea what to say to him.

Sam reached a hand out to Lily. "Come on out of there, sweetie." She climbed out and stood between us while we knelt by the car. Sam put an arm around her and looked up into her face. "What about you, kiddo? Do you ever hear any whispering?"

She shook her curly head, her eyes big. "No, I don't think so."

Thank God for small favors.

Sam stood. "Come on. Let's everybody get inside the house."

Once convinced that we weren't going to drag him back to Sam's house, Tommy came easily enough, curling against Sam while Lily and I trailed behind. I locked and dead bolted the door behind us, then checked the back door and each window while Sam got both kids ready for bed. Tommy fell asleep as soon as he lay down and Lily curled up with *A Tale of Two Cities*, which she'd found wedged between the wall and her bed.

Sam followed me back out to the kitchen and stood next to the dark, scarred wood table, resting his fingertips on the surface while he looked at me. "What the *hell* just happened?"

I leaned against the wall and faced him, crossed my arms, thinking about what to tell him. Wondering how much of it was connected. "I thought maybe...I don't know, epilepsy or something, and then he grabbed me. The look on his face…" I hunched my shoulders against the sick feeling in my stomach.

Sam shook his head. "I didn't see his face, but that voice…Jesus. I didn't know a little kid could sound like that. Creepy."

I pushed off from the wall, gestured to a chair. "Beer?"

He nodded. I retrieved two Weihenstephaners from the fridge, then sat down across from him.

"Whispers," he said finally. "He said you'd heard them too. But you haven't, have you? You'd have told me if something like that was going on at my house—you did the walkthrough with me before I made the offer." He was talking fast, his hands busy peeling the label from his beer, not looking at me or giving me a chance to answer. "Or you think there's some other reason he doesn't want to be at my place? He hasn't been sleeping well, and he doesn't want to talk to me about it. He always talks to me." Sam paused for breath, then finally forced the words out. "Do you think he's starting to remember Aaron? Is he missing his real dad?"

I felt tears prick my eyelids at the memory of seeing Aaron at William's less than an hour ago. I thought about telling Sam, then decided this was the wrong time, if ever. I reached across and grabbed Sam's hand, stilling the movement. "Sam, look at me. Kids don't remember anything before the age of three, and even then it's sporadic. He doesn't know anything about Aaron, okay? He can't miss him. This is about something else."

His eyes went back to the beer, his mouth turned down, brows furrowed. "But he will someday, won't he? Maybe he just knows, even if he doesn't remember. Maybe that's messing with him somehow. Putting distance between us, making him feel unsafe with me."

This was a topic we'd been avoiding for three years now. The timing sucked, but it had to be dealt with. "You're his dad, Sam. The only one he's ever known, and he loves you." I saw Aaron's face again in my mind, and tried not to feel like I was betraying him. "Yes, someday I'm going to tell him about Aaron, when he's old enough to understand. I owe him that, and I owe it to Aaron. I can't pretend he never existed, that we didn't have a child. But it's not going to change the way Tommy feels about you, and it has nothing to do with what's going on right now. He's scared, Sam. Really scared, and it doesn't have a damned thing to do with you. It's your house."

Sam looked impatient. "There aren't any whispers at my place, Rose. You've been there. It's a good house, a happy one. And before you ask, no, there's no one over late at night whispering with me, okay? I never let—" He stopped, pressed his lips together. "Anyway, he's obviously having bad dreams, like you said yesterday. Just nightmares. And the other—that voice he used—it'll turn out to be something physical, nothing major."

"Oh, for Christ's sake, Sam, you sound like a horror movie extra. Next you're going to tell me it's the fucking wind. You and I both know there's scary shit out there—what's more likely than that my son would be the one to pick up on it?"

He glared at me, his mouth set hard, nostrils flared. "What are you telling me? My house is haunted by whispering ghosts? Something you've never heard, that you, with all your experiences, never picked up on, but Tommy did?"

"No, Sam. Tommy was right—I've heard them before."

His hands stilled, clenched around the bottle. "What?"

"Oh, ease up Sam, I don't mean I've heard them at your place. It was before."

"Before. Back—then?"

It had been a long time since we'd spoken of my experiences in recovery after the fire, and the years following my release from the rehabilitation hospital. It had been our habit, even before those visions ceased, to avoid talking about them directly when they happened. Sam and I both felt it was harmful to give them too much attention. Sometimes I would just stiffen, or turn my head abruptly and leave a room, and Sam would come find me. He would hold my hand and ground me in reality, neither of us speaking.

Which was partly why it was hard to talk about now. The other part was simple denial. It had been bad before, scary as hell at times, and when it ended, our relief made us cautious. Like a family that had survived cancer, we avoided talking about it, afraid to speak lest the spirit world take notice of us again. Over time I managed to suppress the memories that sometimes crept up in the form of nightmares, of being small and trapped with something stirring in the darkness.

Neither of us had considered that the ability, or problem, or whatever you wanted to call it, would resurface in the kids. I'd hoped like hell that it was an aberration, something that would never touch my children. Guilt made my heart heavy. What had I passed on to my son?

Sam spoke without looking at me. "Do you ever, you know, see anything anymore?"

I hesitated, then shrugged. "I haven't for years. Not since before you and I split up. When I made S.W.A.T., it was like that swept everything else away."

His jaw was set, his face unreadable. S.W.A.T., the eternal sore point between us.

I sighed, looked away. "When I said I'd heard the Whispers, I meant a long time ago. As a kid. I think maybe it even started when I was close to Tommy's age."

"They were just noises? Just voices?"

I frowned, trying to find a way to put it into words. The Whispers were a memory of a feeling—of terror, of a pushing, clinging, inexorable *wanting*. Even with everything that had come rushing back to me tonight, I had few clear memories of the sound they made, or individual words spoken. Only the way they made the air feel—cold, heavy, hard to breathe—and the horrid certainty that they were always there, always waiting.

Sam didn't look as though he understood. "They didn't actually do anything? Just sort of made noise and scared you?"

I shuddered. "It was more like they wanted *me* to do things. Like they wanted to be part of me, somehow. Whenever they were there, it meant the other things were coming. The Whispers were kind of a precursor to every other kind of haunting."

"Jesus, Rose."

"And I—I think I saw them, once."

"You *think* you saw them?"

I hunched one shoulder. "There was so much, back then. So many things that came and went, and...but this one time, yeah. I was maybe eight? I was already in the cellar, I'd spent the night down there, and something woke me up. The Whispers, I guess, although I don't really remember. I was just lying there in the dark and hoping they'd go away, and then this...*thing* came creeping up to me and kind of peered at me. I got the impression, the feeling somehow, that it was one of them. The Whispers, I mean."

Sam's blue eyes were big. "What did it look like?"

"Like a...I don't know, it was dark, and looked kind of leathery or something. Wings, I'm pretty sure, and these teeth..." I shuddered. "The face was almost human, but not quite, and its eyes were just black. Dead. But I can't be sure. Of all the times I heard them, that was the only glimpse I ever got."

He shook his head, mouth open. "God, Rose, you poor thing. Every time I hear a story about your childhood, I just want to go back in time and scoop you up, baby."

I shrugged and looked away. "Yeah, well. Whatever. It's over."

"What made them finally go away?"

"Briar Ridge, I guess. I don't remember ever hearing them, or feeling them, after the fire."

He was frowning at me. "I don't understand. We talked about everything else—you told me about the visions, the ghosts. Why didn't you ever tell me about these Whispers?"

I pushed my hands back through my hair, tugging briefly at the roots. "I think it's because they were gone by the time we met, and I didn't want them to come back. I know it sounds nuts, but I always had this idea, even after they'd gone quiet, that they were lurking just out of sight. They were part of my life for so long—every time Dad locked me in the cellar at the farmhouse, they were there. I could hear them through the furnace vents at night, and whispering through the windows when I played outside. It was hell, and I was terrified that they'd come back for me someday." Tears welled up and spilled over, and I dashed them away. "Damn it. I can't stand thinking Tommy's been dealing with that, Sam. I can't accept that his life is going to be like mine was."

He reached across the table and took both my hands, squeezing them in his own.

"Rose, Tommy's life will be nothing like yours. For starters, he has two parents that love him."

The steel that crept into his voice made me smile. My father Paul had died before I met Sam, and he'd never met my mother Cora, but he hated them both with a passion I couldn't match anymore. I felt a rush of gratitude at his loyalty.

Cora and Paul Summers had a unique way of dealing with their only daughter's visions. The spirits I saw with increasing frequency as a child made my parents furious—disgusted with me. They told me it was my fault that I was seeing them, that the visitations were a punishment for my sins. That all I had to do to stop seeing them was behave better.

Dad was especially inventive at coming up with punishments to make me worthy of a spirit-free life. My childhood memories were a collage of creeping ghosts, my father screaming at me, a Bible in his hand. Being thrown down the cellar stairs, getting locked in with the things that haunted me. Freezing baths, hours spent outside in the cold, days spent without food and sleep, doors locked to trap me with my own nightmares. Funny how none of it seemed to scour my soul enough to get rid of the ghosts.

I remembered once when I was only a little younger than Lily was now, crouching in my bed, pressed up against the wall with my covers drawn up to my chin, while something watched me from across the room. It sat in front of my bedroom door, blocking my escape: a great, hulking beast that was barely recognizable as a man. It was dirty, its hair long and snarled, blood caked under long jagged fingernails and at the corners of its glowing eyes. They were bright red and fixated on me. There was no telling myself it wasn't there—I could smell it, a mix of musty grave and rotting flesh. I could hear its ragged, growling breaths. And it was no good telling myself it didn't see me—it followed every move I made with jerky, spastic motions of its huge head.

I had held my breath, bit my lips to keep from screaming for my older brother in the next room, for I don't know how long. It was always a gamble—so often, crying for help would get me punishments worse than whatever was watching me, but it's instinct, isn't it? To call for help in the face of monsters?

So eventually I did, and I had a blessed few minutes of Andy's strong presence, of his arms around my shoulders and his voice telling me it was okay, I wasn't alone. Like Sam, Andy had always believed me, never questioned what I told him. Then would come the furious steps of my father, and into the cellar I went, no matter how hard Andy fought for me. The crash of the lock, my brother's voice raised against my father's, and inevitably, the sound of something creeping down the stairs toward me, sharing my exile.

That was my life until the age of sixteen, when the fire that started in my bedroom gutted the farmhouse, killed my father and brother, and left me scarred and hideous.

Yes, Sam was right. Tommy's childhood would be nothing like mine.

"If he *is* seeing things, like you do, he'll at least have you to guide him, Rose. He won't think he's crazy. But are you sure that's what it is? If there is something at my place, why haven't you seen it too?"

I frowned. Sam had a point. Our family breakfasts weren't confined to my house—I was over at Sam's just as often, so I was familiar with the one-and-a-half-story brick place he'd bought two years ago. I had even helped him move in, and I'd never felt so much as a twitch from that other side.

"I don't know. Maybe I can't anymore, like I've aged out of it." Although the events of the last two days made that explanation unlikely. "Or maybe it's recent." I tried to remember the last time I'd been over for any appreciable stretch of time—things had been busy at work lately and it had been a while, maybe a couple of months since I'd done more than stand in the threshold while waiting for the kids. I could tell Sam was annoyed at the implication that there was anything unsavory about his house. "Sam, do you think you'd notice if something there had changed?"

He let go of my hands and sat back, reaching for what remained of his beer. "Like, if it's haunted or something? I'd like to think I'd have caught that, yeah." He didn't meet my eyes, and I waited. He felt me watching him and finally looked up, his shoulders sagging as he sighed.

"Maybe not. Probably not. There were times, back then, when you would...react or whatever, and I thought I could almost see something. But I never knew whether I was just reading you, so I don't know. If Tommy can see things like you can see things, I can't say for sure I'd have noticed."

"Why did you believe me?" I asked before I realized I meant to.

He frowned. "What do you mean?"

"I mean…you didn't know me. I could have been a nut job. I'd even spent time in rehab, so why did you believe me instead of running for the hills when I told you all this shit?"

Sam cracked a grin. "You're kidding, right?"

I was watching him closely. It had always been the strongest foundation of my relationship with Sam, both before and after our divorce. His unshaken belief in me, in the things I had seen. I'd never asked him why before, but now I realized I needed to know. "I'm not kidding. Why? Why didn't you think I was crazy?"

Sam shook his head. "Rose, I *did* know you. We'd been dating a while by then, and I already knew I wanted to marry you. I knew you'd had a fucked up childhood, and the ghost part, when you told me, I guess it made sense. But even if it hadn't, I knew you weren't crazy. You were the most grounded person I'd ever met. So if you said there were ghosts, then I knew there were ghosts."

I studied him and finally smiled. "I guess I still don't get it. But thank you."

Sam stared back, serious as hell. "Always, Rose."

I said nothing else for several minutes, absently stroking the tips of my fingers through the beaded condensation on the side of my beer bottle and mulling over the problem at hand. "Would you object to me taking a look?" I asked finally.

"Over at my place? To see if you can...see...something I missed? If it's these Whispers of yours?"

"I could go tonight while the kids are sleeping. Just, you know, listen. If it *is* something recent, or just more subtle, that could be why I haven't picked up on it before."

"You want to go by yourself?"

I shrugged. "Unless you'd rather I didn't. I don't want to invade your privacy or anything, I'm just worried."

His shoulders hunched upward. "Damn. There's something to this, isn't there?"

"Maybe." My brow furrowed. "Believe me, I'd rather there wasn't, but I don't like the parallels here between what Tommy's describing and what I remember. And before that, what he said, that creepy voice—what if that's part of it too?" And Charlie Akers, I thought. And Aaron. And whatever Sid and Zack had seen and heard at the house on Union. What the hell was going on? I considered telling Sam all of it, but the sore point of Tommy's paternity was too raw at the moment. I didn't want to tell Sam I'd seen Aaron's ghost that afternoon at William's farm.

Sam was nodding now, and I thought how easy it still was to do this with him, to confide things or try to explain them when it would have been unthinkable with anyone else. After all these years of separation, we were still a team. I thought of Luke, tried to picture him in that chair, imagined telling him these things. I couldn't do it. The image wouldn't come. There simply wasn't anyone like Sam, which was both great and depressing as hell.

He tipped his bottle back and drained his beer. Didn't look at me. "You think you'll be okay over there by yourself?"

I raised my eyebrows. "That's some kind of attitude adjustment, McFarland—from 'there's nothing there' to 'do you need backup'."

Sam looked at me. "You know what I mean, Rose. I'm not talking about physical danger. It's not exactly...good for you to be around stuff like that."

I gave him a half smile. "I don't think it's good for anyone to be around stuff like that. But at least I'll know what I'm looking at, and I'd rather it be me than Tommy. If there's anything trying to make contact with him from that other side, I plan to be standing in the way."

Sam watched me with troubled eyes for another minute, then finally his gaze dropped and he fished a small set of keys from his jeans pocket. As friendly as we were, we didn't keep keys to each other's house. It was a line of privacy we didn't cross.

"You want me to stay here with the kids?" he asked as he worked the house key off the ring.

"Yeah. Keep your phone on you. Call me if Tommy wakes up and says anything else, and I'll call you if I come across anything."

He nodded and held the key out to me. He held on a second longer as I grabbed it, wrapping his long fingers around mine. "I want you to go armed, Rose."

My eyebrows went up. I had planned on bringing my .38—I rarely leave the house without a gun—but I knew how little Sam liked to think about it. It seemed dread was catching.

Sam stood in the lighted doorway of my condo, leaning against the frame as he watched me drive away. He lifted a hand once as I glanced in the rearview of my Charger. As I waved back, I tried not to acknowledge the melancholy remembrance of the way he'd always seen me off on dangerous jobs in the middle of the night. I got the feeling he was trying hard not to remember the same thing.

* * *

For once I drove with no music on. I was trying to keep focused on what I needed to do, and discipline my mind to stay out of the dark places—

the cellar the door it's opening what is that dear God please let me out Daddy

—so I was able to hear my cell when it rang. My stomach dropped when I saw Neal's number on the caller ID—I recognized it from the business card he'd given me. I'd forgotten all about the end-of-weekend deadline he'd given me on Friday until just now.

"Fuck," I muttered, thought about it for a beat or two, then answered the call. Maybe I could put him off.

"Agent Neal—"

He cut me off. "Sorry to call so late, Rose, but the weekend's almost over. I didn't want to cut into your time with your family, but we need to talk."

Time with your family. Was he just assuming, or was he watching me?

"It's not a good time, Agent."

"It's never going to be a good time, Rose, but that doesn't change anything." His tone was tight, angry.

I was tempted to hang up on Neal, but his threats about Briar Ridge worried me. I wanted to know exactly what it was he thought he knew. I turned down a side street and pulled over to talk.

"I'm not trying to put you off, Agent Neal, but I've had something

81

come up tonight. Look, why don't you call me tomorrow, we can set something up after work."

"I told you it wouldn't wait, Rose. It's before the incident review tomorrow, or not at all."

"What the fuck does any of this have to do with my review? I don't even know what this is about. I've had an emergency come up with one of my kids—"

"*Don't* talk to me about that, Rose McFarland. You don't know *anything*."

I was silenced, taken aback by the venom in his voice, the bitter fury behind his cryptic words. I came to a decision. "I'm sorry, Agent Neal, but it's not going to be possible to meet up, and certainly not before the review in the morning. Whatever you have to say, I'd suggest you say it directly to my supervisor."

"I don't think you want me to do that, Rose."

I gritted my teeth. "*Stop* calling me Rose—we are not on a first name basis, asshole. And stop threatening me. I don't know what it is you think you know, but you can't touch me, and you can't touch my family."

"You're making a serious mistake. I can help you, and I need you to help me." He paused, and when he spoke again, his voice was soft, subdued. "My son. Ethan. He's sick. Bad off, and getting worse."

"I'm sorry about your son, Agent, but I'm not a doctor. I can't help you, and I certainly don't need your help."

"Are the Whispers back yet, Rose?"

I felt like I'd been punched, my breath forced out of me. No one knew about the Whispers—no one *could* know. "What did you say to me?"

"They must be back. I can tell by your tone. How long has it been since you heard them? Are the memories coming back now?"

I tightened my grip on the phone. "What do you want, Neal?"

"I want you to stop what you're doing and come here, to the Ashland. Meet me in the bar."

"Not possible."

"You'd better make it possible, Rose. This is only going to get worse. Don't you remember how bad it was before? You can't ignore them, Rose, it only pisses them off."

"And you think you can do something about that?"

"No, I can't, Rose. You're the only one who can, and you need to do it soon, before things get any worse. Not just for my Ethan, either. This is about your kids, too. They're all in danger."

In danger? From the Whispers? They'd never hurt me as a child. But that voice coming out of Tommy tonight...

"Why the hell can't you just say what you need to say over the phone, Neal?"

"Because there are things I need to show you. I'll be waiting, Rose. Finish what you're doing and come over here."

He hung up, and I fought the urge to throw my phone. The thought of having to drive all the way downtown and deal with Neal was exhausting. God knew I didn't trust him, but if he did know something about the Whispers, I couldn't afford to dismiss him. Sam could say what he wanted about my ability to guide Tommy through the new and frightening world he was experiencing, but the fact was, I'd never fully understood it myself. I'd see how things went at Sam's—maybe I'd get lucky and find what I needed there.

Sam had bought the little Cape Cod on North McLean two years ago. It was on the part of the long street between Poplar and Parkway, in a neighborhood filled with young professionals and friendly retirees. The area didn't have quite the same amount of old-world Southern charm as the house we'd shared on Deloach before our divorce, but it did have the benefits of close proximity to the zoo, to my place on Belvedere, and to Second Presbyterian Church, where Sam attended, as well as the Presbyterian Day School where Lily went and Tommy would start in the fall.

The street was comfortably lit when I pulled in. It was nearly nine o'clock on a Sunday night, so there was no visible activity, but each house had the hushed and cheerful feel of life just behind the closed doors and drawn blinds. Sam's front porch light was burning, and I could see a lamp on in his office at the front of the house. A huge holly tree stood in the yard and obscured nearly half the front of the dark-red brick house. The covered porch ran the length of the house, and two peaked dormers gave added light and space in the half-story upstairs.

I let myself in with a mix of guilt and envy, careful to lock the heavy oak door behind me. The door was Sam's own addition, an arched and weathered relic of a tumbled-down church in Louisiana. We'd found it on one of our wandering trips ten years ago, propped in the back of an antique shop and missing the glass from the small window cut in the top. He'd been lugging it around for years now, waiting for the right place to hang it. The first time he brought me to see the house, I saw immediately why he wanted it. I knew that door would fit perfectly, and it had.

Making my way down the front hallway, I decided against turning any lights on, trying instead to get my head in the right place for what I was looking for. I set my purse on the refinished table Sam kept close to the door for mail and keys, pulling out the .38 and holding it down at my side. I stopped outside the door of the office, closed my eyes and tried to listen, to remember how to do this.

It seemed to me that back then, before the spirit world had gone silent, I'd been able to get a feel for places. Walk into a room and determine if it was haunted or carried an unhappy energy, even if it didn't always manifest while I was there. I didn't remember how; I just knew that I'd been able to tell, but it had been a long time since I'd done it. Like Sam said, I'd done the walkthrough on this place with him and I hadn't seen anything obvious, but I wondered how dulled my senses were after so many years of suppression. Would I know if something otherworldly was stalking Tommy here? Would I even hear the Whispers? I had to try, but I wasn't sure how to start.

On the surface was only silence, the light purr of the refrigerator from the kitchen, the slight *chunk* as the air conditioning kicked on, the rhythmic swirl of a ceiling fan on the other side of the door to Sam's office. I wanted to open that door and sit in his worn-to-softness office chair, to see the way the bent desk lamp lit the shadows of the room, how they fell on the neatly arranged piles of paperwork on the monstrous mahogany desk or filtered through the wicker of the decrepit peacock-backed chair he liked to read in. I knew it would smell like his shampoo and deodorant, and the fall candles we both liked to burn regardless of season.

I turned instead and continued down the hall to Tommy's bedroom. Sam's inherent neatness didn't extend to making the kids keep their rooms immaculate, but he did insist on the doors being shut to keep the creeping mess contained.

I stood outside, the fingers of my right hand splayed wide as I held my palm to the door, hovering close to the wood but not quite touching. I saw myself in my mind's eye as a child, doing the same thing. Why? What had it told me?

I frowned, pressed my fingers tight to the door itself. It almost felt like...something. The low thrum of energy between my fingertips and the wood. But what did it mean?

I sighed and opened the door, wondering if this was going to be a waste of time. Tommy's room was dark, but in the light filtering in from the streetlamps, I could see the pale blue walls I'd helped Sam paint, the same weekend we'd done a deep purple for Lily's room and a dark red for Sam's. Pictures of boats and water hung on the walls; some were drawn by Tommy himself, but many were framed photos and paintings supplied by Joy, William, Luke, Sam, and me. Tommy had a love for the ocean that had endured almost since birth, much longer than the fads that came and went in his sister's life. His favorite picture was a painting Sam and I had bought together for Tommy's third birthday. It was a sunrise over a darkened beach in California. Beautiful, but so melancholy, and not what you'd expect a toddler to choose for his room. We'd found it in a gallery of local artists, and Tommy had asked to revisit it week after week, trotting straight to it and plunking down on the floor to stare up at it. It hung frameless over his bed and I stood in front of it now, once more pondering the enigma of my youngest child. Now it seemed impossible that I could have missed signs like this in Tommy's life. What toddler wants a painting for their birthday? I wondered how long he'd been seeing things, and felt an immense and heavy guilt at the idea of such a small child living with the constant threat of intrusion from that other side.

Sitting on his bed, I closed my eyes and tried again. Laid my hand on his pillow, and that was when I felt it go through me—Tommy. His own energy, the feel of his small body in my arms, the little-boy smell of him. It was emanating now from every surface in the room, and my eyes flew open, expecting to see him there in front of me. The feeling was that strong.

But I was alone. I hugged my arms to my chest and smiled at the lingering feel of my little boy. Was this how it had been back then? Was this what I'd felt? This wasn't so bad.

I listened for several minutes longer, put my ear to each wall and the window, laid my head on Tommy's pillow, but I didn't hear the Whispers, didn't see anything he'd need protection from. All I felt in there was him.

I tried Lily's room next, got the same result. Sitting in the midst of her mess, I was able to feel her bright, intelligent energy, and this time I was able to catch the lower notes of her family. A little of Tommy in here, a touch of me. Some of Sam—his calm, the warmth of his protection. It was nice, getting back in the groove of this work, and I wondered why I'd ever stopped. There was nothing scary here.

I stopped outside of Sam's master bedroom at the end of the hall, his door cracked. I reached for it, but stopped myself and turned away. I told myself I had no business invading his privacy, but I realized I was also dreading picking up the sign of another woman in his life. It was stupid—I hadn't imagined that perfume on his collar tonight, and I knew Sam never stayed single for long. He'd moved on far quicker than I had after I left, though he'd never remarried, never even introduced me to a woman. I thought of his barely veiled come-on Saturday night as he stood on my porch, and felt like an ass. He had no problem hitting on his ex-wife one night and hooking up with his new woman the next. Yet another reason it was better for us to keep our distance. I reached out and slammed his door shut, a little harder than I needed to.

If there was anything to be found, I'd expected it to be in Tommy's bedroom, but I did a quick check of the rest of the house anyway. Sam's neat kitchen was full of cozy family energy, and the screened-in porch on the back of the house yielded nothing more frightening than a large wolf spider. I trotted up the stairs to the little loft area that Sam used for an upstairs den and playroom for the kids, but again found nothing of interest, even after listening at all the vents and walls. Whatever Tommy was hearing at night, it had gone silent for now. I sat down at the top of the stairs, laid my gun beside me and pulled out my phone.

Sam answered quickly enough to tell me he'd been waiting for my call. "You okay, Rose? Find anything?"

"All fine here, Sam. Didn't see or hear a thing."

He sighed, and I could hear the relief in his voice. "Good. Nothing even in Tommy's room?"

"Nothing, and I tried every which way to see if it might have been coming from a vent or the window or something."

"Your ghostie senses didn't tingle?"

"Not even once."

"Did you check out the cellar? I was thinking about that after you left. Remember me telling you he won't go down there anymore? Maybe it's the furnace he's hearing at night, and that's why he's scared of the cellar. It'd be louder down there."

The cellar. I'd barely even glanced at the door, standing closed in the hallway across from the kitchen. Something in me, some deep old fear, had made my gaze slide right over it without even seeing it.

I almost lied to Sam. I'd already formed the words in my head, ready to assure him I'd ventured down the stairs and that yes, now that he mentioned it, the furnace *had* sounded quite a bit like whispers. Instead I bit my lip, reminding myself I was here for my son.

If I wasn't going to lie, and the fear was that bad, the thing to do would be to ask for help, right? Of course not.

"Hadn't thought about it," I made myself answer. "Good idea, though—I'll bop down there and check it out, then I'm headed back your way."

If he heard the tension in my voice he didn't mention it. "Okay. You might want to take a flashlight; there's one in the junk drawer in the kitchen, just inside the door and under the microwave. There's a short in the overhead light down there—it goes out sometimes."

Great. "Okay, thanks."

I was sweating by the time I stood in front of the door, trying to keep my breath steady. The big black Maglite I'd found in Sam's junk drawer was tucked under my right arm, my .38 in my hand. I had to wrestle the knob on the cellar door and give it a shove with my shoulder, but it finally opened, the stairs dropping off steeply below in total darkness. Only a small wedge of the first step was illuminated. I reached inside and felt for a light switch on first one side, then the other, but came up empty. Flipping on the Maglite, I swung it in an arc, wondering where the overhead light was. I finally saw a chain hanging a few steps down, and a quick yank provided an anemic yellow glow that barely reached the bottom of the stairs.

Three steps down gave me a clear line of sight past the wall over-hang, and I could see through the rotting wood banister to the cellar floor below. There were a few neat piles of boxes stacked close to the stairs and a hideous green, red, and blue plaid sofa from our first apartment tucked against the far wall. Sam's treadmill and my old weight bench were stranded in the middle of the room. Sam didn't even know how to effectively clutter a basement. At least that made it easier for me to see, and there didn't seem to be anything awful lurking in the shadows. I didn't see the furnace, but guessed it was under the stairs, so I gritted my teeth and ran down the remaining steps as fast as I could.

As soon as my feet touched the floor, something sighed deeply, maybe even the walls themselves. I had only seconds to reflect on the grave mistake I'd made coming down here.

Eyes. They were everywhere, glowing, steady sets of them peering out from every corner, at every height. They never blinked, never moved, just stayed fixed on me in the stillness. Here and there I could make out the shadow of a cheekbone, a sunken eye socket, a pair of dry, cracked, and colorless lips. There was no noise, just the hush of expectation.

It had never been like this before. When I was younger, the things that came looking for me, or lurked in old rooms replaying their long-dead dramas, had come alone, or occasionally in pairs. Here I was surrounded. My breathing was ragged, my skin clammy. I squeezed my eyes shut. "They can't hurt me," I reminded myself. "They're already dead."

A sigh came from somewhere behind me as something dragged itself closer. I opened my eyes wide and spun, at the same time bringing my gun to shoulder level. I could see nothing in the blackness. Something moved in the gloom, a dry shuffling and a gust of fetid air.

"Who the fuck is there? Show yourself." I was working hard to keep the panic out of my voice but I could feel it rising, teetering on the edge of hysteria. Whatever was there stood between me and the stairs, my only way out of what had obviously been a very bad idea. I aimed the gun blindly at the darkness before me, my sniper training keeping my hand steady while the rest of me was going haywire. "Show yourself, goddamn it, or I'm gonna just start firing."

The blond-haired thing that lurched into view from below the staircase was a study in anatomical impossibility. The eyes were glassy and dead, the top of the skull a misshapen mass of brain, blood, and bone. The mouth hung open, a swollen purple tongue protruding. Horribly, the tongue seemed to be the only mobile thing about it, lolling and dragging wetly across the lower lip and chin.

"Akers," I breathed. At the same time some vaguely sane part of my brain was screaming at the impossibility of it, I centered my front sight on him and cocked the hammer back. The thing that couldn't be Charlie Akers stood immobile for a heartbeat, then the dead gray lips peeled back in an empty smile, the yellow teeth reddened with oozing blood. When the glassy gaze found me, fixed on me with a horrid intensity despite the black emptiness of the eyes, I pulled the trigger. I fired twice, tight controlled shots, leaving myself three more rounds. The first was center mass and seemed only to nudge the thing backward as a gust of foul-smelling dust expelled from the wound. The second shot was to its face, tearing away the lower half of the jaw. The tongue, that godawful tongue, remained intact, hanging impossibly far past the chin that was no longer there.

"*Ohhhhh,*" creaked an awful grinding voice from ruined vocal cords. "*Killer, you cannot kill what's already dead.*"

I didn't know a moan had escaped me until I heard an answering moan behind me. I turned my head fast. The darkness had filled, the owners of those glowing eyes stepping forward to be seen. My heart nearly stopped when I realized I recognized them all.

Brett Tabor, a small-time thief who'd blundered into the big time when he'd robbed a bank two years ago. He took hostages and ended up with one of my bullets in his chest. He stood before me now, the wound still gaping, black blood oozing through torn flesh, accusation in his dead eyes.

Tammy Ratliff, a meth addict and sometime dealer who had threatened the lives of her own small children when a no-knock warrant had been served on her. She'd taken a shot to the left knee, and when that hadn't dropped her, she took two more. Her femoral artery had been severed and she'd bled out in minutes. She grinned at me, her face full of hate, dragging her twisted, ruined leg behind her.

Eddie McQueen, the first life I'd ever taken. It was before S.W.A.T., back when Luke was still my partner on patrol. We'd surprised McQueen during a burglary, and he'd fired two shots at us from a damn hand cannon, hitting Luke once in the vest and dropping him like a stone, the other bullet missing my face by inches. I'd been just over a year on the force back then, certain I'd seen my partner killed in front of me, and my hands had shaken as I took aim in the gloom, but I hadn't hesitated to pull the trigger. Eddie hung on for three days in the ICU before dying. Luke walked away with a bruise.

Countless others stretched away into the darkness of the cellar and Neal's words came back to me: *you've killed so many, they're starting to blur together.*

I took a step back, shaking my head. They couldn't be here, these people I had killed. They were all dead and buried, their deaths righteous and necessary, brought on by their own bad decisions. I knew these things, knew all of this was in my head, but when Akers' cold grip closed on my wrist, it banished any hope of closing my eyes and wishing it all away. It felt so real, the dirty nails digging into my flesh, the stinking breath stirring the loose hairs that fell around my face. I couldn't help it, I screamed. This wasn't right, I shouldn't be able to feel this, but I did, and no matter how hard I pulled, I couldn't get away.

I heard the others shuffling forward, closing me into a hellish circle while Akers held me in place. None of them spoke, and that somehow made it worse, their silence emphasizing the line they had crossed into something less than human.

"You can't be here," I said through clenched teeth.

An awful, guttural laughter filled the cellar, coming from everywhere at once. I felt the breath of a thousand rotted, empty lungs stir my hair. A dead, flat voice came out of the darkness. "*The Guardians are gone, Rose, and the door is open. We can be wherever we want to be.*"

The door. That awful voice that had emanated from Tommy had mentioned a door, too—an open door, and Aaron had been trying to tell me something about a door. Even Sid Angelo had talked about thin walls. I had no idea what that meant, but uneasily felt that I *should* know.

"*Rose the killer,*" came that flat, dead voice again. I was certain I knew the owner of that voice, but what was so much more awful was the idea that *it* knew *me*. I felt the madness again. Just the lightest tug on the edges of my consciousness, a reminder of how easy it was to slip, but it was enough. I brought my free hand up and smashed the flashlight down hard on the thing's wrist, felt the clutching fingers let go at the same moment the light died. I leveled the .38 in the empty darkness. I whirled around and saw nothing but blackness, heard nothing but my own breathing. The shades were gone.

I didn't bother trying to revive the light, just tossed it to the ground and ran for the stairs in darkness. I scrambled upward, the whole time feeling as though grasping hands were closing just behind me, and when I reached the top I slammed the door shut and threw the bolt that had been unlocked when I got there.

I stood leaning against the wall for a minute, catching my breath and fighting sobs of terror. The visions had never been this bad before. Never had anything been able to cause me physical pain, or restrain me in any way. Whatever was going on at Sam's house was much worse than anything I'd ever dealt with, and I had no fucking idea what to do about it.

When I could breathe normally again, I pushed away from the wall and headed toward the kitchen, moving slowly as weariness overtook me. I hadn't taken more than two steps when I heard the unmistakable sound of a footstep thudding heavily onto the bottom of the cellar staircase. I stood frozen, my back to the door, heart pounding out of control, praying, begging God not to hear it again.

My prayer went unanswered. The heavy footsteps started again, this time with hideous speed as something, maybe even Charlie Akers, ran up the steps toward me. I turned away from the kitchen and ran as fast as I could, screaming when something slammed hard into the cellar door behind me when I'd covered only half the distance.

I struggled with the front door before I remembered I'd locked it behind me. Then I was out, out in the air of the night, away from ghosts and whispered nightmares. When I finally turned back to look, the house was the same as it had been when I'd arrived several lifetimes ago. Silent and waiting, cheerful lights burning behind Sam's old door, holding a place for the little family that lived within.

CHAPTER FIVE

Sitting in my driveway, hands clamped around the steering wheel, back rigid and knees locked, I listened to the Charger's engine tick as it cooled. Watched my front door and tried not to think about all those grinning dead faces, or the way my wrist still stung in little crescent-moon gouges.

Killer, they had called me, and it was true, but the recognition brought no guilt or shame. I killed because I had to. I killed because sometimes it was the only thing that could be done, and someone had to do it—innocent lives depended on it, every time. Was I going to be punished for it?

I had passed through my initial terror and elation at getting away from whatever it was that had invaded Sam's house. Now I was left with the disquieting feeling that the bottom had dropped out of my world.

That horribly familiar alien voice made three times I'd been told of an open door, and I was afraid it meant a door dividing this world from the spirit world. Was that what had been waiting on the other side on those horrible, tearful nights locked in my parents' cellar? Had I escaped it all those years ago, only to face it now? Did it mean that any ghost that wanted to could cross back and forth? Did it mean I had no defenses against anything they might choose to do? I wished I could believe the door only led to Sam's house. Remembering Akers' waking corpse at the shootout, that broken singing voice in the parking lot outside Louie's, my hope died.

"Rose?"

I looked up to see Sam at my window. I opened the door and he reached for me, the concern on his face piercing my defenses and making me want to burst into tears.

"Rose, baby," he murmured and gave me a hand out of the car. He wrapped one arm around my shoulder and held his free hand out for my gun. I placed the .38 gingerly in his large palm and he held it out to his side, then walked me up the stairs and into the kitchen, where he tucked it into a high cabinet, out of the reach of little hands.

Sam pulled me into the living room, where he'd been reading in my recliner, a floor lamp scavenged from my office giving the room a softer glow than the overhead light I usually used. He'd found a red throw I hadn't seen in ages and folded it over the back of the couch, unpacked matching cushions from the hall closet and placed them at either end, and arranged my haphazard stack of books back on the shelves. I knew if I looked, they'd be organized alphabetically by author. I gave a short, husky laugh as I sat down on the couch, legs still shaking. Sam sat next to me and took my hands.

"I guess it's good you're laughing, at least."

I shook my head. "It's not really funny, it's just...you. Here, you know? You're on your own for like an hour and you're already alphabetizing shit."

He smiled and waited. I took a breath and tried to think about how to describe what I'd seen.

"I'm sorry to have to tell you this, Sam, but Tommy is not going back to your house. Neither is Lily, and if I have anything to say about it, neither are you."

Sam only registered mild surprise at this, then nodded thought-fully, accepting my pronouncement. "That bad, huh?"

"Bad does not begin to describe it."

He stood and I heard him open the fridge. When he returned he had two beers, and handed me one he'd already opened. I hadn't realized how thirsty I was until I had the bottle in my hand, but I finished half of it before I tried to speak again. I felt the alcohol hit my bloodstream and begin taking the edge off.

"Tell me," he said.

I took a deep breath and ran through everything that had happened. At the end of my recital, Sam looked grim, his brow furrowed and his jaw clenched. He scooted closer and took the empty bottle from me, placing it on the coffee table before wrapping both arms around me, tense with the effort of holding me close. He was crushing the air out of my lungs, but I wasn't going to complain.

"How the hell did you get away?"

I shrugged against his chest. "How do I ever do anything? I opened fire, flailed, and smashed at things until something worked."

He laughed and squeezed me closer. "Thank God for that."

I sat up, looking around me. "Damn—I left my purse there. I set it down on the hall table and must have run right by it."

Sam pulled me back. "Don't worry about it, Rose. I'll get it for you tomorrow."

"Like hell, Sam. Were you listening to me at all? Whatever you've got down there is not something you want to mess with. None of us is going back there."

His smile was rueful. "Rose, you're talking about my home. I have to go back at some point. These things—you know they never affect me like they do you. I'll be okay."

"Are you talking about going back to stay?" I sat up again, pushing away from him so I could see his face. "You've got to be fucking kidding me. There's no way I'm letting you take the kids back there."

"I never said I was taking them back there. I agree with you completely; they don't need to stay there until we figure out what's going on, especially Tommy. But at the very least I've got to get their stuff for them, and for myself. We're not going to solve anything by just locking the door and abandoning the place."

I put my head in my hands, sighing. "I know. Sorry. It was just so.... bad." I looked back up at him. "That's the first time I've ever felt real danger from something like that, Sam. I think...I think they could have hurt me, if they'd wanted to."

"Hurt how?"

"It was more...physical, I guess is the word. Used to be, the only thing I'd feel would be, like, cold. A couple of times, I felt something kind of brush me as it passed. But this..." I looked down at my wrist. "That *thing* grabbed me, and I felt it—felt his nails, felt the dirt on his hand, the chill of his skin. *I couldn't get away.* Do you understand how bad that is?" I was shaking again and I clenched my fists, clamping my mouth shut.

Sam reached for my hand and squeezed it. "It's my fault, Rose. I'm an ass for letting you go over there alone. I just can't believe...how could I have missed this? How could it have gotten this bad without me noticing? Poor Tommy—what must his nights have been like over there?" A shudder went through his big shoulders. "No wonder he didn't want to go down those stairs. Thank God I didn't make him."

"Akers," I said, sitting up.

"What about him?"

"What if he's the key to all this? You asked how it could have gotten so bad without you noticing. What if he's the one who set all this off? What if none of it started until I killed him?"

Sam frowned. "Maybe...although no, that doesn't fit. Tommy's been having trouble with the cellar for a few weeks now."

"But what if Akers is what made it worse?"

"Why would that be?"

"I have no idea, but it's worth looking into. I'm going to see what I can find out about him tomorrow." I needed more than ever to talk to Zack about what he'd heard, and felt a fresh wave of worry at his continued radio silence.

Sam nodded, thought. "You said he mentioned a door. What door—what did that mean? Is that how things get here? Do they pass through some kind of a door?"

I sighed, rested my head in my hand. "I don't know. Maybe. Maybe it's like in *Poltergeist* and they have to move toward the light, who knows? We know spirits cross over at least one way, from this life to whatever comes next, so that's got to be it. There must be an Ellis Island for the spiritually disenfranchised."

"You're saying if something happened to this door, it could mean spirits could pass back through again to our world?"

I thought about Aaron. Was that how he'd been able to appear to me at the farm? Had he too taken advantage of a newly opened passage into our world? Maybe that was what he'd meant by saying he shouldn't be there—and if he could cross over, that meant worse things could, too.

I shrugged. "It makes a certain kind of sense, right?"

Sam was frowning. "Do you think that has something to do with why he—that *thing*—could touch you? Hold onto you like that? Did something happen to make him more powerful? More corporeal?"

It sounded reasonable. "Maybe. I hadn't thought...but maybe. But if there is something that's opened a door, what was it? How do we close it?"

"Maybe you're right. Maybe it has something to do with Akers." Sam gave a half smile. "Maybe he picked up a discount Ouija board somewhere and invoked the devil."

I snorted. "He looked about bright enough for something like that."

After sitting in brooding silence for several minutes, exhaustion overcame me. I'd barely slept for days now, and it was catching up with me. I rose unsteadily, wanting my bed, hoping like hell I'd be able to close my eyes without those nightmare images coming back. "Come on, Sam. I think we've done all we can tonight. Let's regroup in the morning, okay?"

He nodded and stood. "Of course, you need some sleep. I'll just go take a last look at the kiddos before I head out."

"Head out where? I thought we decided you weren't going back."

He lifted an eyebrow at my tone of command. "I'm not. I'm going to go to Mama's and sleep in her guest room. If you want to bring the kids over in the morning, we can talk again then."

Don't leave me alone was what I wanted to say, but wouldn't. Instead I shook my head and pretended I wasn't still terrified. "Don't be an ass, McFarland. Why don't you just stay here tonight? It's getting late and your mom's probably already in bed."

Sam raised both eyebrows. "Where exactly did you want me to sleep?"

"In my bed. I'll sleep out here on the couch."

We argued briefly, but Sam finally agreed to stay, provided he took the couch. I was annoyed at myself for the relief that flooded through me—I didn't want to need him like this. I rummaged in the linen closet and came up with a couple of extra blankets and pillows, then helped him make up the couch.

"Got anything for me to sleep in, or should I just go commando?" He waggled his eyebrows at me and I grinned, but shook my head.

"I'm sure I have something that will work."

He stood in the doorway of my bedroom while I opened drawers, looking for something that would fit Sam, hoping Luke hadn't left anything the last time he spent the night. Eventually I found a worn pair of flannel pajama bottoms that seemed big enough, and handed them over along with a wrinkled but clean UK Wildcats shirt. Sam took both with a quizzical look.

"I'll give you credit for the shirt, since you're the only person in Tennessee foolish enough to cheer for the Cats, but these are definitely not your pj's."

I froze, trying to remember who I might have stolen them from. When I looked up, he was smiling.

"Do you have any idea how long I've been looking for these, Rose? They were my favorite."

I sighed and returned his smile. "I'm pretty sure they were in the separation agreement, Sam. Didn't I get them in return for leaving the big screen with you?"

He shook his head, frowning. "No, no, I think you traded the TV for the pillowtop mattress." He nodded in the direction of my bed. The look in his eyes when they met mine again was definitely suggestive.

I knew I should have broken the moment. I should have hustled him off to bed, closed and locked my door, and put him out of my head. After all, it was clear I wasn't the only woman in Sam's life, and with the kids, sex with Sam could only complicate things. But when I looked up at him, his smile turning into something more intimate, his eyes traveling over me appreciatively, I didn't want to close the door. When he leaned in to kiss me, I didn't turn away.

There was always something about kissing Sam that felt like coming home, even our first kiss. I remembered that night, in the halogen-lit parking lot of C.J.'s Cafe in the dark hours before dawn, during a late shift on patrol. It was our third or fourth meeting, a quick cup of coffee while Luke took the cruiser to get gassed up and give Sam and me a little time alone. The smells of cooking grease and something burning, the sounds of drunks on the street behind us, the pavement reflecting an oily sheen from the buzzing streetlight made for an unromantic locale, but that wasn't the part I remembered best. It was Sam's uncertainty that touched me, this tall, good-looking guy five years my senior. I remembered the way his hand traveled reverently through my hair and down my neck, and the way I hadn't flinched when his fingers brushed my scars. It had felt right, the way it did now, standing in my messy bedroom and letting him worship me.

"Rose," he murmured in my ear, and I reached up to wrap my arms around his neck. He was half lifting me, carrying me to the bed and sweeping the pile of comforters onto the floor.

"Sam," I sighed as he sank to the mattress beside me. The big bad world didn't seem so big or bad anymore, and I gave myself over.

* * *

I lost track of time and details, but both of our shirts were off and Sam's jeans were unbuttoned when I pulled away and put a finger over his protesting lips.

"*Mommy*," came the plaintive cry again. Sam heard it too, and rolled off me with a sigh but dragged his shirt back on and followed me to Tommy's room.

I felt waves of fear coming off my son before I even made it down the hallway. Terrified that something had followed me home from

Sam's place, that I would open the door to find Tommy surrounded by the gang of awful specters from my past, I pushed through and hurried to his bed.

He was sitting up, his knees pulled to his chin and a quilt wrapped around him, small hands clapped over his ears. The room was cold, colder than it should have been, and I tried to pull him to me, but his little body was rigid. "*Go away, go away,*" he was sobbing, shaking his head from side to side. Sam sank down on the other side of the bed and laid a hand on Tommy's back but at his touch Tommy began to shake and sob even harder.

"Tommy." I tried to make myself heard over the sound of his cries, but he didn't respond. I grasped his wrists and pulled his hands away from his ears. "Tommy!"

He looked up, his green eyes bright with tears, but it was still a long minute that he stared at me in terror, no recognition on his face. "Mommy," he finally cried, threw his little arms around my neck and tucked his head against my chest while he sobbed.

Sam wrapped his arms around both of us. "Tommy, talk to us. What's the matter, kiddo? You have a bad dream?" Sam lifted his eyebrows at me and looked around the room.

I shrugged. Whatever Tommy was afraid of, I couldn't see it. "Tommy, honey, you're safe now, okay? Mom and Dad are here and we aren't going to let anything happen to you." I felt his small hands clutching at my shirt and hugged him tighter. "What happened? What scared you, was it a dream?" Please let it only be a dream.

"Not a dream, Mommy," he sniffed, his voice muffled against my chest. "I *saw* you."

Thoughts of being caught in bed with Sam by my son made me cringe. "Uh, saw me? Where, here?"

"No. You were in the dark place, with the gray people."

His words made me cold. "The gray people?"

I felt him nod against my chest.

"The bad gray people. They were standing all around you, and they were mad. They came through the door."

"The door."

"The bad door, Mommy. It's not supposed to be there, but it is. You can't see it, not like you used to, but it's open again. It's where the gray people come from, but there's something else in there too. Something even badder than them. I thought it was going to get you, but then the radioman came and you got away."

I opened my mouth, shut it again. There was no doubt in my mind that Tommy had somehow seen everything that had happened to me in Sam's cellar. The gray people—easily identifiable as the way a child might have seen those awful ghosts, and yet another reference to the open door.

"Tommy? Who's the radioman? What did he look like?"

Tommy tucked his head under my chin and shrugged. "He was hard to see—like a shadow, kinda, but not like the other ones. Not a bad shadow. He seemed real sad, though."

"Why do you call him the radioman?"

He shrugged again. "That's who he is."

I met Sam's troubled eyes over Tommy's head. What did it mean that Tommy had been able to see these things, and what would have happened to him if I hadn't gotten away? Could those things have killed me? Would he have had to watch me die? Would he have been safe himself, or would whatever window he watched through have opened wide enough for something to pull him through? I shuddered at the possibilities, but when Tommy looked up at me, I put on my best reassuring Mom smile.

"Hey, I'm safe now, kiddo," I said, pushing his soft dark hair away from his sweaty forehead. "Those gray people might be mad, but I'm meaner than them, and meaner than anything else that might come along. Just ask Dad."

Tommy giggled, and Sam smiled at me.

"I'm glad you're mean, Mommy."

I bent and touched my forehead to his. "Good thing, since there's not a lot you can do about it. Yep, you and Lily got the meanest Mom on the block."

He snuffled and smiled up at me. "Can I sleep with you tonight, Mommy?"

Sam's rueful look matched my own. It was probably for the best.

"Sure, kiddo. Let's get your blankets. Where's Tabby?"

My son lifted the blanket beside him to reveal the worn stuffed donkey he always slept with when he was at my house. "Tabby was hiding. He was scared too."

"Tell Tabby it's safe to come out now."

Sam lifted Tommy over his shoulder and carried him out, making pig-snorting sounds in his ear and pretending to gobble him up. Tommy giggled hysterically in that full-bellied way that only children can, and I followed, trailing blankets and pillows with Tabby tucked under my arm.

While Sam was getting Tommy settled in my bed, I took the opportunity to duck into the bathroom and change into a pair of pink and black striped pajama shorts and an oversized Pink Floyd shirt, from the Gilmore "Momentary Lapse" tour. I climbed into bed, and Sam bent to kiss Tommy good night, but a little hand reached out to stop him from leaving.

"Will you stay too, Daddy? Please?"

With another kid, you might suspect them of manipulation, but Tommy had never known Sam and me as a couple. He'd always accepted that Mommy and Daddy lived at different houses, and his sleepy face was guileless. Sam hesitated, his eyes meeting mine, and I shrugged.

"That way we can both protect Mommy, okay?"

Tears pricked the back of my eyelids. I'd thought Tommy wanted to stay with me for his own comfort, and instead my four-year-old was intent on keeping me safe.

Sam relented. "Okay, buddy, just for tonight. I'll go get my pj's on." He collected them from the floor where he'd dropped them earlier, and disappeared down the hall in the direction of the main bathroom.

I lay on my side and curled around my son, watching his eyelids droop even as he struggled against sleep. I wanted to ask him how he knew the things he knew, how often he'd seen otherworldly sights, and why he seemed to have so much more control over the images that came to him than I'd ever had, but those questions would have to wait, maybe even until he was older and better able to express himself. Though I wouldn't have chosen to have these things visited upon my son, I felt the oddest sense of comfort, the lifting of the weight of isolation I'd always carried. Then I felt guilty, knowing that my comfort came at Tommy's expense.

"Tommy, can you tell me any more about the radioman? Do you know who he is? Have you ever seen him before?"

He yawned, his green eyes squeezed shut. "You know him, Mommy. He plays the music to make you feel better."

I frowned. Was Tommy talking about *my* music? Andy's music? Could the radioman be my brother? My heart lifted at the thought that he might be looking out for me, as I'd half believed all these years. That even though I hadn't seen him, Andy had been with me in that cellar—I hadn't been alone. "How do I know him?"

His chin drooped. "I don't know. Mommy..." His voice was small and sleepy.

"I'm here, baby."

"Don't let them in, okay? They want in—they always do. Keep them out, Mommy."

Goosebumps rose on my bare arms despite the warmth of the room. "Let who in, Tommy? The gray people?"

His eyes were closed, lashes long against his cheeks. "No, Mommy. Not them."

His head drooped and his breathing deepened, and I knew he was asleep.

I pulled him closer, tucking his head under my chin. I'd do whatever it took to keep him and Lily safe, no matter how much it scared me. I said a silent prayer of thanks for Sam, glad that whatever I had to do, at least I wouldn't be alone.

By the time Sam reappeared, Tommy was snoring. Sam hit the overhead light, leaving only a small lamp burning on the nightstand close to him, then hesitated. "He's out now, Rose. I don't have to stay if you don't want me to."

"Just get in, McFarland."

With the lamp out, I couldn't see Sam as he made himself comfortable, but I felt him rolling around, arranging the covers just so on his side of the bed. It made me smile, remembering how finicky he'd always been—a minimum of two pillows of appropriate firmness, no more than two blankets, no duvets, and nothing covering his feet. Sam was a pain in the ass, but it was still nice to lie next to him, and better since we hadn't actually crossed the line and slept together. Thanks to Tommy, I could dismiss the sense of guilt I otherwise would have felt. I still figured I'd have trouble sleeping, worrying about what our family was facing and knowing Sam was only an arm's length away, but I was nearly unconscious when I felt his fingers skate lightly through my hair.

"Night, Rose."

"Night, Sam."

* * *

When I opened my eyes the next morning, sunlight was peeking around the edges of the blackout curtains, though it was early and most of the room was still in shadow. I looked over and saw that Tommy had managed to make a 180-degree turn in his sleep, and his head was now at the foot of the bed, his bare feet on my pillow. Tabby was squashed under his head, and every last blanket and sheet had been commandeered and dragged over to Sam's side of the bed, where he slept cocooned in comfort. Must be nice—I was freezing.

"What are you guys *doing*?" came a voice from my bedroom door. Sam stirred and grumbled next to me, but Tommy didn't budge.

I propped myself up on my elbows. "Hey, kiddo, you're up early."

Lily was watching me with an eyebrow cocked, head tilted to one side, glasses crooked and sliding down her nose. "Did Daddy sleep here all night?"

I yawned. "Yes, he did. There's a little bit of a...problem over at Daddy's house, so it was safer for everyone to stay here last night."

She looked skeptical. "What kind of problem?"

"Bugs," I lied. "Silverfish."

"Ewww!"

I looked over at Sam, grinning sleepily at me from within his blanket cocoon.

"Yeah, well. They're gross, I know, so that's why everyone's staying here for now, until we figure out what to do about the silverfish.

Go get ready for breakfast, okay? And get your stuff packed up, remember you're going to Grandmommy's for the day."

She scooted out the door and I could hear her repeating, "Silverfish, ew ew ew, silverfish," as she headed back to her bedroom.

"That was unscrupulous," murmured Sam. "Preying on your daughter's silverfish phobia."

I threw a pillow at him. "I didn't prey on it. Preying on her phobia would be releasing silverfish in her room to make her clean it. Besides, I'm a scruple free zone before I've had my coffee." I started to get out of bed, but Sam grabbed my arm and pulled me back. I wobbled, trying not to squash my unconscious son. "What do you want, McFarland? It's time to get up."

He pulled me to him, tucking his long body against my back. "I just want thirty seconds to lie here with you and not think of anything. Can you handle that?"

I could lie there, but as far as not thinking went, I was a total failure. I thought of how close we'd come to crossing the line again the night before, and how bad I'd been hurt the last time it had happened. I thought about the women I'd seen hitting on Sam all throughout our marriage, the ones who flirted in full view of his wife, and wondered how many of them he'd invited into his bed. I thought about whoever it was he'd spent the day with yesterday, who'd left perfume on his collar. I wondered if she was pretty, and if he loved her.

Even so, I gave it the full thirty seconds, plus a few more, because there were times I still indulged the same fantasy that Sam was this morning. The one where we were still married, and a real family, the kind that lived together all the time and didn't date other people. I opened my eyes, pulled away and stood up, ignoring Sam's deep sigh.

Sam's mother Joy was a widow who lived alone on Sledge Avenue in a two-story brick house built in the 1940's. Sam's dad TJ, a beat cop on the Memphis PD for almost thirty years, had died on the job just before Sam left for college, a little over twenty years ago now, and Joy had never remarried. I'd never met TJ, but there were pictures of him all over Joy's house—my favorite was one of TJ and Sam when he was tiny, less than two years old. Neither one was looking at the camera, but at each other, frozen in a moment of laughter over who knows what, Sam's little blond head tucked close to his dad's.

I pulled into the driveway behind Sam, the Charger bouncing over the bumps in the asphalt. Joy's bright red front door was opening before the car even stopped, and she was coming down the steps with a welcoming smile on her freshly painted lips. Both kids scrambled out and ran to her, folding themselves into her open arms, wearing grins to match her own. You'd never know the woman saw them at least five days a week—every time I dropped them off she gave them the same welcome, like she hadn't seen them in a year. Sam was an only child, so Lily and Tommy were it for grandkids. They could simply do no wrong—if they were bad, they had to sit on the couch, watch cartoons and eat chocolate while they thought about what they'd done. Every kid should have a grandparent like Joy.

When she'd released the critters and shooed them into the house, Sam stooped to kiss her hello. He'd gotten his height from his father—Joy barely topped five feet. She was heavyset and favored brightly colored jogging suits, but she had her hair fixed every week and colored every six. Joy McFarland was everything a Southern mother should be.

"Rose! My Rosie girl, come over here and get some sugar, baby."

I squeezed her hard and was rewarded with a kiss on my cheek. I grinned, knowing I'd have to remove a lipstick stain before I went into work.

"Y'all come on in and get some coffee. Just made a fresh pot."

Sam shook his head. "Sorry, Mama, we can't today. Got an errand to run before work."

She placed her manicured hands on a set of broad hips. "What, both of y'all? Where you going so early, children?"

"We've gotta run by my place and get some things for the kids. They're going to be staying with Rose for a little while."

Now the well-shaped eyebrows lifted. "What's wrong with your place?"

"Bugs," he replied, not looking at me.

"Bugs?" Joy made a little moue of distaste.

"Yep, silverfish. You know how Lily feels about silverfish."

She shuddered dramatically. "Who can blame her? All those legs, ugh. So they're spraying your house?"

"Yes, ma'am. We're gonna get some stuff out before the exterminators come. You mind if I leave my car here until we get back?" Joy shook her head and Sam bent to kiss her again. "One of us will be by to pick them up tonight. Thanks, Mama."

I echoed his thanks and meant it. Most parents would kill for a setup like ours. We both received another noisy kiss, and we were almost to the car before she called to me.

"Rose! I nearly forgot, sugar. Zack came by early this morning, looking for you."

I frowned, turned back to the porch where Joy stood. "Looking for me? He knows where I live—I was at home this morning." I checked my cell; no missed calls. "I've been leaving messages for him all weekend—why wouldn't he just return my call? Why would he come looking for me here?"

Joy shrugged, but looked troubled. "He *said* he was looking for you, but to tell the truth, he seemed more interested in where the kids were. Wanted to know if they were coming here today."

I didn't like the way her words made my stomach flip. Zack was my good friend, a man I trusted. He knew my kids and had never been anything but great with them, but I hadn't shaken the creepy feeling I'd gotten from that odd phone call on Saturday night. I needed to get hold of Zack. I had the strangest fear that he'd somehow been tainted by his contact with Akers.

"Listen, Joy, if he comes by here again I want you to call me, okay?"

She nodded, one eyebrow raised.

I chewed my lip while Sam watched me, then yielded to impulse. "And it's probably best if you don't let him in. Just tell him the kids are with me, okay?"

Both eyebrows went up, and her red lips pursed as she looked from me to Sam. "Is there something I should know, children?"

I met Sam's eyes. "No. I'm just...humor me, would you? I'm probably being paranoid."

"All right, Rosie. It's your call. We won't be at home to visitors today."

"Thanks, Joy."

As I waited at the end of Sledge to get back into the flow of traffic, Sam touched the back of my hand. "What was all that about Zack?"

I hunched one shoulder. "I'm not sure. He was a little...off, after the Akers thing."

Sam frowned. "Off how?"

"He was spacey, kind of. Kept talking about something being in there with Akers—something he heard over the headset."

"Are you so sure he didn't? You're the one who said Akers might have been some kind of catalyst."

"No, I'm not sure. I think it's looking more and more like Zack was right. But I don't like that he was here at Joy's, instead of calling me like he was supposed to. He said he was going to go over the recordings this weekend and let me know what he found. I've tried calling him several times, left him messages, but he doesn't answer or call me back. Instead he comes to your mom's place, asking about the kids. Something's wrong there, and until I know what it is, I'm not letting him near them."

Sam looked worried. "Just how big is this thing, Rose?"

I sighed, rested my forehead on the steering wheel. Cars were still rushing by, but none were stacked behind me. "I wish I knew. Sam?" I said after a minute.

"Yes?"

"Where are we really going?"

"We're really going back to my place. I wouldn't lie to my Mama."

It's amazing the way Southern men can say "Mama" and not sound ridiculous.

I lifted my head, gripped the steering wheel. "I thought we talked about this. Agreed none of us were going back to your place until we figured out what was going on."

"Rose, you're not going back in there. Just me. I told you I needed some stuff from my place, so I want to get this over with in the daylight, and you better believe I'm not going anywhere near the damn cellar. I'll get in, get out, and lock it up after. I only want you there to be a landline, of sorts. If I don't come back, you can holler for help, okay?"

I was already sweating, my heart thudding. I'd barely escaped with my life last night, and now Sam wanted to go back. I didn't bother asking who the hell I was supposed to call for help. "No, it's not okay. What do you have to have from there? I'll buy you a new one, whatever it is. I'll buy you a whole wardrobe and stuff for the kids too, just don't go back, okay?"

Sam took my hands. "Rose, honey, you know these things don't—can't—hurt me the way they do you. Besides, you left your purse, remember? Do you want to have to file for a new badge?"

Fuck. I'd forgotten. On the heels of the Akers shooting, I was going to be facing enough scrutiny without having to explain how I'd lost my badge. Getting a new one wasn't as simple as asking for it—a valid deputy's badge in the hands of the wrong person could be a dangerous thing. The loss would not be taken lightly.

I scrubbed the heels of my hands over my eyes, telling myself to suck it up. A glance at the dashboard clock told me I had thirty minutes to get to work, and traffic wasn't getting any better. "Fine. Let's get this over with." I pulled the Charger into the stream of cars without looking at him, and we didn't speak on the short trip over to McLean.

I pulled into the drive and sat, scrutinizing the house for any signs of last night's disturbance. I don't know what I'd expected—maybe that the whole thing would have folded in on itself, or developed an Addams Family vibe. But the house looked normal, just like any other turn-of-the-century Cape Cod in the area. The porch light was still burning, the lamp in Sam's office the only other light visible from the street.

Sam was already climbing out of the car.

"In and out," he said with a smile, before slamming the car door and loping up the driveway, his long strides eating up the turf. He pushed the door open and gave me a thumbs up before being swallowed by the blackness beyond.

As soon as he disappeared from my sight, I wished I'd told him to forget it, I'd be happy to file for a new badge. Hell, I'd be happy to quit my job and move to Alaska if that was what it took to keep my family out of that place. I leaned down and felt under the seat for the case where I kept my 9 mm. I checked the magazine but kept the safety on, feeling too jittery to have my weapon hot. "He's safe, he'll be fine," I muttered to myself, wishing I could believe it. Sam might think I was the only lifeline he would need, but remembering how close I'd come to losing myself the night before, I wasn't so sure. But who else was there? I was a S.W.A.T. sniper for God's sake—we *were* the heavy artillery.

"Oh, fuck it," I said, and climbed out of the car.

As soon I was outside, I could feel that something was different—the air felt thick, viscous in my lungs and against my skin. It slowed me down, made me fight for every step, and as I glanced up, I saw that the sky had grown unnaturally dark. Nothing moved on Sam's street—it was morning rush hour, but I might as well have been on the moon. I flipped the gun's safety off, my hands steady now as I approached the house. I stopped on the little front porch and tried to peer inside the glass-sided door, but the hallway was in full shadow.

The door was standing open. Just a couple of inches, but I was certain I'd seen Sam pull it closed behind him. Inside, the hallway was empty and silent. "Sam?" I called, stepping over the threshold. I glanced at the hall table and saw my purse was gone.

"Sam." Louder this time—maybe he was upstairs, or in his room with the door shut. I stopped to listen again.

Movement. The rustle of something living. I turned slowly. It was coming from Tommy's room. The door was shut as I'd left it last night, but it looked different. Off kilter, warped somehow, the white paint smudged and browned around the edges. And something smelled.

I stood, stepped closer, reached a hand out to the door like I had last night, wondering if it would work this time. I touched it and recoiled immediately, bile filling my throat. This time the feeling was immediate, knock you on your ass strong, and it wasn't Tommy anymore. Gone was my son's sweet signature. Now whatever was in Tommy's room was black, rotting, and cold.

When the door swung open, I wasn't prepared—my gun was only halfway up when Sam reached for me.

"Rose, what the hell? I thought you were going to stay in the car."

"You were gone forever, and I got worried. Have you seen anything?"

Sam's shoulders slumped. "Nothing moving, no. But Tommy's room..." He stepped back from the doorway so I could see around him.

I sucked in a breath, and the stench of rotting flesh mixed with a charred, acrid undertone made me gag.

"Holy shit," I said, wondering how in hell I could ever have garnered an impression of *cold* from this room. It was anything but.

Every surface was charred, the walls blackened where flames had leapt up the curtains, crawled across the ceiling. The paint had bubbled in places and the hardwood floor crunched underfoot, the first few layers carbonized and covered with the ashy remains of toys, books, and whatever clothes had been scattered around the room. Smoke curled upward, visible in the bands of sunlight that streamed through the soot-smeared window, and heat came off everything.

Something caught my eye, and I knelt. Tommy's wooden train set, the one we'd given him for his last birthday. He'd spent many quiet hours playing with it, putting the segments of grooved tracks together in patterns that only made sense to him. Now it was splintered, burned black and barely recognizable, little globs of melted plastic adhering to the sides.

"Aw, hell," Sam sighed.

I stood and turned, my stomach dropping when I saw what he had.

The seascape painting above the bed, Tommy's favorite. It was ruined beyond repair, the canvas hanging in great strips. It had been ripped in at least five places.

Sam turned to me. "I don't get it. How did a fire start here? How could it possibly have been contained to just this room?"

"While we're at it, Sam, how the hell did it get put out? There's no foam or anything from an extinguisher." I knelt again, rubbed my fingers against the floor. "It's not wet either."

I had a crawling, sick feeling in my belly as an old fear wormed its way back into my consciousness. *Yes, Rose. How did the fire start?*

I crab-walked over to Tommy's ruined bed and bent to check underneath. There it was—the familiar odd circle of carbonized wood flooring. No candle, no matches I could see, no lighter or any other incendiary. Just that circle. Just like eighteen years ago.

* * *

"Tell me what you're thinking, Rose," Sam said.

We were sitting in the driveway, both of us staring blankly at the front of Sam's house, our minds on our son's ruined bedroom.

"I'm thinking," I began, with the longstanding habit of telling Sam everything and letting him put it in perspective for me, but I stopped.

I'm thinking maybe I started this fire in my four-year-old son's room, Sam. I'm thinking that because of that weird little charred circle of origin under his bed—I recognize it because there was one just like it under my bed after the fire that killed my father and brother and left me a walking horror.

I looked at Sam's well-loved face. Pictured the way his expression would change from concern to fear, maybe even to disgust.

"I'm thinking I'm glad no one was home when that fire started," I said, cranked the engine and backed out of Sam's driveway.

He sighed. "Me, too." There was a short silence, then, "But I'd still like to know what you were really thinking."

Saved by the phone. I checked the ID—it was work. "McFarland."

"Sarge, it's Ben. Taylor's looking for you." Ben's voice was tight. Taylor was Assistant Chief Deputy Al Taylor, who was over Special Operations, which included S.W.A.T.

"Shit. Yeah, I'm sorry, this morning's been nuts. I've just got to—"

"Sarge, listen, you need to get in here. Like, *now.*" There was a rustling, and I pictured him covering the phone. When he spoke again, his voice was lowered, almost whispering. "They found something in the house—something of Akers'. Now they want to know if you knew him beforehand—they think there's some kind of connection."

"*What?* What kind of connection?"

"I don't know, Sarge, they're playing it pretty close to the vest, but it's not looking good. Just get here, okay?"

"Yeah, okay," I agreed as I pulled into Joy's driveway.

Sam was watching me. "Everything all right?"

I sighed, rolled my shoulders. "No. No, it sounds like not. Ben says they found something in Akers' gear, and now they think I knew him. I've got to get over there."

Sam's blue eyes were worried. "Could they know something? About the way he's been appearing to you?"

I frowned. "I don't see how. I can't think…"

I stopped, feeling cold as I remembered Evan Neal's threat the previous night. Before the review or I'd regret it; that was what he'd said. I hadn't made a conscious choice to blow him off last night, but after what happened at Sam's house, I'd never even thought of Neal. Could he really know something that would cause trouble for me? He'd mentioned Briar Ridge, talked about the Whispers, but my stay at the Ridge was in my personnel file, anyway. It showed up as rehab and physical therapy after the trauma of the fire, and hadn't disqualified me from active duty or S.W.A.T. If Neal tried to tell my superiors about the Whispers, all I'd have to do would be deny it, and he'd end up looking like a nutcase.

"Do you want me to stay with the kids today while you deal with this work stuff?"

I looked at him, but for once there was no judgment in his voice. "Can you? Tommy's got his doctor's appointment at 10, and I'd feel better if Joy wasn't on her own with them."

"Because of Zack? Or something else?"

I chewed my lip. "All of the above, Sam."

"You think something else is coming?" His voice was quiet, worried. "That it's not just something wrong with my house? I thought hauntings…I mean, it always seemed before like ghosts were attached to a place, right?"

I looked out the Charger's windshield at Joy's cheerful red door, the sunlit street, the promise of the morning. I wanted to tell Sam he was right, that whatever was wrong couldn't pass beyond the threshold of his house, but I knew that wasn't the case. Charlie Akers wasn't confined to a place, not if he was the one who'd stalked me in the Louie's parking lot. Neither were the Whispers, whatever the hell they were, and Tommy's problems needed to be dealt with.

"Something's coming, Sam. I don't know what, or why, but whatever it is, anything we thought we knew about the old rules doesn't apply anymore."

* * *

I rolled into the sheriff's office parking lot twenty minutes later. There was no sign of Neal there or in the lobby, and I breathed a little easier until I saw the B.P.S.I. investigator, Bonnie Skylar, through the open door of Interview One. She was alone, seated on the wrong side of the table—the interviewee's side. She was sitting painfully straight, her thin shoulders thrust backward, a white-knuckle grip on the briefcase in her lap.

As though she felt my eyes on her, she looked up and over at me. I gave her a nod and a small smile. In return she pursed her lips and gave me a terse shake of her head before turning back to face the empty wall.

I stared at her, the sinking feeling in my stomach getting worse. When I'd last talked to Bonnie on Friday, everything had been fine; she'd given no indication that my debriefing had raised any problems for her. Now she wouldn't even look at me.

Ben was in the bullpen when I rounded the corner. He was at his desk next to mine, looking busy and worried. He gave me a quick wave and a grimace, then jerked his head in the direction of Taylor's office.

I dropped my purse at my desk and glanced around the pen. The room was windowless and decorated in a uniform gray, full of loud phone conversations and the smell of bad coffee. Most of the desks were full at this hour, my team pecking away at paperwork while they waited for the next call out.

I responded to greetings as I made my way to my boss's closed door and knocked once.

"Come in," came the curt reply. "Close it after you."

"Al? Ben said you were looking for me."

Taylor looked up and pushed his reading glasses to the top of his head, where there was precious little hair to get in the way anymore. He didn't smile. "You're late, McFarland."

"Yeah, I'm sorry about that. I told Ben when he called that something came up with Tommy." Usually anything having to do with my kids was a free pass with Taylor, one I took care not to abuse. Thanks to the combined efforts of Sam, Joy, and William, it was rare that my family life interfered with my job. Taylor's own failed marriage and strained relationship with his grown son made him more sensitive to his officers' family dynamics. Under normal circumstances, he was more apt to give me grief about *not* going home to be with my kids.

Taylor leaned back as far as his ergonomically challenged chair would allow and folded his hands over a substantial belly, his dark eyes assessing me while I tried to keep my expression neutral. The silence went on long enough to make me squirm, fighting the impression of being called to the principal's office.

My relationship with my boss was usually benign. Al Taylor was a good man and a good chief. A thirty-two year veteran of the Shelby County Sheriff's Office, he'd long ago mastered the art of walking that fine line between bureaucratic politics and actually running his departments. His thick black eyebrows and the deep lines carved on either side of his mouth often intimidated people who didn't know him, as did his deep, rough voice, complete lack of verbal filter, and tendency to exercise his quick temper regardless of the setting. Anyone expecting to be treated with kid gloves didn't last long under his command, but if you had a spine and could square up to the man, he was a loyal and protective eight-hundred-pound gorilla to have in your corner.

Right now it didn't feel like he was in my corner.

"You gonna sit down, Rose?"

"If I'm in trouble, I think I'd prefer to stand." When he didn't respond, I finally dropped into a chair. "Jesus, Al, what the hell is going on? Ben said something came up about the Akers shooting."

"In a manner of speaking. You want to tell me about it?"

I set my jaw. "It was a good shot, Al."

"I know that, Rose. You don't take any other kind."

"Then what the hell—" I started to ask.

"Tell me about Charlie Akers, Rose," Taylor interrupted.

I blinked. "What about him? He's dead."

"Besides the obvious. What do you know about him? Who was he to you?"

What the hell had Evan Neal said? What could they possibly have found in Charlie Akers' stuff that would place me under suspicion? "What do you mean, who was he to me? Al, I don't know a damn thing about Charlie Akers—he was just some fucking perp. I followed the rules, I let Zack have his turn, but when shit went sideways I took Akers out."

"Without a direct order from Llewellyn."

"Hey, that's on him. He should have called the shot, ask anyone who was there. We were all waiting for it, and he just took too long. It doesn't matter anyway, Al, it was imminent danger, no doubt—all the elements were there."

S.W.A.T. teams adhere to strict protocol. The entire point of having a dedicated team like ours is to respond to incidents out of the ordinary, to provide tactical support to other divisions when they run into situations they aren't equipped to handle. We prepare for those incidents with a hell of a lot of training—daily workouts, constant drills, roundtable discussions on any kind of possible scenario we might come up against—all so that when we're faced with the unexpected, which is all the time, we can react quickly. It's also to build trust as a team; we don't have to waste time and energy worrying about whether someone else is going to be able to do their job. Everyone has a part to play, and we're all damn good at it.

Snipers like me are supposed to watch and wait. We spend the majority of any S.W.A.T. incident crouched in uncomfortable positions, trying to maintain a viable shot on our target and providing bird's-eye intel to the S.W.A.T. commander. The goal in any S.W.A.T. incident is to avoid using snipers altogether—a non-violent resolution to each deployment is how they phrase it in the training materials. We take shots when we have to, but nearly always on direct orders from the team leader. The only exception is the imminent danger rule. If a sniper can see that a hostage, a civilian, or a teammate is in imminent danger, and we're in a position to take a shot without further endangering anyone, we may do so. It's supposed to be a rare occurrence—S.W.A.T. is no place for a cop with authority problems, so anytime a sniper takes a shot without a direct order, there's a lot of scrutiny after the fact. When it came to the Akers shooting, I was fine with scrutiny. I was ready to defend my actions.

Taylor hadn't answered me; he just sat drumming his thick fingers on the file in front of him and watching me.

"Al, come on, what is this? Does Llewellyn say otherwise? He got a problem with what I did?"

"He didn't, Rose, when he thought he had all the facts. But this guy Akers...you sure you didn't know him? That the only time you ever saw him was at the standoff?"

The image of Charlie Akers shuffling out from under the staircase in Sam's cellar, coming for me with those dead eyes, made me hesitate a fraction of a second, and Taylor noticed. I leaned forward, my hands on the desk. "Taylor, I swear to God, the first time I ever laid eyes on the guy was through the scope of my rifle. Ben said you found something, but I don't see how that could be. I swear I didn't know him."

Taylor sighed, shoved the file across his desk at me. I yanked it closer and began flipping through it. Two pages in, I froze, feeling like my heart had stopped. I flattened my palm over the pictures that were clustered tightly across the page, as though I could obliterate them. I looked up. "What the *fuck* is this, Al?"

"You can see our cause for concern, Rose. You may not have known Charlie Akers, but he sure as hell knew you."

* * *

I twisted my fingers together in my lap, my stomach sour. The photos in the file were of other photos—shots of pages from what might have been a scrapbook, pictures arranged chronologically, with descriptions penciled in tiny writing I couldn't make out, flanked by unidentifiable items glued in place. Some looked disturbingly like human hair; others were just trash—bits of food wrappers, ticket stubs, receipts—a hoarder's scrapbook. There were two pages toward the middle that looked like crumpled black construction paper.

"Shooting range targets," Al said when I looked up at him. "Good ones, too. Near perfect marksmanship. Look like yours?"

"How the fuck would I know, Al? You have any idea how much time I've spent on the range?"

He grunted, and I turned back to the evidence shots. Whoever had taken them hadn't done a great job—much of the detail in the original pictures was obscured by glare, fuzzy and hard to make out—but I could see enough to know I was looking at myself. Lots and lots of shots of me. I looked up at Taylor again and leaned forward, my eyes steady on his. "Where did you get these?"

"Charlie Akers' place. The original book is in evidence lockup."

"How many people have seen this?"

"Just the ones who had to—the evidence techs that collected them, Llewellyn, me."

"Nobody else?"

Taylor sighed. "That's the other thing we need to talk about, Rose. Do you know a guy named Evan Neal? He's an FBI agent based in Louisville."

Damn it. "Barely. The guy approached me at the Akers scene, said he needed to talk to me. I got a cagey feeling about him, pointed him toward Llewellyn."

"That it?"

I sat back in the chair, crossed my arms over my chest, tried to keep my temper in check. "No, he followed me to Louie's on Friday too, then called me last night. Told me he wanted to meet up before the review this morning."

"And you agreed?"

I shrugged. "At first, yeah. I said I'd try to meet up, if I could work it out. I wanted to know what he was talking about. Besides, he's a fed—I didn't want to make inter-agency trouble for us." The last part wasn't true, but it sounded better than bringing up Briar Ridge.

Taylor snorted. "'Preciate that, Rose."

"Anyway, as it turned out, I couldn't meet up—this thing with Tommy started last night, Sam and I were occupied with him and... other stuff. But I didn't have a good feeling about Neal. He threatened me, Al."

"*He* threatened *you?*"

"Yeah. Said if I didn't find time to meet up before today's review, I'd regret it. Like I said, he kept dropping little veiled hints about my family, about knowing something."

Taylor sat forward. "What about your family?"

"I don't know. He said it was about the Summers side, my dad's family. Nothing beyond that. But he kept mentioning Sam and the kids, kind of like he was trying to show how much he knew about me."

Taylor's eyes were keen now. "Did anyone else hear him make these threats?"

I shook my head. "I was alone when he called last night, and when he approached me at Louie's. I know he talked to Ben and some of the other guys, I can see if they heard anything specific."

"You do that, Rose. It could be important. Because according to Neal, you were the one making threats."

I shot to my feet. "He said *what*? What the hell? What was I supposed to be threatening *him* about? I don't even know the guy."

Before Taylor could answer, the office door flung open hard enough to bounce off the wall with a bang. I flinched and turned to face my S.W.A.T. leader, David Llewellyn, looking extremely displeased.

Llewellyn was in his early fifties, came through the sheriff's academy at the same time as Luke Harris. Unlike Luke, he'd kept up his training and maintained a solid, trim build on his six-foot frame. His head was clean-shaven above a set of thick black eyebrows and a thin face. He was known for his even temper, which at the moment was nowhere in sight.

"McFarland, this is not a good day to be late to work."

I straightened. "I'm sorry, Lieutenant. I just—"

"And Taylor, you were supposed to call me when she got here."

Al stood more slowly, resting his hands on his desk. "Calm down, David. She's here now—I was just giving her a rundown of what's happened."

Llewellyn stalked the rest of the way into the room. "I thought we agreed we'd do that together. This is serious, Taylor. It's not just the Sergeant's job on the line, it's mine, too."

"Wait, *what*? My *job*? Why the hell would my job be on the line over this, let alone yours? It was a good shot, Loo, and you know it. In fact, I'd still like to know why the hell you didn't call it yourself— Zack was down, Akers was within seconds of—"

Llewellyn turned on me. "McFarland, back it off. You're out of line—and you have to know that no matter what the circumstances were, you had *no* business at that scene at all, let alone behind a rifle. *Fuck*." He ran a hand over his smoothly shaven head and glared at me.

"I don't get it—what do you mean I had no business being there? Just because some psycho was collecting pictures of me—how the hell was I supposed to know?"

"You're familiar with the concept of conflict of interest? Because I'd say this qualifies."

I looked back and forth between Llewellyn and Taylor, waiting for something to make sense. "Again, how the hell was I supposed to know about the scrapbook, guys? It's only a conflict if I knew about it, isn't it?"

"It's the family relationship that causes a problem, Sergeant Mc-Farland," Evan Neal said as he closed the office door behind him. "No matter how justified the shooting may have been, the fact that you and Charlie Akers shared a father makes all your actions suspect." His hands were clasped behind his back and he smiled. "Surely you can see that?"

* * *

I stared at Neal, numb. "Charlie Akers...was my brother?" It came out quiet, but in my head I was shouting. It was wrong—Neal couldn't be right. "My brother" could only mean Andy—the golden boy who'd died eighteen years ago. It couldn't have anything to do with a wife-beating creep I'd put a bullet through.

All three men were watching me now. Neal with that same irritating smile, Taylor with what looked suspiciously like pity, and Llewellyn with barely contained anger.

"What the fuck," I said carefully, "are you talking about?"

Neal was still smiling. "Charlie Akers was your brother," he answered just as carefully.

"I'm not deaf. I'm asking you why the hell you would say something like that?"

"Because it's what he told me, Rose."

Llewellyn and Taylor started talking at once, but Taylor's booming growl won out. "You're saying you knew this guy? You talked to him before?"

"In the course of a federal investigation, yes."

I flung my hands up. "So that's it? You're making accusations that could have a serious impact on my career, based on the word of a guy who was demonstrably off the deep end? Where's your actual proof?"

"Proof?" Llewellyn took a step closer. "You're denying it?"

"I don't even know enough to deny it. I never met Charlie Akers in my life, never saw him before last Wednesday afternoon when we were called out to Union. My father never mentioned him, sure as hell never said he had another family somewhere. So yes, I'd be interested to know if Agent Neal has any actual proof that this guy's related to me, and on top of that, why I'm being accused of withholding information I didn't have."

Taylor turned to Neal. "That's fair. I'd like to know what the feds have got on Akers."

"And why you didn't see fit to say anything until now, when it's too late to do anything about it."

"That's enough, McFarland," said Llewellyn.

I was hoping to see a crack in Evan Neal's shellacked exterior, hoping he'd turn on the crazy like he had before, but he just kept smiling. "I'm sure I'll be able to share some information with you, Chief Taylor, although you understand that some of what I have on Akers is privileged—part of other ongoing investigations. Akers was an informant of sorts. I'll need to go back to my hotel for the files, and make a couple of calls to my office to see what I can get cleared for release to you. I can be back a bit later this afternoon, if that's all right?"

Taylor watched him for several beats, and I could tell my boss didn't trust Neal any more than I did. "Fine," he said. "And if I feel the information is incomplete, I'll be happy to make a call to your superior officer to see if that will help things along."

Was it my imagination, or had Neal's smile faltered at the mention of his superiors?

"I'm sure that won't be necessary, Chief. I'll see you back here this afternoon." He turned to go. "Sergeant. Lieutenant." He nodded as he left.

Taylor shut the door behind Neal and muttered something under his breath that sounded like "pretentious fuck" before turning back to me. "In the meantime, Rose, how do you feel about submitting to a DNA test?"

I crossed my arms over my stomach. "Yeah, sure. Whatever it takes."

"Good. Go across the street to the private lab, it'll be quicker. I don't want this getting lost in our lab's backlog—it won't be considered a priority."

There was a long seething silence that I finally had to break. "What happens now? The incident review board, do they know about any of this?"

Llewellyn shook his head. "No one knows except for us, and that investigations woman, Skylar."

Skylar knew. That explained her presence in Interview One, and probably her attitude as well.

"I plan to keep it that way for the moment," Llewellyn was saying. "There's no way I want either of us in front of that board until we see what Agent Neal comes back with, and come up with a game plan on how to handle it." He exhaled, and put both hands on the back of his head. "Jesus, McFarland, what a clusterfuck. I was *this* close to making captain."

And I was this *close to taking over your job*, I thought, but didn't say.

"Do I need my union rep?" I asked after another long silence.

Llewellyn glared at me, took a step toward me. "Are you fucking kidding me, McFarland? After the mess you've made, you have the nerve to—"

"I think that's a fine idea, Rose."

Llewellyn turned on Taylor. "Damn it, Al, stop coddling her. This is a goddamn mess."

Taylor didn't back down. "What makes you so sure it's her fault? Why are we giving this federal clown more credence than our own officer? What does he have on you?"

For a second, I thought Llewellyn was going to hit him. Then he backed off, turning away from both of us. "I'm giving him credence because he has proof, and because this is *exactly* the kind of bullshit that makes cops look bad."

Taylor sighed. "David, go tell Fischer we need to postpone the review board for later in the week."

"He's going to want to know why."

Taylor shrugged. "So tell him. You can't keep this from him anyway. Just make sure he knows we're not convinced yet, and we're waiting for the whole story."

"Fine." Llewellyn left without looking at me, slamming the door behind him.

I stood still and worked on keeping my temper in check—it seemed Al Taylor was my only ally at the moment.

"Rose." He waited until I met his eye. "I'll ask you this once, and I'll believe whatever you tell me. Did you know anything about this?"

"I most certainly did not, Al." My anger cooled when he nodded and sat back down.

"Okay. So, knowing what we do, where does that leave us?"

I stared at him blankly. "I don't know. Waiting, I guess, to see what Neal comes up with, and for the DNA test results."

Taylor shook his head. "Rose, think about this. If what this Neal asshole is saying turns out to be true, you've been set up, haven't you? What are the odds you'd end up with some long-lost half-brother on the other end of your rifle? That after you're forced to take his life, some federal agent just happens to show up to do his civic duty by bringing the circumstances to the attention of your superiors?"

I sat down, thinking. It had been clear to me that Neal had set me up somehow, but I hadn't thought as far as Akers being part of it. Did that mean he'd committed suicide by cop? To what end? And why had he been watching me beforehand, taking surveillance photos and following my family around?

"I want to see that album Akers had—the original."

Taylor nodded. "Okay. The lab still has it right now, working it over for trace. I'll put in a request. In the meantime, I'll work on finding out who the hell this Agent Neal is, and why he's decided to show up right now."

I raised an eyebrow. "Gonna call his bosses?"

Taylor smiled. "He didn't like the sound of that, did he? Hell yes I'm calling them, he left a card with the desk sergeant, and I'm going to make use of it. Since you've got the day free, why don't you see what you can come up with on Akers?"

Something was bothering me. "Al, who let Agent Neal in this morning? I mean, did he give any kind of explanation of what he's working on, or if he's even here in an official capacity?"

"He came straight in and asked for Llewellyn, told him he was working an open file on Charlie Akers. He didn't say why, but I'd like to know. Then he dropped his bombshell on Llewellyn, and I got called in." He chewed the inside of his cheek. "Rose, I want you to steer clear of him right now. Llewellyn, I mean. Anything he wants from you, I should be there too."

I had no problem with that. "What's his deal, Al? Why did he blow his top like that without even talking to me first?"

Taylor shook his head. "I don't know, exactly. Could have something to do with that shot—his part of it, not yours. Like you said, he should have given the order. It looks bad, one of our negotiators getting hit like that. Maybe B.P.S.I.'s climbing up his ass about it, and he's using the opportunity to turn it back on you."

I nodded, wondering how likely it was that this whole thing was going to fuck my promotion. Decided it wasn't the time to ask.

Taylor cocked his head to the side, considering me. "Rose, was your dad the kind of guy to do this, have an affair and keep the kid secret?"

I thought about a harsh disciplinarian with a house full of secrets. Paul Summers wouldn't have been the first pious man who didn't practice what he preached. I shrugged. "I wouldn't rule it out. The Summers family was never what you'd call stable. Much as I hate the idea, I guess it's possible Neal is right, but I still didn't know."

Taylor turned down the corners of his mouth. "If he *was* your brother, maybe it's a good thing you didn't know him. He didn't exactly seem like the type you'd want to sit across from at Thanksgiving dinner."

I smiled faintly, mostly at the notion of the Summers family celebrating a non-religious holiday. "I wonder how much of what he became was a result of how he was raised, Al. Maybe he never had a chance."

Taylor snorted. "The old 'rough childhood' excuse? Bullshit. You turned out okay."

Only because you don't really know me, I thought.

I stood. "Let me know when I can see the scrapbook."

"I will. And Rose?"

I stopped with my hand on the door handle, looked back over my shoulder at him.

"Be careful who you talk to out there, okay? I think someone's been feeding information to Neal, or Akers, or maybe both. It's too cute to be coincidence, for Neal to know as much as he does about your family. You said he called you on your cell, tracked you to the bar—think about who might have a reason to talk to him."

His words made me feel cold, but I nodded and tried to smile.

Out in the bullpen, I looked at everyone with new eyes. It seemed like a lot of people were looking back at me, but I reminded myself I'd just been called into the boss's office, so they were bound to be curious.

I called the private DNA lab across the street and made an appointment for early afternoon, but was disappointed to learn the results would still take three to five business days after all samples were collected. Which reminded me I needed to call the morgue, and get them to send a blood sample from Akers. It gave me pause, thinking of Akers in Sam's basement last night. He'd seemed like something more tangible than the spirits I'd had truck with in the past, more of a reanimated corpse than something ethereal. Would the morgue call me back and report the body gone? I shuddered, told myself that was crazy. Surely, if Akers' corpse had gone missing, we'd have heard something by now.

I turned my mind back to practicalities and decided three to five business days was too long—I needed to know now. I hunkered down at my desk and tried to think where to start.

Part of that depended on whether I truly believed Charlie Akers could be my half-brother. I turned on my computer and logged into NCIC to see what I could find. Neal had said Akers was some kind

WHISPERS IN THE DARK

of informant, which likely meant he had a record.

Bingo—there he was. Charles Cotton Akers, age twenty-eight. There was no information on his criminal record, or what charges the feds might have brought against him. It looked like his file was flagged for higher security clearance than mine, which I supposed could make sense if he was informing on high-profile cases. Vital statistics was all I could pull.

If Akers was twenty-eight, that made him six years younger than me. If he was my brother, he hadn't been the result of a youthful in-discretion—Paul Summers had been unfaithful to my mother. And Cotton...that had been my father's middle name too. Of course, it was a Southern name, but it was old-fashioned. I wondered how many people were named Cotton anymore. Tradition had been important to my parents, they'd named my brother Andrew Paul Summers, and I was Rosemary Narine after Dad's mother, a grayish mouse of a woman I barely remembered.

If my father had another family, would my mother have known about it? It was possible—Cora Summers had believed in her duty as a wife above everything else. Definitely above her duty as a mother. I considered calling her, but immediately rejected the idea. Dealing with Cora always did more harm than good. Let her realize she had information I needed, and she'd twist me every which way to get the most out of it.

I sat up. If Akers and I were related, was that why he'd appeared to me? Was our unacknowledged family relationship the link that had set everything in motion? The worst of Tommy's manifestations had started after I'd killed Akers. Had I brought this on myself?

My phone buzzed, and I checked the ID. "Sam, hey. How are the kids?"

"They're fine, Rose, it's been pretty quiet. I'm getting ready to take Tommy to see Dr. Daughtry, you want to meet us?"

Guilt turned my stomach sour. "I can't, Sam. Things are a little precarious right now. I've got a deadline."

"What's going on?"

I sighed. "Something's come up. I'll tell you about it tonight. Take care of little bit, and let me know what the doctor says, okay?"

I waited for the lecture, but it didn't come.

"I will, Rose. I'll call you as soon as we're done."

"Thanks, Sam."

I hung up, and wondered how Sam would react to the news that I had a sociopathic half-brother I'd shot in the head last Friday. Probably the same way he reacted to every other nutty thing that happened—he'd nod, think through all the logical implications, assimilate the information and move on.

My phone rang again, Luke this time. I debated, then picked up, remembering he'd promised to look into Neal for me. Luke sounded surprised when I answered.

"I was going to leave you a message—thought you'd be knee-deep in bureaucracy by now."

"Schedule's going a little off the rails today, Luke. What's up?"

"Been looking into this Evan Neal guy for you. You heard anything else from him?"

"Unfortunately, yes—he's been causing problems for me. You come up with anything yet?" Taylor had said he was going to look into Neal, but I didn't mind having my own avenue of research.

"I was afraid he might. Guy's known for being a little obsessive, apparently, particularly when it comes to Charlie Akers."

"Obsessive over an informant? That's odd. I wonder what put Akers on the FBI radar in the first place? I took a look at NCIC, but his file's flagged. The only thing our search found when we were looking at him during the standoff was some domestic violence stuff. That seems a little outside the scope of federal jurisdiction."

"Yeah, that's what his superiors thought. He tried to make a case for Akers being a bigger threat than that, maybe some kind of domestic terrorist wacko, but nobody bought it. 'Course, I guess they may be rethinking that after last week, but still."

I snorted. "It was hardly Waco out there, Luke. What do you mean, Neal was obsessive about Akers? Was he trying to nail him for something else?"

"It all sounds pretty odd. According to my guy, Akers got pulled in as part of a larger drug bust. Neal flipped him, which isn't out of the ordinary, since it looks like Akers was a small fish, but no one seems to know what information Akers ever brought in. Then, a little while back, Neal switches gears and starts talking about Akers being dangerous, trying to get the FBI interested in bringing the guy back in. They turned him down, but he wouldn't let it go, just kept pursuing Akers and ignoring his other cases. They ended up coming down pretty hard on him."

"What happened after they told him to back off?"

"Like most obsessive people, he didn't. Currently on administrative leave."

"Administrative leave? Not suspension, or outright firing?"

"Yep. Seems like there's something else going on there—I'm waiting to hear back from somebody. I'll let you know when I do."

"Thanks, Luke."

"Sure, babe, hope it helps. I'll call you later."

If Evan Neal was on administrative leave, he couldn't be here in an official capacity. I knew it didn't completely negate what was happening right now—if he was right about my family relationship with Charlie Akers, Neal could still cause me trouble. But it made him less plausible, and I wondered what his superiors would think if they knew he was in Memphis, still chasing after his obsession. Luke's information at least gave me some leverage with the guy. No wonder he'd looked squirrelly when Taylor mentioned calling his superiors—Taylor would be able to find out the same information in no time. I frowned. In fact, why hadn't he already? He'd given the impression it was high on his priority list, so I wondered why he hadn't already come out and called off the dogs. I decided not to piss him off by hounding him but I kept waiting to hear from him.

I spent the rest of the morning on research. Charlie Akers had been born in Liberty, Kentucky, and his mother was listed under her maiden name of Bethany M. Akers. The father was marked unknown, according to the records clerk I got on the phone. Inconclusive, but a little worrying—Liberty was close enough to the farmhouse where I'd grown up to make it possible for Dad to have carried on a double life, or at least an extramarital affair. I found myself wondering if that was all it had been, if maybe Dad hadn't known about Charlie or had refused to acknowledge him, or if instead he made time to see him. I wondered which option would have left Charlie worse off. I studied the crime scene photos, mentally removing the gunshot damage I'd caused to his head, trying to find similarities between his features and mine, or Andy's. I didn't have any pictures of Andy, all of that had perished in the fire, so I closed my eyes and tried to conjure his face for comparison.

I thought of him the way I remembered him best, standing in his bedroom at his desk, tinkering with some project or another. His blond hair falling into his eyes, his brow furrowed, gray-green eyes squinted. I opened my eyes, looked again at Charlie, but I still didn't see it. I sighed. This wasn't exactly productive, and I wondered if the vague familiarity I'd noticed had to do with some kind of family resemblance.

Sam called around noon to let me know Tommy's doctor hadn't found any cause for concern during his visit. He'd pronounced my son in excellent health, but had scheduled some additional neurological tests to be sure. Sam sounded worried, but he stressed that Dr. Daughtry had only done so as a precautionary measure—he thought Tommy was fine. I pretended to accept his assurances, just as I was sure Sam had pretended to accept Daughtry's, thanked Sam and told him I'd be home as soon as possible.

I was finishing a pastrami sandwich I'd picked up on the way back from the DNA place when Taylor leaned into my cube. "Trace is done with the album for now, if you want to see it."

I thanked him and waited a tick. "Um. Any word back from Neal's people in Louisville?"

Taylor shook his head. "Nothing yet. Left a couple of messages. If I don't hear back before the end of the day I'll follow up." He gave me a sharp look. "You haven't been kicking the hornet's nest, have you?"

"No, sir." I followed Taylor over to the lab and settled into a corner, pulling on gloves before I opened the large brown album one of the techs had laid out for me. Taylor stayed in the room but gave me some space, leaning against the far wall and watching me. I lifted the heavy cover, drew a sharp breath. I'd known a little of what to expect from what I'd seen in the evidence photographs, but it hadn't prepared me for the sheer quantity, or the level of care that Akers had taken.

It was me. Lots and lots of me. Me lying flat on a rooftop, rifle in hand, the photo taken from street level. Me at Louie's, holding a beer, a sheen of sweat on my smiling face. Me at the grocery store, me running, me lifting weights. The zoo, mid-stride following Tommy. Standing next to Sam at the park across from Lily's school, leaning into him while we watched our kids.

That part was bad, really bad. Every shot had been taken without my knowledge, by a voyeur who'd somehow managed to fly under my radar. I didn't like that he'd been near my family, that he knew what my kids looked like and where we liked to go. So yeah, those shots made me cold and angry at the same time, but they weren't as hard to explain as the older ones. Like a trio of portraits taken at various places around Briar Ridge when my hair was still growing back in, the red shininess of my scars making me wince with remembered pain. Or one of me in a hospital bed, my torso and arms still bandaged, a crispy fuzz of charred blonde hair haloing my head. Me at my high school, at my middle school, at the church we'd attended, sullen-faced in the back row.

Me as a baby, as a toddler, as a chubby-faced kindergartner. None of this made any sense—anything like this would have been long gone. Even if I accepted that Charlie Akers and I shared a father, Paul Summers had been dead by the time I entered Briar Ridge, and there certainly hadn't been anyone snapping family shots of me in my hospital bed. I sat numbly in the hard molded-plastic chair and tried to piece together what this thing was, what Charlie had planned on using it for.

"You all right, Rose?"

Taylor's voice made me jump, I'd forgotten he was there. I looked up at him. "Yeah, I'm okay. I'm just a little..."

I stopped, catching a glimpse of something in the glare from the overhead lights. Reaching for a small desk lamp, I clicked it on and dragged it closer, tilting the shade up. In the brighter lighting, the surface markings were easier to see—on every photo a little arrow was drawn, sometimes two or three, sometimes accompanied by a question mark. I traced the arrows—they all seemed to be pointing to what would have been my line of sight in each picture. I leaned back, trying to take the whole thing in, and realized that I wasn't looking at the camera in any of these shots. In most there was a pensive, sometimes troubled expression on my face, even when I was small.

There, in the middle of all this, was a picture of Andy and me, about ten and eight respectively. We were in Easter outfits, Andy handsome in a dark blue suit and red tie, me in a light pink dress with ruffles, a straw hat with a matching pink ribbon, ruffled socks sticking out of shiny black Mary Janes, white gloved hand tucked into my brother's as he smiled easily at the camera. Not me, though. Not our Rose, I could almost hear my mother say in that tone of deep disappointment. No, eight-year-old Rose was staring hard at something out of frame. Eyes intent, I seemed to be leaning toward it, my free hand reaching out ever so slightly.

I remembered that day. A shadow on those church steps. A darkness that crowded out the sunshine, that chilled me as something watched Andy and me. Something hungry. It came to me then, as I looked at the Easter picture, what all these photos had in common. In each one of them, I was haunted. I felt a moment of intense regret and sadness for the little girl who looked so damned unhappy, then a flash of fear for Tommy. I wasn't going to let his childhood turn out like mine.

I slammed the book closed as Taylor pushed his bulk away from the wall and ambled over.

Taylor leaned a hip against the table, his arms crossed. "Pretty screwed up, huh? Where the hell did he get all that stuff?"

"Fuck if I know, Al. What've we got on Akers so far? I mean, anything tell us what the hell he was *doing* with this?"

He shook his head. "The trace guys just got finished collecting samples—we don't know much yet. Maybe your pal Neal knows something about that too."

"He'd better not. If I find out he knew Akers was stalking me, I'll skin him."

Taylor leaned over my shoulder and flipped the album open to the middle. "You were an awful cute little kid, Rose. Lily looks just like you."

I smiled faintly. "Do you think at some point, I might be able to get copies of some of these? The older ones, I mean, of me and my brother. I don't have any pictures of him, and I'd like to be able to show Tommy and Lily their uncle."

His heavily lined face softened. "Of course, Rose. I'll talk to somebody in evidence, we'll get you copies of whatever you want. What'd you make of all the news stories?"

"The what?" My mind was moving slow, trying to process everything I'd seen, rolling through old memories.

Taylor turned pages until the contents changed from photographs to yellowed news clippings. "Here. All of a sudden it goes from the Shrine of Rose to the damn firebug news archives."

"Firebug?" My stomach dipped and I bent over the pages, scanning the headlines. They were in chronological order, with the first clipping dated more than twenty years ago. The earliest ones were from Kentucky, the more recent ones from Tennessee. Taylor was right—every story dealt with fire. Homes and businesses, fatalities, arson and unexplained. The articles ran the gamut. The only thing they seemed to have in common was proximity—to me, to wherever I was living at the time. Did Charlie think there was some kind of connection? But many of these had been solved, or the cause was easily discernible, right there in the titles. *Mulch Fire Leads to Loss of Business; Lightning Strike Starts Blaze, Killing Two.* Why would Charlie have included these?

I thought of Tommy's room this morning, the way it looked like there'd been some kind of contained fire. I thought of the farmhouse eighteen years ago, and of the vivid dreams of burning I'd had for as long as I could remember. There was that old feeling again—that familiar, sick fear that maybe my parents had been right to be afraid of me. Afraid of what I could do.

"We'll sort this out, Rose, I promise. You're one of our own. Llewellyn may be pissed right now, but you need to remember this whole unit is going to take it seriously. You're not alone, okay, kid?"

I smiled mechanically as I stood to go. I wanted to believe him, but the more I found out, the more alone I realized I was.

CHAPTER SIX

The thing that had been Charlie Akers crouched outside the broken window to hear his father's words. He wasn't allowed inside, not yet, and it rankled, but he didn't let it show. He would continue to be the good son for now, and his father would know, and appreciate him.

"*Did you set the fire?*"

"*I did.*"

"*Like I told you?*"

"*Yes. Only the boy's room was burned.*" It had been more than burned—Charlie had gotten carried away in there, seeing all the things Rose and Sam had provided for Tommy, feeling their love for the child. That stupid painting over the kid's bed. He'd done more damage than was strictly necessary, but his father didn't need to know that.

"*You left the mark, as I told you?*"

"*I did. It wasn't easy, making it look like nothing started it. I can't do it like you can. If they investigate, they'll find the accelerant.*"

A grinding noise that could have been a cough or a laugh. "*She won't investigate. She'll be too afraid to have her suspicions confirmed.*

How did she look when they were leaving?"

Charlie grinned. *"Sick as a dog."*

"Good. That's good."

Charlie almost told his father about the scrapbook, the collection of stories on fires. He hadn't had a plan for the book at the time he'd started it, just a way to feel close to a family that wasn't his. The fire stories had been his own theory, back when he was tracking his half-sister. Back when he'd believed Rose had been the one with the power. He knew better now; those fires were nothing more than what they'd appeared to be, chance blazes. But the articles were a nice touch, would play perfectly into Paul's instructions, and Charlie thought his father might be proud. But if he learned of the rest—all the pictures of Rose, of her family...what would he think? That Charlie was weak, pathetic, the lesser son as always. No, he would keep the scrapbook to himself.

Charlie sidled closer to the window, craned to see inside. *"Can I stay here for a while? I'm tired, Dad. It's harder being...like this. I want to hear more stories—stories of the Summerses."*

The voice was cold. *"There are no more stories. You exploited the ones I told you—shared them with that halfwit bureaucrat."*

"I'm sorry, Dad. That was before I knew..."

"It doesn't matter. That may yet turn out the way we want it—he's malleable. Overweening love of a child makes a man vulnerable. Remember that, Charlie."

"Yes, Dad."

"Now, I have more for you to do. What did you drive up here?"

"My car—the Toyota."

"Get rid of it, you idiot. You think no one's going to notice a dead man driving his own car?"

"What should I drive, then?"

"Go to the mountain, to the home place. Find my wife, give her my instructions. You may drive my old car."

Charlie stared through the window, stricken. *"Your wife? Why? We don't need her—we can do this ourselves."*

"Don't question me, boy. Do as I say. I have work for her, and more for you. So listen close."

Hatred burned in the dead man's eyes, but he ducked his head and listened.

CHAPTER SEVEN

Something was coming. When Cora Summers' eyes flew open, it was with the certain knowledge that whatever it was, it was getting close. She sat up, her neck and back stiff from falling asleep in the rocking chair, her heart thumping as she looked around the neatly swept front porch and yard. When several minutes passed and nothing moved, she sighed and allowed herself to relax.

Cora closed her eyes again and tried to remember the dream, her fingers twisting the cross at her neck. The fire. Always the fire. The old farmhouse lit in patches by the unholy glow as flames found their way to windows, to doors, to cracks in the home's stone facade. Watching the open door her son had disappeared through when he realized his sister was still inside, where Paul had furiously followed when Andy didn't immediately return. Praying to see the two come back through safely. Praying she wouldn't be left alone.

Cora dreamed of the Whispers, too. She'd never heard them in waking life; for years she'd doubted they were even real. The fire had shown her how wrong she'd been, but it was too late for regret. The Whispers had found her. Haunting her sleep with increasing frequency and intensity, filling her dreaming mind with such a crescendo of angry sound she thought she'd go mad. She knew they could do that to a person—she'd seen firsthand the damage they could cause to a fragile mind.

The memory made her cold, and she missed her husband. Paul had been her strength ever since he'd come into her life when she was a girl of sixteen—the same age Rose had been when she'd lost the battle with her demons. Paul had been the only one to see Rose for what she truly was, the only one with the fortitude to do what was right, no matter how painful it was.

There had been times, back then, when Cora had wanted to cry out against the harshness of Paul's punishments. When Rose was a little girl of five or six, tears streaming down chubby cheeks as Paul marched her to the cellar, she would raise those brimming eyes to Cora's. It was hard not to answer the plea in those eyes, hard not to join Andy in yelling at Paul, begging him to stop, she was only a child. But Cora never had, and by the time Rose was eight, she'd stopped looking at her mother. It had been a relief, really.

Cora knew now how right Paul had been to fear Rose. Knew that no matter how horrible it had seemed at the time, his solution had been the only one possible. Even as she'd stood on the lawn, watching the flames build and waiting for her daughter to die, Cora had trusted Paul. It hadn't been his fault that things had turned out the way they did. Rose had been more dangerous than even he'd realized. A murderer, that's what she was, and no one safe from the things she could do. The damage she could cause, when she was angry enough. Just look at what she'd done to her own brother and father, leaving her mother with no one.

Cora stood, feeling every one of her stiffened joints, the dull ache in her lower back a constant these days. She looked up at the sun—time to start dinner. She would pray first. If the Whispers were back, she was going to need help.

Easing the door shut behind her, she stopped, conscious of a prickle of unease. She turned and squinted to see beyond the porch, her vision not what it used to be. There was nothing out of place, no movement beyond the lazy sway of the tall grass out by the treeline. But still. Something felt wrong. For the first time, Cora felt uneasy in her isolation.

The little one-story cabin had been in the Summers family for over one hundred years, and before that, it had been rebuilt at least twice. It had been painted many times, but the last had been long before Cora had arrived here, a widow mourning her husband and son, trying to forget she had a daughter. The greenish-gray paint was peeling now, the tin roof faded and covered in dead leaves from the towering oaks that surrounded the cabin. It was nestled in a natural hollow, the long, steeply curving gravel drive ensuring that visitors didn't drop in on her. It also meant she was miles from her closest neighbor—miles from anyone who could help.

"I don't need anyone's help," she muttered, slamming the door and heading for the back bedroom.

The inside showed significantly more care. The rooms were sparsely decorated, but the small sofa and side table in the front sitting room were clean, the sofa's fabric neatly mended. The kitchen was to the left, the white counter tops gleaming, the large double-sided sink washed daily. Shuffling along the scrubbed and waxed wooden floors and humming to herself, Cora retrieved Paul's weather-beaten wooden cross from her bedside table and laid it on the threadbare quilt that covered the twin mattress. She placed the Bible next to the cross and knelt, wincing at the creak in her arthritic knees. Folding her hands together on the edge of the bed, she bent her head, her faded hair falling over her face, a pale memory of the shining curls she'd once had.

"Dear Heavenly Father," she began, though the face she saw was Paul's. "Your humble servant asks for your help. I know that trouble is coming again. Last time I had my husband by my side to tell me what to do, to help me be strong. Now I must stand alone, but I ask for your guidance, and I know that I will never truly be alone. Lord, please tell me what to do."

Cora hadn't been expecting an answer, so when something sighed her name from out in the hallway, she began to shake.

Eyes open, she pushed back from the bed. No one was there.

She looked at the other nightstand, twin to the one she used. It had been Paul's, and his revolver was still locked in the top drawer. Cora didn't care much for guns, but she hadn't been able to bring herself to get rid of it after Paul died.

A thump reverberated through the house and she screamed. It had come from the opposite wall, the locked room she never entered, filled with godless, archaic relics of a time when evil had roamed this mountain. Before Paul's great-grandfather, Jacob Summers, had taken control of the family and steered them to the path of God. Paul had shown it to her once, making her stay in the doorway. The room was dark—the only bulb had burned out, and the single window was blocked by a looming wardrobe. She'd been able to see enough to know why the door stayed locked. Mortars and pestles, glass jars filled with unspeakable liquids and unidentifiable floating lumps—body parts, perhaps, or freak-show fetuses. Crumbling parchments and bound books, strange carvings—Cora's only question had been why these items had been allowed to remain. Why hadn't the Summers men simply burned them all?

"To remind us of how far this family fell at one time," Paul told her. "Of the dark arts in which they dabbled—looking for healing and power beyond that which God can provide. Sinning in pride. In case we're ever tempted to shrink from our duty to this family, we must always remember what the consequences will be."

Now, something was awake in there.

Cora stood and crossed to the nightstand, staring down into the top drawer at the gun. In eighteen years she'd never touched it, moving the furniture that had survived the fire without unpacking. She picked up the unfamiliar weapon, wondering if it still worked. Did guns rust? Did they go bad with age? She supposed it didn't matter—it was what she had.

Cora stepped into the hallway and stopped, listening. Her hands began to shake when she heard ragged, heavy breathing from the next room. The door was closed, and no sunlight crept from beneath the door jamb, but something was in there. Cora didn't know if she could make herself open the door, wasn't even sure she could move another step. She thought of Paul and began to sing in a thin soprano, her voice lilting upwards at the end of each verse, stretching the syllables.

"What a friend we have in *Jeeee-zuss*, all our sins and griefs to *bayyyyerrr*." She took one step toward the door, then another. "What, a *priv-il-ege* to *care-ryyyyy*, everything to God in *prayyyyerrrr*."

Another thump, this time shaking the door in its frame, silenced her singing. Breathing hard, she held her cross necklace in one hand and the revolver in the other. She stood in front of the door, but the room had fallen silent. Finally, she released her grip on the chained cross to reach for the knob. The door swung open before she could turn it, the unoiled hinges creaking before the base thudded against the stop on the wall behind. It was as dark as she'd remembered, a cloying, organic smell filling the musty air. She thought of the things floating in those glass jars and shuddered. Tried not to imagine their eyes opening, turning to watch.

Cora edged further inside and peered around, trying to put a name to what had fallen and caused those thumps. It didn't take long. Sunlight from the hallway glinted on broken glass and some kind of viscous liquid. One of the jars had fallen and shattered, spilling its contents in a fan-shaped stain across the wood floor. Cora recoiled at the thought of cleaning it up, whatever it might be. She braced herself for a stench, some kind of rotting smell or maybe formaldehyde. But the room smelled sweet, redolent of an herb she couldn't identify that quickly dissipated the musty odor of the room. She looked closer at the object on the floor, expecting to be repulsed, but it looked like nothing more than a dead flower.

Relief making her giddy, Cora went to the cedar closet in the hall where she kept her cleaning supplies, stopping first to return Paul's revolver to the nightstand. She was singing again when she returned with a small broom and dust pan. Kneeling stiffly on the hard floor, she caught a glimpse of a reflection in a clouded mirror leaning against the heavy wardrobe. She jerked, cutting the web of her hand on one of the larger shards of glass.

Someone was behind her.

Cora turned quickly, holding her cut hand against her flat chest, blood already staining the front of her dress. No one stood in the hall behind her, but when she turned back, she could still see a shadow in the smoky glass.

It was a woman, her hair long and curly, hanging nearly to her waist. The image was too hazy to tell the color of her eyes, but they were dark and sad. Cora could make out little beyond the woman's pale face and hands—the rest of her seemed to lose resolution whenever Cora tried to focus.

Her heart was thudding, her breath coming fast. *A ghost.* It must be, Cora knew, though she'd never seen one before. Panic began to set in. What had she done wrong? How had she allowed herself to slide so far into sin that she would start seeing these unholy creatures? For the first time in her life, Cora was glad Paul was dead. She couldn't have borne the shame of him knowing.

She turned her back on the apparition and began to pray, her blood-slicked hands clasped, head bent and eyes closed. A shadow crossed the room behind her just as she reached the last line of the Lord's Prayer. Cora looked up and was relieved to see only her own reflection in the mirror.

A sigh, a whispering shuffle, and a stench like rotted meat surged, overwhelming the sweet herbal scent of the contents of the shattered jar. She knelt in trembling silence, her body growing cold.

When she heard nothing else for a long minute, Cora tried to stand.

She was immediately pushed back down, a hand reaching from behind to squeeze her frail shoulder in a painful grip. Her scream was choked off when another hand covered her mouth.

Cora gagged. The hand pressing hard over her lips was rotting, yellowed bone starting to show through in places, nails ragged and nearly black with dirt. She tried to push the hands away, tearing at the loose skin with her own nails and retching as strips of flesh came away under her fingers. She stopped when the crushing grip on her shoulder moved to her throat. Something leaned in close behind her, its rancid breath stirring the fine hairs at the nape of her neck.

"What a friend you have in Jesus..." it croaked. Her head began to pound as the grip tightened on her neck, and breathing became more difficult.

"*Cora...*" it rasped into the delicate whorls of her ear.

She raised wide eyes to the mirror and screamed against the stench of the hand across her mouth. The creature squatting behind her was much more substantial than the sad shade of the woman she had seen. He grinned at her in the mirror, a hideous grimace through a useless, dangling jaw. Sunken eyes that might once have been gray glowed darkly from beneath a skullcap that had been blown away. While she watched, he dragged his hand from her mouth to her hair, leaving a foul scum across her lips. She scrubbed the back of her hand against her mouth, then met the creature's eyes in the mirror again.

Her eyes widened. "You," she spat. "You can't be here." She'd wanted it to sound strong, commanding, but her voice was a barely audible tremor, terror robbing it of any force. "You may have been my husband's son, but you were never mine, you little bastard. Do you hear me, Charlie Akers?"

It chuckled, a wet, choking sound. "*Cora...time to bring her home, Cora.*"

"What? Who—bring who home?" She squeezed her eyes shut when the thing began to nuzzle its ruined head against her neck.

"*Rose.*"

"No." Her voice was shrill. "I don't want her here. This is *my* home—neither of you are welcome here."

The hand in her hair tightened, wrapping the long strands around bony fingers and pulling her head back painfully. Cora cried out. Its voice was in her ear again. "*You'll bring her home, Cora. To the first home. You'll bring her home, or you'll burn.*"

She screamed, struggled in the thing's grasp once more, and this time managed to pull free. She fell forward, cracking her head on a wooden table piled with bottles, scraps, and ancient tomes. Cora sat up, scrambling sideways in panic, then stopped.

She was alone again.

She stood and stumbled from the room, slamming the door behind her with a sob. She didn't stop running until she reached the kitchen, then collapsed at the table and cried.

When she was finally calm, Cora found herself gazing intensely through the tears on her lashes, staring at the old cream-colored phone she'd had installed when she moved in after the fire.

She stood, walked to the wall and lifted the receiver. She began to dial a number she knew by heart, but had never called.

Bring her home, Cora...

"Rose?" Cora said, forcing a smile into her voice.

In the darkness, something smiled.

CHAPTER EIGHT

After my disturbing trip down memory lane with Charlie Akers' stalker scrapbook, I headed outside for some sunshine. I leaned up against the brick, letting the heat soak into my shoulders, my eyes closed and face to the sun.

"Rose?" came a calm voice, and a second later a shadow fell across me.

I opened my eyes, stood up straight, and glared at Evan Neal. Peaceful moment terminated.

"What do you want, Neal?"

He cocked his head, his face a picture of polite concern. "I'm sorry about this morning, Rose. It was an ugly necessity. I had to get you to listen to me."

I gave him the full benefit of my resting bitch face.

He lifted a thick file tucked under one arm. "I got what you asked for on Akers. Shall we go somewhere to talk?"

"What about Taylor and Llewellyn?"

"I don't think that's a good idea for either of us, Rose. What we have to discuss doesn't concern your superiors. Give me half an hour of your time, then decide for yourself what to tell them."

I said nothing for as long as I could, trying to put off the necessity. I hated giving in, but Neal had already shown me the damage he could do.

"We can go somewhere public, if you're worried I might hurt you."

That did it. I pushed off the wall, got into his space. He didn't move. "CJ's cafe—two blocks from here. You get ten minutes, and if I'm not convinced, then we'll come back here and tell Taylor everything, and fuck the consequences."

Neal nodded and expanded his smile. "Fair enough."

"And Neal?" I stabbed a gloved finger into his chest, hard enough to push him back a step. "You wouldn't get the fucking chance to hurt me."

The cafe was close to the precinct, still in my territory. Neal hurried to keep up, pushing through the glass doors just as a waitress with improbable eyebrows was leading me to a corner booth. Neal eyed the greasy tabletop, then matched my order of black coffee before settling in across from me. I waited until we both had cups in front of us before prodding him.

"Tell me how you know about the Whispers, Neal."

"I've heard them, Rose. I've seen what they can do."

I searched his face for anything slippery, but all I saw was quiet sincerity. "What do you mean by that, you've seen what they can do? How can you hear them when no one else can?" I looked at him intently. "Are you...do you see other things too?"

There was pity in his eyes when he shook his head. "No. No, I'm not a...I'm not like you."

I sighed, hunched my shoulders against the cracked back of the booth. Looked out at the dirty parking lot. "Then how do you know anything about the Whispers?"

"From your brother, Rose."

I smashed my fist down on the table, making our mugs jump. The waitress glanced at us, then away again. "Stop calling him that, Neal. That *thing* was not my brother."

He leaned in closer. "Rose, I'm sorry if it distresses you. If it helps, he wasn't always like that. Charlie was a good man when I met him."

I thought of Akers shooting Zack, trying to bait me with his own daughter. "Your judgment seems suspect, Neal."

His clear eyes were intent, and he shook his head. "I mean it, Rose. Something happened to him—changed him. When I first met him, he was pretty normal. He'd had some problems with the law in his home town, had a little bit of a record, but nothing violent. He was one of those petty crook types, the poor schmucks who end up holding the bag after the smarter guys get away."

I leaned forward. "So start with that. How *did* you meet him? What had he done that put him on the FBI's radar?"

He settled back in the booth, wriggled around trying to find a comfortable spot on the lumpy plastic. "Drug bust. Big meth operation, running through Bowling Green on the way to Tennessee. Charlie was low man, a runner. Got caught with the big fish, otherwise we'd never have crossed paths. On his own, he was too small-time."

"Akers was a dealer?"

"On the fringes, yeah. Trying to make ends meet. Back then, his daughter was less than a year old, his wife pregnant with his son. Charlie never went to college, didn't have any job skills."

Damn. Charlie's kids—my niece and nephew, if what Neal said was true. Orphans now, thanks to me. I shook it off. That was on Charlie.

"That's sad, Neal, but since you're a cop too, I'm sure you can appreciate that drug dealers aren't harmless criminals. Even if Akers wasn't making the shit himself, and didn't take part in any violence, he was peddling methamphetamines. You have any idea how many families that shit's ruined? Am I supposed to feel sorry for this guy because he couldn't hold down a fast-food job?"

Neal waved a hand. "No, I'm not saying that. All right, you've got a point. Akers was a loser. Not the kind of guy anyone wants dangling from their family tree."

"So how did you get involved with him? After you arrested him, I mean."

He stared down into the opaque surface of his coffee. "He made me an offer. We made a trade."

"He offered to be an informant?"

"No, but that's what I told my superiors. I needed a reason to cut him loose but stay close, so that worked as well as any. No, what Charlie had to offer me was worth a hell of a lot more than information. At least, I hoped it would be." He was staring out the window, looking anywhere but at my face. "I told you my son was sick. I didn't mention that my wife had been ill as well. Cancer."

"I'm sorry to hear that."

"Yes. She was...it was getting close to the end. Breast cancer, but none of the usual treatments had worked. Chemo just made her weaker; surgery didn't get it all. By the time I met Charlie, Kathleen was only days away from death."

I wondered, but didn't ask, what the hell he'd been doing at a drug raid with his wife that close to the end.

"I don't know how, but Charlie...he was able to tell, just by looking at me, that something was wrong. He told me later it was part of his 'gift.' He asked me about it while I was processing him, and I found myself telling him everything. I don't know why, even now, except that when I looked at him, I felt this incredible empathy coming from him. Like he was really concerned, really wanted to help. Charlie had kind eyes, Rose." He finally turned back. "They were a lot like yours."

I thought of that dead, flat gaze staring out at me from the darkness of Sam's cellar. Squeezed my eyes shut, pushed the image out of my mind, opened them again. "What was it that Akers offered you, Neal? How could he help your wife?"

"He said...that special talents ran in his family. Your family, though at the time I didn't know anything about you, or the rest of the Summerses. He said he'd inherited a special...connection, of some kind with the spirit world. That he could see things most people couldn't." Neal looked at me. "Starting to sound familiar?"

Connection? What the hell kind of connection had Charlie Akers had to the spirit world that made him think he could help Neal's wife?

When he realized I wasn't going to answer, Neal shrugged and continued. "Charlie told me this ability was something that had run in his family for years, though for a long time only the women had been born with it. Sometime a few generations ago, it jumped to the men. Not everyone got it—it usually skipped siblings, and not everyone's gift was the same. Some of them were a little less benign—predictions, the ability to sway other people's judgment." He looked at me intently. "Fire starting."

I clenched my jaw. Fire starting. Was it true, then? *Had* I been the one to start that fire eighteen years ago? What about Tommy's room—had I done that, too? If so, why didn't I remember it? Did I have any control? "Did Charlie happen to mention how these special talents worked, Agent Neal?"

"The way Charlie talked, it was kind of personalized. It usually had to be honed. He said healing was part of his gift, and he offered to help Kathleen in exchange for me getting the drug charges dropped, and some cash payments."

I raised an eyebrow. "You bought into this? You'd just met the guy, a confirmed criminal. He tells you he can do a—what, a faith healing or something? Lay his hands and cure all your wife's ills?"

"Yeah, I know it sounds nuts. At first, I *didn't* buy it. I mean, there was something different about Charlie from the start, that empathy thing, but that didn't mean I believed he could talk to spirits and get them to heal Kathleen. But then he showed me."

I was starting to get queasy and shoved my coffee away, leaning back against the booth. "That's how he did it? He asked spirits to heal your wife?"

Neal nodded, both hands clenching his cup. "He said it was a matter of tapping into the right place, controlling the right powers."

"*Controlling* them?" Such a thing had never occurred to me—the most I had hoped for was to make them go away. "You said he showed you. How?"

Neal lifted his left hand from the mug, flexed his fingers, rolled the wrist. "During the raid, I cut the back of my hand pretty bad. Sliced it on some jagged glass, all the way from here to here." His blunt finger traced a line from his ring finger knuckle down to the base of his thumb. "It was bleeding like crazy, even with the bandage, and hurt like hell. With all those chemicals from the meth lab in there, I was worried it would get infected, take a while to heal." He lifted the hand, palm facing himself. There was no scar, no hint that the skin had ever been damaged.

"We were alone in the room. He asked me to turn off the camera, so I did. He gets this real glazed look and starts this kind of guttural noise. There was a rhythm to it, so it may have been an invocation or what-ever. I didn't notice him for long, because the room was getting dark. I mean, we're pretty buried underground in the interview room, but the lights start to go. Not just that; it was like shadows were...gathering, or something. It got cold in there, freezing, and the air was...heavy, somehow. I heard this crazy rush of noise. As it got louder, I was really hearing them—it was all this whispering, from nowhere. Like I said, I couldn't exactly see them, but it seemed like I could have touched them, if I'd tried. The whole time, Charlie's doing this glazed chanting bit, looking less and less *there*, like he's just floated into the ether him-self. He grabs my hand, rubs his thumbs over it, over the bandage and everything. The noises get louder, fill my head—it seems like they're *in* me somehow, and then it all just stops. I look across and Charlie's kind of waking up, seems groggy but he's smiling too. Tells me to take off the bandage, and I'll be damned if the thing wasn't healed. Dried blood all over, but not a *scratch*. Unreal." He kept looking at his hand, the fingers splayed, wrist bent.

I was looking at it too, trying to make my mind work, wrap my head around what Neal was telling me. I wanted to dismiss his story—I had no reason to believe he'd been injured as he claimed, so the smooth skin on the back of his hand didn't mean a damn thing. What did, though, was his description of the Whispers. The way they'd shown up, a gathering of shadow and sound. It rang true, down to the way they changed the texture of the atmosphere. I didn't think Neal could have ad-libbed that part, or guessed. Either he'd experienced the Whispers for himself, or he'd gotten a detailed account from someone who had.

I sat forward, cleared my throat. Neal looked back at me, dropping his hand back to the table.

"If Charlie was capable of something like that—if he was an honest to God healer, why wasn't he using that to make ends meet, instead of dealing drugs?"

Neal shrugged. "I asked him the same thing—he said he did, from time to time, but that he had to be careful not to overuse it. 'Dip from the well too often', that's how he put it."

"So what happened?" I asked. "You agreed to a trade with him, his freedom for healing your wife. Did it work out like he said it would? Did he repeat the miracle?"

His face darkened, his lips tightening. He dropped his eyes to the table again. "At first, yeah. Kind of. I brought Charlie to my house, introduced him to Kathleen. She liked him, too. He had that empathy-charisma thing going, she was smiling at him, trying to follow what he was saying even though it was costing her—the drugs and all. I will say, he didn't try and bullshit me—it wasn't any kind of con where he tried to put me off, or ask for more money once I'd gotten him there. He got started right away, same thing as before." Neal's hands were clasped tightly, the thick veins on the back standing out in sharp relief. His voice dropped, and in the sudden cacophony of a dropped tray through the open doors of the diner's kitchen, I had to lean forward to catch his words.

"I could tell immediately something was different. It happened much faster, for one thing—it took no time at all before the room went dark and the air got thick. But it also—it just *felt* darker, angrier. Scary. Like the Whispers were...mad, or something. Charlie seemed to struggle with them a little—had to start over on the chanting thing a couple of times, get louder, like he was trying to be more commanding or something. Then he got calmer, and he reached for Kathleen."

I was surprised to see tears drop from Neal's bent head onto the scuffed tabletop.

"She was scared. I hadn't been looking at her while all that build-up was going on; I was looking at Charlie. But when I did, because he reached for her, I saw this terror on her face." He brushed at his eyes, his movements jerky. "I'll never forgive myself for that. She was terrified, and I didn't help her—I didn't stop it."

I found myself feeling sorry for Neal. I looked away from him. "She was afraid of Charlie?"

"No—I don't know. Maybe. But it seemed to me, when I thought about it later, that she was looking past him. At something I couldn't see."

I thought of all the things Kathleen Neal could have been looking at as Charlie called the Whispers.

"It didn't work?" I managed to ask.

He laughed, though it trailed off at the end, a broken sound. "No, it did, actually. When they did the autopsy, the pathologist told me her cancer was completely gone. Not a trace. Surgical scars were gone, too—just like the cancer had never happened."

"What the hell happened?"

"Her heart stopped. Just completely seized up. She died with Charlie's hands on her, that expression on her face, staring at something neither of us could see."

"It was...shock?"

Neal raised his head, looked at me from hard and reddened eyes. "It was crushed, Rose. Her heart had been completely crushed."

The waitress came back, brandishing a pot for refills, but I shook my head, forced a smile, told her we were fine. I turned back to Neal.

"Did Charlie—was he able to say what had happened? Did he know what went wrong, or did he do it on purpose?"

"No—no, not on purpose, of course not. You have to believe that, Rose. It's true, what I said before, about your brother being a small-time criminal, not one of the real bad guys. I think he did want to help. He was more upset than I was, almost hysterical."

Maybe, I thought. Or maybe that was what Neal wanted to believe, so he didn't have to be the guy who brought a psycho home to murder his wife.

"What was his take? What happened?"

Neal shrugged, impassive again, the mask of propriety in place. "He lost control, that's what he said. He lost control of the Whispers. He blamed the hell out of himself, you know. Couldn't get over it. Kept saying he should have known better than to attempt something like that on his own. That he didn't have the power, the discipline to hold them for that long."

"On his own? Did Charlie mean he had someone else to help him?"

Neal clasped his hands again, looked grave. "You won't like this part, Rose."

I gave a short laugh. "You think I've liked any of this shit so far? This is a fucking horror show, Neal."

He sighed. "I know. None of this is pleasant. If I could have it to do over again..." He trailed off, looking out the window. "It was Charlie's father helping him, Rose. Your father."

"My father," I repeated flatly.

"Yes. Charlie said Paul was the one who trained him when he started exhibiting signs of the gift at the age of four. When he got older, Paul told him about the history of the Summers family—everything he knew about where the gift came from, how to control it, what it could be used for."

I shook my head. "That's—it's not possible, Neal. If nothing else, that right there proves that either Charlie Akers and I didn't have the same father, or that Akers lied about where he learned this shit. My father has been dead for the last eighteen years. In any case, Paul Summers didn't believe in the 'gift.' He thought of it as a curse. Told me I was evil, that the things I saw proved it. He did his best to rid me of it."

Neal reached across the table, laid his hand tentatively on mine. I pulled it back, put both my hands in my lap.

"I'm afraid it's true, Rose. For whatever reason—maybe it was a gender thing, I don't know—though he tried to crush your abilities, he honed Charlie's while he was alive; that's what he meant about someone helping him. Believe me, I've learned enough since then to know it's true."

"Great. Good for you. You've got the rights to the Summers family saga. Someone somewhere might give a shit, but not me. I've spent most of my life learning how to forget about that family—why the fuck would I want to come here and have you fill in all the lovely details?"

"I'm sure you don't, Rose. It's no joy to me to recount my personal tragedy to a virtual stranger. But like I said before, we need each other. I need your help for my son, and you need the information I got from Charlie in order to help Ethan, and your own kids. There's no other way."

"Neal, what exactly is wrong with your son that you need my help? Don't tell me he got a cold or something and you let Akers take a shot at that, too."

Neal flinched. "No, not quite," he muttered. "Both of us knew better at that point—even if I'd asked him to do it, I doubt Charlie could have been convinced to try another healing."

"What, then?"

"The damage had been done, Rose. We didn't know it at the time. In fact, Charlie said he didn't even know something like that could happen. He'd never seen it, and Paul never told him. We figured it must have been a side effect."

I didn't like where this was going. "Neal, was Ethan home when you guys decided to have your little healing session?"

He nodded miserably. "He was in his room, with the door closed and the television up loud. Charlie said Ethan wouldn't see or hear anything from in there, that the Whispers were more localized than that. I didn't have any reason to disbelieve him."

"You didn't have much reason to believe him, either."

"I know. I realize it was stupid now, but at the time, I just...I was ready to try anything. I loved her, Rose. I wanted my wife back, wanted Ethan's mother back."

"What happened to him?"

"I went to his room later, after everything with Kathleen had been...cleared up. One of our neighbors had stayed with him while we took her to the hospital, so Ethan wouldn't have to come, wouldn't have to see her like that. When I got back, it was late and he was sleeping, seemed okay. But he woke up several times during the night—terrible nightmares."

"It could have just been a result of his mother's passing. Doesn't mean it had anything to do with what Akers did."

"That's what I thought too, at first, until Ethan began having trouble sleeping. He told me there were people keeping him awake at night—he could hear whispering, all night long. He said he couldn't tell what they were saying, but they scared him."

The people whispers, Mommy. The Whispers in the dark.

But why would Ethan Neal have heard them? I'd been working on the assumption that Tommy had inherited the ability directly from me, so I could have bought it if Charlie's kid had started hearing the Whispers. How could Ethan Neal have fallen victim?

"I took him to counselors, Rose. To doctors, chiropractors, anyone I could think of to help him. Even Charlie, after I got desperate, but he refused to get involved. Until the seizures."

"Seizures." *Tommy...*

"Yes. Ethan was having these spells where he'd go all blank, wouldn't respond to anything, like a sleepwalker. Sometimes he would drum his feet or flail around, kind of groan. That was bad enough, but when he started speaking in these crazy voices—that's when Charlie agreed to get involved again."

Crazy voices? This had to be a nightmare. "Why would you even think of exposing your son to Charlie Akers after what happened to your wife? Are you nuts, or just a fucking sadist?"

Neal's voice was hard, angry. "I had no choice, Rose. There was no one else I could turn to. Ethan was getting worse all the time, and the doctors couldn't find a damn thing wrong with him. I knew Charlie had healing powers; I'd seen them. I—we both hoped that what was wrong with Ethan would be an easier fix than Kathleen. That Charlie would have a better chance of controlling the Whispers."

"Did he understand why it had happened at all? Why they'd latched on to your son? Is it just proximity? Is that all that's needed for them to take anyone they want?" My voice had been rising and I cut off, put the heel of my hand over my mouth. If that were true, I had no chance of keeping my kids safe.

"Not then, no, he didn't get it. He said it had never happened before, that usually they just came and went at his request. It was later that he told me..." Neal shook his head. "We weren't completely irresponsible, Rose. We tested it first. I sent Ethan to stay with Kathleen's mother, up in Cincinnati—I hoped that would be far enough. I sliced my other hand open, on the palm this time, and Charlie tried to call the Whispers again."

He laid his right hand on the table, palm up. There was an angry red wound in the middle, a cut that had gotten infected at some point, wasn't healing well.

"So it didn't work this time."

He clenched his hand into a fist. "No. This time it was even worse. The Whispers showed up almost immediately, like they'd been waiting. It got pitch dark in the middle of the day, and not just in the house—it was like the whole neighborhood went dark. Charlie, he was rigid, convulsing. I couldn't get him to stop, to respond. Meantime, everything was getting louder, angrier—it was like being in the middle of a tornado." He shuddered. "Like standing at the gates of Hell."

"Yeah," I said softly. "It can be a lot like that."

Neal nodded, then fell silent.

"How did it end, Neal? How did you manage to stop them?"

"That's just it, I didn't. Eventually everything just kind of went quiet, and Charlie woke up. He said he didn't remember anything, didn't know what had happened. But he seemed...different. Colder. That charm he'd had, the empathy, it was gone. I asked him what we should do next, if there was anything that could help Ethan. That's when he told me about you, Rose."

"He knew about me? What did he know?"

"Just what Paul had told him, I assume. Charlie knew you had some of the same talents, said you'd be the best one to approach. That with your abilities, you'd be able to help."

I shook my head. "Neal, listen to me. I don't know what Akers thought he knew about me, but it's bullshit. I don't have any *talents*, I had a living hell for a childhood. I can't control those things—Jesus, I'd say it's pretty clear from what you've told me that *nobody* can, and I'd be nuts to try."

Neal leaned forward, getting worked up. "You're wrong, Rose—you've got the goods. You're a healer, I could tell the first time I saw you. I knew Charlie wasn't wrong about you. You can help."

"I'm not a healer, Neal, I'm a fucking *killer*, in case you haven't noticed. The first time you saw me, I'd just blown the head off your little spirit guide. So explain to me, Agent Neal, how the fuck it is that my long-lost half-brother just happened to end up creating a hostage situation in my jurisdiction? And why the little creep had a damn *stalker* scrapbook of me and my family?"

Neal winced. "I realize it looks bad out of context. But you have to understand, Charlie wanted to know his family. Paul had told him about you and Andy for years, but never let him meet you guys. The first photos are ones Paul brought him, part of the family history, I guess. Then Paul died when Charlie was only ten, so Charlie felt even more isolated, wanted to know more about you. So he added to it over the years."

"By stalking me? That's ridiculous. There are pictures of me at Briar Ridge, and in the hospital, after the fire. How could Charlie Akers have gotten hold of those?"

He shrugged. "I don't have all the answers, Rose. I'd only known Charlie a short time, and I can't account for his actions before I met him. He didn't show me the photo album until he told me about you."

"And his little news archives?"

Neal watched me gravely. "I think that's pretty self-explanatory, don't you? Charlie thought someone was setting fires."

Me, of course, and I could tell from Neal's face that he knew it. "Why would he care about that?"

"He wanted to know what you—your family—what you could be capable of. The extent of your powers, compared to his."

I broke eye contact first, looking out the grimy window into the parking lot, my stomach doing nervous flips. I wanted someone to tell me those fires had nothing to do with me, but Neal wasn't the right person to seek reassurance from.

He finally cleared his throat. "As for the rest—him ending his life the way he did, taking Laura and his kids—I can't answer that either."

I thought I could. The Whispers had come close to driving me mad when I was a teenager. I couldn't imagine what kind of havoc they could wreak on a person who tried to control them.

"I don't know if Charlie had the specific intent of getting you involved, or if it just worked out that way," Neal went on. "All I know is, after the last time we tried to call the Whispers, Charlie changed. He got secretive, weird. Impatient. He kept leading me on with all this information about you and the Summers family, but he wouldn't commit to a timetable for approaching you. Then he stopped returning my calls. He moved almost overnight—his wife split with the kids, came down to Memphis. He stayed up in Kentucky, but he didn't come back to their apartment. It took me a while to find him, and once I had, he wouldn't talk to me, pretended not to know me. That's why I was tracking him through work again—I thought if I had some leverage on him, he'd have to help me. By that time..." Neal's voice wavered; he dropped his gaze to the table again. "By that time, Ethan was in a coma. Totally unresponsive, and the doctors still had no explanation. I knew I had to get help from Akers, or someone in your family—it was my only chance." He swallowed, hard. "He called me, the day before everything went to hell on Union. Said he knew how to get to you, bring you on board. He told me it was what they'd wanted all along. It was why my boy had been taken by them—to lead us to you. That Ethan wouldn't have a chance until we brought you to them."

I stared at him. "Brought me to them? Jesus, are you...and this whole thing with his wife? The shootout? You think that was his plan to get my help? Put himself in front of my gun?"

Neal shook his head. "No, no, I'm sure that wasn't it. Like I said, I don't know why Charlie ended up doing what he did. I didn't even know what he'd done until I read about it in the papers on Thursday morning. I was already in Memphis because of Charlie's call, and I came to the scene because I wanted to know what the outcome would be. To me it seemed like blind luck that you were there at all."

"Luck." I laughed hollowly. "Yeah, I feel very lucky right now."

"You should, Rose, even if you can't see it. How else would you have known what was going on with your kids? Why they're getting sick?"

"They're not sick. My kids are fine," I said. I'd been trying my damnedest throughout Neal's narrative not to draw parallels between his son's illness and what was going on with Tommy. Looking at Neal's pitying expression, I knew he saw right through it.

My phone vibrated in my pocket and I pulled it out, not sorry for the distraction. It was a text from Luke.

Need to see you. You off work?

Will be shortly, I tapped back. *Meet me at Louie's in ten.*
K.

I stood, pulling a ten-dollar bill from my pocket and throwing it on the table. It would more than cover the coffee, but we'd been camping at the poor server's table for an hour by now. "I've got to go, Neal."

"Rose, please." His voice was panicked, and he reached out for my wrist. He stopped just short of touching me, but his hand hovered close. "After everything I've told you, you're not seriously going to walk away, are you?"

"I've got to think through all this, Neal. You've just unloaded years' worth of family drama onto me, and I need time to process it. But if I were you, I'd be looking for another solution."

Neal's brows descended and his jaws bunched. I spoke before he could start in on me.

"I'm not saying I would knowingly refuse to help an ill child, if it was in my power to do so. What I *am* saying is that you have to be prepared for the possibility that I'm not going to be *able* to help your son. You're counting on the words of a crazy man—you think it makes any damn sense for the Whispers to take your son just to get to me? Why would you believe that?"

"Because I have to. Because it's all I have—I've tried everything else. The Whispers want you, Rose. You've denied their power too long, and your own. You're the only one who can do this."

I leaned in. "You said it yourself, Neal. My father may have honed those skills in Akers, but he crushed them in me."

Neal's face relaxed and he smiled, his perfect white teeth on full display. "I know you can do it, Rose. I have complete faith in you."

I stepped out of the booth, ignoring the hand he extended toward me. "Like I said, Neal, no promises. I need to sleep on this. I'll be in touch."

"And Lieutenant Taylor? What are you going to tell him?"

I sighed. "For now, this is between us. That doesn't mean I won't change my mind, Neal." I wondered what to do if Taylor got the same info Luke had, about Neal being on leave. Would I let my boss kick his ass back up to Kentucky, leave Ethan Neal in his coma?

"Okay, Rose. That's fair." He made no further attempt to delay me, and gave a friendly wave when I passed by the window on the way to my car. When I revved up the Charger and headed for the exit, I gave him one last look. He was on the phone, head bent, eyes hard and narrow. I wondered who the hell had been waiting on his call.

* * *

Luke was waiting in his truck when I pulled into Louie's parking lot at ten minutes past five, rocking out to Kansas with both hands drumming on the steering wheel. We used to squabble over music when we shared a squad car, until we'd finally designated bands we could both agree on, Kansas being one of them. He turned it down and opened his door when I pulled in next to him, but I waved him back in, climbing into his passenger seat with a smile. "Hey there, Wayward Son."

"Hey, darlin'," he said, leaning in for a kiss.

Evidently we were going to pretend our fight on Saturday morning hadn't happened. I gave him a peck on the lips and swiveled sideways to face him, one leg cocked and tucked under me.

"What's up?"

He leaned against the far door and smiled. "You climbin' in my truck, sittin' just like that and asking me what's up makes me think it could be thirteen years ago."

"If it were thirteen years ago, wouldn't you still have that mullet?"

"It wasn't a mullet. I have never worn a mullet."

"Whatever, Billy Ray Cyrus. You were all business in the front, party in the back when I met you."

"What about you with that damn eyebrow pencil? Lookin' like some kid took a black crayon to your face every night, took me forever to realize you were doing that on purpose."

I reached over and flipped his shoulder. "No one taught me makeup, I had to figure it out on my own. I think I misinterpreted something I read in *Glamour*. Anyway, you got something for me on Evan Neal or what?"

He nodded. "That's one bad dude, Rose. I heard back from my guy today. Not a whole lot in the way of detail—you know those feds are pretty tight-lipped."

I smiled. Luke thought anyone north of the Mason-Dixon was tight-lipped. "What *did* he say?"

"Like I told you earlier, Neal met Akers quite a while before this showdown happened. Some kind of drug bust, and it was the first time Akers was on the federal radar. Neal claimed Akers agreed to flip, was going to inform, and he was low man on the totem pole anyway, so Neal's bosses signed off on it."

"Did they think anything was hinky about that?"

Luke shrugged. "Not at the time, but the thing was, no one was ever able to track down any intel Akers brought to the table. It doesn't seem like he was a real useful informant, in any case. Made it a lot weirder when Neal tried to steer the department toward tracking and arresting Akers more recently. But the shadiest stuff has to do with Neal's family."

"What'd you find?"

He twisted around to rummage in the back seat and came up with a crumpled spiral-bound notebook, a slim green one-subject, the same kind he'd used for years on patrol. He flipped to the middle and stabbed a thick finger at the page, and I scooted over to see. "Wife Kathleen Neal, aged thirty-three. Died fourteen months ago. She'd been sick with cancer, or at least that's what Neal told everyone at work. When she finally dies, coroner finds no sign of cancer, but her heart's crushed. Arteries clean as a whistle, but the thing looks like it's been smashed with a sledgehammer."

I frowned. So far, Neal's story was being corroborated, but Luke's phrasing brought another scenario to light—there never had been any cancer, and Neal had lied about it. "Did they have any thoughts on what could have caused that kind of damage?"

"Nothing real likely. Chemotherapy can weaken the heart muscle, but for the most part, heart conditions are chronic. Kathleen Neal had no history of any. Collapse of the heart muscle—hang on, lemme find it—okay, here we go, so collapse can sometimes be caused from a forceful stab that penetrates the muscle with enough force." Luke made a fist with his right hand and mimed stabbing himself in the chest. "'Course, there was no evidence of a wound that would have done that in Kathleen's case. There've also been instances where intense pressure changes—like altitude, I guess, or going under water—have caused heart muscles to collapse. But pretty much any other scenario involves gettin' hold of the heart itself and squeezing."

I pursed my lips, not liking the imagery. "So what's your guy's thought? Neal caused his wife's death somehow?"

"Maybe. He was a little squirrelly on being pinned down on that. Also said Neal's son is sick. Been in a coma for six months now, doctors don't know what's wrong. Again, this is what Neal says. No one else knows for sure."

"So why the administrative leave? To take care of his son?"

"Nope, although the FBI offered him compassionate leave. No, it evidently goes right back to this Akers dude. Neal got obsessed, wouldn't leave it alone. They found out he was using federal resources for his own little crusade, shut him down fast."

"Hm." I stared out the windshield, thinking. It matched up with what Neal had just told me; it made sense that he would have been obsessed with finding Akers to help Ethan if Akers had dropped off the map. But there were different ways to tell the truth. It hadn't gotten me any closer to a solution, but I hoped what Luke had found out would at least give me some leverage with Neal.

Luke cleared his throat, leaned closer. "What do you think, Rose? Any of this help you?"

"Maybe. Still working through some of this stuff. It's been a messed-up couple of days." I filled him in on what had gone down that morning, the ambush by Neal about Charlie Akers possibly being my brother.

He leaned back, his thick brows drawn together. "Ho-oh-ly shit, Rose. Think there's any truth to it?"

I shrugged. "I can't rule it out—I took a DNA test, but it's going to be a few days."

He shook his head. "That motherfucker stirred the beehive but good, didn't he? You piss him off in a past life or what?"

"I didn't know rednecks believed in karma."

"That's what you get for making elitist assumptions. How bad you think Neal has it out for you? You heard anything else from him? He still trying to get you to meet him?"

"Actually, yeah." I told him the bare bones of what Neal and I had discussed, leaving out the ghost details. Instead, I told him Charlie Akers had been trying to use old family secrets to help Neal's wife, and that now he thought I could help too. It sounded lame, but Luke barely even noticed that part.

He stared at me, his brown eyes huge. "You actually met with this asshole? Alone? Before I got a chance to check him out? Jesus, Rose, if I ever met anyone who could get into trouble faster than you do. What the hell happened to letting your partner back you up?"

"Things changed after this morning, Luke. Neal said he could cause trouble for me at work, and he did. Big time. I didn't feel like I had a choice. Besides, it sounds like the people in the most danger from him are related. That leaves me out."

"Yeah? What about Akers? He wasn't related to Neal, and look how he ended up."

I gave him a measured stare. "That was my doing, in case you don't remember. Not Neal's."

"Rose, from everything I've found out, Charlie Akers was a pretty normal guy before running across Evan Neal. My FBI contact looked into him after Neal got weird. Akers was a small-time loser, sure, and it looks like the drug bust was legit, but his family life was pretty good. Everyone that knew the Akers family said Charlie and Laura had a good marriage—high school sweethearts. And he loved those kids—no way he'd endanger them the way he did last week. What happened in just over a year to make a friendly small-time time loser turn into a gun-wielding psycho? What did Neal get him into?"

"What are you saying? Evan Neal somehow caused Akers' behavior? Turned him into a wife-beater or something?"

"I don't know, Rose. But why meet with him? Why take the chance? He screwed you with the family thing, sure, but he's already done his worst. What else are you afraid of? What does he have on you?"

"Jesus, Luke, nothing that I know of, but that's just the problem, isn't it? He seems to know more about me than I do—I didn't believe that the first time he told me, and look what happened."

It sounded good, even reasonable, but I could tell Luke wasn't buying it. He'd known me for too long, heard too much of my bullshit to be convinced. He watched me with worried eyes before leaning forward, reaching across and taking my hands. Before I knew what he was doing, he slipped my gloves off and held my bare skin to his own. Whatever I'd been thinking went straight out of my head, and the only thing I could see were my gnarled, scarred hands in his smooth ones.

I don't know why it was different, here, now, than it was when I shared a bed with him. Maybe because it was usually dark, or because we were distracted by our libidos. All I knew was how on edge I was, and how badly I wanted my gloves back.

"Luke—"

"Rose, I know something's going on." He pulled my hands into his lap, rubbed his thumbs over my scars. "I know Neal is threatening you with something—you've been distracted, upset. We've known each other for years—why can't you trust me with it?"

Because you're not Sam.

I didn't say it, but he must have seen something in my eyes. I remembered what William had said about every thought I had marching straight across my face, and I felt bad.

Luke dropped my hands and handed my gloves back, turned away again. When he finally spoke, he wasn't looking at me, staring out into the empty parking lot instead.

"Can I see you tonight, Rose? I've got somewhere I need to be in an hour, but I'll be done by seven-thirty, eight at the latest. I could come by after."

Part of me wanted nothing more than that, to jump back in bed with Luke and let him distract me from everything that had gone to shit today. But I thought of Sam, sharing my bed last night with Tommy between us. I didn't owe Sam anything, but I couldn't very well kick him out to the couch in favor of my friend with benefits. "I can't tonight, Luke. I've got the kids."

He frowned. "It's Monday. I thought Sam had the kids until Wednesday."

"He does, normally. But they're spraying for bugs over at his place this week, so I've got them." I looked at the dashboard clock, reached for my door handle. "I've got to go pick them up."

He gave me a long look that I couldn't interpret, his deep brown eyes serious, his mouth turned down. "All right, Rose. I'll talk to you later. Have a good time with the kiddos tonight."

"Listen, Luke, thanks for the info on Neal, really. I appreciate what you've done for me." It sounded oddly formal, and I searched for something better to say, something to bring us back to where we had been. "I'm sorry about tonight."

He waved a hand, smiled. "Hey, you know me, a woman in every port. Don't worry, I'll find somethin' to do. Just don't go gettin' jealous on me, remember I gave you first pick."

"You have no idea how flattered I am," I said as I hopped out of the truck, feeling better. When I turned to wave as I pulled out of the lot, he was still sitting, watching me drive away.

* * *

The bullpen was dark and quiet when I got back to the precinct. It was still plenty light outside, but that didn't penetrate to the center of the building where my desk was. Most of the day shift guys had already gone home, and second shift must have been out on a call—there wasn't a soul around. Llewellyn's Explorer was still in the back of the lot, but I didn't run into him. Al Taylor's door was shut, light coming from underneath, but I couldn't hear anything. I decided I'd wait to fill him in on Neal until tomorrow—it would give me time to figure out who should know what, and how much. If he thought it was suspicious that Neal hadn't showed back up that afternoon, he hadn't said anything to me about it, so I figured I could wait.

I was halfway across the room when a loud hissing froze me in place.

"*Shhhhhh...*"

It was coming from my desk.

"*They're here.*"

Whimpering, as of small children. The voice was familiar.

"*Be very, very still. They only want bad children.*"

I thought I might be sick. It was Akers. Charlie's voice, my father's words. Heart pounding, I stepped around the cubicle wall.

There was no one there. A small tape recorder was sitting in the middle of my desk, illuminated in a pool of light from the lamp. The tape was still spinning.

Tearful, muffled crying. The sounds of toddlers trying to master their fear, to keep themselves safe from the bogeyman who shared the shadows with them. Charlie's children.

A wet sound then, like something soft and fleshy being ripped. More crying, interspersed with moans of "Mommy." Bile rose in my throat, thinking of Laura Akers' desiccated corpse. All that missing, abraded soft tissue. What the fuck had happened to her, there in the dark, in front of her children?

I was frozen, staring at the spinning tape deck, realizing this must be the playback from all those hours over on Union. I was terrified of what I might hear next, powerless to make myself reach out and turn it off.

Rushing silence was all that played for another minute or more, punctuated only by those unspeakable wet sounds. Then:

"*What a friend we have in Jesus...*"

I slammed my fist on the buttons of the deck, killing the recording.

Someone was there. In the sudden quiet, I could hear breathing behind me.

I turned, the hairs rising on the nape of my neck. A hulking figure stood a few feet away, hidden in shadow.

"Zack?" I braced a hand on the side of my desk, my legs shaking. "Jesus, Zack, you scared the shit out of me. What the fuck are you doing? Did you put this tape player here?"

He didn't answer. Didn't meet my eyes, stared instead at the floor in front of him.

My relief drained away as I looked at Zack.

It had only been since Friday that I'd seen him—three days. I knew it hadn't been the best of times for him. He'd gotten shot and lost a hostage taker, so I didn't expect him to be chirping merry, but the change in my friend was disquieting. Always a large guy, Zack's normally full face looked gaunt, his cheeks hollow and shadowed.

His beard had straggled out from its kempt shape; his eyes were bloodshot. His clothes looked like they'd been slept in for more than one night.

"Zack, man, what the hell?"

He looked up slowly, his anemic smile looking like it hurt him. "Sorry, Rose," he said. "Zoning out a little at the end of the day." At least he was looking me in the eye.

"Okay," I said slowly. "What the hell are you doing here, lurking in the dark? Why did you play that tape?"

"Huh?" His eyes were feverishly bright, at odds with his lethargy, but his gaze kept bouncing away from mine. I realized I could smell him—a faint musk of body odor, sweat, and dirty clothing.

"Zack," I said louder, and his eyes finally locked back onto me. "Seriously, Zack, what is *wrong* with you? You look like hell. Did you even go home this weekend?"

"Of course," he answered after a pause, an odd little grin playing across his face. "Home is where the heart is," he said with a giggle.

I wondered if he was drunk.

He shook himself, reminding me of a Saint Bernard. His smile grew bigger, but still failed to reach those oddly bright eyes.

"I *am* tired—had a hard time sleeping the last few nights. Got... things on my mind. I wanted to talk to you before you left tonight, though." He took a step toward me. "Alone."

"Is that why you came looking for me at Joy's this morning? Why didn't you just call me?"

His eyelids dropped, his gaze skewing sideways. "I lost my phone. I needed to talk to you."

"Why didn't you come to my place?"

He ignored me. "I finished going through the recordings from Union Avenue. From the nights Charlie Akers was in there, you remember me telling you about that? Him talking to himself?"

I looked at the silent tape deck. "Yes, Zack, I remember. Was there something you wanted me to hear?"

He didn't answer me. "I heard all *kinds* of things on there, Rose. And the thing is, I think Charlie was *onto* something."

It was Charlie now, I noted, not Akers. "What was he onto?" I asked, keeping it conversational, taking a step back when he took another toward me.

"You believe in ghosts, don't you, Rose? Not just an afterlife—the idea that spirits can come back to us—can interact with us again." He didn't wait for an answer. "I wasn't sure if I did, before last weekend. I wanted to. I lost my brother when I was a kid, did you know that?" Zack was suddenly solemn, the manic grin that had played across his features disappearing briefly before creeping back. "I always kind of hoped, you know, that I'd see him again."

It was a hope I could relate to. "And...and did you, Zack?"

"Yes! I did!" The smile looked painful now, stretching his features grotesquely. "What I didn't want to say at the time was, I heard him that night. Matt, my brother. I can't tell you, Rose, how wonderful it was to hear his voice, after all these years, to know that he wasn't mad at me anymore." Twin tears rolled down his face, and he made no move to wipe them away. "Can you imagine the joy of it? You've lost people, haven't you, Rose? You lost a brother, too. Andy, right?"

Warning bells were going off in my head. I had never mentioned Andy to Zack—I didn't talk about my golden brother and what had happened to him.

Zack nodded as if I'd spoken. "I know what that's like, Rose. To lose your brother young. To feel bad about it, to feel like it's your fault somehow, like you have something to make up for. I never thought I'd have the chance to make up for it, but I was wrong. Because Charlie, he figured out how. He tapped into it."

Tapped into what? If what Evan Neal had told me was true, Charlie had gotten in way over his head with the Whispers. But what the hell were the Whispers, anyway? Voices, sure, that much I knew. I'd always assumed they were the voices of the dead, but they were impossible to differentiate into their separate parts, so I'd never given much thought to who they might have been. Was it possible Zack was right? Was Matt Dayton now part of that faceless horde? If that were so, would Zack be able to communicate with his brother the way he thought he could?

"What do you mean, Zack?"

He reached out and grabbed for my hand. I flinched as, for the second time that day, someone who should have known better tried to touch me.

"Come with me, Rose."

"Come where, Zack? What the hell are you doing?"

"I want to show you. I want to help you see him, Rose."

"See *who?*"

"Andy, Rose. See Andy again. Haven't you always wanted to?"

I hesitated. Because however off-kilter he might be right now, Zack was right—I did want to see Andy again. I wanted to know that he was all right, that he didn't blame me for what happened to him. I'd half believed for years that he was watching out for me, but I'd never seen him, didn't know for sure. Maybe if all those references to an open door meant what I thought they did, Andy would be waiting for me. And if what I feared was right, that Matt—and by extension, Andy—had become part of the Whispers, maybe I could help free them.

"Where do you want me to go, Zack?" I finally managed out of a dry throat.

"We have to go back, Rose. To where it began." He was squeezing my hand, hurting me, but I didn't let go.

The phone rang. A shrill, harshly electronic sound, popping the little bubble of solitude Zack and I had been in for the past few minutes. Zack didn't move. When I reached for the receiver, he squeezed my hand harder. I felt the bones crunch together and cried out.

"What the fuck, Zack?"

He leaned in across the desk, getting within inches of my face, his features locked in a snarl. He was breathing hard, filling my nostrils with a rotting stink that seemed like more than just a few days without use of a toothbrush, and I recoiled.

"Don't answer that, Rose. Come with me, now."

I looked at the caller ID. "Zack, it's your wife. Don't you want me to get it?"

"*No.*" He picked the receiver up with the hand not currently crushing mine and slammed it back down.

"Zack, let me go. You're hurting me."

He released my hand and I stepped around to put the desk between us.

Zack tried for a reassuring smile. "I'm sorry Rose, I'm just excited to see Matt again, and I know you want to see Andy. But there's only a small window here—we have to go now, or we'll miss them. Maybe forever."

"Go where, Zack?" I glanced over my shoulder, wishing Taylor would open his door, but it stayed shut tight, more than thirty feet away. Would he hear me if I yelled? Was he even in there, or had he just forgotten to turn the lights off?

"We have to go back to where it started, Rose."

"To where *what* started?"

"All of this. Everything. The door—the crossing. To where all of it began, to where you made it possible."

"Zack, I don't understand. I think we need to—"

He lunged across the desk, grabbing my gloved hand in another crushing grip. This time he tried to pull me across the desk, and I hit hard with my hip. I struggled but couldn't get loose, and he was moving like a freight train. I had to scramble across the desk top to avoid being dragged.

"Damn it Zack, stop! Let me go!"

He didn't look back, just pulled me along behind him, headed for the front door. "I can't wait for you to see it, Rose," he said conversationally. "It's incredible, what's waiting for you."

"Zack, what the hell is wrong with you?" I dug my heels in, trying to get traction. I needed leverage to disable him, and I wasn't going to get it stumbling along behind him. Where the hell was Al?

Zack began to sing.

"*What a friend we have in Jesus,*" he sang in a strong tenor.

I stopped struggling, instead following numbly, tripping over my own feet. "That song," I whispered. "Why are you singing that song?"

He turned to face me, his mouth only inches from mine, his smile a horrifying rictus. "*All our sins and griefs to bear...*"

Almost before I heard the gathering of the Whispers, I felt them. They were like sharp, jagged fingernails at the edges of my brain, clawing and prying, trying to get in. I clutched at my skull, pressed hard with the heel of my hand.

Zack kept on singing in that crazy, manic voice. I didn't know where he was taking me, but by now it was clear that whatever had happened to my friend, the Whispers were part of it.

I grabbed his wrist with my free hand and yanked back hard, at the same time digging my feet into the gray industrial carpet. He stopped and was carried back by my momentum, and I used the opportunity to kick at the backs of his knees. His legs went out from under him, and he hit the floor with an *oof* as the breath was knocked out of him.

He was still holding on to me, and my arm was pulled nearly out of its socket as I fought to remain upright. I kicked at his arm and he finally let go, only to lunge immediately for my right ankle. I was turning to get out of range, but he was too fast. Down I went, hitting hard.

He was dragging me again, toward him across the rough carpet. This was crazy—Zack was no slouch, but he wasn't S.W.A.T.—he didn't spend the hours in the gym and on the range that I did. I should have been able to break free easily, but I couldn't. I flipped over on my belly and flailed for something to hold onto, kicking as hard as I could with my other foot.

There was a grunt as my boot connected with something solid that then gave with a sickening smoosh. My ankle was released—Zack had stopped struggling, and the Whispers went silent.

I gasped in the relief of their absence, scrambling backward just as a door banged open somewhere along the back hallway. "Who the hell is out there?" shouted Al.

"It's Rose," I managed to say in a shaky voice. When Zack stayed still, I braved a closer look. He was out; the right side of his head was already swelling where I'd gotten him with the toe of my boot. I checked his pulse.

Nothing.

"Oh, fuck." I scooted closer, laid my head on his chest. It wasn't moving.

"Rose, what the hell are you doing here in the dark? Where are you?" There was a loud *thunk* as Al walked into something. "Ow, damn it. I can't see anything in here."

I stood, my ankle aching where Zack had grabbed it, my hip

hurting from where I'd landed on it. "Al, I'm up here, near the door. I need help. I think I've hurt him pretty bad."

A stunned silence, then Taylor could be heard crashing through the bullpen. "Hurt who, Rose?"

I gestured behind me helplessly. "He's—he was attacking me. Out of his head—I didn't know what else to do. I don't think he's breathing."

Al leaned to peer behind me. When he met my eyes again, he had that wary look I had dreaded as a child—the one that meant someone was afraid of me.

"Al, you have to believe me—he was crazy, trying to get me alone. I don't know what he was planning to do, but I didn't mean for this to happen."

"For what to happen, Rose? There's no one else here."

CHAPTER NINE

The sun was down by the time I pulled into my driveway behind Sam's Ford. I'd called from the office and given him a shortened version of what had happened with Zack, told him I'd be later than I'd thought while I tried to figure out what was going on with my friend. Sam, bless him, had only said he'd keep dinner warm for me, for whenever I got home.

I'd told Al about Zack's appearance and his attempt to get me out of the building with him. I'd even told him about Zack's brother, too tired and stunned to come up with a convincing lie. We'd both gone over the whole building and found no sign of Zack, or of anyone else who'd seen him. His car was gone from the lot. The security camera footage from the parking lot showed his Trailblazer there one frame, and gone the next, something neither Taylor nor I could explain. Did it mean Zack had never even been there? Was my friend a ghost now, or somehow being controlled by Charlie Akers? I wondered which option was worse.

I'd handled the call to Zack's wife, Anna. She'd left me a voicemail, having called back shortly after Zack hung up on her. She hadn't seen him since the night of the Akers shooting. Evidently he'd stayed in touch by phone at first, telling her he wanted to go back in and review the tapes over the weekend. Then he'd stopped answering the phone, and she hadn't talked to him since late Saturday night.

I told her he'd been at the station that night, and had seemed upset about something, but I left out any description of his attempt to get me out of the building. I said we'd be looking for him, and would be in touch with her.

I'd spent the next couple of hours looking for Zack, hitting all his favorite spots in town, everywhere I'd ever known him to hang out. I ran by the Akers crime scene on Union, but Zack's truck wasn't there, so I moved on, telling myself it wasn't because I was scared. There was no sign of Zack anywhere. Al finally told me to pack it in, that Zack clearly didn't want to be found.

I was glad I'd told Al; it felt better not to be alone in my knowledge.

With that conclusion, I decided I'd fill Sam in on everything. Tonight, without further loss of time; I didn't want to be alone in any part of whatever nightmare was building around me. Even if the only thing in the world I wanted right now was to finish off a six-pack and pass the hell out. I sighed, grabbing my purse and bag out of the back seat. Maybe after the kids went to bed.

I stopped on the porch, the fine hairs on the nape of my neck rising as I tried to listen. Ever since my foray at Sam's house, I'd been trying to relearn the skill, using it whenever I could. It wasn't always pleasant, being prey to whatever energy was floating around a place, but I could see a lot of merit in not being taken by surprise. I thought there was a good chance if I'd been more alert when I got back to the station house tonight, Zack wouldn't have gotten the jump on me.

There was nothing out of place for a Memphis summer evening, and when I turned to scan the street, I saw nothing to concern me. I closed my eyes and reached further, and for a moment I thought I felt something draw back from the touch of my mind, but I couldn't be sure. I reached again, but there was nothing. Had I even felt anything?

My mind felt ravaged, ragged from the earlier attack by the Whispers, an occurrence I was trying like hell not to think about.

Finally I pushed through the front door, engaging the deadbolt behind me, kicking off my shoes and shedding clothes as I went down the hall. The whole house smelled like good barbeque, and I realized I was starving. I locked up my service weapon and turned, noticing a bottle of wine standing next to two glasses on the bar. Wandering over, I peeked at the label and smiled—sweet white muscadine, cold. Not every store carried it, but it was my favorite. A big brown paper bag was on the kitchen counter next to the fridge, grease spots telling me my evening was looking up.

On the way back to my room to change clothes, I peeked in the kids' rooms but found them empty. "Sam?" I called.

"In here," he replied from the master bath.

I stripped off my long-sleeved tee, but left the black ribbed tank I wore underneath. I knocked with one knuckle on the partially closed bathroom door. "You decent in there, McFarland?"

"Come on in, Rose, all the naughty bits are covered up."

The mirror was steamed and the tub was filled with thick foam, the air redolent of my favorite and seldom-used cranberry apple bubble bath. Sam was sitting on the edge, one hand in the water, testing the temperature. He wore a white linen button-up top, the sleeves rolled to his elbows, and a pair of dark wash Levi's that looked good on him. His big feet were bare on the black and white checkered tiles. He turned and gave me the kind of smile that makes a girl want to say yes, whatever the question might be.

"Hey, you. I was starting to wonder if they'd ever let you come home."

My smile was more tired than enticing, but I meant it. "Long day."

"Sorry, hon. Any news on Zack?"

I shook my head. "Nothing. Anna hasn't seen him since the morning after the Akers shooting."

"I'm sorry, Rose. I know you're worried about him."

I nodded. "Where are the kids?"

"They're still with Mom, having a pizza night. Before you say anything, William's over there too. Two adults with at least one firearm each, so Lily and Tommy are safe, okay?"

I frowned, then looked around the bathroom, noting the low lights and the CD player he'd brought in from my office. A moment later I was able to make out the low strains of cello concertos coming from the speakers.

"What is this, Sam? Getting rid of the kids, bubble baths? And I thought Don Henley was your go-to seduction music."

He stood and dried his hand on a fluffy towel before reaching for my hands. "It's not seduction music, Rose, it's relaxation music. Seduction comes later." His eyes smiled into mine as he pulled me forward. "This is all you, babe. Bath should be the right temperature, got your music, your candles, your bubbles—I will shortly bring you a glass of wine and get out of your hair." He disappeared into the bedroom, humming as he went.

Deciding ulterior motives were a secondary concern, I wasted no time getting out of my clothes and into the bath. I piled my curls on top of my head and leaned back, closing my eyes and sighing as the water covered me up to my chin. A minute later I heard the door ease back open, then a click as Sam set a wine glass on the edge of the tub within my reach. I opened one eye. "Is there chocolate?"

"Would I forget? 77% dark with chili peppers. It's behind you. And whenever you're ready, King's Palace ribs and pulled pork for dinner, with all the trimmings."

I closed my eyes again. "Whatever the hell you're buttering me up for, Sam, the answer is yes."

He bent and dropped a kiss on the top of my head without even trying to peek beneath the bubbles. "Holdin' you to it. See you when you're done."

Stalkers. Threatened careers. Irritating feds, estranged parents, killer ghosts. I wondered how shallow it made me that ten minutes in that tub, half a glass of wine, and two squares of dark chocolate made all of that recede into the distance. The taut muscles of my shoulders and neck, which never seemed to release, slowly loosened up as I soaked and splashed, amusing myself by kicking bubbles over the edge onto the tiles. By the time the water was growing tepid, my sense of responsibility returned and I regretfully surfaced. I stood carefully and stretched, letting the water sluice down my body before reaching for my towel.

"Heyo, Rose—you ready for dinner or did you drown?" The door swung open and Sam stopped, his mouth open. After a speechless moment, he swallowed audibly and blinked. "Wow."

I could feel myself blushing, and hurried to wrap the towel around me. "See something you like?" It came out much less sarcastic than it sounded in my head.

"Everything." His voice was low, and because it was Sam, I didn't think about the gnarled, ruined horror that was my flesh from the neck down. Instead I believed him, and was able to see myself through his eyes.

He took a step toward me and held out a hand to help me out of the bath. I'd forgotten to warn him about the bubbles I'd splashed onto the tiles, and it was just as I was stepping out that his feet went out from under him. Neither of us had enough balance to keep the other from falling, and Sam hit the tiles hard, twisting to keep me on top and cushion my landing.

"Ow," he groaned. "My ass."

I giggled, and he glared at me.

"All these years I thought it was the kids who soaked the floor at bath time."

"Fooled you. The rubber ducks were mine, too." I tried to push off him, but he wrapped his arms around my waist and held me close. I resisted for only a few seconds before deciding to just let go. I'd promised myself full honesty tonight—maybe that could apply to my complicated relationship with Sam. If I was being completely honest, there was nowhere I'd rather be than in his arms.

He was still smiling at me, one hand stroking my bare back. "Rose."

"Hmm?"

"Rose, I've missed this."

"Falling in bathrooms?"

"Can you let me say this, please?" His blue eyes were intent now, his expression serious as he twisted to look at my face.

My stomach fluttered, my mouth dry. I laid my head on his chest so I wouldn't have to hold that bright blue gaze.

Sam took a deep breath and I felt his grip on me tighten. "I've missed us, Rose. I've missed you, missed being a family. I know we have a good thing going—we get to see each other all the time, do things together with the kids, be a parenting team. All of that is great, it really is, and I know neither of us wants to jeopardize it. Hell, it's a lot more than I thought we'd have when we got divorced, and I've been grateful for it. But it's not enough anymore."

"Sam..."

"Just listen for a minute, okay?" He waited; then, when I offered no further protest, he took another breath. "When you married Aaron, I figured it was over at that point. There was no getting you back. I knew you loved him, and I knew he'd never get on your back about the job the way I did. Then, when he died...Rose, I don't want you to think I was happy, because I wasn't. I liked Aaron, and I would never have wanted you to lose someone you loved. But there was a part of me that wondered if there was hope for us."

He struggled into a sitting position, propping himself up against the cabinet and tucking me next to him, one arm around my shoulders. "I know we both tried to move on. You had Aaron, and I've been with other women."

Although his admission came as no surprise, it hurt to hear out loud. I felt a rush of anger at him for bringing it up at all. Then I thought of Sam congratulating me on my engagement, dancing with me at my wedding to another man, hugging me when I told him I was pregnant with Tommy, and I tried to swallow my resentment. Tried, and failed.

"You were with one this weekend, weren't you?" I asked, trying to keep my tone light.

Sam frowned down at me. "What are you talking about?"

"Sunday? I smelled her perfume. It's fine," I said when he started to answer. "It's not my business, okay? Obviously, since you never introduce me to any of them. It's just, you making it sound like you're sitting around pining, it's bullshit. Doesn't she have a right to know about this?" I gestured at our entwined bodies, tried to pull away.

Sam wasn't having it. He pulled me closer, looked into my eyes. "No, she doesn't. She's not a part of my life, not like you are. Like you've always been. You want to know why I never introduce you to the women I date? It's because I know they won't measure up, not to you. The first time I got in your patrol car—when I met your eyes in the rearview—since then there's been nobody else for me, and I know now there never will be." His arm was tight around my shoulders, and I could hear his breath coming fast.

I concentrated on the tile floor, my face flushed as I thought of all the hurt I'd tried to push away for the last six years. "You—it took you five minutes to get someone else in our bed, Sam. You didn't even wait for the dust to settle. You didn't try to get me back." Tears fell; weak, stupid tears as I remembered seeing the slim redhead leaving Sam's driveway, our driveway, early on the morning I'd come to talk.

Now he was looking at the floor, too. "I didn't know you knew about that."

I wiped the tears away with the heel of my hand. "Yeah, I knew. I came by. I thought we could talk, that it had been long enough for our emotions to settle, and there she was."

He squeezed his eyes closed. "Shit. Shit, shit, shit. You came back—you came back to me, and I—oh, Jesus. Oh, hell."

I cleared my throat, tried to stand but he still wasn't letting go of me. "It's fine. It was for the best, okay? We weren't right together, and Sam, as good as this might feel right now, nothing's really changed, has it? We're still the same people we were."

"No, Rose, no. I fucked it up. I get that. Things were great, we loved each other, we loved Lily...and you loved your job, too. I know that now. I know it doesn't mean you love me any less. And whatever you might have thought, seeing that woman—"

I winced and he squeezed me tighter. "I was always faithful to you. Always. I never wanted anyone else, but when I thought I couldn't have you, I just wanted a distraction." He swallowed, brushed at tears of his own. "I can do better this time, Rose, I promise. You know I'll never be able to stop worrying about you." He gave me that crooked smile I'd always loved. "It's in my genetic code. But I'm trying—trying to learn how to express that in the right ways, and not turn it into a guilt trip or a blame session. I know I can trust you to take care of yourself on the job like I trust you to take care of our family—and I think that will be enough."

I looked at him, my heart pounding uncomfortably fast, my stomach in knots. Sam was right; we had a good thing going, and it would be folly to risk that. But how much worse to risk this? For the first time since I'd left, I allowed myself to think of letting go of my hurts, of going back, being together again. I realized how badly I wanted it, and that scared me, too. I'd been kidding myself that I was over Sam, that there was nothing left for us but friendship and co-parenting. When I was with Luke, or any of the other men I'd dated since my divorce, I couldn't picture the same kind of partnership I'd had with Sam. None of them made me want to be married again, to commit to them fully, because none of them were Sam.

Which gave me all the answer I needed. I was way too cool to cry, but I threw my arms around his neck and kissed him hard and deep. Somewhere in there I managed to lose my towel, but I didn't care.

* * *

I was curled against Sam with my head on his bare chest while he stroked my hair, listening to the quiet of the house. When the landline rang in my office, we looked at each other.

"Ignore it," Sam said. "Anyone who matters can reach you on your cell."

I sat up and stretched. "You mean the one that's in my purse in the kitchen?"

He made a face. "Duty calls, I suppose."

"I just need to make sure it's not the kids, Sam. If it's work, and it's not an emergency, I'll tell 'em to get bent." I swung my legs out of bed and grabbed a t-shirt, pulling it over my head on the way to my office. Sam yawned cavernously, but was struggling to sit up by the time I was in the hall.

I made it to the door just as the answering machine kicked on, the generic robot voice inviting the caller to leave a message after the tone. I stood in front of my desk, waiting to hear the message.

It seemed like a long time before I heard anything. There was a sigh, and a voice I'd never expected to hear again came tremulously through the tinny speaker. "Rose. I hoped you'd be there, I'd like to speak with you. There are some things I need to tell you." I winced as a shrill, shrieking whine cut her off, then static. Silence again, then she was crying. "Please, Rose—I'm at the home place. We don't have much time." A fuzz of more static, then rising feedback. A sharp crack cut the connection, and the dial tone began to hum.

I stood staring numbly, my hand reaching out at first to play the message again; then I pulled it back and hugged it to my chest. My knees were shaking, and I plunked down on the bean bag chair I kept in front of my office window. My fingers were in my hair, twirling a curl tightly around and around. I turned when I saw Sam's shadow in the doorway.

"Who the hell was that?"

I took a shaky breath, but my voice was steady when I answered him. "That was my mother, Sam."

Twenty minutes later, we sat next to each other on bar stools at the counter, our backs to the living room, watching the empty street and working on plates of barbeque. We weren't talking, our mouths full of ribs, but I could feel Sam watching me. When we'd finished, Sam took the dishes to the sink and refilled my wine glass. He hitched up the robe he was wearing—a ratty Victoria's Secret terrycloth he'd bought me for our first Valentine's Day.

I smiled as he sat back down beside me. "You know, pink and cream is a great color combo for you, Sam. I don't know why I never thought of it before."

Sam shook his head. "All those hints I dropped, and all you ever did was buy lingerie for *you* to wear. Talk about selfish."

"I was always pretty oblivious." I stared down at my wine and kicked my dangling feet. Bar stools aren't designed for shrimps—I'd mostly bought them for the kids, who loved to twirl on them while I cooked.

"So, your Mom."

"No, *your* Mom."

He reached out and flipped me on the shoulder. "Real mature, Rose. You going to tell me about it?"

I shrugged, drank half my glass in a swallow. "What's to tell? You heard the messages, so you know as much as I do." After we'd listened again to the most recent one, we'd checked and found three more from earlier in the day, increasing in desperation as the day wore on, but all with the same request. *Call me, I need you.*

"In thirteen years, that's the first time I've ever known your mother to get in touch with you."

"It's been more like seventeen." My voice went flat, and I tried to imagine going seventeen days without talking to one of my kids. "What can I say? We're not exactly close. I didn't even know she had the number to the landline—she's never called it before."

Sam stared down at the wooden counter top, his mouth turned down and his jaw clenched. "After all this time, she's finally decided to reach out. Where's she living?"

"She said the home place—it was Grammy's house, been in the Summers family for years. Mom moved there after the fire—I think it'd been abandoned for years before that." I drank more wine and checked my cell for the time. "Do we need to pick the kids up to-night?"

Sam shook his head. "No, Mama expected them to spend the night. I'll go over there in the morning." He reached for my hand. "Rose, are you going to call your mother back?"

I stared at him. "Are you kidding me? Have we met? Why the hell would I do that? I think I've got enough on my plate right now without dredging up all the old bullshit."

He was watching me gravely. "She sounded pretty upset, Rose. Scared even."

"So what? She's not my problem anymore, Sam. We've got plenty of our own troubles without letting Cora drag us into hers."

He gave me a troubled look I tried to ignore. "Okay Rose, but what if she can help us?"

"How the hell could my mother possibly help us?"

"I guess I'm wondering if her calling now, after..." He trailed off. "Well, after what's been going on with Tommy, and over at my place...do you think it's coincidence, or do you think she could know something about it?"

I gave him a skeptical look.

"Hey, you're the one who brought up the possibility of genetics in all this. If you passed it on to Tommy, who's to say your mom didn't pass it on to you?"

I sighed, sat back on the bar stool, ran a hand across my face. "Because I don't think it came from her side, Sam. I think it came from my father."

"What makes you say that?"

I filled Sam in on the events of my morning: the disconcerting stalker scrapbook, Evan Neal's appearance, and most of what he'd told me about Akers. Part of me still wanted to keep Sam and the kids out of it, but if Sam was serious about starting over together, then I needed to stop trying to protect him. He listened in silence, his brows drawn together, though he nearly choked when I got to the part about Akers being my brother.

"Wow," he said when I finished.

"Yeah." I took a deep breath, surprised at how much better I felt for having told him everything. I got up to refill my wine.

"Do you think it's true? About Akers being your brother, I mean," Sam asked, holding his glass out for a top-off.

I shrugged. "My first thought when I heard it was hell, no. But the more I look into it, the more plausible it seems. I heard one of the recordings from the Akers incident. He was using some of the same phrases on his kids that Dad used to use on me. And singing this song—this fucking song. Christ, they used to sing it at me all the time. How else would he get hold of those old family photos? He had to have gotten them from my father."

Sam's blue eyes darkened. "That crazy fuck. He was stalking you? Had pictures of the kids and all?"

"Yes. I may never sleep again. But at least the motherfucker is dead now." I swallowed. "Deadish, anyway."

He looked at me, then we both cracked up. It was high-pitched, manic laughter that had more to do with fear than genuine amusement, but it still made me feel better.

Sam cleared his throat, dropped his gaze. "What about the newspaper articles, the ones he collected about the fires? What do you think that's about?"

181

I dropped my gaze, my face flushed. "I'd say that's pretty obvious, wouldn't you? Charlie thinks I'm a firebug."

I could feel Sam's eyes on me again.

"Why would he think that, Rose?"

I hesitated, once again considered telling him my fears, once again chickening out when I thought of how it might change how he looked at me. "I don't know, Sam. If Charlie spent much time with my father, he'd have been predisposed to think all kinds of awful things about me. I guess my proximity to the fires would've been enough to make me look guilty." My mouth twisted in an attempt at a smile, and I gestured to my ruined skin. "Although I'm the last person who'd want anything to do with fire, wouldn't you think?"

"Of course, Rose."

He was silent so long I didn't think he was going to let it go, but he finally changed the subject.

"I hate to beat a dead horse here, but if this 'gift' thing is genetic like that Neal guy claims it is, it might be that much more reason to get in touch with your mother. Maybe she saw the same kinds of things you did—maybe she knows family secrets you don't, stuff your dad told her."

"She didn't, Sam. Mom never saw anything I saw. I'm not saying it isn't genetic, but trust me on this, Sam. Mom can't help us."

"How can you be so sure? Rose..." He scooted closer and grasped my wrists when I tried to pull away. "Rose, come on. We're up a creek without a paddle here, aren't we? You said yourself, you don't know enough to guide Tommy through this ghost shit, and I'm as good as useless. All you've got is what this Neal guy is telling you, which is partial and third hand at best, and outright delusional at worst. What's the harm in just calling her, seeing if she has anything to offer? It's not like it obligates us to invite her over for Christmas dinner."

"Sam, I don't want her having anything to do with Lily or Tommy." My voice hardened. "Going through that childhood once was bad enough. I'll be damned if I give that bitch a chance to hurt my kids. To make them feel like any of this is their fault."

His eyes softened, and he ran both his hands up my arms to rest on my shoulders. "Rose."

I pulled away, hating the tears that were pricking my eyelids. "It's fine, Sam. It was a long time ago. I'm over it. I'm just trying to protect us—all of us."

He looked like he wanted to say more, then finally shrugged. "Okay, Rose. Just tell me what you want me to do."

"We'll deal with it tomorrow, Sam."

I wish we'd had the chance. Maybe it could have changed things.

CHAPTER TEN

I was up early the next morning, well before Sam, with a sense of buoyancy that was only marginally negated by the memory of my mother's calls the day before. Having Sam in my bed, feeling like I'd regained something lost so long ago, I began to believe we could make it through everything that was threatening our family. I decided to let him sleep and crept from the bedroom, my clothes and boots under one arm. I made coffee and sat in my kitchenette, trying to make a plan for the day.

One thing was for sure, I wasn't calling Cora Summers. Whatever Sam might think, I knew we'd never be able to trust anything she said. It's damn near impossible to explain to someone with two loving parents how completely dangerous sociopaths are, and I'd come to believe over the years that's what my parents were. I might have felt the weight of their blame as a child, but I was a grown fucking woman now with kids of my own, and I knew there was nothing I could have done at that age that would have justified their sadistic treatment of me. Sam might think he could control a meeting with my mother, steer it to protect us and get what he wanted out of her, but I knew he was wrong. You can't plan for the machinations of a mind that moves in such alien, reptilian ways.

As the sun came up and morning light began to creep across my living room from the big picture window, I finally noticed the small cedar chest William had given me sitting in the middle of the coffee table. I spent a long, cold minute staring at it and wondering how it had gotten there. I hadn't looked at it since stuffing it in the trunk of my Charger the night I'd gotten in. I certainly hadn't brought it in the house, and Sam didn't even know of its existence. What was it doing here?

My heart thudding, I made my way to the couch and sat down, my eyes on the chest. It was a beautiful piece, worthy of Aaron's best work, and I could picture him carving it in his father's workshop on the farm. Lovingly planing the edges, sanding where it was rough, putting his heart and soul into the wood. The latch was iron and old, almost certainly something he'd picked up at a builder's supply store. Aaron liked working with old wood, pieces that had history and could be born anew.

I reached out with a trembling hand and lifted the latch, opening the chest's lid. It was heavier than I expected, and the warm rush of Aaron's scent filled the air before dissipating. I bent to see what it was he'd preserved so carefully.

My wedding dress, I realized as I lifted the ruffled white fabric, my heart full. And underneath, the tuxedo vest Aaron had worn, a burnished gold color, and the light pink flower-girl dress Lily had quickly grown out of. The wedding had been small but elegant, a late summer ceremony on William's farm with dancing well into the night. We'd dressed up against my inclination, because Aaron felt it was important to Lily, and he'd been right. I'd worn the mermaid-style dress of delicate ivory lace, stripped it off at the end of that long, perfect night, and couldn't remember seeing it since. I hadn't given it another thought until it came time to move after Aaron's death, when I couldn't stand to stay alone in the house we'd shared. I'd been packing up mementos, and it had crushed me that I couldn't find these things. My dress, Aaron's wedding clothes, any of the precious reminders I should have been storing up myself but never seemed to get around to.

I held my daughter's tiny dress in my hands, thinking of how little she'd been back then, how proud, dancing with her father and her new stepfather. It should have made me feel guilty, I supposed, this loving preservation by my dead husband with Sam sleeping in my bed, but it felt like a gift. A reminder that we'd always done a good job of blending our families, and it didn't have to be different now that Aaron was gone.

Beneath Lily's dress was something crackling and dry—my bouquet, and Aaron's boutonniere. I touched them lightly, not wanting the petals to crumble beneath my fingers, and then I saw there was something still underneath: a document of some kind, the paper as brown and brittle as the flowers that rested on it.

It took some doing to get the parchment out without damaging it, and when I had, I carried it to the island bar where I could see better.

The script looked old-fashioned: long sloping letters, the spellings archaic. I was surprised the lettering hadn't faded more than it had—it was a little labored, making sense of the phrasing and some of the letters, but I could still read it.

Guardian's Contract, it said at the top, and my interest was piqued. Aaron had liked old things, and sometimes he would buy antique case reporters or legal documents and display them in a glass case in the office he shared with his father. This must have been something he'd picked up and forgotten about, or maybe it was symbolic, packed up with our wedding things. Maybe he'd meant to make it a gift to me, for an anniversary we'd never made it to. I settled onto one of the bar stools and read, but it wasn't long before such comfortable notions were dispelled. Wherever Aaron had come across this thing, it wasn't symbolic.

I, Bella Summers, do hereby pledge my own life and those of my descendants forthcoming to the service of Guardianship of the Dead, one Guardian a generation, for the span of that descendant's life. Beginning at age four, such descendant shall devote their existence to shepherding the wandering lost to the final resting place of all souls. Each chosen Guardian shall be gifted the ability to see the Dead, in all forms and manifestations, and to communicate with them as is needed. The presence of the Guardian shall act as a beacon to guide lost souls to themselves, in order that they may find the path.

In exchange for this service, each Guardian shall be further gifted as suits their temperament and the necessities of their time. It shall be the sole responsibility of the previous generations' Guardians to instruct the others in their gifts.

On pain of death do I sign my name and make this pledge.
Bella Summers

I stared sightlessly out the window, then turned back and skimmed through the document, looking for the punchline. Bella Summers? Who the fuck was that? I'd never heard of an ancestor named Bella, but my father hadn't talked about women in the family at all. There'd been a Jacob Summers he'd seemed pretty proud of, some insufferable jackass who'd effected some kind of cleansing over a hundred years ago. Dad had loved to talk about that guy, how he'd snatched the family from the jaws of paganism or some bullshit. I'd always thought Jacob sounded like a zealous twat, but I wondered whether his cleansing had anything to do with the Faustian contract Bella had signed.

I shook my head, pushed away from the bar. Why was I assuming this Bella had anything to do with me at all? Summers wasn't that uncommon a name, and the document had been with Aaron's things, not my parents'. It was a fluke, something he'd probably found in some dusty drawer in an antique shop and brought home to show me as a curiosity.

Only he hadn't shown me. He'd never mentioned it at all. What would have prompted him to bury it at the bottom of a cedar chest with sentimental reminders of our wedding day? Why had William suddenly been moved to give it to me? It wasn't as though the contract's references to the wandering dead weren't pretty fucking on point, as far as my life went. I'd taken Sam to task for trying to write off Tommy's ghostly experiences as coincidence, and I couldn't afford to be that naïve myself. However this contract had gotten here, it wasn't an accident. Something had brought it straight to me, and I was willing to bet neither of the Matthews men had ever seen it. Not while living, anyway, but did I believe Aaron had brought this to me? Or was it something more sinister?

I came back to the counter and looked over the contract again. It wasn't the first time I'd heard reference to a Guardian, and I shuddered, remembering that flat, alien voice in Sam's basement. Something about the Guardians being gone, or dead, or something. I hadn't known what it meant at the time, but now I wondered. Was that why things were going to hell in Memphis? Because something had happened to these Guardians of the dead, who had the ability to see and speak to spirits? Lost souls...people who had died and not found their way to the other side? I thought back over a lifetime of rooms filled with spirits in some form of distress or other. Some filled with rage, others an overwhelming despair that permeated a room, filled it with poison that leaked into my own mind. It made sense, if that was what they sought—guidance, and I hadn't given it to them.

The presence of the Guardian shall act as a beacon....

I shivered. Was that why so many of the dead had found their way to me over the years? Was that what I was, some kind of spirit guide without a manual? One a generation, and Andy hadn't had my abilities. I thought about Charlie, about what Neal had said about it being unusual for more than one Summers in a generation to hear the Whispers. Was that who Bella had signed the contract with? There was no signature line for another party, no indication of who Bella was signing her soul away to, but I was afraid I was right. Was that why they wanted me? I'd been ignoring my duties as Guardian of the Dead? But no one had told me—who had the previous Guardian been? Who was supposed to teach me?

Bella had done more than sign her own soul away. For her descendants forthcoming...what the hell had she been thinking? What could have been worth a promise like this? And what the hell was the part about a gift? It was written vaguely, and I didn't understand it—suiting the temperament and the necessities of the time. What had Charlie told Neal? That healing was his particular part of the gift. If that were true, I was sure mine must be something else. I had no power to control the Whispers as Charlie had done, unless you counted suppression. What was my gift? Fire I couldn't control? What was Tommy's? If I was meant to train him, how could I do so if I didn't know what the hell I was doing?

I paced, my coffee growing cold. This was bullshit, it had to be. A literal, physical contract with the dead. No way. Some removed part of my brain that remembered contract law from Sam tried to analyze whether such a thing would be binding on parties who had received no consideration but I shook my head when I realized what I was doing. I stifled a hysterical giggle at the thought of taking it to court, of being sued for breach.

I read it over several more times, but there was no further information to be gleaned. I realized that in spite of my incredulity I was taking this seriously—it answered too many questions. "Bella, you fucking bitch," I swore as I looked at the thing. "What the fuck did you do? What did you do to my family?" My hands were shaking, and I wanted to scream, to punch something until I bled. All these years. All these long, horrible years of feeling like I was responsible. And now my son, my sweet young son tainted by the touch of the dead.

Was Bella one of the wandering dead, now? Would she come through that open door? "Show your face," I snarled, my hands clenched on the counter top. "I'd love to tell you what I think of your fucking contract."

It took a lot of cussing and a few sets of pushups before I could calm my fury enough to think rationally, but even once I had I wasn't sure what to do. I thought about waking Sam and showing him, but I knew it would reinforce his determination to get in touch with my mother, and I was just as determined to keep her out of it. Who the fuck could I go to? Neal knew more about the Summers family than anyone else, but I didn't trust the man, and I wanted to limit my interaction with him. Luke was in the dark about my ghosts, so he wouldn't be much use.

Zack believed, though. Something had happened to my friend, something had made him off-kilter, unbalanced, skewed his perception and actions. He'd been going on about seeing his brother, so whatever else, I knew he'd been in contact with the spirit world. He might not know anything about the Summers family or the Whispers, but if I could get him to explain what he'd seen, what he meant about going back to where it began, maybe that would give me a place to start. I needed to find him anyway, get him some help, so tracking down Zack made the most sense right now.

I cast one more glance at my closed bedroom door, then carried the contract to my office and slid it into a drawer. It was too fragile to take with me, and I didn't want to leave it lying around for Sam to find. I could fill him in later, when I'd found us another way through this thing. I'd stop in at work, check in with Taylor to make sure Zack hadn't been in contact, then set out to look for him myself. I had a pretty good idea of where to start. Before I left, I packed up the chest, carefully replacing the wedding clothes and carrying it upstairs with everything else that reminded me of Aaron.

I pulled into the station lot on Madison a full thirty minutes before my shift, and my stomach did an unhappy flip when I saw Luke's truck parked near the back. He was standing next to the hood, his left arm resting on it while he talked to someone out of my line of sight. I hesitated, frozen by guilt when I realized I'd never even thought of him before falling into bed with Sam last night. It was true we hadn't made any promises to each other, and he'd several times made jokes about his other women, but that didn't mean he wouldn't be hurt. I at least owed him honesty, but I dreaded the conversation. Then Luke shifted his weight, and Evan Neal stepped into view.

I frowned. What the hell was Luke doing talking to Neal? After Luke's warning the day before, I wouldn't have expected to find the two anywhere near each other. I tried to read their body language— maybe it was a confrontation of some kind, Luke warning Neal to stay away from me. I wanted to hear raised voices, or see tension, or even watch Luke sucker-punch Neal, but nothing like that happened. I couldn't see Luke's face, but he was leaning, relaxed, and Neal was wearing one of those wide, slippery smiles.

The two men shook hands, Neal reaching out to clap Luke's meaty shoulder before breaking contact and turning away. Before they could see me, I zipped the Charger into a spot near the front between a white panel van and a black Escalade, then sat with my hands clutching the wheel, wondering what the hell I'd just seen.

I watched the exit, an eye on my dashboard clock. Neal pulled out two minutes after I parked, but Luke's truck had yet to move. What the hell was he doing?

A tap on my window made me jump, bumping the Charger's horn. Luke was smiling down at me. I grabbed my purse and sidearm, opened the door and stepped out.

"Hey, Luke."

He was standing too close, crowding me, so I took a step back. "Hey, Rose. Sorry, babe, didn't mean to scare you." He ducked in for a kiss that I broke away from, taking a step back.

"Seriously, Luke? Not here, okay? What are you doing here, anyway?"

Luke sighed, stepped back, leaned against the panel van parked next to my Charger. It was the kind with no windows that looks like it was designed to be used by kidnappers.

"I came to see you, Rose. I missed you last night. Is that a problem?"

"Is that all?"

"That's all, Rose. You're worth the extra trip." A suggestive smile, a shift of his hips. Nothing in his expression to indicate he was hiding something from me.

"What was that about just now? Your meet and greet with Evan Neal?"

His brows went up. "That? I was waiting for you, saw the guy hanging around, and thought I'd see what I could find out for myself."

I considered him. "And?"

He shook his head, looked grim. "No dice. Doesn't seem to matter what you say to the guy, he just slides around it. At least I got him to leave, I was worried he might have been sticking around to bother you." He was watching my face closely. "You remember what I told you—stay away from him, okay?"

I watched him but didn't answer.

Luke frowned, leaned closer. "Rose? Promise me you'll stay away from him. I know what you're like, and it's not a good idea to try to handle this guy on your own."

He sounded so much like he used to when we'd worked patrol together, always looking out for me. I relaxed and smiled, told myself I was being an idiot. "Duly noted, Luke. Look, I've got to go, I need to get to work."

He grabbed my elbow as I tried to pass.

"Rose, hang on. I haven't gotten to spend time with you since Saturday morning."

I crossed my arms under my breasts and stalled. "I know, I'm sorry. Things have been a little nuts lately."

"I'm sorry this week's been so shitty for you." He smiled and leaned in closer, ran a hand up my arm to my shoulder. "I can think of a few ways to make you feel better. How about tonight?"

Guilt made my stomach sour. How in hell did people carry on full-fledged affairs without keeling over from anxiety? "I can't, Luke, I've got the kids all week."

"Okay then, how about I grab a couple of pizzas and we can all watch a movie? It ain't like they don't know me."

I sighed. "Luke, we talked about this."

"I know, but I can just be Uncle Luke while they're awake, can't I? They don't have to know any different."

"I don't think that's such a great idea."

He dropped his gaze and didn't say anything for a minute, while I tried to think of what to say, how I should phrase things. I was being a coward, and that wasn't me—I made it a point to be direct in my relationships, because it was how I wanted to be treated. But I hadn't considered the long-term consequences of my fling with Luke. He wasn't some guy I could put out of my life and my head when things didn't work out, he was my best friend.

"Rose, I like your kids. Hell, I love your kids, and you know they love me."

"Of course they do, Luke." I took a breath. "Look, there's something I need to tell you."

He looked up again and reached for me, putting one hand on my lower back, using the other to push a stray curl out of my eye. He acted like he hadn't heard the last part of what I'd said. "Maybe I want them to start connecting the dots. Maybe I'm okay with them seeing me as something other than Uncle Luke."

I stared at him, wondering how the hell I'd managed to read this situation so badly. This was Love 'em and Leave 'em Luke, the man who'd had a different woman for every night of the week when we worked together. He never got invested in relationships, never looked at the long term. After Aaron died, the idea of dating had made me exhausted, and the last thing I'd wanted was a romantic entanglement. I'd thought this thing with Luke was perfect—no strings, no expectations, nobody gets hurt. I didn't want this, and it must have shown on my face. He let go of me and took a step back, dropped his gaze again as his ruddy cheeks flushed.

"Look, I know what you're going to say. I know you want things to be normal for the kids, don't want to change too much. But let's give it a shot, okay? At first we can just try it, you and me, see how it goes, maybe go somewhere together in daylight." I heard the note of resentment and wondered how I could have been such an idiot.

I took a deep breath. "Luke, I'm not ready to do something like that. I'm sorry if I gave you the impression that I was."

"Can we at least talk about it?"

"Not now. I've got to get to work."

"I can stop by tonight, maybe after the kids go to bed."

"Sam's staying too," I blurted out.

"Sam? At your house? Are you...were you even going to tell me?"

I held his gaze, my jaw set, fighting the urge to dissemble. "I'm telling you now."

He stared at me, his mouth working; then he shook his head. "Fine, Rose. I understand." His tone was flat. He turned and headed back to his truck with quick, jerky steps, hands dug deep into his pockets, shoulders hunched.

"Luke, wait, don't go like this."

He didn't turn around, just raised a hand. "Don't worry about it, Rose. I get it. No strings, right? Just how I like it."

"Damn." I smacked the heel of my hand against the Charger's roof and glared at my distorted reflection.

CHAPTER ELEVEN

Sam woke to bright sunlight and a feeling of well-being he couldn't immediately place. When he stretched his long arms overhead, he noticed the slats of Rose's four-poster bed overhead and smiled. Not a dream.

He rolled over to find Rose's side of the bed empty, but there was a sticky note on her pillow with a smiling hippo drawn on it, and he grinned. Rose often drew lopsided animals on notes in the kids' packed lunches. He checked the time and saw it was after eight. He called his mother and Joy picked up almost immediately. She told him the kids were fine, and that William had spent the night, but was on his way back to Millington to feed the farm dogs.

"He said he's coming back this afternoon, though, gonna get one of the neighbors to look in on the dogs for tonight. Y'all doing all right today?"

"Yeah, Mama. Rose already went to work, but I just got up."

"You stay over with her again?" Joy asked with interest.

"I'll see you in a little while, Mama. Thanks for taking care of the kiddos last night."

"Samuel McFarland, are you ignoring your mother?"

"No ma'am. Love you, Mama."

She sighed. "All right, honey. Be safe. I'll have breakfast waitin' on you when you get here."

Sam called his office for messages and let his secretary know he might work from home again. He returned a couple of calls to clients, then tried Rose on her cell. It went straight to voicemail. He left her a message telling her he'd be at Joy's, then tried her work line. No answer.

When he got to the kitchen, he found Rose had left the coffee on for him, and poured himself a cup into his favorite blue mug. He padded around the townhouse in socked feet, looking at Rose's things but resisting the urge to open any drawers or cabinets. He stopped when he circled back around to the island bar, the scrap of notepaper with Cora Summers' phone number on it catching his eye.

Sam stared at it for a few minutes, tapping the crumpled paper lightly with one finger. Rose would be pissed, but he thought she might be relieved, too. He knew she hated the idea of talking to her mother, but he thought she was beginning to see the necessity. Whether Cora could help them or not, the call needed to be made, and that was one burden Sam could carry for Rose.

It was probably safer for him to make the call anyway. He didn't know Cora, so she couldn't hurt him. He contemplated calling Rose and telling her what he planned, but decided it was better to ask forgiveness than permission.

It took a long time to connect; then the line rang six times with no answer, and no machine picked up. Sam waited through several more rings. Just when he was going to hang up, he heard a click, then labored breathing.

"Hello?"

"Rose?" slurred a woman's voice.

Do I sound like a Rose? "No, this is Sam. McFarland. Is this Cora Summers?"

A long pause. "I need Rose. My...daughter. Get Rose." The woman sounded old, and heavily drugged.

Sam frowned. Rose hadn't mentioned her mother having any substance abuse problems, but then, Rose wasn't likely to know something like that. He felt vindicated in making the call—she didn't need anything else on her plate.

"I'm calling on Rose's behalf, ma'am. You left some messages, said you needed to talk to her. That you needed help."

"Need *her* help—not you. Get me Rose."

Sam winced away from the earpiece—the slurring voice had grown painfully loud. "With all due respect, ma'am, that's not up to you. I'm not putting Rose on the line—she's not even here. You can talk to me, or you can forget it."

There was a long silence, and Sam began to wonder if she'd passed out. A rustle over the phone, then a muffled question and answer. Was someone else with Cora? Maybe she'd remarried.

"All right, Sam McFarland. I suppose you'll have to do. Where can we meet?" Cora sounded more alert, business-like, the slurring gone.

"I don't think we really need to, ma'am. Why don't you just tell me what you want over the phone?"

"Listen here, young man. You're not going to call all the shots. If you called me, I assume it's because you want something from me, too. I'll take you in place of Rose, but we're going to meet face to face."

Take you in place of Rose? What an odd way to put it, thought Sam. "I don't have time to drive up to Kentucky, ma'am, so why don't we—"

"That's just fine, Sam McFarland. I happen to be in Memphis. Where can we meet?"

Sam didn't answer at first, feeling uneasy. "I thought I was calling you at the...home place. That's where you said you were in your messages."

There was a pause. "I've had the calls forwarded to a cellular phone. I couldn't wait around anymore."

Cora was in Memphis? Why? Rose would be pissed. She'd want to know. Sam decided he could meet with Cora, then tell Rose as soon as he was done. "What's close to where you're staying, ma'am?"

"There's a little coffee shop just across the street from here. Looks like a bit of a greasy spoon, but it's close, and won't be crowded this time of day. The sign says CJ's Cafe. It's on the corner of Madison."

Now he was really uneasy. That coffee shop had been the scene of many of his dates with Rose when they first began seeing each other. Open 24 hours, and close to the station; they'd often met there. It was even where they'd shared their first kiss, out in that scuzzy parking lot. Was it just coincidence that had Cora staying so close to that coffee shop, and to Rose's work? Sam knew Rose wouldn't think so. He was beginning to seriously regret making this call.

"Well, young man?"

Sam hesitated again. The woman was acting oddly, that was for certain. But she was older than him, and likely frail. How much damage could she do? Didn't he owe it to Rose to shield her from things like this?

"All right, I'll be there. What time?"

"How about now?"

* * *

Sam called Joy on his way out the door, letting her know he had an appointment to keep and not to hold breakfast for him. She clucked at him for missing a meal but said little else, reporting that William was already on his way back and the kids were doing fine. Sam promised to come by later.

Weaving his way through mid-morning traffic, he glanced at his phone and thought again about whether to tell Rose first. He didn't like that this meeting was taking place across the street from where she worked—there was too much likelihood of her, or one of her teammates, seeing him and wondering what was up. In the end, he decided against it—she'd just come barreling over to protect him. Rose was never able to believe anyone but her could handle anything complicated or unpleasant. It was a conviction Sam hoped to change.

The clanging of the bell over the glass front door of CJ's Cafe made a waitress and two solo male customers glance up. The only unaccompanied female was an older woman seated against the glass toward the back of the restaurant. She had to have been waiting for him, but she sat staring rigidly out into the parking lot. As Sam got closer, he saw that her lips were moving, her thin hands clutching a mug of tea.

Sam had a chance to look her over as he approached. It was surreal—he'd never met a member of Rose's family before, so it was odd to see a lank, graying version of Rose's wild, bright curls, and a duller copy of her gray-green eyes on this sour-looking old woman. Cora looked a lot like Rose, but at the same time, nothing like her. As she finally turned to face him, he realized this was how Rose would look if someone sapped the life and energy from her.

The woman seemed older than she likely was, painfully thin, her skin a pallid, crepe-paper gray. Her lips were thin and compressed, colorless and dry. She wore no makeup, but Sam didn't think it would have helped anyway. L'Oreal or Cover Girl couldn't paint on a soul.

"Cora Summers?" he asked as he reached the table.

She looked him up and down. "It's Mrs. Paul Summers," she finally said.

Sam resisted the compulsion to roll his eyes. "All right then, Mrs. Summers. May I sit down?"

She gave a curt nod, and he settled into the booth across from her. They spent another minute sizing each other up before the waitress came over. Sam asked for black coffee, abandoning his plan to eat breakfast. He'd rather go hungry than eat across from this cantankerous old bat.

Cora waited until the waitress brought his coffee before she spoke again. "So you're Sam. Her first husband, yes? What are you doing making calls on her behalf, hmm?" Her syrupy voice made Sam's skin crawl.

"Oh, I still look out for Rose," he said. "I try to handle the unpleasant chores for her—you know, taking out the trash, squashing bugs, that kind of thing." His smile was as false as hers.

Cora's thin eyebrows shot together. She said nothing for a minute, then changed tacks. "How is my little Rose these days, Sam?"

"She's just fine, thank you, ma'am."

"And my grandchildren?"

The ones you've never met? thought Sam. "They're fine too, ma'am. In fact, I need to be getting back to them, so can we get down to business here? What is it you need from Rose?"

Something slid across Cora's face, a slippery, cunning expression, there and gone so quickly he couldn't be sure he'd seen it.

"Why don't you go first? What is it *you* need from *me?*"

Sam hesitated, wondering how much to tell this woman. He decided to start on easier ground. "How about you tell me what you know about Charlie Akers?" he asked, leaning back against the booth, arms crossed.

Cora's eyes widened, and her gaze darted somewhere behind Sam. Frowning, he turned, but saw nothing. When he turned around again, she looked composed.

"Charlie Akers," she said softly. "That's a name I haven't heard in quite some time."

"You knew about him?" asked Sam, sitting forward.

She nodded, a sad smile hovering at her thin lips. "Not well, you understand. He was Paul's son, not mine, but I often thought of him."

If her husband fathering a child as a result of an extramarital affair bothered her, she didn't show it. "Poor boy, his mother did the best she could, but she wasn't all there. Parenting is hard, as I'm sure you know. Sometimes love means being strict, and I'm afraid Charlie's mother wasn't good at that."

An image flitted across Sam's mind, of Rose's haunted eyes when she spoke of this woman's parental love. He found himself squeezing his hands into fists and crossed his arms tighter. "It's true, then? He was Rose's half-brother?"

Cora nodded. "Yes, I'm afraid so. Unfortunately, I believe he inherited some of the same...defects that Rose did."

"Defects."

"Yes. He saw things, heard them, like Rose. Though, from what I understand, nowhere near as often or as intensely. And Charlie didn't turn out to be dangerous." Her voice dropped to a discreet whisper. "Not like Rose."

Sam thought about a man who could flay his own wife, kidnap his children, and keep them for three days in a house with their mother's rotting body while a S.W.A.T. team pointed rifles at his head. And this woman said *Rose* was dangerous?

"Dangerous how?" he asked, trying to keep his tone even.

"The fires, Mr. McFarland." She leaned in closer, lowering her voice as though she spoke of something shameful.

"You mean the one that killed your husband?"

"That one, among others. Rose was quite the little firebug, you know. Paul knew she was a danger, but you never think...your own child, you know..." She trailed off.

"You're telling me Rose had something to do with that fire?"

"Rose had everything to do with that fire, Mr. McFarland," snapped Cora. "My Paul, my darling Andy, both gone. My poor little Rose, disfigured that way." She sighed. "It all started when she was four." She looked up, her expression blank. "Isn't the little boy—that other fellow's son, isn't he about four now?"

Sam felt sick, and furious with himself. He should have known better than to come here, to give this woman any kind of opening. Rose had been right; there was nothing to gain from Cora Summers. He didn't believe for a second that Rose was responsible for the fire that killed her brother, but he knew she would believe it easily enough. Cora couldn't be allowed to get close enough to Rose to drip this poison in her ear.

"You're saying Rose set the fire?"

"Of course she did, Mr. McFarland. Oh, not on purpose, at least I don't think so. It was just that she had such a temper, and no control over it. It was enough for her to get mad over something, and things would go up in flames. It was all part of the curse of what she was."

Sam stared at her. "You're telling me you think Rose can set fires with her *mind*?"

"I've seen it myself, young man," she said. "Are you telling me you haven't?"

"Of course not," Sam said contemptuously, but the image of Tommy's ruined room came to mind unbidden. A contained fire, with no visible means of starting or being put out...

Cora leaned in closer. "It was in her room, you know. Paul never let Rose have any matches or candles, it was too dangerous, but it still started under her bed. There was a perfect circle charred in the wood, exactly in the middle of the floor under there. That was all they ever found."

Rose in Tommy's room yesterday, bending down to peer under the bed. Standing up, looking stricken. Sam remembered knowing she was holding something back from him. It couldn't possibly be...why would Rose have kept this from him? What reason could she have had for starting a fire in Tommy's room?

Unless she truly had no control over it.

Sam looked across the table at Cora, wondering exactly what in hell her agenda was. To sow doubt in Rose's mind, maybe drive a wedge between her and Sam? Was that all? Wasn't it just a little too perfect, her showing up now with everything else that was going on?

"Did you know Charlie Akers was dead?" he asked.

Her eyes didn't change, the faded green holding his as her thin mouth widened, her head tilting to the side. "Is he?" she asked, and Sam knew she was lying.

His phone vibrated in his pocket and he pulled it out, grateful for the interruption. It was Joy. "Excuse me, I need to take this." He stood, bashing the underside of the table with one knee and sloshing coffee. He took a few steps toward the front door.

"Mama?"

"Sam, honey." Her tone was calm, but the bottom dropped out of Sam's stomach. He knew that voice—it was Joy's bad news voice.

"What's happened? Rose? The kids?"

"Rose is all right, honey, and so is Lily. It's Tommy. He's sick or something."

"Oh, God—what's wrong with him?"

"Now, I don't want you to panic, Sammy, because we're already with the doctor. The paramedics say he's stable."

Paramedics. Jesus. "Rose?"

"I called you first, honey. She's next on my list."

"No, I'll call her, Mama. She'll want to hear it from me."

"Sam, I don't want you trying to call her while you're driving—not while you're upset, you hear? I'll take care of it, and ask her to meet us. You just worry about getting yourself here safely."

Sam squeezed his eyes shut. "Which hospital?"

"Le Bonheur Children's, honey. Now, Sam, you drive careful, you understand? Your family needs you, so don't go runnin' into anything. You want me to have William come and get you?"

"No, Mama, I can drive myself. I'll be right there." Sam felt a light touch on his shoulder as he hung up, and turned to find Cora uncomfortably close.

"Bad news?" she said with an approximation of sympathy.

"I have to go." He dug in his pocket for his wallet. "Here—"

She shook her head. "No, don't you worry. I've taken care of it. You go on now, okay? We'll pick this up some other time."

"Fine," was all Sam could trust himself to say. He pushed through the door and headed for his car at a dead run, not looking back.

He didn't see Cora fish the little flip phone out of her purse and dial it.

"I got what you wanted," she said when she heard ragged breathing on the other end. "I know where they're going to be."

CHAPTER TWELVE

The derelict house on Union looked even lonelier than the last time I'd seen it. Crumpled crime scene tape had been added to the detritus that dotted the straggling, weed-choked lawn. Several windows had been broken in the intervening days—kids, most likely, drawn to gawk by the ghoulish tragedy that had played out here.

This part of the street was mostly foreclosures now; I only saw signs of life in three or four of the houses. The rest had the same abandoned air as the one in front of me. Down the street, a small gaggle of children were riding their bikes in circles, but they were too far away to break the eerie silence where I stood.

I hadn't forgotten Sid Angelo's warning on the night I'd killed Charlie Akers. He'd told me not to come back here, no matter what. That the walls were thin, and anything at all could come over. How the hell had he known that? Had something spoken to Sid in the dark of night as he stood guard? Maybe Zack hadn't been the only one to make contact. However it had been, standing here now and feeling the darkness of this place, I thought there was a good chance Sid had been right. So what the fuck was I doing here?

I'd looked for Sid this morning, wanting to see if he had anything more specific to say or if he even remembered the conversation, but I hadn't been able to find him. In fact, when I asked around, no one could remember seeing Sid since that night at Louie's. Another worry to add to my list.

Even without Sid's warning, I knew it was stupid to come here alone. It was exactly the kind of dumbshit move that could get me my own sheriff's academy "what not to do" video, but I couldn't square it with my conscience to expose anyone else to what might be here. There was a time when the presence of someone else might have held the spirits at bay, but after what happened at Sam's house, I couldn't count on it.

I'd have to settle for someone knowing where I was. I'd checked in briefly with Taylor, so he knew I was heading out to look for Zack, and Luke had called on my way over. That had surprised me after our tiff in the parking lot this morning. I didn't want to get into it with him again, but I'd answered. I didn't give him time to speak.

"Not a good time, Luke."

"I only—"

"I'm sorry, but I'm on the way over to Union. I can't talk now."

There was a short silence. "The Akers site? Why are you going back there?"

"I'm looking for something. I'll try to call you when I'm done."

"Oh. Okay." Now he sounded surprised.

"I shouldn't be long," I said, and clicked off, feeling guilty. I'd answered Luke's call with the sole purpose of setting up a safety net. I knew he'd be waiting for my call, and if he didn't hear from me, he knew where to find me. And I knew he'd come looking. However pissed he might be, the habit of looking out for his partner was too longstanding to break.

Now I holstered my 9 mm and locked the Charger, walking up the drive to the retaining wall where my half-brother had lost his life. Where I had killed him with a well-placed bullet to the brain. I stared down at the broken pavement, waiting to feel something, but there was nothing. No guilt, no anger, no sadness for the loss of life. But then, there never was. Not from me. I'd never thought much about it, figuring it was simply because I knew my work, had faith in my job. Maybe it wasn't normal, but either way, I'd chosen my profession well. Now I wondered if it made me something less than human. A killer, no different from the people I sighted through my scope.

I looked up, movement in one of the upper-story windows catching my gaze. I stood still, watching, waiting for it to move again.

Nothing but the lazy billowing of a ragged pink curtain through the shattered lower pane. I exhaled, willing my heartbeat back to normal.

Zack's truck wasn't anywhere in sight, but maybe he'd parked and walked. I made a careful circuit of the house, checking for signs that anything had been recently disturbed. I was already familiar with the layout, having studied it closely for two long days while we waited to see what Charlie Akers would do. There was the front door, crossed over several times and sealed at the edges with unbroken crime scene tape, so no one had entered that way. Two small windows at ground level led to the below-ground basement, but those appeared intact as well, and certainly too small to allow a man of Zack's size to squeeze through.

That left the sunken staircase on the right side of the house. I walked around to it and peered into the gloom. More dirt and trash littered the stairwell and gathered at the concrete pad outside the door. The wooden door looked warped, which could explain why it appeared to sit open, but I didn't think that was it. It looked like Zack might well be here, waiting on me to catch up.

I pulled my weapon out, holding it at my side as I crept down the stairs, giving up any attempt to be quiet as my boots crunched and scraped. I peered through the dirty glass at the top of the door, but saw nothing.

As soon as I pushed the door open and stepped onto the gritty basement floor, I was hit with vertigo, queasy from the cloying stench of decomp. I choked, pulling my shirt up over the lower half of my face. How could Zack have borne any kind of time in here? It smelled like a slaughter house in midsummer—if the air conditioning had gone out.

I waited until I felt steadier, then ventured further into the gloom, the smell getting worse the deeper I went. Flies were abundant, their buzzing growing louder the closer I got. Jesus, what the hell *was* that smell? Had something crept in here to die? Or had what happened to Laura Akers just left its indelible reek on the place? I'd seen the crime scene photos; she'd been flayed, her skin shredded and missing in patches. Then left to rot in the Memphis summer heat—that could do it, but I wouldn't have expected it to be this strong, not this long after crime scene clean up.

A board creaked overhead, and I froze. The minutes stretched out in silence, and I wondered if someone was up there listening too. I looked behind me—the outside door was only a few feet away, and stuck open. If anyone came down the inside stairs from the kitchen above, I'd have the advantage—they'd be vulnerable as they made their way down into the gloom.

"Zack?' I called. "Is that you? Are you up there?"

Another creak as someone made a quick, startled movement. I waited for more, my muscles taut as I held myself completely still, using my sniper breathing, slow and steady. I was concentrating so hard on the floor above me that when the sound came from beside me, I nearly screamed.

I turned, but the shadows beside me were empty. I stared hard into the gloom.

There it was again—the scrape of a shoe against the gritty basement floor. It was coming from the far corner of the room, up against the wall on the left side of the house, past the inside staircase leading up into the kitchen. Squinting, I could just make out a figure standing there. Tall, but somehow diminished, he held his arms close to himself, bent at the waist like a man in pain.

Not Zack, I realized—there wasn't enough of him to be my large friend. So who? My breath was coming hard—visions of Charlie Akers lurking beneath the staircase in Sam's cellar. Wouldn't that make sense here more than anywhere else? This was where Charlie had hidden, where he'd brutally murdered his wife. Where he'd died. Had I walked into this trap a second time?

I moved closer. "Hello? Who's there? Are you all right?"

He moaned softly, his head dipping.

Another two steps. "Sir? Are you in need of assistance?" *Call it in, dumbass*, yelled the sensible part of my mind. But there was something about this guy that seemed familiar, and I didn't want him to disappear. "Sir?"

"R-Rose?" came the trembling voice from the shadows. A familiar voice, from long ago.

Damn it, what was it? Why couldn't I shake the memory loose?

I stepped closer. At the same time, he moved into a wedge of light from one of the half windows. I gave a little gasp, oddly breathless now.

"Andy," I whispered.

It was my golden brother, no doubt. His blond hair was lank and dirty, his body thin, nearly skeletal.

No, not nearly—it *was* skeletal. I could see yellowed bones through the charred flesh of his right arm. Most of his face was gone, melted off in the fire, the way that tender flesh does, as I knew so well. All that remained of his handsome face was a small patch of waxy-looking skin under his left eye, and those bright gray-green eyes.

"Oh, Andy." Tears pricked my eyelids. Zack had been right. He'd wanted to take me to my brother last night, and I hadn't believed him.

But in all the eighteen long years since I'd seen him, in all the aching sadness of missing my big brother, I'd never pictured him like this. Burned almost beyond recognition, he was clearly suffering—bent, his bony hands clutching his stomach. There was agony in those eyes—a terrible, long agony, mixed with what I'd always feared to face—accusation.

"Rose, help me," he rasped, shuffling closer.

I holstered my gun and hurried to his side. My gloved hands outstretched, I hesitated to touch him. Would I hurt him?

"What can I do, Andy? How can I help you?"

"End it, Rose. You have to end it, please."

"End it?" I repeated, my voice weak. Did he mean he wanted me to end his life—kill him? That wasn't possible, was it? He couldn't have been alive this whole time—no one could have made that mistake, could they?

"What do you mean, Andy? End what?"

"End *this*, Rose. You have to make it stop. I'm suffering—the pain, the burning, it never stops. I'm trapped."

"Oh, God, Andy, I'm so sorry—I never dreamed...I thought—I thought you'd be at peace." Tears streamed down my face. What an idiot I had been all these years. That music, my music, could have nothing to do with my big brother in the state he was in. He couldn't have been looking out for me, not like this, and why the hell would he even want to? The loss was crushing.

"Peace?" His tortured eyes shone brightly in that ruined face. "There's no peace for me. There never will be, until you can make all of this stop. You have to close the door, Rose. No matter what it costs, you must close the door."

"How, Andy? How do I close the door?"

He leaned in close, and I smelled his fetid breath. I tried not to recoil, tried to breathe shallowly.

"You have to go back, Rose. To where it began. To where you made this all possible—where you opened the door."

They were the same words Zack had used last night, nearly verbatim. I'd thought he meant to come back here, where everything with Charlie Akers had begun.

"Where *I* opened the door? What do you mean, Andy?"

"You have to go back to the fire, Rose. To the first fire. To the night I died. You have to go back there to close the door, or I'll be trapped like this."

There was a thud of quick footsteps down the outside stairs and I turned, pulling my gun from its holster.

A man stepped into the gloom of the basement, his features hidden by shadow and backlit by the bright morning sun beyond.

"Who's there?"

"It's Evan Neal, Rose. Dispatch has been trying to reach you—you haven't been answering your cell phone." He peered around behind me. "What are you doing down here?"

I whirled, but Andy was gone. I turned back to Neal, narrowing my eyes. "How the hell did you know dispatch wanted me? And how did you know where I'd be?"

208

There was that slippery look again, meeting my eyes briefly before sliding off to the side. "Don't be mad, Rose."

People seemed to be saying that to me a lot. "Who's been talking to you, Neal?"

"Look, it's more important that you know—"

"*Who?*"

"He only wants what's best for you, Rose. He cares about you, you know."

Only three people had known where I was headed this morning, and only one of them had been talking to Evan Neal that morning.

"You're talking about Luke Harris." Even as I said it I wanted to be wrong, wanted him to shake his head and tell me who it really was.

"I mean it, Rose, he was just worried about you."

If he was worried, I knew the last person Luke would send after me would be Evan Neal. If it was Luke, he'd have another reason. Like being jealous and pissed off at me, I supposed, but that didn't fit either. Neal had been getting information well before Luke and I had fought. I set my jaw. "I don't believe you, Neal. Luke wouldn't give you the time of day."

Neal sighed, showed me his cell phone. Punched a couple of buttons and I heard a recorded voice time stamping a voicemail about ten minutes ago. *One saved message.* Luke's voice, buried in static, but his inflection unmistakable.

"*She's on her way to Union. Dispatch can't reach her and neither can I—you'd better head over.*"

I looked at Neal and felt the weight of Luke's betrayal. I shook my head, trying not to believe it, but the image of him with Neal that morning pushed its way to the front. His cagey attitude about the FBI agent, telling me over and over to stay away from the man. Was this about Sam? Was Luke jealous enough to sabotage me over that? Friends with benefits, that's all we were, all we were supposed to be. I wasn't stupid, it had become clear over the last few days that our relationship meant something more to Luke. Did that mean he'd be capable of this?

The timing didn't make sense, but I'd been operating under the assumption that Neal had been getting all his information from the same source. But everything he knew about my family, he'd gotten from Charlie before he ever came to Memphis, and as far as finding me at Louie's that first night after the standoff, it wasn't exactly privileged information—any number of people knew that was where my team went. It was possible that Luke's intervention was new. But it still didn't make sense—why wouldn't Luke have just come to get me himself?

As though Neal had read my mind, he placed a hesitant hand on my shoulder. "He didn't think you'd talk to him after your fight this morning. He's hurting, I'm sure you can understand that, but he still wants to make sure you're safe. He's a good man, Mr. Harris."

Neal knew about our fight. He couldn't have overheard, I'd seen his car leave the parking lot before Luke and I exchanged a single word. How could he have known unless Luke told him? But why? What possible sense did any of it make? What the hell was Luke up to?

I felt like I'd been gut-punched. Stood there in the semi-dark without a clue what to do.

"Like I said, Rose, he was worried about you coming here." Neal looked around the dingy basement. "This place isn't exactly healthy to be in. Besides, it was urgent that someone find you—you weren't answering your phone."

I felt my pants pocket. Empty. "I must have left it in the car," I said, scrubbing a forearm across my face, off-balance and still trying to understand. I focused on the only part of what Neal had said that made any sense at all. "What does dispatch need with me? Do we have another incident?"

Neal stepped closer, shaking his head. "No, Rose, it's not that. I'm so sorry, I've been trying to tell you."

Fear kicked my heart into overdrive. "What, Neal? What is it?"

"The Whispers. I was hoping it wouldn't come to this. I thought we'd have more time."

"Goddamn it, Neal, *what?*"

"It's Tommy, Rose. A 911 call came in from Joy McFarland's home, and an ambulance has taken them to Le Bonheur. The code was unresponsive child."

210

CHAPTER THIRTEEN

I paced the hall outside Tommy's hospital room, tired but unable to sit still for more than a few minutes at a time. Sam was slumped in a chair too small for his lanky frame, head down and hands dangling between his knees. Joy sat next to him, one hand running in endless comforting circles against her son's broad back. She was watching both of us.

"How the hell much longer before I can see my son?" I stopped outside the room and tried to peer inside for the umpteenth time.

The ER had already admitted Tommy and sent him up here by the time I'd arrived at the hospital. He was in a single room in the NICU, the sliding glass doors closed and covered by long slatted blinds. I could hear machines beeping and the murmur of adult voices. As far as I could tell, Tommy was still silent. My music came softly now and then, another waiting room relative bringing comfort, but just as quickly a sense of loss. If it wasn't Andy, then who? I wondered if Tommy could hear it, if it would bring him peace.

Joy reached out and patted my arm as I stalked past again. "Give it some time, sugar. You want them in there helping him, don't you?"

"Yes," I sighed, collapsing into the chair next to Sam, resting my head in my hands and willing myself not to panic. Sam reached for me, one big hand on my closest knee.

"He's going to be okay, Rose."

I said nothing, trying hard not to believe the worst, but all I could think about was Ethan Neal, locked in a coma for all this time. Was this the same thing?

As if he'd followed my thoughts, Sam cleared his throat and asked, "Do you know—is this the same thing that's wrong with that other little boy you were telling me about? The FBI agent's son?"

I closed my eyes. "I don't know. It could be. Neal seemed to think it was, but all we knew was that Tommy was unconscious." I wished I'd thought to ask Neal more questions about Ethan's symptoms and disease progression when we'd spoken at the diner. Today I hadn't said another word to him, just raced past him to my car and peeled out, nothing in my panicked mind but the need to see my son.

Unresponsive child. Was there a worse phrase in the English language?

I checked my phone: no signal. There were signs all over the place forbidding cell phone use within the hospital anyway. "I'll call him when I can. See what else he can tell me." I felt a momentary flash of anger at Luke, but his betrayal seemed a distant problem now. Even the horror of seeing Andy again, like that, had paled in the wake of Tommy in that hospital bed. So small, so unnaturally still, with his little arms folded across his chest. I'd had to banish the thought that he looked like he'd been laid out for burial.

If Tommy was suffering from the same thing as Ethan, and if Neal were to be believed, the only way to reach either boy was through the Whispers. If it was this guardianship of the dead business that had them stirred up, then fine, I'd do what they asked, live up to the terms of Bella's contract. The thought turned me cold, but things were different now. I would do whatever Tommy needed me to do, even walk through Hell itself. Which wasn't an unreasonable comparison.

"Did he say anything, Joy? Before he...before he collapsed?" My throat closed on the words, and hot tears coursed down my cheeks.

Sam turned and wrapped both arms around my shoulders, pulling me to him. I twisted awkwardly in the seat to tuck my head against his chest. Joy's cool hand pushed my hair out of my eyes.

"He didn't say anything out of the ordinary, honey. He was just being Tommy. Watching cartoons with Lily, and then after a while he seemed to lose interest and wandered away toward the toy box. He kind of stared at it for a minute, then he just—fell." Joy's voice broke, but she lifted her chin and met my eyes. "When I got to him, he was having some kind of seizure and I couldn't wake him up. That's when I called 911."

Sam's grip on me tightened.

"Did you see him when they brought him through? God, he just looked so pitiful."

"He's okay now, Sam—he's going to come through this." I wouldn't allow myself to imagine any other outcome. We both turned to look at the closed glass door to Tommy's room.

Joy cleared her throat. "I'm gonna go get some coffee, children. Give you two some time alone."

We sat in silence after she'd left, willing the door to open, willing Tommy to wake up and be okay. I felt Sam sag against me.

"God, Rose, I am so sorry. I should never have left them over there. I was supposed to keep them safe."

"Shut up. This is *not* your fault. We don't even know what's wrong with him. It could be something else, something purely physical—there's no reason to assume it's related to...the other stuff."

His look told me he didn't buy it any more than I did, but he didn't say anything.

We both turned when we heard the door slide open and Dr. Daughtry sidled into the hallway.

Allen Daughtry had treated both my kids since their previous pediatrician had retired two years earlier. I didn't know him well, but what I knew, I liked. He was great with kids and adults both, and in addition to being a great pediatrician, he worked several shifts a week at Le Bonheur Children's Hospital in the NICU, treating severe childhood illnesses.

Daughtry was compact and energetic. He was a few inches taller than me, maybe five-six or seven, but he carried his fit form in a way that made up for his lack of height. He had the broad shoulders and flat stomach of a fitness fanatic, and his open, handsome face was framed by thick salt and pepper hair that kept falling over the pair of rimless glasses he wore. Just now he looked tired.

"He's stable," he said before we could speak. "It's too soon to tell if there's been any kind of permanent damage as a result of the oxygen deprivation, but I don't think it's likely."

Sam groaned, and Daughtry gave him a brief smile. "I'm sure it seemed a lot longer to your mother, Sam, but we think it can't have been more than a minute or two that he wasn't breathing. We won't know for certain until he wakes up, but that's not usually long enough to cause major problems, especially in an otherwise healthy little boy."

"How long before he wakes up?" I asked. "What caused this?"

"When I know the answer to the second question, I'll be in a better position to answer the first, Rose. He's not exhibiting symptoms of any of the common pathogens, and his CT scan was clear."

"That's good, right?" Sam asked.

Daughtry shrugged. "In some ways, yes. We know it's not meningitis or something of that nature. On the other hand, until we do know what it is, we have to be conservative in our treatment. We'll be handling his symptoms and making sure he's comfortable while we run tests. For now, try to stay calm and think positive, okay? In the meantime, are either of you aware of any genetic abnormalities or inherited diseases that run in your families?"

Sam and I exchanged a look, then his gaze dropped and I watched his expression go wooden. I turned back to Daughtry. "Nothing on my side that I'm aware of, but I've been out of contact with my mother for years. My father died eighteen years ago."

Daughtry's forehead wrinkled, but he didn't offer me the knee-jerk condolences most people felt the need to. "Disease?" he asked.

I shook my head. "Fire. I don't know of any genetic illnesses in his family or my mother's." I doubted it would help him to know that seeing dead people was a Summers family trait.

Daughtry's quick gaze took in what scars were visible above the neckline of my shirt and nodded, then turned to Sam. "What about you?"

I squeezed Sam's arm. "Tommy's biological father died three years ago. Car accident. I know Tommy's grandmother passed away from breast cancer, but other than that..."

"Okay—are you still in touch with any of his family?"

"Sure. William is Tommy's grandfather—he's staying with Lily right now. I'll call him."

"Great. I'll have him talk to one of the residents to get a medical history." Daughtry turned to Sam. "How about your daughter? How's she feeling? Was she exhibiting any symptoms, anything at all?"

Sam shook his head. "Nothing today when I checked on them, and Mama said she was acting fine. Do you think it's something contagious?"

"Like I said, it's impossible to know at this point, but tell—William, is it?—to keep a close eye on her, okay?" Daughtry smiled again. "Go on in and see your son. I'll be back soon."

Sam took my hand and led me through the sliding glass doors into a large room occupied by a single bed and a lot of equipment. A nurse had her back to us as she adjusted a monitor.

At first I thought the bed was empty. Tommy's little body was almost lost in it, his thin chest barely disturbing the white knit blanket. His eyes were closed, but he wasn't peaceful. No longer still, his eyebrows were knit over his snub nose and he was spasming all over. Kneeling beside him, I took his little hand, dry and feverishly hot, and reached out to smooth his dark hair. As I watched, he thrust his head back violently and his mouth opened, as though he were trying to speak.

"Tommy?" I said, keeping my voice low and soothing, hoping he would recognize it and be calmed. He turned his head in my direction, but his twisting body didn't grow still.

"Here, honey."

Sam had dragged a chair over to me. I pulled it closer to Tommy, and made room for Sam when he brought another chair. We sat in silence, watching Tommy and trying to take comfort in his small movements. I felt Sam's hand on my shoulder.

"You don't really think this is unrelated to the thing with the Whispers, do you?"

My shoulders sagged. "No. I don't think it's unrelated. I think that would be too damn easy."

Sam's hand clutched my shoulder harder. There was real fear in his eyes when I turned to look at him.

"What are we going to do, Rose? How do we help him? Help you?"

I turned away from him, shaking my head. "I don't know, Sam. I've never known."

* * *

At some point I must have slept. I woke with a jerk, my arm sliding from the hospital chair's uncomfortable oak armrests and my heart pounding from a dream already fading from memory. There had been fire again, I knew that. I shook it off. There were worse things than dreams to deal with now.

Sam's chair was empty, and Tommy was finally still. I moved closer and crouched next to him, laying my hand on his chest. It rose and fell steadily, and he seemed to be resting more peacefully. I stood and stretched my cramped back and shoulders. A glance at my watch told me it was almost three in the morning, and I wondered where Sam was. Joy had gone home earlier to be with Lily and William, though she had called often for updates.

I eased aside the vertical blinds hanging across the glass front of Tommy's room and opened the door to peek out into the hallway. The floor was deserted, silence from the adjacent rooms and no one at the nurse's station. The fluorescent panel overhead buzzed and flickered, the sporadic light casting eerie shadows. I resisted a childish urge to slam the door and crawl into bed with my son. Instead I went in search of coffee, telling myself I wasn't looking for Sam. I glanced back once to make sure Tommy was still sleeping, then slid the door closed as quietly as I could behind me.

After a few minutes, I managed to locate a coffee maker in the empty family lounge at the opposite end of the NICU floor. The pot was on, half-full of a deep black sludge that had probably been cooking on the burner for hours. I sniffed it and decided it was better than taking the time to brew a fresh pot. I already felt anxious being away from Tommy this long.

The nurse's station was still deserted when I walked past it on my return, but there was movement out of the corner of my eye. Someone had just turned the corner out of view on the opposite hallway. I glanced up at the signs showing room numbers and directional arrows. My heart sped up when I realized the figure was headed for Tommy's room.

It's Sam, I told myself as I began to sprint. Or some other parent. Or a nurse. No reason to think it's anything bad. I turned the corner in time to see the door to Tommy's room sliding closed, the blinds rustling with the movement of someone passing through them. Sam, I thought again, but it didn't stop me from hurtling down the hall as fast as I could. There had been something about the movement—jerky, dragging, deep in shadow.

My heart filled with dread as I thought of Charlie Akers—the open door. *Please, not here.* I fumbled at the door one handed. It wouldn't budge.

I dropped the cup, hot coffee splashing my shins and boots. Grasping the handle with both hands, I tried again, but the door wouldn't move. I could see nothing in the darkness beyond, and smacked the glass with the heel of my hand before trying again. Tears were starting to my eyes, and my breathing was ragged and heavy. I took a step back and kicked at the glass with as much force and precision as I could muster, but all I managed to do was send a bolt of pain shooting up to my knee. "Tommy!" I cried, pounding the door with both hands. "Someone please help me, you have to get me in there. Something's in there with my son."

I spun around, hoping to see a nurse or doctor coming my way, but the floor was still empty. Where the hell was Sam? Where were the damn nurses? This was the NICU, they had to be on hand for emergencies. I turned back and saw that in the seconds my attention had been elsewhere, the glass had frozen over, the surface opaque with condensation that crystallized into frost before my eyes. I took a step backward as something behind the door sighed, the exhalation of a corpse on an autopsy table. A wet, sliding squeak as an unseen finger began to trace a pattern on the other side of the glass.

Rose.

Launching myself at the door again, I pulled with every ounce of my strength, and was nearly knocked on my ass when the door slid open easily. The room was still frozen and shrouded in darkness, but I was next to the bed in two strides. Tommy was lying motionless under the covers, looking much as he had when I'd left him a few minutes ago. The only difference was the blanket, now drawn over his dark head. I scanned the dim room, ducking to check under the edges of the bed, but it was one of the hydraulic models and there was nothing but machinery underneath.

Slow breaths, I told myself, hoping to calm my hammering heart. I had been so sure, and never more glad to be wrong. I turned back to my son and smoothed the blankets, tucking them in against his little body, my hands shaking with adrenaline. I frowned.

Why was the cover over his head? Had Tommy pulled it up in his sleep, reacting to the sudden drop in temperature or the noise I'd been making outside? My hand trembled as I reached for the cover to pull it down, some barely defined dread slowing my movements. I saw the covers rise and fall with shallow breaths. I knew he wasn't dead, but I still wasn't reassured. My fingers had just brushed the cloth over his face when I heard the door slide open behind me and turned to see who had entered. A small, dark-haired boy stood there, backlit by the lights from the hallway.

"Mommy?"

* * *

"Tommy?" With the light behind him, it was impossible to see his face clearly, but his small build and the tilt of his head belonged to my son. "Oh sweetie, you're awake—thank God. Are you okay?"

Even as tears of relief sprang to my eyes, warning bells were going off in my head. Something was wrong. If Tommy was standing here, who was in the bed?

I tried to scramble sideways, but a rotted, ragged-nailed hand rose with nightmare speed and clutched my wrist in an impossibly strong grip. My scarred flesh was burning where it touched me, even through the glove.

"No, no, no, not again—not here." I tried to pull away, but the horror in the bed was rising to a sitting position, the blanket sliding off the far side of the bed. A wide, dead grin, missing lower jaw, wet purple tongue.

Charlie.

"Run, Tommy." I was screaming on the inside, but kept my tone as calm as I could for my son. "Run and find Daddy, tell him to come, but you stay away from here, do you understand?" I didn't turn but heard the door slide open and closed again behind me.

I was nearly yanked off my feet when the hand clutching me began pulling me toward the bed. My boots scrabbled on the slick floor.

"*Rooooose,*" came a dry and creaking voice from the bed. The room grew steadily colder, filled with the by-now familiar stench of decomposing flesh.

"Fuck." I looked wildly around for something to break the rigid grip on my wrist. My service weapon was in its holster, folded into my jacket near the other end of the bed, if I could only reach it. Stretching to the end of my arm span with the fingers of my free hand, I was able to graze the edge of my holster. Swinging as hard as I could, I knocked the whole pile to the floor, and by extending my right leg as far as it would reach, I managed to kick the belt within range.

There was a hiss from the bed, and I ducked to free my 9 mm. With a shaking hand I pointed it at Charlie.

He smiled wider. "*Go ahead, killer. Shoot me some more. Kill me again.*" His voice was a gargling horror.

My finger on the trigger, I hesitated. A vivid memory of everything I'd seen over the past few days filled me with doubt. How the hell could I be sure I was seeing what I thought I was seeing?

Charlie leaned in quickly, baring what teeth he had left. "*Shoot me, Rose—do it. It's all you're good for, so do it while you can.*"

Why was he so anxious for me to fire?

The dead, sunken eyes darted behind me. The glass door was sliding open.

He looked at me. "*Too late now, Rose. Tommy belongs to us.*"

Before I could move, he had lunged out of the bed past me.

I turned, aimed, ready to fire this time.

"Rose, what the *hell?*"

It was Sam in the doorway, a steaming Styrofoam cup in each hand.

There was no sign of Charlie.

"Sam, thank God." I sagged against the bed, my knees shaking, lowering the gun to my side. "Did Tommy find you? Is he okay?"

He took a step toward me. "Find Tommy?" His voice was flat. "Was he missing, Rose? Did he go wandering from that bed, comatose and hooked to a dozen machines?"

I was puzzled by his combative tone. "No, not missing—he was here, and I told him to go and find you—to run and bring you back."

Moving slowly, deliberately, Sam edged around to the small side table and set both cups on its surface. He looked down and saw my scattered S.W.A.T. gear, then looked back at me. "Why would you send Tommy to get me, Rose? Why wouldn't you look for me yourself?"

"I, I couldn't—there was..." I gestured lamely at the empty bed.

"There was what, Rose?"

I stared at the bed, then looked at my wrist as though the imprint of that hand would still be there. I could still feel it—the burning cold and vice-like pressure—but it hadn't left a mark. I gripped the edge of the bed rail with my trembling hand and spoke without turning to face him. "Charlie was here, Sam. When I woke up, you were gone and Tommy was sleeping, so I got up to stretch my legs. When I came back someone was in the room, keeping me out. When I got inside it was Charlie in the bed, and Tommy came in behind me. I sent him out to keep him safe."

I was angry at the way my voice was shaking, at the tears that pricked the back of my eyes. I was angry at how badly I wanted Sam to believe me like he always did, to tell me again I wasn't crazy. He said nothing for long minutes that stretched in silence, while I waited in forlorn hope to feel a comforting hand on my shoulder, an arm around my waist, his chin resting on my head.

Sam stayed where he was and I finally turned.

He was close enough now for me to make out his features, illuminated by the green and red glow of the hospital monitors. I had braced myself to see confusion, disappointment and mistrust in his eyes. What was there was worse—it was wide-eyed fear. Sam looked at me like he didn't know me—his eyebrows up, his blue eyes tense and his jaws clenched tight. My eyes traveled down to his waist, where his hands were raised, palms outward in supplication.

"Sam? What's wrong? Why are you looking at me like that?"

I realized his stricken gaze wasn't on me, but fixed on a point just behind me. My pulse sped and I turned, expecting to see that horrible figure rising again and reaching for me, but instead I saw my son. "Tommy?" I reached a shaking hand to touch his face, to convince myself it was him. Sam slapped it away.

I stepped back, stung. "Sam! What's wrong with you?"

He shoved to the head of the bed and positioned himself between Tommy and me. "You can see him now? He's magically back in bed without a sound, without making a move? Does that make sense to you, Rose?"

I put a hand to my head. "No. No, it doesn't. I can't..." The bed had been empty when Sam walked in, I was sure of it. Had been empty the whole time we were talking. Before that, it was Akers in that bed—not my son. It couldn't have been. I took a step towards the bed and Sam put his hands up.

"Don't you take another goddamn step towards him, Rose."

I blinked. "Sam, what the hell is this?"

"Just put the fucking gun away, right the hell now."

My eyes followed his furious gaze to my other hand, still wrapped around the handle of my 9 mm, the bolt in place and a round in the chamber. My legs went weak and I bent double, fighting nausea. I had been within seconds of pulling the trigger on the bed's occupant. I had almost shot my son.

I stared at Tommy's sweet face, and didn't let myself turn away from the image of the damage I'd have wrought. The same thing

I'd done to Charlie Akers—taking the top of his head off, smearing brain behind him—that would have been Tommy. It would have been my son if Sam hadn't come in when he did. I gagged, swallowed, fought the rising tide of self-hatred.

I looked down at the gun and thought, in a removed kind of way, that the best thing I could do for my family now would be to turn it on myself. Put the barrel in my mouth, aim for the top and pull the trigger, make sure I'd never be in a position to hurt them ever again. I thought about it for a long time, tried and failed to find a reason not to. My son. I had almost killed my son. I looked back to the bed and thought the least I could do was take it somewhere else, not make my last act a burden my son might have to bear.

Hands shaking, I ejected the magazine from the semi-auto, followed by the chambered round. Turning the barrel toward myself, I laid it on the cold tiled floor and pushed it toward Sam, straightening slowly but keeping my hands above my waist and visible.

He bent and snatched the gun when I got far enough away, held it at his side, his chest heaving. "You pulled a gun on our child, Rose. What the hell were you thinking?" His voice rose as he spoke.

"I—"

"*What were you thinking?*" he screamed at me, shaking with fury.

Tears were spilling down my face as I tried to make him understand. "There was something in the goddamn bed, Sam. Something was there, and it wasn't Tommy. I would never hurt our son, never. You have to believe me."

He took a step toward me, brandished the unloaded gun at me. "Except that's exactly what you were primed to do. You had a cocked and loaded gun on your son. You almost killed Tommy, Rose." He clutched at his head with his free hand, his eyes squeezed shut. "Oh, Jesus, I should never have left you alone with him."

"Sam, please—I'm sorry—it wasn't, I didn't—"

Sam paced in front of the bed, looking like he might be sick. "I *have* believed you. For thirteen years I've trusted you, bought into everything you said about ghosts and the other side. Even though I never saw anything, I trusted you. But I never thought it would lead to this—putting the kids in danger."

My world was crumbling out from under me. I tried to answer calmly, get him to understand I wasn't hysterical. "Sam, please. I'm telling the truth, and you know damn well something's going on. The Whispers, Charlie Akers, they're here. However angry you are, you can't ignore that, please."

He wasn't listening, caught up in his own fury. "All those years. All those fucking years, wondering where that division was, where that line lay for you. How you could get up in the morning and put a bullet between someone's eyes and come home at night and be someone else's mother. But there isn't a line, is there, Rose? You're just a killer. Just a trigger-happy, uncaring killer."

I stared at him, felt like I'd been punched. Words crowded my mind; hurt, angry words about the unfairness of what he was saying. But how could I refute it? How did it get worse than someone who could kill their own child?

Sam's eyes met mine, and they were like flint. "Get out, Rose. Get out of here now, and don't come back. Whatever else is going on, Akers, whoever, they couldn't be a bigger threat than you. You can't be trusted."

I choked on my words, pressed the back of one hand against my mouth. Dropped my gaze from his so I wouldn't have to face the disgust in his eyes. "I'll deal with it, Sam," I said in a low voice. "Charlie, and the Whispers, whatever's coming, I'll find a way to fix it. To protect them, from a distance. Just, keep them safe, Sam."

He never looked up as I backed out of the room.

* * *

I dressed as I walked, jamming my ball cap low on my head and tugging on my long-sleeved t-shirt. I strapped my gun belt back on and immediately missed the comforting weight of the semi-auto I'd left with Sam. Hated myself for the weakness of wanting it. I couldn't be trusted. If I'd needed anything more to convince myself I was the monster my parents had always said I was, the evidence was back there in that hospital room. Sam certainly believed it.

It was early morning, not quite 4 am. The earlier eerie emptiness of the NICU floor was gone. Other parents and a couple of nurses roamed the halls, but I avoided eye contact and headed for the elevator.

When the doors slid closed in front of me, I choked back a sob—I couldn't break down here, I needed to get farther away. Focusing on the vague smear of my reflection in the polished metal before me, I bit my lip and forbid myself to think about what I'd almost done. When I closed my eyes I saw Sam's face, the warmth and concern I unconsciously expected from him replaced by fear and anger. I told myself to be grateful that he was looking out for our kids, grateful that I could trust him when I couldn't even trust myself, but there was a part of me filled with fury. I hated that he hadn't tried to help me, hated the unfairness of his words, the totality of his disgust.

The doors slid open on an empty hallway on the first floor. A white sign with a red arrow guided me to the exit, and I followed the hallway down a gradually descending slope. I met no one there or in the lobby on the way out; even the security desk was unmanned. When the automatic doors to the outside slid closed behind me, I couldn't stop my tears anymore and headed blindly in the direction of the parking garage, where I'd left the Charger, wishing I could go numb, feeling bereft without my gun.

I made myself keep moving, told myself I had no business with a firearm anyway. There was simply no way I could trust my own senses anymore. I had known, absolutely known, that it had been Charlie Akers, not Tommy, in that bed, and I had known he was a dangerous threat. Sam hadn't experienced any of the awful things I had seen and felt, but even now I wasn't sure what would have happened if I'd fired. Maybe it would have been Tommy, maybe it had been him all along—a thought too hideous to contemplate. But how could I possibly have known? Charlie had been so real to me—had he truly been there? Or was it just what he wanted me to see?

I still couldn't wrap my head around what was going on. Ghosts I understood. Maybe I could even buy that Charlie Akers had become something else, not living, not yet part of the ethereal. I was still working on that. Was it because he was a Summers? Because he'd been in contact with the Whispers, had they somehow granted him life beyond the mortal? But why would they do that? What were the limits of his power?

It seemed like the world had gone mad, that some portal to hell had opened and released every creeping nightmare ever made. Anything was possible, and all of it was bad. I wished for a guidebook, old family stories. A wise teacher to walk me through what I was going to have to do. All I had were Cora Summers and Evan Neal, and a crumbling parchment I didn't understand, signed by an ancestor I'd never heard of, and to whom I could find no reference. Nothing that could tell me how to fight these things, how to send them back where they came from.

I stopped when I caught sight of a shadow extending beyond the rounded bumper of my car. It was impossibly long, stretched by the angle of dim moonlight. I couldn't hear anything but the distant sound of traffic passing outside the hospital grounds. A second later my nostrils caught the acrid tang of cigarette smoke.

Real or imagined? I asked myself, with no way to answer.

"Who's there?" I said.

The broad shoulders jerked upward, then he turned. "Hey, Rose."

"Luke?" I released a trembling sigh. "Jesus Christ, you scared me. What the hell are you doing here?"

He took a step toward me. "You never called me back before, from Union. You weren't answering your phone, so I got worried and called the station. They told me about Tommy, Rose. I'm so sorry. How is he?"

I leaned against the car and folded my arms across my middle. "He's still unconscious. They don't know what's wrong with him." Tears began to spill down my cheeks and I felt again the horror at what I'd almost done in Tommy's hospital room, saw Sam's look of distrust and fear. He was right to fear me.

Luke moved close and wrapped his arms around me, holding me tight. "I'm so sorry, Rose," he said, his mouth close to my ear. "What can I do?"

For a minute I let myself sag against him, cried my heart out against my best friend's broad chest while he stroked my scarred back and told me it was going to be okay.

I buried my face against his chest at the same time I pushed against it. "You—you can't do anything, Luke. He's...no one can help him, and I—I almost, I came so close to—oh, Jesus, Luke, what the hell is wrong with me?" Sobs overtook me and I couldn't speak, only cry.

Luke pulled me closer and murmured in my ear. "Sweetheart, Rose, honey, there's nothing wrong with you, why would you say that? Shh, shh, it's okay, baby."

I looked up at him. "There is, though. Something terribly wrong— I'm..." I shuddered. "I'm a terrible mother, Luke. A terrible person. I wish, oh God, I wish I'd died in that fire, Luke. I wish I was dead."

He tightened his hold on me, looked down into my eyes, his own growing intense. "No. Don't you say that, Rose, don't you dare say that. You're a good person, a good mother. The best I know." He pushed a sodden curl behind my ear. "Whatever's happened, honey, we can get through it. I promise you. Haven't we always? Tell me."

I held his gaze and wondered if I could. Over the last thirteen years of friendship and working the streets together, Luke had seen the worst of me. He'd seen me scared out of my mind, over-confident and cocky, naïve, drunk, hungover, sick as a dog. He'd covered for me when I'd fucked up, helped me learn from my mistakes. If anyone could still love me after what I'd just done, it would be Luke.

The memory of Neal's disclosure returned, the realization of Luke's betrayal, and the grief of yet another loss threatened to take me under.

I pushed away and took a step back, wiped my eyes on my sleeves. I didn't have the luxury of losing control over this, over any of it. No matter how horrible, I still had work to do. "Nothing. It doesn't matter. I—I have to go, Luke."

He took a step back as well, his hands hanging loose at his sides, watching me with a puzzled expression. He sighed. "Okay, Rose. You don't have to tell me. But sweetheart, there's something you should see..." Luke stepped aside, revealing the back left tire of my Charger slashed deeply across the entire radius, flattened to the ground.

"What the *fuck*?" I pushed him out of the way and dropped to a crouch, placing my fingers on the edge of the cut. The tire was cleanly sliced through.

Luke's knees cracked as he knelt next to me. "I was looking at it when you came up—I didn't know if you'd seen it."

"No, I didn't know about it—I drove in on this thing. It must have happened while I was inside."

He shook his head. "They got some bullshit security around here, I'll tell you that much."

I stood and stepped back, giving him a level look. "Do you know anything about this, Luke?"

He was still peering around the wheel well as though it was going to tell him something but he looked up at this. "What? I know as much as you know. I parked over there—" he jerked his head to indicate his truck two spaces over, "—and when I walked by your car, I saw the tire. I got here two minutes before you did."

I stared down at him, feeling like I was looking at a stranger. A dangerous one. I'd been partnered with Luke Harris for years and had trusted him with my life a thousand times over. I knew it was still possible that Neal was lying about Luke, but it fit too neatly for me to ignore. I didn't know what Luke's motivations were, but that didn't matter.

Luke's thick brows knit over his crooked nose, broken at least twice since I'd known him. "So do you have a spare? I can help you change it if you want." He placed a hand on the Charger and used it to leverage his bulk back to a standing position. I stepped back as he loomed over me.

"Rose, what the hell is wrong with you? You're lookin' at me like you don't even know me."

"I'm not sure I do anymore, Luke."

He frowned. "Is this about before? Listen, I'm sorry about that. I didn't mean to get all huffy. You were right. You told me from the start you didn't want anything serious, and I should have listened." He dropped his eyes and shrugged. "I got carried away, I guess. I've always been a little jealous of Sam, but I'm sure you knew that."

I stared at him, fighting a rush of fury. "Luke, my *son* is upstairs in that hospital, completely comatose. The doctors have no idea what's wrong with him or if he'll ever wake up and you think I give a shit about your goddamn *feelings?*"

"Hey, Rose, it's going to be all right." Luke took a step toward me and tried to put his arms around me again, but I pushed him, hard. I was riding the wave of my anger now and it felt a hell of a lot better than despair.

"Stay away from me, Luke. Why the hell are you here?"

"I told you—I came by because I heard about Tommy. Taylor told me what had happened when I called the station looking for you. For fuck's sake Rose, I'm your best friend. Why else would I be here?"

"You didn't do that to my car?"

Luke's eyes widened, then narrowed to angry slits. "You could ask me that? You think I'd slash your tires at a time like this, just to.... what, give myself an opportunity to play your knight in shining armor? I love you like crazy, Rose McFarland, but I'm not that nuts." He was breathing hard now, his face flushed a ruddy shade of pissed off. If he was acting, he was doing a damned good job of it.

When I didn't answer he threw up his hands, turned and paced away a few steps, then came back. "What the hell is all this about, Rose? If anyone has a reason to be pissed, it's me. You've been shutting me out for days, and now you act like *I've* done something wrong. I don't deserve this. Even if—" His gaze dropped and pain spasmed his features. Then he looked back up, and when he spoke again his voice was quiet, calm. "Even if you're done with me, as a lover, I don't want to lose your friendship. If this is about Sam—if you guys are getting back together, just tell me. I won't pretend to be happy about it, but I can take it." He held my gaze, his jaw clenched.

"Tell me about Evan Neal, Luke."

His brows shot up, he took a step back. "Neal? What the hell does he have to do with anything?"

"Why didn't you tell me about meeting with Neal this morning? I asked you—gave you a chance to tell me what you were doing. You lied and said you hadn't found anything else out."

"Damn it Rose, I didn't lie. I *didn't* find anything else out. Yeah, I approached the guy when I saw him out front. I struck up a conversation with him, even told him I knew you, just to see what he would tell me. I told you that, damn it."

I shook my head, folded my arms even tighter. "I don't believe you."

Luke ran one hand back through his curly hair, tugging it as he did. "I don't believe you. After everything we've been through, you find it so easy to think the worst of me—"

"I *didn't* find it easy, Luke. I tried to convince myself that what I was seeing had to have some other explanation, that the guy who'd trained me, partnered with me, stood as godfather to my daughter, shared my bed, wouldn't betray me just because he was jealous of my ex-husband."

He threw his hands up. "Betray you? How exactly was I betraying you? What possible reason would I have for talking to Neal other than getting information for you?"

A car door slammed on one of the levels above us, followed by a large engine cranking up. I stepped closer to him, lowered my voice. "Someone's been giving information to Agent Neal. Al Taylor told me as much—Neal knows things he shouldn't. Any thoughts on who might have been responsible for that?"

Luke straightened. "So you know about that."

His words hurt more than they should have. I'd been mostly convinced of his guilt, but I'd been hoping he'd prove me wrong. I felt like my entire world had been turned upside down—I'd lost everyone I could count on in the space of one night.

"Fuck you, Luke." I brushed angrily at the tears spilling down my cheeks again, turned away and began walking. I didn't know where I was going; all I cared about was getting away.

"Damn it Rose, stop, will you?" He caught up with me, stepped in front of me and held his hands out. "I wasn't giving information to Neal. When you saw us in the parking lot, that was the first time I ever talked to the guy. I knew somebody had to have been talking to him, and I was trying to figure out who. I was throwing names out, trying to get him to slip up and tell me who he knew."

"What about the phone call, Luke?"

"What fucking phone call?"

"The one you made to Neal right after we spoke, when I told you I was on my way to the Akers site. I tell you, you call him, he shows up."

"I don't know what you're talking about, Rose. I never made any damn phone call to Evan Neal, I don't even have his phone number."

"I heard your fucking voicemail, Luke, it was your damn voice on his cell phone. How the hell else does that happen, huh?"

He slammed an open hand against the concrete column beside him. "I don't fucking know, Rose, but all I can tell you is, you must not know me as well as you think you do, if you believe I'd do something like that. I never called Neal, I never left him any goddamn message, and *I never betrayed you.* I never fucking would." He stood there panting and glaring at me, angrier than I'd ever seen him.

I searched his face, tried to read him. He looked guileless, like a man who was telling the truth—meeting my eyes, steady gaze, seriously pissed off—and I wanted to believe him. But it was that very wanting that I distrusted. Maybe he was telling the truth, maybe he was covering his ass. But I'd heard the message on Neal's phone. It was Luke, I had no doubt. What reason would Evan Neal have to lie about Luke's involvement?

I looked back at my car, at the shredded tire. Turned back to Luke. "Are you carrying?"

He faltered, confused by the change of tactic. "Yeah, always. In the truck."

I wiped my face again, raw from hours of on and off crying jags. "Give it to me."

"Why?"

"Because my gun is up there with Sam, and I need a weapon. I don't have a spare here for the Charger, so I need you to take me home to get my .38, and the rest of my gear." I still didn't think I should be trusted with a gun, but no more could I trust anyone I once had. As long as I stayed away from my family, they at least would be safe from what I might do.

"Of course I'll take you home, Rose, whatever you need." There was relief in his eyes, and his face relaxed into a smile. "Come on, honey."

"No. Give me your keys, and your gun." I held out my hand.

"What?"

"I'm driving, and I want to be the only one armed. I'd like to trust you right now, Luke, but I don't have the luxury."

He said nothing for a long minute, just looked at me. Then he shrugged, went back to the truck for his .45, and handed me the gun and keys without further comment. He climbed into the passenger seat and faced out the window, his big shoulders tensed, his anger palpable.

I climbed into the driver's seat and tucked Luke's .45 into the side panel pocket on the door. I didn't feel completely safe, and I wished to hell I wasn't in a position to have to be alone with him, but I would keep vigilant. If Luke was lying and I found myself in danger, I would shoot him. After all, it was nothing I hadn't done before.

CHAPTER FOURTEEN

Sam sat alone in the darkened hospital room, watching the shallow rise and fall of his small son's chest and waiting for dawn. He slumped in the uncomfortable hospital chair, shoulders and neck aching, eyes feeling like sandpaper every time he blinked, wanting to be numb. He felt like he should be, after everything that had happened over the last week, but his mind was still sharp. It kept replaying the impossible image of Rose with a gun trained on Tommy, of the confusion in her face, and the hurt when he sent her away. It kept whispering to him about fire—about inexplicable, contained fires occurring only around Rose. It mercilessly circled back, over and over, to the scene in the parking garage that he had watched from Tommy's window. Luke, waiting for Rose by her car, taking her into his arms. Some kind of argument, both of them heated, then Rose climbing into Luke's truck and driving away.

Sam told himself it didn't have to be what it looked like. He was well aware of Luke's feelings for Rose—Sam had often picked up on jealousy from the other man, and since Aaron's death he'd been afraid

Luke might do something about it. There had even been times during Sam's marriage that he'd worried about Rose's relationship with Luke. Everyone knew how close partners could get. But he'd always trusted Rose, and she'd always treated Luke like a brother.

Now, though, Rose wasn't bound by marriage. Sam had gotten the impression in the last few weeks that she might have started seeing someone, but it hadn't stopped her from falling into bed with him last night. He figured it must not have been serious, just like his current fling wasn't serious. Luke would be a different story—the one man Sam knew could stand as a real rival. Rose and Luke been partners and friends for years—sometimes it even seemed like they were reading each other's minds. And Sam knew damn well Luke would never get on her case about the job. So no, it didn't have to be what it looked like, but Luke showing up here, only minutes after Sam had banished Rose from Tommy's hospital room, didn't look good for Sam.

It was that exile that made Sam so afraid. He and Rose had found each other again only a day ago, and it had been the best feeling of his life. He'd promised Rose, and he'd promised himself, never to let anything get in the way again, but here he was alone. It didn't matter how rational it sounded when he told himself it was what Rose herself wanted him to do—he knew that Rose would sacrifice her own life and happiness in a heartbeat for her kids, and she fully expected him to do the same. But he saw the hurt in her eyes over and over again, and would not be comforted. He squeezed his eyes shut. How could he have said those things to her? Called her a killer, a bad mother? After years of trusting her, believing her, and knowing how much that meant to her, he'd thrown it all in her face. He'd been terrified, walking in to find her like that, her gun on Tommy, and his fury had come quickly on the heels of his fear. It wasn't an excuse, though. He might have been right to send her away, but there was no justification for what he'd said.

When the glass door slid open behind him, Sam jerked upright, his heart beating fast, the book he'd been reading to Tommy sliding to the floor with a clatter. He stood and turned quickly, trying like hell not to hope, but he was still unbelievably crushed when it wasn't Rose. He wanted, more than anything, a chance to make things right with her.

"Zack," he said, trying to keep the disappointment from his voice. "Wait, Zack? Where have you been, man? Everyone's been looking for you." Sam took a step back as Zack shuffled forward and a strong miasma of body odor came with him.

"Zack. What's up with you?" Even in the dimly lit hospital room, Sam could tell something was wrong. Zack's beard was unkempt, his clothes wrinkled and visibly dirty, his dark hair oily. His eyes were bloodshot behind smeared glasses. He looked dazed, spacey, standing there swaying while he watched Tommy.

"Hi, Sam." Zack stepped closer, his movements jerky, uncoordinated. "I came as soon as I heard. How is he?" He settled his glazed expression on Sam's face, acting like he hadn't heard a word.

"No change." Sam moved to block Zack's view of the bed. Rose had said Zack had gotten violent the last time she'd seen him. Sam was pretty sure he could overpower the other man, but he hoped it wouldn't come to that.

"Zack? Are you all right?" He looked around for a nurse call button while he talked. "Rose told me you'd taken a shot to the vest on Friday. You healing up okay?"

"Huh? Yeah, fine. No real damage." Zack rubbed absently at his chest, looking through Sam.

"Good." Sam waited, his back and shoulders tensed, but Zack said nothing else. "Zack? It's good of you to come by, but Tommy needs rest. Maybe you could call Rose later."

"Right, of course." Zack finally looked up, seemed to focus on Sam for the first time. "Where is Rose? She was supposed to be here."

Sam tried to keep his expression neutral. "She...headed out a little while ago. Needed a break."

Zack frowned. "That's not right. She should be here. Where did she go?"

Sam crossed his arms over his chest. "She was here for a long time, Zack. She wouldn't have gone anywhere if I hadn't been able to stay. We have a daughter too, you know."

Zack's eyes narrowed, grew darker. "She's with Lily? Where are they?"

Sam stared at him, feeling the hairs prickle on the back of his neck. Something was wrong here. "Zack, Tommy needs rest. If you need to find Rose, you should call her cell phone." But not before I have a chance to call and warn her, he thought.

Zack wasn't listening anymore, at least not to Sam. He had turned away, his head tilted, staring at an empty corner of the room.

Sam tried to search the darkness, his skin crawling. Something was there, moving in the shadows. Something slow, something sly, the dry rustle of flesh on cloth. Of course he couldn't see it—he needed Rose.

"Zack," he said as the silence stretched on, taking a step toward the other man. "I really have to ask you to leave now, okay? Tommy's sick, and I—"

The snarling face that turned on him didn't belong to Zack at all—it couldn't. "I was told Rose would be here. *Where is she?*"

The gun, thought Sam. Rose had left her 9 mm with him. It was sitting on a chair against the wall to his left, under Rose's jacket. He lunged for it, making the most of his long stride, and scrabbled for the pistol. He felt nothing but the cloth of the jacket for a nervewracking moment, then closed his hand around the barrel. He turned the gun around, flipped the safety off with his thumb, and whirled to face Zack.

Before he could raise his arm, something hard cracked across his temple. He lost his balance, falling heavily, his vision starred. Zack stood over him for only seconds before turning his attention to the bed.

Sam struggled to stand. "No, get the fuck away from him!"

Without turning around, Zack kicked backwards, knocking the gun from Sam's hand. Sam felt his fingers crunch under the other man's boot.

"It's not my fault she wasn't here," said Zack, his voice a mewling whine. "I did what you asked me to. When can I see my brother?"

Sam lunged up from the floor, grabbing for Zack's shoulders, trying to pull him off-balance. He didn't see when a dark shape resolved itself from the shadowed corner, didn't see the stumbling horror until it was too late. Something smashed against the base of his skull, and he fell.

Just before his vision tunneled to black, he saw the grinning, rotting skull above him, watched skeletal hands reach for his sleeping son. She'd been right, Sam realized. Charlie Akers had been here.

"Rose," Sam mumbled as darkness took him.

CHAPTER FIFTEEN

Cora drove slowly from the hospital to the little house on Sledge Avenue, trying her best not to choke on the smell coming from the back seat. The ancient, rusted Cutlass was still in Paul's name—she'd never had the heart to change that. It drove like a land yacht but was still low-mileage. She'd barely left the mountaintop for the last eighteen years, and her weekly grocery trips were just enough to keep the car in good condition.

When she parked and killed the headlights, the sun was coming up but the tree-lined street was still dark. Five a.m., too early for anyone to be up. She sat watching for another few minutes, saw no movement behind the pale curtains.

"*Go,*" growled the voice behind her. The lack of a jawbone turned it into *gah.* "*Kill the woman, bring me the girl.*"

Cora straightened, met the thing's glowing yellow eyes in the rearview mirror, shuddered.

It laughed.

"When do I get to see Paul again?" she asked, her voice trembling.

"*Soon. He's busy right now, but I'm sure he'll come and visit you.*"

"And the boy? You're going to bring me the boy?"

Waiting in the shadows of the doctor's lot at the hospital, Cora had watched Charlie hand off a small, sleeping bundle to a large, furtive man in a dirty white shirt. "Is that man going to bring him to me? Paul said—"

"*I know what he said. There's been a change in plans.*" The yellow eyes narrowed. "*Go. Now.*"

Cora bit back a retort and popped the glove box, filling the car with the smell of aging, dusty plastic. Paul's revolver, however, was well-oiled and loaded.

She eased the Cutlass door open but it screeched a protest, making her heart kick up several notches. She cast a furtive glance up and down the silent street, but if anyone had heard, they weren't coming to check it out.

Cora was nearly to the porch when the light went off and the front door swung open. She froze, one foot on the first step, trying not to breathe.

A man stepped out. He was tall, but too thin to be Sam McFarland. Who, then? Had the little slut already found another man to do her bidding?

It didn't matter. She had only seconds before he would turn and see her—she had no cover. She took the steps quickly, raising the revolver as she did.

The man turned, a murmur of surprise all he could muster before Cora shoved the gun into his gut and pulled the trigger, the shot ringing in her ears.

He groaned, pressed a hand to his belly, and slid to the porch. A sliver of light from the rising sun reflected on a pair of silver glasses, a swatch of dark hair falling over glazed eyes.

Cora kicked his legs out of the way and swung the front door open, slipping inside as quietly as she could.

Not that quiet was going to do her much good—the whole street must have heard that gunshot. Cora bolted the door behind her. She didn't want any interference from her dark passenger—not that a locked door would stop the likes of that creature.

The house was pitch dark. Dawn hadn't breached the windows yet. The man she'd shot must have good night vision, she thought. She crept along the wall, feeling her way until she made it out of the front room and into a darkened hallway. Here she paused, wondering where her granddaughter's room would be. There were three doors along the passage, and all were closed, with nothing to tell her who slept where.

She licked her lips, steadied her gun hand, and slowly opened the first door. A master bedroom painted in shades of light blue. A messy queen-sized bed, slept in, but empty. Probably belonged to the dead man on the porch, she decided, and closed the door behind her. The next door opened onto a small windowless bathroom, also unoccupied.

That left the door at the end of the hall. Cora crept down to it, pausing to listen. No sounds came from the other side, and she smiled to herself. This was easier than she'd expected.

She pushed the door open, the hinges emitting a low creak as she did. There was a pair of twin beds, one on each side of the room. The one on the left was empty, the bedclothes tucked in smoothly. Someone was sitting up in the one on the right.

"Lily," crooned Cora. "Lily, come see your grandmother."

A metallic snick from the bed.

Cora froze.

A cultured Southern voice lilted through the darkness. "I don't think so, you dried-up old bitch."

Five rounds from a snub-nosed .38 special punched their way into Cora's stomach. She collapsed to the carpet in a groaning heap.

Joy sat catching her breath, her heart thudding, feeling sick. She was a light sleeper and had heard William get up from the couch. She'd heard the gunshot, and the thud of a body hitting the porch. Seconds later she'd been in Lily's room, her husband's old revolver in hand, hiding her granddaughter and praying she could do what needed to be done.

Joy supposed she needn't have worried. She thought T.J. would have been proud.

William. She hoped like hell she would be in time to help him. She extricated herself from the blankets and bent down, reaching a shaking hand under Tommy's empty bed. "Come on, sugar," she said as calmly as she could. "Don't look at her, okay?"

Lily wriggled out, taking her grandmother's hand. Joy did her best to block Lily's view of the body, tucking the girl's head against her side. They gave Cora a wide berth, and Lily looked up at Joy when they reached the bedroom door, her blue eyes wet behind crooked glasses.

"I did like you said, Grandmommy," the little girl said in a choked whisper. "I didn't make a sound."

Joy pulled the door as far as she could and knelt to hug her granddaughter, hoping the girl wouldn't feel the sickening thud of her own heartbeat. "You were very brave, Lily girl. I'm proud of you. It's okay to cry, sugar, it was a scary thing."

"I, I don't want to cry," Lily hiccuped on a sob. "She, she was a mean lady and she wanted to hurt me."

"That's all right sweetheart, you just let it out. Can you come out in the kitchen and call your Mama on the landline? I have to go help your grandfather."

Lily's bright blue eyes looked up at her, red-rimmed and wide. Joy hated what this night was doing to her family.

"What's wrong with him?" Lily asked. "I thought I heard—"

"I don't know yet, sugar. Hand me that cell phone, I'm calling 911. Be strong now, Lily."

CHAPTER SIXTEEN

Luke and I didn't speak during the short drive back to my place. He sat staring out his window at the passing scenery while I concentrated on the road ahead, trying to think what my next move was. The streetlights on Belvedere had gone off by the time we got there, the horizon pinkening with the dawn. I pulled up in the darkened street in front of the condo, threw the truck in park and reached for Luke's .45.

He grabbed my wrist. "Rose, stop. Look."

I looked where he was pointing. At first all I saw was the hall light bleeding through the frosted glass next to the front door. A shadow glided smoothly across, the shape indeterminate. Someone was definitely in there.

"Damn."

I looked up and down the car-lined street, but didn't notice any vehicle that was out of place. Not William's farm truck or Joy's little gold Mazda, and they were the only ones with keys, other than Luke.

We watched for a minute or two, but nothing else moved. I reached out hesitantly with my mind and immediately felt an answering brush—either I was getting better at this, or whatever was in there was strong as hell. Feather-light though, completely unlike the violent, grasping claws of the Whispers. It also didn't feel like anything I'd ever experienced. Living or dead, I couldn't tell. But did that mean anything? My judgment was clearly fucked.

Luke turned to look at me, his dark eyes unreadable.

"What do you want to do, Rose?" he asked in a low voice. "Should we call for back-up, or do you want to deal with this on our own?"

"No back-up. I don't want to involve anyone else in this."

He didn't question it. "Front or back?"

"It'll have to be the front. I don't have a key for the back door, it's a latch that only works from the inside."

"Okay." He reached for the door handle, but I stopped him with a hand on his elbow. He turned back, eyebrows up, his gaze mistrustful.

"Luke, you don't have to go with me."

He just looked at me, brown eyes steady, his face impassive.

"I mean it, Luke. Whatever else is going on...I don't know how to explain this to you." I looked back at the house, tried again to get a feel for what was there. Nothing this time.

I turned back to him, dropped my hand from his arm. "What we find in there...there's a good chance it won't be human, okay? It could be dangerous. Something you've never faced, and won't know how to fight."

His thick brows drew together, he shook his head. "I don't follow you, Rose."

I sighed. "I know. I don't think there's a good way to prepare you for this, so maybe it's better if you stay here. You might not even be able to see what's there, but that doesn't mean it can't hurt you."

He looked at me, finally shrugged. "It doesn't matter what's there, Rose. I'm your partner, whatever you might think of me now, and I don't want you getting into trouble by yourself. I'm coming with you." He climbed out of the truck, and after a minute I followed.

I knew I should still be pissed at him, and part of me was, but I'd trusted him implicitly for more than a decade. It was hard to break the habit of feeling safer with Luke Harris watching my back.

We crept up the walk, stopping on the porch to listen. There was no sound, but the door swung slowly open.

No one was in the hallway beyond.

Luke didn't give me a choice, pushed his way in first. I followed close behind and felt it as soon as I crossed the threshold. The atmosphere was heavy, sound from outside the house muted, as though we'd traveled a long distance.

"Cold in here," whispered Luke.

I nodded.

We both looked around, but there was no one in the main living area.

"Where next?" he asked softly.

I looked up. A shadow stretched from the rarely used second floor. Someone was up there, at the head of the staircase. Dead still.

"There."

We moved to the foot of the stairs, and this time I pushed my way to the front. I was, after all, the only one with a weapon, just on the off chance it could do us any good.

The shadow didn't move. Though we were now directly below it, I couldn't make out any detail. I felt watched, measured.

"Who's up there?" I said finally. I felt Luke flinch beside me at the break in eerie silence.

"*The Guardian comes.*"

It was a woman's voice, deep, like mine. And sad.

I shivered. The Guardian—was she talking about me?

She seemed to glide down the stairs, faster than I was prepared for, and I fell back a step, stumbling into Luke.

He steadied me, but I could feel his hands shaking. The shade had stopped on the second step.

I was certain I'd never seen the woman standing before me, but I knew her all the same. She was shorter than me, her hair honey blonde and curly like mine, but worn much longer, nearly to her waist. Her gray-green eyes were sad, her cheeks wan under long dark lashes that reminded me of Tommy's.

When I tried to clear my vision and focus on her, I found I couldn't.

It was impossible to tell what she was wearing; she lost definition around the edges. Her skin was pale white, nearly luminescent even on the dimly lit staircase. Everything seemed darker around her, as though she were infecting the very air. It felt like the temperature had dropped twenty degrees.

We stood in silence for a long time, watching each other, then I felt that feather-light touch again, brushing the edges of my mind. She smiled.

Your defenses are strong, Rose of the Summers. That's good. You will need them. Tommy will need them.

Luke's hold on me tightened. "Back it up there, lady. What the hell are you doing in Rose's house?"

I twisted to look up at him. "You're seeing this?"

Luke's eyes stayed fixed on the figure on the stairs. "I'm seeing *something*." His voice was shaking, only the barest tremor.

I turned back to the ghost. "You're Bella, aren't you? The one who signed the contract?"

She nodded.

I am Bella Summers, the first of the Guardians, the shepherds of lost souls—the only hope for the wandering dead, the guardians of the passage between this world and the next.

"I'm fucking glad to have this opportunity, Bella, because I've been wanting to ask you—*what the fuck were you thinking?* What could have possessed you to sign something like that? To give your descendants no choice—what could have been worth that?" I'd been afraid before, but now I was trembling with fury.

Her gaze narrowed.

Can you think of nothing, Rose Summers? Nothing that would be worth that sacrifice? I had a son once. Matthew. He was dying, and it was the only way to help him. Can you say you would not have done the same? That there is anything you wouldn't do to gain the power to heal your own son?

Would I have signed that contract? Made promises for people not even born or thought of? To save Tommy or Lily, you're damn right I would. I didn't answer, but she heard it anyway.

You have little time, Rose. It is the Guardians who hold the Whispers in

243

check, and it has been too long since a true Guardian kept the gate. The passageway has been shut too tightly for many years. The pressure builds, and eventually becomes great enough to breach. That is why the dead are crossing now—far too many to be contained, and stronger than they should be.

Stronger. "Charlie?" I said, touching my wrist where he had clawed at me.

She nodded.

Because of the breach, and because of his contact with the Whispers.

"The part about the Guardian being a beacon for the dead, that's why they keep showing up? Why they did when I was a kid?"

Seeing these things, Rose of the Summers, is the gift of the Guardians. You are their keeper. The only one who can guide them home.

"Gift," I repeated with a hollow laugh. "Yes, it's been some kind of gift."

Yes, Rose. There are gifts, meant to offset the heavy responsibilities. For many generations, each Guardian developed a special talent, as well as the ability to see and assist the dead. For many it was healing. For some it was Sight—dreams and premonitions of the future. Still others could control the elements.

"Like fire," I said softly.

The gifts were always meant to be used for good, and for many years they were. Until Jacob Summers came to the mountain, until he coveted his wife's gifts for himself.

I frowned. "I don't understand. Jacob Summers...I've heard of him before. But if his wife was a Guardian, then how—"

How did he carry the Summers name? It was tradition. The Summers clan was close, of necessity. Each family took the Summers name, and passed it on to their children, to stay close to their roots. Jacob was not a Summers by blood. He wanted to take by force what he could not rightfully have.

"How did he do it?" I asked. "If the Guardians always have these gifts, wouldn't they have been more powerful?"

Jacob chose his time well. There is always only one Guardian. The next generation develops their gifts early, beginning at age four.

Tommy.

But they are taught to use their gifts, and to grow stronger, by the elder

Guardian. The mantle and full potential is only passed upon the death of the current Guardian. Jacob Summers' mother-in-law was the last of the great ones. She died young—there was a great storm, and the valley flooded. She drowned.

"And the next Guardian..."

Was Jacob's own wife, Rebecca. He had for many years been controlling her, chipping away at her confidence. When her mother passed, Jacob tightened his control. He used physical force to keep her in line, threatened to kill her if she did not suppress her abilities.

"Still," rumbled Luke from behind me. "If she had these powers, like you say, he couldn't control her all the time, could he? Couldn't she just, I don't know, cast a spell or something while he was sleeping?"

Bella's gaze, when it fell on Luke again, was not benevolent. Her face darkened, the room grew colder.

There are no spells. That is not what we do.

She returned her attention to me.

Rebecca Summers' talent was of the passive sort. She was a healer.

"Each to their temperament and necessity..." I loosely quoted.

She nodded.

Rebecca had no power to harm. As I say, Jacob and his kinsmen chose their time well. Rebecca's daughter Anna was only six, too young to use her talents to help her mother, even if she'd been allowed to train them.

From that point on, Jacob Summers and his ilk gained control. They kept the Summers name because of the respect it garnered, but they crushed any sign of the Guardian's gifts in every generation. Anna was the first to have her growth stunted in that way, and that's been the practice ever since.

"I don't understand," Luke said. "How could they do that? How did they crush them?"

"Systemic abuse," I answered softly. "Physical pain any time the...*gift* manifested. Associating punishment with its use, whether intentional or not." I looked at Bella. "That's it, isn't it? That's what my parents were doing. Trying to train it out of me."

I felt Luke's hand on my shoulder, but I didn't look at him.

Yes. That, and making you fear it. Rather than tell you what was happening, teaching you how to control the visions and visitations, they taught you to fear them. Over time, your only goal became to suppress them.

So that was it. That was why every time the bogeymen had come to visit, I'd been locked in with them. To make me terrified, make me hate the visions. It had worked.

"What about my father? How the hell did he know how to train Charlie? Why would he want to, if it was supposed to be evil?"

Because Charlie Akers was a male child. Jacob's goal was to turn the gift of the Guardian over to the men of the Summers family. Your father was the first to show that talent.

It took time to process what she had said, and even when I did, I couldn't believe it.

"You're telling me that Paul Summers—that *he* was a Guardian?"

Yes. More than that, Rose of the Summers. Even in death he still clings to the role, to the powers he used to have. He is who you must face to end this.

"No," I whispered from a dry throat. "It's not possible. He can't still be..."

Alive? He is not. He straddles the door between life and death, growing stronger as the barrier thins.

"Oh, God." My knees weak, I slumped to the floor at the foot of the stairs. This was worse than anything I'd imagined. In the back of my mind, since I'd been sixteen years old and finally grasped that my father was dead, there had always been the thought that no matter what else life threw at me, Paul Summers could never hurt me again. Now I was being told that he was back, that he'd never truly been gone, and my little girl fear of him returned. I would rather take down a field full of gunmen, rather spend a night in the most haunted graveyard than face my father again. I pulled my knees to my chest, hugged them tight and shivered like a child.

Luke crouched next to me, a hand on my shoulder. "It doesn't matter if he's around or not, Rose. You don't have to deal with him—you never have to see him again. No one can ask that of you."

It is asked of her—she has no choice. Rose must end this struggle—only she can do so.

"Why?" he asked, his voice hard. "Why the hell is it so important for Rose to save the damn world, huh? Hasn't she done enough, been through enough?"

It must be her. She is the one who caused the rift, and she is the only one who can fix it.

246

I looked up at her, tried to keep the tremor out of my voice. "How? I keep telling people I don't *have* these goddamn talents. All I've ever had are the visitations, and they made my life a living hell. I was glad when they stopped, and I'm not going to let Tommy live like that. How the hell am I supposed to do anything? I can't heal people, or see the future, or whatever you think I should be able to do. I'm not even a particularly good person—I'm a killer, okay? I'm fucking deadly with a sniper rifle, or any other gun in my hand, and that's what I am. It's all I am, and I don't even feel bad about it when I'm done. Does that sound like the kind of person you want saving the world? Someone who doesn't even have enough humanity to feel bad when they put a bullet through another human being?"

You are a killer, Rose of the Summers. Your aim is true, you do not hesitate, and you do not torment yourself once the die is cast. That is exactly what is needed now—that is your gift. Jacob chose his time well when he 'cleansed' the mountain. So have we chosen our time well. We have been waiting for one who could restore the balance, and it is you.

I stared at her, my mind numb. A killer, like Sam had called me. A robot who could murder without guilt, could train a gun on her own son. This was my gift?

It was Luke who spoke. "What if she doesn't? What if we just leave here, and never look back? What if we tell you to find someone else?"

The room grew colder, and darker. Bella seemed to draw the shadows to herself, to grow larger, looming above us.

The darkness over this city, and the shadows, will grow absolute. The dead who are lost have wandered too long on this earth, and many who have already crossed over have found their way back through the opening. The dead already outnumber the living here, and soon that darkness will be everywhere, in every city.

I thought of Zack, telling me he'd seen his brother. Of Aaron at his father's farm, telling me he shouldn't be there. Of Andy—or not Andy, I really didn't know—at the house on Union. Wondered how many other signs I'd missed.

"Why here? Why Memphis?"

Because you are here, Rose. You and Tommy. The Whispers are drawn to you, as they always have been.

"The dead will walk the earth. Will have strength, and numbers."
It sounded biblical.

Can you doubt it? She made a dismissive gesture toward Luke.
Even this one can see that things are not as they should be.

I stood, facing her. "What do I have to do? Just find Dad, kill him
again, patch the drywall or whatever to close this damn door?"

You must restore the balance—you must release the pressure.

"Okay, fine, and how do I do that?"

*You must let them in, Rose. The Whispers. You must let them take you
over.*

"Let them in," I repeated. Dread made me cold. "I have to let
them...what, possess me? Is that what they want?" It made a certain,
blinding, terrifying sense. All that wanting I'd felt over the long years
of my childhood, those claws at the edges of my already frayed mind.
It was what they'd always wanted.

*Yes. The Whispers are the source of the Guardian's power, the guiding
force behind our shepherding of the dead. Without them, we would not
be. Without us, the dead who are lost would stay lost—there would be no
chance for them to find their way. There are times that the Whispers must
take the Guardian's form.*

I was starting to feel panicked. "I'm supposed to let them use me?
What if they don't leave? What if I don't come back?"

*You are the only one strong enough to hold them, Rose. It must be you.
If you do not, Tommy will. It is as simple as that.*

I glared at her, my fists clenching at my sides. "You mean if you
can't make me do it, you'll coerce my four-year old son to do your
bidding?"

*It is not I who will do so. The Whispers have already found him. They
are in there with him, in his mind, as he sleeps. He does not have your
defenses, Rose, and he will fall to them soon. He may not make it back.*

The Whispers already in my son—it was a horrible thought. An
image of Tommy in his car seat, his sweet face twisted, an awful
voice that couldn't be his telling me we both belonged to them. Then
so shortly after, the coma. Had the same thing happened to Ethan
Neal? But how, if the boy wasn't a Summers, had nothing to do with
the Guardians? Could the Whispers get to anyone, anywhere? What

were the limits of their power?

Reading my thoughts again, Bella shook her head.

The Whispers were driven into the Neal boy, Rose. Your brother, under the aegis of your father, twisted their power, tried to use them against their will. Their strength was great and uncontrolled; the boy was sleeping and defenseless. Had his father not exposed him to your brother, he would never have been harmed. But the Neal boy hasn't your abilities, and Tommy has not been trained. Neither of them will be able to drive the Whispers out on their own. You are the only hope for either child, Rose.

Neal had been right. I had to let the Whispers in to save our children. I wondered if he knew this part, if he was only disclosing information in bits and pieces for some reason of his own.

"How," I started, then choked, my throat dry with fear. I tried again. "How do I start, then? How do I get them to come to me, to leave Tommy?"

Bella tilted her head at me.

You must find a way to call them, to open yourself. Go to where you feel the closest to the other side, where the walls are thinnest. Where they will have the power, not you. Then you must let go, and let them in.

CHAPTER SEVENTEEN

Joy handed the phone to Lily, crouched next to her on the dark porch. "Keep hold of that, okay, sugar? Answer if it rings."

Lily nodded, her eyes big behind smudged glasses. "Should I try calling Mom again? She didn't pick up."

"Give it a minute, hon. 911 might call back—I want to keep the line open."

Joy kept up the pressure on William's stomach, the way the emergency operator had told her to. He was getting cold, his breathing shallow. Where was the ambulance?

She watched his face, praying to see his eyes open, to see that blue shade fade from around his lips. He'd been so still, his breathing so shallow, that at first she'd been sure he was dead. She'd found a pulse, but it was weak, thready.

She wished she could shoot Cora all over again. She'd never taken a life before, had expected to feel...something. Guilt, regret, something. Maybe she was in shock, who knew, but at the moment, all she felt was fury at the woman who'd hurt her family. She wondered if this was how Rose felt when she was forced to kill. She looked over at Lily, watching solemnly, the phone pressed to her skinny chest. Joy was proud of her granddaughter.

She didn't hear the back door of the old Cutlass open. Didn't see the lurching figure climb out and shamble furtively across the street in the gray pre-dawn light.

The creature slipped around the back of the house unseen. The back door was locked but easily forced, and it was soon inside. It stood in the hall, sniffing, its purple tongue lolling wetly. Its lifeless eyes focused on the door at the end of the hallway, the same one Cora had chosen with such unfortunate results.

The door stood open, a bare foot sticking out into the hall, the battered black shoe it belonged to lying a few inches away.

The creature grinned wider. *Shot out of her shoes.*

It dragged itself to the door, pushed it open until it thudded into something on the other side. There was a groan from the floor. The creature shuffled the rest of the way into the room. Knelt clumsily next to the prone woman, getting soaked in her blood in the process, long past caring.

Cora whispered something. The creature leaned closer and she pulled away, gagging.

"*What's that?*" it crooned.

"Paul," Cora whispered. Her life was ebbing, he could feel that. "I did...what I promised. Give...him to me. Give me Paul."

Rotted fingers lovingly caressed hair from her eyes. "*Oh, but he doesn't need you anymore, Cora. Doesn't need any of your family, not now. I'm his son, the only one he has left, and from now on we'll work together. I've waited in the wings long enough. When you're gone, and Rose, and her children, then he'll see how much he needs me. We'll be together forever.*"

Cora frowned. "No—you can't—you promised. He promised. Do as you were told. Bring me..." But she couldn't hold to consciousness, drifted into darkness again. The smell of gasoline woke her.

She opened gummy eyes, but couldn't see. The agony in her belly had dulled. She realized she couldn't get enough air and began to panic.

Where was that *thing*? Where was Paul? She'd been promised.
She heard movement again behind her, and hope flared. "Paul?"

There were no more words, no more promises, just the harsh scrape
and sulfur stench of a lighted match from somewhere above her.

Then hope died, and the flames lived again.

CHAPTER EIGHTEEN

"Rose."

I looked up, disoriented. Bella was gone, and Luke was in front of me, bent close, looking at me with worried eyes.

"Rose, what the hell happened? What was all that?"

I straightened, went to the front window to look out at the street. It was still dark out there, the city locked in pre-dawn light, the air heavy with that feeling I knew so well by now. Something was coming. Was already here, if Bella Summers was to be believed.

"It was exactly what it looked like, Luke." I moved past him to my gun safe in the cherry bookcase by the door.

Luke stood impatiently behind me while I got my gear out.

"What it looked like...it looked like a damn ghost, Rose. Are you telling me that's what we're dealing with here? Ghosts? That's what we're fightin'?"

I gave a short laugh, pushing past him again to get to my office closet, where I kept two large flashlights and my extra ammunition. "I wish it were that simple, Luke. I really do."

He kept pace with me, one step behind. "Damn it, Rose, will you please stop and talk to me?"

"I can't, Luke. I don't have time. I don't have time to stand here and argue with you about the existence of the paranormal. You saw what you saw, and you heard the same thing I did. You can either accept it and keep up, or forget it happened and go the fuck home, but I won't be the Mulder to your Scully."

He stared at me for a moment before breaking into reluctant laughter, and I found myself grinning, too. It felt good to laugh with my friend.

"All right, Rose. I'll follow where you lead. Any chance I can get my gun back now? Unless you've got an extra proton pack or somethin'."

I considered him. His betrayal hurt, but it had become such a small thing in the face of everything else. If Luke was coming with me, I didn't want him completely unarmed, even if bullets didn't do much good.

I was handing it over when my cell phone rang. I checked the ID and frowned.

"Joy? Is everything okay?"

"Mom," Lily cried, her voice high and breathless. "They came—they found us, they came for us. They're here—you have to come help. Grandpa Will—he's hurt, really bad." Her voice dissolved in tears.

God, no. She had to be safe. I'd thought, of all of us, Lily would be the safest—no touch of that other side, in the care of two capable adults who loved her. I forced myself to sound calm.

"Okay, baby, Mom is on the way. I'll be right there, Lily."

Luke had heard, and we were both running for the truck. I tossed him the keys when we got outside—he had more experience handling his own vehicle, and I wanted my hands free.

He peeled out, tires squalling.

"Lily, honey, Mom and Uncle Luke are coming—are you okay?" But the line was dead.

* * *

Another nightmare drive through my darkened city. More whispered prayers that I would find my family safe. I called Joy's house, but the line had been disconnected. Her cell phone went straight to voicemail, and so did William's. I tried Sam over and over, but got no answer in Tommy's hospital room, or on Sam's cell.

Luke didn't take his eyes off the road, his face grim.

As we got closer to Sledge, the wail of sirens grew louder. At first the pulse of emergency lights against dawn-lit houses and the shadows of shade trees made me feel relieved—I knew that even if Lily had been on her own, she'd have called 911 first. It was what Sam and I had trained her to do. Help had arrived faster than I could.

Only...

Why were there so many units?

The first fire truck I saw made my stomach drop.

We couldn't get close. The street was blocked where it joined with Union, neighbors milling anxiously in robes and pajamas. Luke pulled his truck haphazardly up to the curb. He said something, reached for me, but I was already out and shoving my way to the cordon.

A flash of my badge got me by the Memphis PD uniform working crowd control. He wasn't having a hard time of it—the gathered neighbors were subdued, talking in hushed voices, their faces grave. Everyone knew who lived behind that bright red door. Joy was the type of woman who adopted whole families; she made everyone feel like a beloved niece or nephew.

From the outside, it was hard to tell anything had happened to the house. Black smoke rose from somewhere in the back, but the brick I could see was unsmudged, the front porch intact. I thought of the framed picture of Sam with his dad and felt like crying.

I saw no sign of Joy or Lily in the crowd. I called their names. People looked at me with pity, or not at all. It felt like my heart was caving in—I couldn't breathe. Luke was beside me, helping me look. We pushed our way to the steps just as the front door swung open and a pair of FD medics came out bearing a stretcher, a zipped black body bag on top. Small, much smaller than I would have expected for a woman Joy's size.

Lily.

I fought back nausea, forced my legs to work. Stumbled up to the porch, held onto the railing. "Wait," I said to the medic with his back to me.

He turned. "Ma'am, I need you to step back, please. Get off the porch."

"Hang on, Mike, she's sheriff's department."

It took me a minute to recognize the firefighter in full gear standing next to me, his helmet and visor pushed back, sweat and grime covering his harsh features. Grady Combs, a long-time firefighter who often assisted with S.W.A.T. training.

He nodded to Luke, then turned to me. "It's Sergeant McFarland, right?"

I gave a jerky nod. "Yes. It's—is this..." I gestured to the pathetic mound beneath the black plastic.

His brows came together, the natural lines on his forehead leaving incongruous clean streaks in the soot. "Are you family?"

"Yes. This is—was, my mother-in-law's house. I'm divorced, but..." I choked. "My kids—my daughter was staying with her. Are they—is she..."

Combs' eyes softened. "No, no, there were no kids inside. Only the one fatality, and the fella we pulled from the lawn. Wasn't the fire that got him, anyway."

I sagged against the railing, relief making me dizzy. Then I remembered Lily had said William was hurt.

"The guy from the lawn—he's dead?"

Combs frowned. "He wasn't when the ambulance left. He'd lost a lot of blood, though. Gut shot, up close."

"William's alive?"

"Like I said, he was the last time I saw him."

My gaze dropped back to the stretcher. "Is this...is it Joy? McFarland? She's my—the homeowner."

Combs shrugged. "We're not sure—haven't gotten to identification yet. I'm sorry, Sergeant, she's pretty badly burned. We may need to use dentals."

I swallowed hard.

"Can I look? I might be able to give you an ID, and Sam—her

son—he shouldn't have to see her like this."

Combs studied me, lips pursed. Probably thought I couldn't handle it, but he finally shrugged again. "Mike, open it up, will you? Sergeant McFarland might be able to give us an ID."

The medics pushed the stretcher back on the porch. I stepped closer, Luke hovering at my shoulder, waiting for me to lose it. I told myself not to. The sun might be making an appearance, but this night wasn't over for me yet.

With the black plastic pulled back, the stench of charred flesh became almost unbearable. I breathed through my mouth, leaning in closer. The face was unrecognizable, a blackened and twisted skull, flesh and adipose melted to the bone. No hair left, nothing to tell me who this pathetically small burden on the stretcher used to be.

I reached past the guy Combs had called Mike, pulled the zipper down further.

I felt a sliver of hope. The body was small, limbs drawn up against the torso the way bodies do in intense heat. Joy was a short woman, but she had a lot of padding on her. I couldn't be sure, but it looked like this had been a much slimmer adult. A glimpse of dulled metal on the left hand caught my eye. Jewelry—a wedding ring. I knew Joy's didn't fit anymore; she wore it on a chain around her neck. Close to her heart, she often said.

I sighed, looked up at Combs with a tremulous smile. "I don't think it's her. Jewelry doesn't match. See the ring?"

Combs leaned closer, flicked on a flashlight and pointed it at the charred fingers, curled close against the body. "You don't recognize that one?"

"No, I..." I stopped, looked again. Realized I did recognize it—rose gold, with the tiniest of diamond chips in the center.

Nothing ostentatious—our rewards aren't here on earth. This is good enough for now.

"Sergeant?" Combs looked concerned, took a step closer, touched my elbow.

I straightened. "This isn't my mother-in-law. This is my mother."

257

CHAPTER NINETEEN

"*Sam.*"

Sam couldn't tell if the voice had been part of his dream or the noise that woke him from it. Unconsciousness blended seamlessly into reality in the darkness of this place, and though it seemed the voice still echoed, he couldn't be sure.

He became aware of sharp pain at the base of his skull, stabbing down his neck to his spine. He lifted a hand and gingerly felt around, drawing a breath through his teeth when his fingers touched a knot under ragged flesh, sending a zing of agony through his head.

He vaguely remembered waking up before; how long ago, he had no way to tell. He'd felt his way around as best he could, but there had been little to tell him where he was. A cold dirt floor, stone walls. No windows that he could find. A short flight of stairs that led up to a heavy locked door. Was it night or day? What time had it been before he'd lost consciousness? How the hell had that happened, anyway?

Zack, he remembered slowly. Zack at the hospital, early morning,

LAUREL HIGHTOWER

acting strange. Wanting to know where Rose was, getting pissed that she wasn't there. Maneuvering behind Sam at some point. Zack hit me, Sam thought. Then that thing—whatever it was, creeping out from the shadows of the hospital room, where maybe it had been all along. He started shaking, tried to stop, to concentrate. The last thing he remembered was seeing that…seeing *something* pick Tommy up out of the bed. Tommy…

Sam tried to sit up, and was filled with panic when he couldn't move his legs. They felt numb, heavy. He reached out tentatively, felt thick curls under one hand, soft feather-like hair under the other.

Tommy and Lily, both in his lap. He sagged with relief. They were okay and here with him, not alone with Zack or whatever had attacked him. At least he could protect them. He put a hand on each of their backs, took comfort in the steady rise and fall of their breathing. They were both fast asleep, but Tommy was still and peaceful, with none of the restless twitching he'd been doing in the hospital.

Good, Sam thought. *Let them sleep through this nightmare if they can.* He leaned his head back against the cold wall and tried to think, but it was hard to concentrate. He tried to listen in the darkness, to find anything that might give him his bearings, but silence shrouded his small family. He wondered where Rose was, and why the hell Zack had wanted her so badly. Sam hoped like hell Zack hadn't found her.

The thought of Rose nearly overwhelmed him with grief. The type of trouble they were in now was exactly the kind of thing Rose was built for, and at any other time Sam would have just waited for her to kick in the door and start shooting the place up. But he'd driven her away, not trusting her, making her think she was dangerous. Probably pushing her straight into the waiting arms of Luke Harris, he thought bitterly.

Part of Sam still couldn't shake the image of Rose standing with a gun trained on Tommy as he lay helpless in that hospital bed. She'd been convinced that whatever she'd seen there instead of her son posed an immediate threat, and it made him sick to think what might have happened if he hadn't walked in when he did. Even after seeing some of the same horrors Rose must have seen in the hospital, knowing what kind of threat they posed, Sam still wasn't sure what would have happened if she had pulled the trigger. He hated feeling alone, like he couldn't fully trust her. He wanted them to be a team on this, like they'd always been.

Stupid waste of time, remembering the naked loneliness on her face when he'd sent her away, the image of her climbing into Luke's truck. What did that matter now? It hurt to think of, and he pushed it away. Shook his head, winced at the fresh agony the movement brought. Once it subsided, he tried again to think of what he should do. Where the hell was he? How far from help? Would anyone hear him if he called? Would the right people hear him?

Wherever they were being kept was underground, the floor and walls made of cool packed earth, studded with an occasional outcrop of root growth. This place was old, far older than his turn-of-the-century home. Sam wished he had Rose's feel for places, for their histories and their...all right, their intentions. Might as well use Rose's word for it. Sam had an idea that even trapped in silent darkness, Rose would have been able to skate her fingers over the earthen walls and figure out where they were. His heavy head drooped, his eyes closed. He was drifting off again when the insistent voice returned.

"*Sam. Wake up.*"

There was no mistaking it this time. Sam opened his eyes wide, searching the darkness for the voice's owner. For a long time nothing happened.

"Hello?" he called tentatively. "Who's there? Can you hear me? I'm down here with my kids..." He choked, coughing violently against air that seemed too thick. Stars burst against the blackness behind his eyelids as his lungs spasmed.

"*Sam. I hear you. It's time to wake up.*"

Gasping for breath, Sam reached a shaking hand into the darkness. "Where are you? We need help."

He jerked back when he felt a cool hand grasp his.

"*I'm a friend, Sam. You don't have a lot of time. We need to get you out of here.*"

"I can't see you—I can't see anything. Is there a light somewhere?"

"*No. It's best not to draw their attention, anyway. You'll have to feel your way. Stand up, I'll guide you.*"

Sam struggled up, moving the kids gently. "What do you mean, draw their attention? Who?"

When the voice came again, it was close to his ear. "*You're not alone down here, Sam. They're coming.*"

As Sam listened in the blackness of the underground cellar, he began to hear the stirrings.

CHAPTER TWENTY

I stood with Luke beside his truck, outside the cordoned-off area around what had been Joy's house. The sun had partially risen, but the street was still dark. The sky was reddish, providing a half-light, smoke still rising into the hazy atmosphere. I didn't know if I was giving weight to the banal because of what Bella had told me, or if it was just the return of all my old bad senses, but the world seemed heavy with something. Expectation, maybe, or just plain fear. *The dead will walk the earth and outnumber the living*... Whatever was coming, it was coming fast. I wondered if I'd be alive to see tomorrow's sunrise.

We'd found no trace of Joy or Lily, and Joy still wasn't answering her cell phone. William was in surgery and hadn't regained consciousness in the ambulance or in pre-op, according to the ER nurse I'd spoken with. I'd tried Sam's number again with no luck, and no one was answering at the NICU desk. When I called the main switchboard and asked to be connected, they transferred me twice and disconnected me twice. It seemed sinister, but I hoped it was just hospital run-around.

Grady Combs had assisted Luke and me in talking to the neighbors, asking if anyone had seen where Joy and Lily went. No one had, but several people reported seeing a strange car parked across the street shortly before the fire, and the closest neighbors said they'd heard gunshots before the fire broke out. At least two people had called 911 in addition to Joy's own call.

Tom Allen lived directly across the street from Joy in a two-story red brick. He told me he was sure the car had been an old Cutlass 88. Dark-colored, but not black. Dark blue or gray.

"Or emerald green?" I asked in a flat voice.

He thought about it, then nodded, cinching his bathrobe tighter. "Yep. Could have been green, sure. Was kind of rusted around the edges."

I thanked him. When he'd gone, I told Luke that at least answered the question of how Cora had gotten here.

"It was my dad's car. He didn't drive it much. Parked it out in an old horse barn. It must have escaped the fire."

He looked down at me, his expression unreadable. "Your mom kept it all these years, drove it down off a mountain in Kentucky, crept into Joy's house, and shot the place up. Then she burned herself alive. Is that what happened here?"

My mother burned herself alive. I probed the thought carefully, wondering if it bothered me to know Cora Summers, my last remaining family member, was dead. I was an orphan. Even that knowledge didn't elicit any kind of an emotional response. What kind of person did that make me? Was I as one-dimensional as I'd represented myself to Bella? Just a killer cop, no humanity left? And why hadn't that thought bothered me either?

I looked at Luke, then up and down the street again. "Problem with that theory, Harris, is that the car's gone."

He grunted, leaned against his truck. "Maybe Joy and Lily took it."

"Without bothering to call me, and leaving William behind?" I shook my head. "No way."

Someone spoke up from behind us. "Charlie came with your mother."

We both turned.

263

"Neal."

My tone was unwelcoming, but as usual it didn't make a difference. The FBI agent came striding through the crowd, his slippery smile absent for once as he cast a glance over his shoulder at Joy's house. When he looked back at me, I could see how tired his eyes were, and he'd missed a patch shaving his jaw.

Part of me was glad to see him—he was the only one of us with any firsthand knowledge of the Whispers. Bella had seemed to bear out Neal's story about his son and how he'd been caught in the cross-fire, but I still didn't trust him.

"What are you doing here?" I asked.

"I came here when I couldn't find you at your place or the hospital." He turned to Luke. "Good morning, Mr. Harris. Nice to see you again."

Luke crossed his arms across his broad chest and said nothing, turning his back on Neal and staring at the smoking husk of Joy's house.

I chased away the creeping disappointment I'd felt since realizing Luke and Neal had been working together. It didn't mean they couldn't both be of use to me now.

I turned to look at Neal. "Why? Why are you so sure it was Charlie? Why would my mother be with him? What was it they were trying to accomplish?"

"I think they're both operating under the influence of someone else, Rose. I think whoever it is wants you corralled. Wants to either get you to do something they want, or prevent you from doing something—like helping Ethan and Tommy. They're going after the people you love, Rose. That's what I think."

Corralled. That was exactly how I was starting to feel. Andy, or something pretending to be Andy, had told me to go back to Kentucky, and I believed that was where Bella was sending me too. *Where the walls are thinnest.* That had to mean the old farmhouse. It was where I'd first heard the Whispers, where they'd concentrated their efforts. Where they were strongest. Corralled by who, though? Paul Summers? Could Bella be right? Was that what waited for me at the end of this long road? My father? I shuddered. To end this, I would have to face my father.

I looked at Luke.

"You're calling the shots, Rose," he said.

Was I? Somehow, it didn't feel that way. I had the uncomfortable suspicion that I'd been two steps behind the whole time.

"All right then, road trip it is. Back to my old Kentucky home." I hoped the dread I felt didn't come through in my voice.

"Let me come with you, Rose. I can help you." Neal's face was guileless, even frightened. His green eyes were strained. "Please, Rose. I'm the only one who knows anything about what you're dealing with—and the only person with as much to lose."

I studied him. I wanted to say no; I didn't trust Neal, but he was right. He was all I had.

"Fine. Get in the truck. But Neal?"

He turned back to me, his smile fading as I backed him up three paces.

"You fuck with me, or you endanger my kids in any way, and you're a grease spot, you understand me? No second chances."

I didn't wait for a response, but held my hand out to Luke for the keys. Both men climbed into the truck without a word.

I knew I couldn't leave town without seeing Sam, even though the thought made my stomach dip. Making sure he and Tommy were safe while I did...whatever the hell I was going to do. I didn't have to come inside the hospital room, and I'd leave all my weapons in the car. Fear of Sam's rejection made my hands sweaty on the steering wheel, but I knew I couldn't leave things the way they were between us. There was a good chance I wouldn't be coming back, whatever Bella's plans entailed.

The city was deserted on the short drive back to Le Bonheur. Traffic should have been picking up; it wasn't quite time for the morning rush hour yet, but there should have been plenty of cars on the road. The sky was still that odd overcast gray and red, as though the sun had gotten stuck halfway up the sky and stopped. A sense of unreality settled in when I swung into the hospital parking garage and saw no one out and about. There was only one other vehicle on the ground floor, parked up against the far wall.

I climbed out of the truck and turned back to Luke, handing over my weapons while he watched, his brows raised.

"What the hell is this?"

"Hospital policy," I said. "Stay here with him, okay?" I nodded towards Neal. "I'll just be a minute."

"Not afraid we'll be plotting against you while you're gone?" Luke asked.

He spoke calmly, but I could see the bitterness in his face. I wondered if I could have been wrong.

"Whatever, Luke. If you're not going to help me, then just save me the time and piss off while I'm gone, will you?"

I turned my back on him and hurried up the walk back to the hospital. I hadn't even made it up the sloping hallway to the elevators before Allen Daughtry found me.

"Rose," he said. "Finally. Did you get my messages?"

"No, I didn't." I pulled my phone out, but back in the hospital there was no signal, and I saw no messages or missed calls. "I just came back to check in with Sam and Tommy." I felt nervous, wondering what, if anything, Sam had told Dr. Daughtry about my absence.

"Shit," said Daughtry, raking his hair back from his forehead. "So you don't know."

"Know what?"

"They're gone, Rose. Both of them. They've been missing since early morning."

* * *

Luke was dozing in the front seat. He jerked awake when I wrenched the driver's side door open, blinking at me through bleary brown eyes.

"Rose? Are Sam and Tommy okay?"

I threw myself in and sat clutching the steering wheel. "They're gone. They're both gone."

Luke sat up. "How the hell did that happen? Did Tommy wake up?"

I shook my head. "The doctor doesn't think so. He checked the last information the machines recorded and said the vitals didn't support that. He also has no idea why the alarms didn't go off when Tommy was disconnected from the monitors, or why no one noticed them walking out."

"No one saw *anything*?" asked Neal from the back seat.

"He says not, but he also said things were weird in there—he can't find any of his regular staff, and people were acting oddly. I didn't go anywhere but Tommy's room on the NICU floor, but he's right—it's a damn ghost town in there."

Luke leaned forward, peering out the windshield. "It's a ghost town out here, too, Rose. Everywhere we've been so far this morning, except Joy's house. Did you notice the traffic on the way over here?"

I nodded, chewing my lip. "A weekday, and nobody on the road for rush hour." Just as Bella had said, Memphis was on the receiving end of whatever was coming through that open door.

"The sun, too," said Neal. "Whatever's going on, it's getting worse."

"What the hell do we do now?" asked Luke. "You think they're with Joy and Lily? Or should we check Sam's place first?"

I shook my head slowly. "No. They won't be there. Bella was right—there's only one way to make this stop, to get them back safe. We have to go back to where it started."

* * *

The charred skeleton of my family home came into view as we crested the low rise halfway up the drive, Luke's pickup crunching over gravel made sparse by time and erosion. There was no blinding recognition, no sense of familiarity or coming home. The two-story farmhouse squatted in a slight dip in the ground, the outer structure still intact, the stone walls darkened around the edges by soot. The roof had fallen in on the right side, leaving the top floor open to the elements. The front entrance gaped, the tall wooden door burned and rotted long ago, and there was no glass left in any of the front windows. There was a large, treeless area encircling the burned wreckage—I remembered the landscape being heavily forested in my childhood, but it was dead now. Nothing stirred, and whatever unearthly element kept these blighted acres shrouded in darkness seemed to glide aside, letting weak sunlight spill in a wide circle around the house. It could almost have been beautiful, if you didn't know what hell it had been to live there.

I killed the headlights as I coasted up to the crumbling stone gateposts that stood at the top of the rise, pulled over to the right of the entrance, and turned off the engine. From here we would go on foot.

Luke climbed out of the truck without looking at me. The drive up from Memphis had been eerie—the sun still refused to rise and the roads were empty. Whatever was going on was obviously already spreading. The six-hour drive had been mostly silent, Luke having run out of arguments before we reached Nashville.

I had listened to him without interruption, and when he finally talked himself to a standstill, I said, "You're right. Everything you're saying is right. It doesn't change what I have to do. Come if you want, not if you don't."

He'd spent the rest of the drive staring out the window in silence, but he hadn't asked to go back.

Now he was around the side of the truck, loading up on ammo for the .45 in case we ran into something with a pulse. I didn't plan on putting him in the way of anything we might meet out here, but if I were successful in calling the Whispers, who knew what might come with them?

Neal climbed out and stood staring down into the dark valley. He'd said little on the drive—he probably didn't need to, now that I'd agreed to his plan of action. I still didn't trust him; I didn't like the way he'd been parceling information out to me when it suited him. I doubted he'd told me everything, and I planned to keep an eye on him.

I took my .38 from the glove box and put it in the spare webbed holster I'd unearthed from my bedroom closet. I added my .22 semi-auto pistol, then stood looking down into the hollow and listening, reaching out with all my senses.

Even with my mind as wide open as I could manage and my concentration focused on my search, I felt no trace of my family, or of anyone else. It didn't mean I could trust that we were alone—I didn't know how far my senses extended, or how reliable they were, but this place felt empty, and I was glad.

The stretch of stinking land behind those gates was hidden by a psychic darkness that matched the fevered shadows and muttering threats of the burned-out trees and charred grasslands. It was easy to see why this place had been left to rot—no family could be happy here, no crops would ever grow. None that would be fit for human consumption, anyway.

Luke laid a tentative hand on my shoulder. "Rose?"

I looked up at him, but couldn't see his eyes in the dim light. "Yeah, I'm ready."

Neal walked over to us. "Rose, you need to be prepared for whatever you find down there."

I studied him. "What is it I'm going to find, Neal?"

"I don't know for certain. I just know you won't be able to trust your senses, okay? You might see some things that seem incredibly real, but they won't be. You can't let them sway you from your purpose, do you understand?"

Luke snorted. "You just stay where I can see you, got it?" He turned back to me. "Get behind me, Rose. I'll go down first."

"Not this time, Luke. I go first. Keep your eyes open." I turned my back on him before he could argue, took a breath, then passed through the gates, sidestepping the gravel drive. I crunched over dry, brittle grass, moving cautiously and hoping not to trip over a fallen tree or catch my foot in a rabbit hole. It was mid-afternoon but might as well have been midnight—the half-light of the hidden sun couldn't penetrate the farm's darkness, and the moon hung pale in the sky above.

There was a nagging buzz of discomfort in my head that quickly grew worse. A dull pain throbbed unpleasantly and made me feel muzzy, disoriented, getting worse as I got closer to the farmhouse. I turned my head from side to side, listening hard, but there was nothing, only a maddening impression of sounds just outside the reach of my hearing. I was flying blind, the silence disconcerting.

I passed the remains of the smaller farm fence that had marked the boundaries of my old front yard. No good memories here—only punishments, pain, fear. Stark loneliness hit me as I stopped just shy of the dark doorway.

Something was wrong.

I turned, saw Luke and Neal only a few feet away, and realized what was missing. I couldn't feel them either, and I should have been able to. Living people in close proximity gave the brightest signals of all, but it was like I was alone. Something about this place was dulling my senses.

"Wait," I said. "There's something wrong here."

A shrieking cry sounded, dragging out into a hoarse yell. Human? The sound echoed through the little valley where the farmhouse sat. It was impossible to pinpoint where it came from.

We froze, scanning the hills above us for movement, Luke and I with guns in hand.

"What the hell was *that*?" rumbled Luke.

Neal looked at me. "Rose? Are you getting anything?"

I shook my head. "No. Nothing. That's what I was getting ready to say—I'm not picking up on *anything*."

Luke looked at me uneasily. "What are you talking about, Rose? Are you saying you can read minds or something?"

"No, nothing like that. It's more like...energy signatures, I guess. I can tell if someone else is around. Right now I can't feel anything."

"That's a good thing, right?" Luke asked.

"No, it's not. I'm not even getting anything on the two of you, and I should be. That means something here's blocking me. There could be anything here—anyone."

Neal said nothing, just looked grave and turned away again.

"What does that mean?" asked Luke. "What do we do?"

Before I could answer, something burst through the overgrown hedges to our right with a sound somewhere between a snarl and a scream.

Whatever it was took Luke down with a meaty thud, followed by a gristly sound I couldn't identify. Neal went sprawling, well out of reach.

"Luke!" I reached him in two long strides.

He was face-down, struggling weakly against the weight of

something large on his back. A man, I realized, though the filthy, matted creature snarling and clawing at Luke was barely recognizable as such. I leveled the .38 at his head.

"Get the fuck off him or I'll blow your goddamn head off."

He didn't flinch, didn't even look at me. The murky half-light glinted off something wickedly sharp in his hand. He dug his fingers into Luke's curly hair and yanked his head back.

I squeezed off three shots in quick succession. The man's filthy, once-white button-down shirt bloomed red and he slumped to the ground without making a sound.

White button-down shirt?

I stepped around Luke and knelt next to the man I'd shot, fighting a bad feeling as I turned him over.

Zack.

My friend, so troubled the last time I'd seen him, going on about seeing his long-dead brother. Trying to drag me back to the house on Union, for God only knew what purpose. Something bad had happened to him, had changed him, and I hadn't found the time to help. Now he lay motionless on the cold ground, his smudged glasses catching a glare of weak light, blood trickling from his open mouth. Blood spread rapidly on the grass beneath him—I'd hit him with all three shots. He was gone.

I couldn't feel anything but numb.

Luke was still lying face-down, not moving. I turned away from Zack, tried to roll Luke onto his side. He groaned, his eyes shut tight.

"Luke?" I struggled to get him onto his back so I could look him over. "What's wrong? Are you hurt?"

Luke didn't answer. He opened bleary brown eyes, looking puzzled, and raised a hand slowly to his chest. The hilt of a second blade was protruding at a steep angle. His hand came back soaked a dark red, and he blinked at it.

Everything seemed to slow down, panic just out of reach, pressing in against me in my bubble of strange calm. I pushed it back, something in me insisting that this could be fixed.

Luke's blood-slicked hand found the hilt but I pushed it away.

"Luke, damn it, leave it alone. You know better than to pull that shit out."

"It—hurts," he said.

"No kidding. You think it's gonna hurt less if you pull that knife out?" I moved around to his head, lifting it to cushion him on my lap. I reached forward and felt lightly around the wound, careful not to nudge the knife. Luke drew in his breath with a hiss.

My hands were sticky with blood, but I could see nothing of Luke's wound, so I carefully unbuttoned his shirt and peeled back the torn, sodden material. My fingers were steady, but the panic was getting closer. I wasn't a medic, but I'd gone through the requisite first aid training for S.W.A.T. members. I knew Luke's biggest risk was a tension pneumothorax—trapped air in the chest cavity, which could eventually collapse his lung and put pressure on his heart. How quickly that would happen depended in part on whether his lung had been punctured by the blade, and how big the opening in his chest wall was.

Luke's breathing was labored, but I didn't hear the telltale wheeze or see any bubbles around the edge of the blade, so I thought there was a good chance it had missed his lung. I needed to close off the wound's airflow, but didn't have my S.W.A.T. gear with me. It wasn't even back in the truck; I'd left it in my Charger back in Memphis. I stripped my overshirt off, pressed it against the wound with as much pressure as I could muster.

I was trying to think, figure out what to do next, but my mind had slowed down along with everything else. After a moment that stretched into eternity, I thought to fumble my cell out of my pocket. It took an age for my fingers, slippery with Luke's blood, to work the screen, but when I did, there was no signal.

Of course there wasn't. Nothing was going to go right tonight, I realized. Nothing would be easy.

Luke's breathing grew louder, and I looked down to see his eyes open, watching me. I tried to smile reassuringly.

"That...bad?" he wheezed.

"Fucking flesh wound, Harris. Don't be such a pussy."

He tried to laugh, was wracked with spasms of coughing instead, blood flowing from the edges of his wound.

"Hey, stop moving, okay? You're going to make it worse."

"Can it get worse?"

"Are you breathing okay?"

He knit his brows. "I—I think so. Everything hurts. Feels heavy. Wish you'd quit pushing on me like that."

"Fine then, you do it. We need to keep pressure on it, keep air from getting in, okay?"

Neal appeared, gave me an unreadable look. "I just went up the hill to try for a signal. There's nothing. Do you know if there are any neighbors? A landline we could use?"

I shook my head. "Back then the nearest farm was at least five miles, but that doesn't mean anything now. I can take the truck, go get help."

"No," said Luke, his voice low but strong. "You have to go, Rose. Do what you came here to do."

I frowned, tightening my hold on him. "Not a chance, Luke. I'm not leaving you here."

Neal knelt next to me, put a hand on my shoulder. "There's no time, Rose. You've got to get in there."

"Look, I can't just leave him out here alone."

"He won't be alone. I'll take the truck and go for help—he'll be okay."

"No," I said, but Luke pushed my hands away, put his own over my sodden shirt.

"Rose," he wheezed. "Go. Get in there—do what you have to do for Tommy. You heard what that ghost lady said—he's almost out of time." He pressed tightly on his chest. "I got this, okay? I'll be fine."

Neal squeezed my shoulder. "Tonight could be your last chance to make this right, Rose. Your family can't wait."

I looked from Luke to Neal and back again. I knew I needed to go, that time was growing short for all of us, but leaving felt wrong. I was missing something, but my mind was still encased in molasses.

Luke shoved me again, feebly. "Go," he rumbled. He tried to smile, but a stab of agony twisted his mouth instead.

I put my hands over his. "Keep strong pressure on it, you understand me? You need to keep air from getting in there. And don't move the knife." I looked back at Neal. "You're going for help, right? Because he can't last like this."

Neal nodded. "Of course, Rose."

I ran a hand through Luke's thick curls one more time, my eyes dry. "I'll be back for you." I said, and bent down to kiss his cool forehead. I stood and turned my back on my partner for the last time.

I stood in front of the yawning darkness of the open door. Then I stepped across the threshold, and straight into hell.

CHAPTER TWENTY-ONE

Luke watched Rose get swallowed up by the darkness beyond the door, fighting an overwhelming feeling of loss. He was a fuck-up. He'd planned to walk into hell with her and make sure that she, at least, came out on the other side. Now she was alone, and so was he.

Darkness was beginning to tug at the edges of his vision, the pressure heavier with every breath. The excruciating pain in his chest had dulled somewhat, which was worrying in a removed sort of way. He felt feverish, except for the place where Rose had kissed him, which still felt blessedly cool. He'd even had the ridiculous fancy that when she'd touched him, the pain had receded. Stupid. He'd never been realistic where Rose was concerned. Not from the first day she'd walked into his life, a solemn academy cadet with a wicked sense of humor and a steadfast loyalty he'd never seen in anyone else. He hated knowing what she believed about him—that he would have betrayed her to Evan Neal, or to anyone else. He simply hadn't been able to find the words to make her understand; in his typical blundering fashion, he'd just made things worse.

Luke dragged his narrowing gaze from the spot where Rose had disappeared to where Neal stood, a monumental effort.

Neal loomed over him, watching speculatively, making no move to get to the truck. Luke wasn't surprised.

"That was selfless of you, Mr. Harris," Neal said, sidling closer. "I was hoping you'd do something like that."

Luke was only able to keep his eyes open with great effort. "Like what?" he finally managed.

Neal turned away to watch the dark hole that Rose had stepped through. Luke followed his gaze, then blinked.

The opening was gone. In its place was soot-stained stone, looking like it had always been there.

Neal gave no sign that he'd noticed. "Like leaving her alone," he answered. "Whatever else happens, Rose needs to face this alone."

"Why?" Luke asked after what seemed like a terribly long time.

Neal still wasn't looking at him. "I didn't ask."

Luke had been fading, pulled along on a tide of darkness and exhaustion. He knew he was dying, from blood loss if nothing else, but right now it seemed like a secondary concern. Neal's words dragged him back from the edge, reminding him that there was something left to do. The pieces were clicking together now, too slowly to save himself, but maybe he could still be of use to Rose. It had been Zack, Luke realized. Zack had been the one giving Neal information from the first night. If Zack and Neal were working together, for Charlie Akers or someone else, then Rose was in deep trouble. Luke tried to shake his head and clear it. When that didn't work, he struggled to sit up.

That did it. Fresh agony rolled through his entire body, his chest a fire all its own. His vision sharpened, though he knew it was temporary. "Ask who?"

Neal turned, his eyebrows raised. When he saw Luke struggling, he smiled. Luke wanted to punch that smile right off his face.

"It never mattered to me," Neal said. "Either way it happened, if Rose could help Ethan, that would be fine. I don't particularly wish her any harm. Although," he said, frowning, "I hope I would have been more helpful to another parent who came to me for help."

It was so hard to focus. "What the hell are you talking about?"

Neal was smiling again, watching Luke curiously. "You know, it's odd, how little she shared with you. You don't know anything about her family at all, do you? You've known her longer than anyone— longer than Sam, even. I thought partners trusted each other with everything."

Luke said nothing.

"You don't even know why we're here tonight, do you?"

"I don't...need...to know. Never have."

"Admirable, I suppose," observed Neal, though his tone suggested it was anything but. "Maybe every woman needs a doormat. Who knows. In any case, this is one time you probably should have demanded an explanation. At the very least, it might have spared you, well, *that*." He gestured to Luke's blood-soaked chest.

"Why?"

"Why what? Oh, why we're here? Suddenly taking an interest, are we?"

Luke said nothing, breathing shallowly, conserving his strength. At least, he hoped that was what he was doing.

Neal turned his back on Luke again, facing the blank stone wall, tapping his open palm against his leg. "We're here so Rose can fulfill her destiny, Mr. Harris. She should never have walked away from that fire eighteen years ago. She wasn't meant to. Everything that's happened since then, it's been a mistake. That's the real reason everything's so fucked up now. That's the reason all those horrible things are roaming the earth. Why my boy is sick. She threw the balance off, and as long as she's alive, Ethan won't get better. But tonight, everything's going to be put right again."

"Put...right?"

Neal still wasn't looking at him, which made it easier for Luke to ease over on his right hip. He bit his lip as agony rolled through him, but after a struggle he was able to get to the .45 wedged against his left thigh.

"Yes. She'll heal my boy—when she lets the Whispers take her, he'll be freed. Then she'll burn."

Luke growled low in his throat.

"I'm not the bad guy here, Mr. Harris. If Rose had believed me, if she'd been willing to help of her own accord, this could all have gone very differently. We could have worked together, been partners in saving our children. I haven't asked her to do anything she hasn't come to willingly. It may not have been what Charlie wanted, but I gave her a choice. If she'd agreed to help Ethan from the beginning, instead of poking around at the FBI, having her bosses call my bosses and getting me fired..." Neal's voice grew hard, his open palm clenched into a fist.

Luke wanted to laugh, but he didn't have the strength. "If you thought she'd...respond to threats...you know her less than you think you do. You're a...crazy fuck, and she knew it from the first."

Neal's body relaxed. "My conscience is clear, Mr. Harris. I've done very little. It was Charlie and Cora who took the little girl and burned down the old lady's house." He smiled. "Charlie's been busy. It was he and Mr. Dayton there who took the little boy and Mr. McFarland." He nodded over at the bloody mess that had once been Zack Dayton. "He's been quite helpful, ever since he heard what he wanted to hear over on Union Avenue. I could never have gotten as close to Rose as I did without him passing along helpful information."

"You...bastard. You made her think...it was me. How?"

"Oh, I *am* sorry about that, but the thing was, I needed her isolated, and you were too close to her. You'll be glad to know it took a hell of a lot of convincing. In the end, I had to have some help—the folks I work with are pretty good at making people see and hear what they need to push them in the right direction. The touch of a button and there it was, your voice on the recording. Until she heard that, she was calling me ten kinds of liar. I hope it's a comfort that even though she doesn't love you, she trusts you implicitly. Or at least she did."

Actually, it was a comfort. It lifted Luke's heart to know that Rose had needed supernatural intervention before she'd believe ill of him. "If...everyone else did the...heavy lifting, what the fuck...did they need you for?"

"My only role was to help get Rose here, alone, and make sure she didn't get back out this way."

Luke was panting, his vision starring as he struggled to raise the gun. "How...are you going to stop her?" he growled.

Neal turned, that slippery smile on his face. Whatever he'd been going to say died on his lips, right along with his greasy grin.

Luke pulled the trigger, a prayer on his lips.

Evan Neal's face was lost in a spray of blood and brain matter. He slumped sideways, his body hitting the hard ground with a thud.

It was the last thing Luke heard—his world went peacefully quiet after that. He breathed a final sigh, and stared up at the darkened sky.

CHAPTER TWENTY-TWO

I walked into silence so complete I feared I had lost my hearing.

I'd braced myself for battle as I crossed the threshold to my old home. The Whispers had increased in intensity each time they'd appeared, and I'd assumed that here, where the walls were thin, they would be at their zenith.

Instead, I was surrounded by the hush of a sleeping house. Everything looked the same as I remembered—the wood-paneled walls in the parlor where I stood, the faded yellow flowered wallpaper below the chair rail. The furniture was sparse; a set of hard seated ladder-backed chairs arranged in a semicircle in front of the cold hearth, two side tables pushed up against the far wall, a woven rug on the polished wood floor. Above the mantle hung a particularly gruesome depiction of Jesus on the cross.

No television, no radio. Electric wall sconces turned down low, leaving the room in deep shadow. The low glare caught the glass on a set of portraits that hung to my right, marching up the wall that supported the narrow staircase to my parents' bedroom.

I moved closer to the photos, ignoring the central piece—an unsmiling wedding photo from the day Cora and Paul Summers said their vows. Instead, I headed straight for the ones of Andy.

Andy. My golden brother, two years older. My protector. The only reason I'd survived that night—he'd been outside already, safe from the fire, but he'd come back for me. He'd opened my locked bedroom door, rolled me in a rug to put out the flames that had already consumed my cotton nightgown. I remembered it clearly, all of it. The pain of the flames, the terror of being trapped in my bedroom with the raging fire.

The fire...

This was wrong—of course it was wrong. None of these things could still be here. The fire had ravaged this place eighteen years ago. All our possessions had been lost, save for the things in my parents' room upstairs. The house had been destroyed, leaving only the blackened stone shell I'd seen from the outside, the roof caved in, the windows broken out. This was impossible.

I turned, expecting the house to melt into the horror I knew lurked beneath this vision.

The scene remained unchanged.

I closed my eyes, shook my head, tried to clear it, but when I opened my eyes again, it was still there.

I went to the front door, but the latch wouldn't lift. I shook it hard, putting every ounce of my strength into moving the handle, but it wouldn't budge. I peeled off my gloves for a better grip, but stopped before I touched the door, gazing down at my hands.

My clean hands. My smooth, unblemished hands—hands I hadn't seen for more than half my life. I held them in front of my face, staring at them, waiting for this vision to fade, but it didn't. Cautiously I touched the back of my left hand with the fingers of my right.

Smooth, just like it looked. My hands shaking, I pulled my shirt up and looked down.

My scars were gone. Tears started to my eyes, and I wished Sam could see me like this.

"Sam," I whispered. Sam was in trouble—the kids—something. I didn't know; my mind was hazy.

A board creaked in the hallway overhead, and a door shut. I looked up, my heart thudding too fast. Daddy was awake.

I backed away from the staircase, a hand over my mouth to quiet my breathing. Daddy couldn't find me up at this time of night—I had to get back in my room, back in my bed before he saw me. When I looked down to watch where I stepped, I saw my feet were now bare, the hem of a long cotton nightgown brushing their tops. I crept silently through the parlor to the back hallway that led to my room, stopping at the threshold to listen.

There was a long silence, and I allowed myself to hope I'd gone undetected.

Then a crashing of heavy footsteps, thundering along the upstairs hall and down the stairs at a run.

I knew I'd been discovered, and my only thought was to get away, back to my room, and shut the door, try to block it with the bed until the worst of Daddy's rage had spent itself. I turned and ran, my feet cold on the wood floor, terror robbing me of breath.

The lights went out, plunging the whole house into darkness. I tripped on the edge of the hall rug, crashed into the wall as I tried to catch myself and fell to my knees.

I stayed there, disoriented, trying and failing to silence my breathing. I listened, but couldn't hear movement anywhere. Where had he gone? He'd been just behind me—*where was he?*

I heard the *whump* and hiss as flame leapt to life only a few feet in front of me, lifted my eyes to see where it was coming from.

His face was only inches from mine when I met his empty eyes. For a moment I was sure it was Charlie, but as the small flame dancing in his hand bathed his charred and darkened features with sporadic light, catching the shadowed hollows of gaunt cheekbones and grinning spaces between his few remaining teeth, I saw that he still had his jaw. Long patches of hair hung limply in places, but mostly his skull was a wizened, blackened mass. Impossibly, the gold wire-rimmed glasses he wore in every memory still perched on the edge of his nasal cavity, the earpieces melted to the place where his ears used to be.

"Daddy?" I whispered.

Past and present merged again.

He was so terribly still that for a frozen breath I dared to hope it was just a husk, a burned-out lifeless body that should have been buried eighteen years ago but had somehow found its lonely way back here. I saw the sideways flicker of the dying flame as he closed his palm around it at the same time I felt his hot breath graze my hand.

"*Rose*," came the terrible, creaking whisper as the tiny flame burned out.

I scrabbled backward in the pitch black, feeling for the wall, hoping for a door. I could hear him moving, feel the air rush as he came for me, smell the stench of his charred and rotted flesh.

I clutched at the handle of a bedroom door. It might buy me only minutes, but I would take anything. I twisted it and fell backward into the room, slamming the door shut in my father's face, reaching for the knob to lock it, sobbing for breath.

I heard him crash into the wood, rattle the handle.

"*Rosie*," he crooned. "*My little Rosebud...*"

I shuddered at that endearment, fighting a surge of nausea. I looked down, hoping to find reality restored, but I was still wearing that thin cotton gown and nothing else. Somehow I'd been transported back eighteen years, or at least I was meant to think so.

There came a creaking from outside the door, a light tapping, and then he spoke again. "*My little Rose came back to me*," he croaked in a voice rusty from years of silence.

I heard a sigh, and the grinding of joints long dried and dead. I pictured him on the other side, settling himself on the floor to torture me through the closed door. I scooted away, back against the far wall as I tried furiously to think.

"*Brave little Rose. Walked through fire and made it out the other side.*"

Fury rose within me as I thought of my handsome older brother, who hadn't come out the other side. I knew my survival that night had nothing to do with bravery—at least not my own—and everything to do with sacrifice. My dearest Andy, his promising life cut short by the actions of a madman we'd both called Dad.

Dad had set the fire that night—I knew that now. With all my other memories, that one had returned as well. The flames had started in my room, but they were his flames. Paul Summers was the fire-starter, not me. I had doubted it, just as he and my mother had wanted me to do for years. But I'd known for certain when he brought that flame to life in the hallway.

"It's more than you can say, isn't it? You didn't make it out the other side. You died in the fire you set, you sick son of a bitch."

The hall was silent, and I hoped I'd struck a nerve. Did dead men have nerves?

I stood carefully, looking for something, anything I could use as a weapon. "You meant for me to die, didn't you Dad? That's why you locked me in every night. Why you nailed my window shut. You couldn't stand what I was, but more than that, you couldn't stand what *you* were. But you burned instead. And you killed my brother, you fucking bastard."

"Not me, little Rosie. It was you."

"Fuck you, Dad. It was you. If you hadn't done what you did, Andy would never have had to come back for me. Did you really expect him to just leave me to burn? That wasn't who he was." I was searching frantically, but there was only thin furniture—a wooden dresser, a nightstand. The bed was too heavy to lift. I realized I was in Andy's room, not mine, which explained why I'd been able to lock the door from this side.

"You're so sure it wasn't you? You don't even know how it works. You never did. You didn't even realize you were calling them to you—the dead. You were the one that brought them."

"I didn't set the fire, and I didn't kill Andy."

What was that light? There, in the far corner of the room, a soft glow. Too steady to be a flame, so what? I edged towards it, afraid of what I would find, until I heard the music.

My music. That nameless tune that had followed me for years, had shown up to soothe me when I was in danger, or frightened, or at risk of letting my temper get the better of me. The music no one else ever heard, and despite its maddening familiarity, I'd never been able to place.

Until now.

"Andy," I said, stepping up to the light.

He turned and smiled at me. He was in front of the old stand-up desk he'd used for his homework and projects when we were kids. There was a small lamp burning, and next to it, an old radio, the one he'd found in a junk shop ages ago. Dad never wanted us to have televisions or radios, but Andy had hidden it, fixed it himself. He'd taken it apart and put it back together and when he did, it worked. Not well—its range was minimal, only picking up one static-filled station. But on the nights that I'd woken, terrified by something stalking me in the shadows, on the nights when I could get to his room, my brother had played that radio for me. He'd turned it up as loud as he dared while the station played old dance music, jazz songs from another era, and I'd used it to drown out the Whispers, to push them back and keep them out of my head. My music had reminded me of Andy because it was *his* music, the songs he'd played for me.

"Radioman," I said, a laugh of joy catching in my throat. "It *was* you. All this time, you've been there, keeping me safe."

He pushed a shock of blond hair out of his eyes, smiled a crooked smile. "Of course, kiddo. Where else would I be?"

"It was you in Sam's cellar that night? You're the man Tommy saw?"

He just smiled back, watching me.

I stepped closer, reached out hesitantly to touch his shoulder. He felt solid. Tears welled, and I let them fall. "I thought..."

"You thought what, dork?"

I shook my head. "I thought you might be mad. Because...I'm the reason you died. I was afraid, maybe you had suffered—were still suffering." I remembered that creature, lurking and waiting for me in the basement of the house on Union. Of course that hadn't been Andy—how could I have ever thought he'd be so angry at me? It had been an illusion, or an imposter, I didn't know which, meant to send me where Dad had wanted me.

Andy shook his head and gave a sigh. "My little sis. I always said I got the brains of the family, and you got the beauty." He opened his arms, and I stepped into them, wondering how I ever could have doubted my big brother.

CHAPTER TWENTY-THREE

Sam stopped once to wipe blood from his fingers on his jeans, drying them as best he could to get better purchase on the hinge of the door he was working. Though he couldn't see the source, there seemed to be a dim light now in their subterranean prison.

Sam was back at the top of the staircase, guided by the same voice that had wakened him, a voice that in some indefinable way reminded him of Rose, of her speech patterns and inflections. The voice had left him some time ago, with a warning to keep going no matter what he heard, words that chilled Sam.

Although locked as he had expected, the door had been hung backward, with the hinges on his side of the frame. They were old and stuck fast with years of accumulated rust and grime, but patience and the use of his shirt to help grip had rewarded him. The first pin, lowest to the ground, was already out, and the second was finally starting to move. Sam's fingertips were cut to shit despite the protection of the cloth, and sweat dripped freely from his face, but his head was clearer with a task to concentrate on.

"I don't hear any singing," he called over his shoulder.

Lily was sitting on the stairs a few feet away. She had wakened groggily at some point, but Tommy remained comatose in the darkness, his breathing steady but slow. At first Lily had seemed inclined to cry, but figuring that having something to do would keep her mind off her fear, Sam tasked her with watching over her brother and singing songs to keep him motivated. It was something Rose had done with her when they were first teaching her to pick up her room. When Lily had started tremulously with the first verse of "Rain," Rose's favorite Patty Griffin song, Sam had to bite his lip and blink back tears.

She's not gone, he told himself. She's fine, and Luke's just helping her. I'll get the chance to make it right.

Sam attacked the hinge with renewed vigor, ignoring the burning pain of his cut fingers. "Lily? Come on, honey. Dad needs some motivation."

"I'm tired, Daddy."

"I am too, baby girl, but I'm still working. That's why I need you to sing to me, so I don't fall asleep." Sam also figured if he could hear her, he would know she and Tommy were all right. They were within easy reach, but the stirrings he'd heard before were getting louder, and there were times he thought he could make out voices.

He fought back a wave of panic as the noises grew louder. So far he hadn't heard anything on the stairs, and he clung to an irrational hope that the steps were some kind of home base, a ghost-free zone where none of the creepies could get them. He heard Lily whimper behind him.

"C'mon, Lily, Dad's gettin' tired. Sing for me now. Sing for your brother."

"I don't know any more songs, Daddy," she said in a small voice.

Sam bit off a curse as his hand slipped and the edge of the rusted pin sliced into his wrist. He took a breath and tried again. "I know your Mom taught you more songs than that. She sang to you every day, even when she wasn't home, remember? She sang to you on the phone. Just think of one—it's okay if you don't know all the words, just make 'em up like she used to, remember?"

There was a long silence before he heard Lily's wavering soprano.

"*Red is the rose…that in yonder garden grows.*"

Sam stopped to listen as his daughter sang a song she'd learned not from Rose, but from him.

She faltered on some of the less familiar words, then found her stride again. "*Come over the hills, my bonny Irish lass.*"

"*Come over the hills to your darling,*" Sam whispered with her. It was the song he had sung for Rose on their second date, an old Irish tune to make her fall in love, one he'd learned from his father. It had worked, and Sam had kept it for her ever since. He'd sung it to her when they were alone, and she'd never seemed to notice that he was tone deaf, or that it was a cheesy thing to do—she'd just smile and lay her head on his shoulder and listen. He couldn't remember the last time he'd sung it. Lyrics that spoke achingly of lost love had taken on a different meaning, once Rose was gone.

Lily was stumbling through the last verse when Sam finally pulled the second hinge free. The kids always remembered this part best, and Lily's voice swelled as he stood to tackle the final pin standing between his family and freedom, the singing drowning out the stirrings from below.

"*'Tis all for the loss of my bonny Irish lass, that my heart is breaking forever.*"

The last hinge was coming easier, despite the uncomfortable angle. Sam had nearly worked it loose, when his nostrils were filled with the acrid, unmistakable smell of smoke.

CHAPTER TWENTY-FOUR

"Hey, sis."

"Yeah?" I said.

"It's not over, you know."

I lifted my head and stepped back. "I know."

My brother looked down at me. "You need to know something. Sam and the kids, they're here. In the cellar."

I pushed away from him. "What? Oh, Jesus, here with that *creature*?"

Andy clasped my hands between his own. "It's okay. They're okay. Sam's nearly got them out. You'll need to find them and get them out of the house first. Things are about to get bad down there."

I nodded, quashing the panic. I needed to act, not give in to fear. "Yes."

"Are you ready?"

My hands began to tremble in his. I knew what he was talking about; letting the Whispers in. Letting them possess me, take me over. Stop being Rose, and become whatever they wanted me to be. "You're sure it's the only way? Isn't that what they brought me here for—Dad and Charlie?"

He nodded. "It's not going to work out like they want it to. Not if you do it your way. Nothing else will stop him. Nothing else will kill him, for good, and restore the balance." He smiled, but it was sad, and I knew he was afraid for me. "You have to be brave now, Rose, for your children."

"Okay." I looked up at him. "Will it hurt?"

"I don't know, sis. Could it possibly be worse than losing Tommy and Lily?"

I straightened, made fists of my hands at my sides to keep them from shaking. "You're right, it doesn't matter. I'm—I'm ready." I took a breath, looked up at him.

"Good." My brother's ghost took me by the shoulders, looked into my eyes intently. "Remember who you are, Rose. Remember so you can come back, okay? Don't get lost out there."

I took a breath, let it out slowly. "Okay."

I closed my eyes, because it seemed like the right way to start. I had no idea what I was doing, and thought it might be hard to get them to come to me.

I needn't have worried.

They had been there all along, a constant presence. Hovering, waiting, wishing—I'd held them off for so long, I didn't even notice them anymore. I'd been strong enough to hold them off all these years, but now I was letting go. Now I was letting them in.

At first there was a rush of sound and breath, as I'd come to expect. A hundred thousand voices speaking at once, trying to be heard. It felt like chaos had surrounded me, was trying to drag me under. The air changed, became cold and heavy, impossible to breathe. I choked, gasped, fought for air. I looked for Andy, but he was gone, lost to the whirling maelstrom of the Whispers.

I began to see them, as I had only once before in my life. That had been a stolen glimpse, a sliver of a suggestion. This was all of them at once, headed straight for me. Ancient winged things, with barely human faces. Leathery-skinned and dark, they flew at me, eyes black as pitch, all claws and dark toothy mouths. I felt the tug and tear of them as they took me over, clawed their way inside my body, my head, my soul. It was agony not to fight back, to give myself over to it, but as soon as it had begun, it was over.

Silence now, deeper and darker than any I had known. I looked around the empty bedroom, unable to believe the pain had ended, my breath returning to normal, my heartbeat steadying. There was only ash where the furniture had been, and the wall that had separated Andy's room from mine was falling to bits. Through the gaps I could see the charred and rusted metal bed frame where I'd slept for all my long childhood, and the circle of blackened wood beneath it, where the fire had started. I turned my back on it. My quarry wasn't there.

I lifted my hands and looked at them, wondering if I'd still have any control over my body. I had feared being pushed to a corner of my own mind, a prisoner, unable to act, but that didn't seem to be the case. My arms obeyed, and I saw my gnarled, scarred hands returned.

Good. I wanted to be Rose McFarland, not Rose Summers, for what I needed to do next.

Andy had gone, but I could hear my father moving around in the main part of the house. I realized I could see him, too—he was out in the parlor, trailing a thin line of flame behind him, headed for the kitchen in the back of the house.

I could see through walls now?

No, it wasn't that. It was the Whispers—I had their consciousness. Some of them were in here, with me, but others still whirled outside, watching. I saw them now, felt their anger, intense and throbbing, a low ache. They hated him more than I did. What he'd done was an abomination—twisted the role of the Guardians, imprisoned the Whispers, tried to shut them out. No one could control the Whispers. The power to contain them hadn't existed on this earth since the day Bella Summers made her bargain. I saw it through the Whispers. I saw their prison, deep in the earth, and I felt their joy when their power was released, when they joined the living once again, to guide the wandering dead.

Go now, they said, so I did. I opened the door onto the dark hallway. I was coming for Paul.

CHAPTER TWENTY-FIVE

Sam felt the heat rush forward as he stepped through the door. Smoke filled the narrow space and made the darkness all the more disorienting. He leaned against a counter to adjust the weight of Tommy on his hip and move Lily's clasped arms away from his throat. Lily whimpered as the heat and smell of smoke reached her through the muffling barrier of his torn, wet shirt.

As soon as he'd smelled smoke on the stairwell, Sam had fashioned makeshift masks for the kids from the halves of his shirt. Finding a patch of standing water at the base of the steps, he had soaked both before draping them loosely around Tommy's head, then Lily's, then used what little water was left to damp their clothes and the bottoms of his own jeans.

Tommy had woken unexpectedly as Sam gathered him up. The boy began coughing, and seemed to remember nothing of what had happened before he fell unconscious, but Sam had little time to rejoice in his son's recovery.

Now he stumbled from the cellar carrying both kids, hoping the restless ghosts wouldn't follow as he searched for a way out. Fire climbed the walls, up the remnants of cabinets and countertops, crawling across the floor of what had once been a kitchen. This place had burned before, and Sam had a good idea of where he was. Not that the information helped—he'd never been here.

There was no door to the outside in the kitchen, and between Sam and the rest of the house was a wall of flame, growing higher. He thought someone was standing on the other side, watching him, but as quick as he saw it, the shadow was gone. He thought uneasily of the creature that had brought them here, but he had to get through the fire first.

"Guys, lift your feet up. Pull your legs up closer and hold them there, okay?"

Tommy and Lily clambered up his body as best they could. Sam took a deep breath, then succumbed to a coughing fit as his lungs filled with smoke. Moving blindly, he turned into a dark hallway along the back of the house, and smashed into someone coming the other way.

"Rose?" Sam said as she grabbed his arms to steady him. Elation made him feel giddy; he laughed and wished he could hold her, but his arms were full of kids. "You're here."

"Shh," she whispered, pressing a finger to his lips.

"Mommy?"

Rose put her arms around all three of them. "Hush, guys. Mom's here. I need you to be quiet, okay?"

Sam looked at her, torn between relief and unease. It was Rose, certainly, but there was something off about her. "Rose, did you see? Tommy's awake—isn't that incredible?"

She looked at him, her eyes calm and depthless. "Yes, I know. We let him go."

"We? What the hell—"

She turned to the kids. "Dad's going to take you somewhere safe now, okay?"

"Rose, no, we all need to get out of here. I don't know if we can get to the front door—are there ground floor windows?"

She gestured back the way she had come. "There are two bedrooms back there. Take them to the first one on the right. The window's still blocked on the other."

"You have to come with us—I can't leave you here."

She shook her head. "There's something I have to do."

As Sam watched, something stirred behind those eyes. The flesh of her face seemed to ripple, and then it was Rose, and only Rose, looking at him.

She kissed him once, hard, then pushed him away. "Get them out, Sam. Don't come back, no matter what you hear, no matter what you see. Get them out and as far away as possible."

"Rose, no—"

"Go, damn it." She turned her back on him, and was gone.

Sam stared after her, arms and shoulders aching, Lily and Tommy getting heavier by the second. Finally he turned and staggered down the hall, to a room that opened off to the right. The first door, like Rose had told him. The room beyond was empty, save for the detritus left behind from the first fire: blackened furniture, crumbling into ash, and unidentifiable hunks of twisted metal, things that might once have been bed springs. In the far corner, a sagging stand-up desk with a melted globule on top—the remains of an old radio.

Sam set the kids down. They both reached up and pulled the wet cloth from their faces, blinking in the darkness.

"Where are we, Daddy? Where'd Mom go?"

"We're safe, honey. Mom had to go take care of something, but she'll be back."

"She's not safe, Daddy, we have to help her. She's not alone." This from Tommy, his little face solemn but scared.

"I know, buddy. I know she's not."

Sam looked around the room, saw a narrow window several feet off the ground on the far wall. The glass had been broken, but jagged shards remained in the blackened frame. He wrapped the halves of his shirt around his elbow and told the kids to cover their eyes, then smashed the rest of the glass out.

The crash seemed impossibly loud. Sam held his breath, listening. Nothing.

He cleared the broken glass as best he could. It was still dangerous, but he passed the kids over one at a time, careful to keep them away from the edges until they could step onto the sagging remains of an old back porch. Lily went first, then Sam handed Tommy through to her.

"Okay, Lily, hold Tommy's hand. I'm right behind you, but no matter what, you two stay together, got it?"

Lily's face was soot-stained, tear tracks running down her cheeks, her glasses smeared and sitting crookedly on her nose, but she only nodded and sniffled. She held Tommy's hand tightly, her other arm around her brother's shoulders. "Hurry, Daddy."

Sam squeezed carefully through the small window, cutting himself on the glass only once. He caught the inside of his right thigh and it tore through his jeans, slicing his skin open. He sucked in a breath to keep from cursing, and landed clumsily on the other side.

The air was much cooler out here. Sam looked around, then headed to the left side of the house, away from whatever trouble Rose had been walking into. He saw no one.

"Okay, guys," he whispered. "I want you to stay right here, at this corner of the house. If the fire looks like it's going to get to here, go out farther." He squinted into the darkness. "Go all the way out to the treeline, you see it? Wait for me there. Stay quiet, even if you see somebody. Only come out for your mother or me, you understand?"

They both nodded, but tears welled in Lily's blue eyes. "Please, Daddy, don't go. I want to stay with you."

"I have to go back for your Mom, Lily. I'll come back, I promise. Keep your brother safe." Sam hugged them both, then hurried back to the window.

He knelt beneath the sill, peering into the dark room. The door to the hallway was shut, just as he'd left it. Things were quiet, and the fire hadn't reached it yet. The porch sat low, so it was harder climbing back in, his shoe getting stuck on a shard of glass. He fell hard, whacking into the hardwood floor and cracking his forehead. He rolled to his back, pressing a hand against the wound and trying not to cuss.

It was as he was lying there, getting his breath back and looking at the room upside down, that he heard a crash from out in the main part of the house.

Sam scrambled to his feet, wheezing. He reached the bedroom door and pushed it open, peering into the dark and smoky hallway.

His heart stopped. The house was engulfed in flame—the remains of the upper story had collapsed into the front parlor. No one could have lived through that, he thought numbly.

Then something was moving out there, pushing aside the burning lumber and striding through fire without flinching.

Sam held his breath, hoping like hell it would be Rose.

"*Sam...*" came a guttural nightmare voice as a blackened shape lurched into view.

CHAPTER TWENTY-SIX

The parlor was living flame. It climbed the walls and up the stairs, made its way into the kitchen and across what remained of the cabinets. The wood was dry, the structure of the house weakened, and it provided ample kindling.

I stepped out of the hall and over fire. There was a rumbling crack, and I looked up to see one of the heavy wooden ceiling beams crash down. It landed in a shower of sparks and smoke, blocking the way back, and any chance for Sam to come charging to my rescue. That was just fine. I wanted Sam well out of this, and I had no expectation of leaving this place alive. It didn't work that way.

The heat was growing intense and I felt my scarred flesh tighten, beginning to itch. There was no sign of Paul Summers or Charlie Akers. I didn't think they were gone, though. My father, at least, would want to see this through.

Where?

I felt the clutch of talons on my neck, turning my head to the left. I saw the gaping entrance to the cellar, the door off the hinges and lying to one side, already burning.

Of course. The haunted cellar of my childhood, last bastion for nightmares. I walked through fire and the Whispers walked with me, clearing a path. Leathery wings flapped beside me, claws and teeth prickling at my insides as they stirred.

I stepped over the threshold and down the stairs to the place where I'd spent so much of my childhood, crouching and hiding from the phantoms I didn't understand. It should have been terrifying; this cellar had lived in my nightmares for most of my life. I was seeing it with new eyes now.

It was a highway. Teeming with activity, souls moving back and forth through a shining gap that was hard to look at. Many on this side of the divide were lined up for their turn to cross over, and many more were passing back through to earth. It was an endless stream of dead-eyed shades, filing past me only to fade from sight as they reached the far wall of the cellar. Sam and the kids had been trapped down here with all of this? Something must have protected them from the brunt of it, and I smiled, knowing my big brother was still looking out for me and the ones I loved.

The gazes of the ghosts seemed to pass through me, and I hoped it stayed that way. I had known from a young age how bad it was to catch the attention of a wandering spirit. I never again wanted to feel those empty eyes fixated on me, wanting.

Even in a cellar packed with corpses, my father was easy to find. He stood near the head of the line on this side, unnoticed by the dead. Even now, he looked different—more substantial, his cooked flesh standing out in more detail than these faded specters. He was watching me, grinning. Or maybe that was his default expression, now that so much of his face was gone.

"What now, Dad?" I called across the divide. "What's the last chapter? You've got me here. What the hell do you want? What was the point of all this?"

"*To take it back, little Rosebud. It's time to give it back to me.*"

"Give what back? What have I got that you want?"

"*Your life, Rose. I want your life.*"

He gestured at the gap behind him, at the roads from the other side that led to this cellar. Because of me. The Whispers, the ghosts, they'd all followed me here when I was a child. As soon as the Guardian's abilities began to manifest in me, that was when they were called to my side. The wandering dead, because I was their beacon, their only way home. The Whispers because I was their tool, their focal point. They'd all gathered here, around a scared little girl. That was why, when my father had burned to death eighteen years ago, he'd been able to stay right here, waiting for me. Even then, the boundaries were weak, allowing him to stay on in this haunted place, getting stronger.

"I don't understand. What good's it going to do you to kill me? You're already dead. You can't come back. What does it matter?"

A subtle shift in the dim light, the feel of air moving across my face, made me look around. The dead were beginning to notice, to see me. To watch.

"*Your death will give me back the power of the Guardians, what is right-fully mine. You took it from me.*"

"Guardians have to be alive, Dad, or did you miss that part of the lesson? It won't do you any good dead."

"*Oh, you're wrong about that, Rosebud. I've learned so much since pass-ing. So much by hanging around here, watching what came through. Things you couldn't imagine. Once the power is mine again, there's no limit to what I can accomplish.*"

Could he be right? Had Paul Summers learned something that would let him transcend the barriers of life and death? I didn't think so, but what the hell did I know?

"What if you're wrong? Then you've murdered your own child for nothing. What about that?"

He was next to me in an instant, though I never saw him move. He leaned in, his noseless face pressed close to mine, his rotted breath stirring my hair.

"*It would still be worth it, Rose. Your line is an abomination—it should never have been. It would be worth it to snuff you out for good. I'll do the best I can by Tommy, but if he can't be trained, then I'll kill him too.*"

I felt a hot flash of fury, the kind that had so often led to me mak-ing rash decisions. As soon as it came something reeled it in, choked it back: a sharper scratch of those claws and teeth.

"You won't get Tommy, Dad. Do whatever you want to me, but my kids are safe. You'll never touch them."

"You stupid bitch. You really don't get it, do you? Your precious son isn't safe at the hospital—I had him taken. Your brother brought me your daughter and your ex-husband, but he gave Tommy to your mother to take back to the mountain. She'll keep him there for me, Rose. He needs supervision, training, to control what he'll become."

I smiled. "Mom's dead, Dad. Didn't you know? She burned to death this morning. Tommy's safe with Sam—they got away. Charlie didn't bring Tommy to Mom, he brought him here. Now they're all gone."

He went still. *"It's not true."*

"It is, Dad. Looks like your protégé didn't follow your instructions. All those years of being the second-string kid, I don't think he was ready to give up his spot to my son."

His dead, dull eyes—those black shark's eyes that had stared at me without pity while I burned—flashed rage and I knew I was right. Charlie had always been in second place. God help him, he had loved my father in his twisted way, and in death they were closer than they'd ever been. Resurrection or not, he wasn't going to lose what he'd wanted for so long, so he'd planned for Tommy to die with the rest of us.

I threw a hand up. "Whatever the hell you've got planned, Dad, it's over. A fucking washout. I didn't come here because of you, however much you tried to manipulate me. Neal, Zack, Charlie—none of it mattered." I started to laugh, thinking of all those machinations, every twist and turn of Paul Summers' mind, just to get me where I was always destined to be. "Whatever you thought was going to happen is done. I'm here to finish this."

He was silent for so long I almost believed he was going to agree. Then he looked up, hate on his withered, shrunken face.

"It's not finished until you're dead, Rosie. You're going through that door, one way or another."

Before I could move, he lunged at me, grabbed hold of my wrist and began pulling me toward the door.

CHAPTER TWENTY-SEVEN

"Oh, fuck," said Sam.

The lurching corpse was grinning at him. Its lower jaw was missing, the top of its head blown off.

Rose's work, Sam thought with satisfaction, then ducked backward, scrabbling for the door to slam it closed. The frame was swollen and the door wedged tightly shut.

Did he have time to get back out the window? It was ticklish, getting his broad shoulders through the small opening, and he sure as hell didn't want that thing getting to him while he was wedged and helpless. Besides, Lily and Tommy were out there. If Sam headed back toward them, he'd lead this creeping horror right to his kids. He looked around the room, searching for anything that he could use as a weapon, but everything had been reduced to ash and crumbling wood by flame and time.

Smoke curled under the door, and it was getting hard to breathe. Sam knew he only had minutes before the fire reached him, but he was out of ideas. He'd noticed a small closet tucked in the far corner. There was no door, but the space would provide a certain amount of concealment. He knew hiding would only gain him a couple of minutes at most, but it was all he had left.

Seconds later, the bedroom door flung open. Smoke rolled into the room and flames crept down the hallway, an eerie backlight to the figure in the doorway. Sam held his breath.

The dead thing passed him by without a glance, but Sam's relief was short-lived. The corpse was headed for the window, making a horrible snuffling sound that made Sam think of a bloodhound. When it stopped at the frame and leaned out, Sam realized that was exactly what it was doing: following the scent of his children. He remembered too late about Rose's newfound ability to "feel" the signatures of Lily and Tommy—it looked like this thing could, too.

When it poked its head through to the outside, Sam took a deep breath, then lunged into view, yelling at the top of his lungs.

"Over here, you fucking creep—I'm right here, come and get me."

The thing pulled back into the room and turned to face him, purple tongue lolling in what might have been a grin. "*This only ends one way, Sam.*"

"Uh." Sam hadn't thought his plan through any further than drawing the dead thing's attention away from the window and his kids. He had nothing in hand, nothing to fend off the creature that was dragging itself toward him. He stumbled back two paces, but it moved too fast.

It was on him in a second, its gaping, jawless mouth pressed up next to his face. Sam squeezed his eyes shut, turning his head away from the stench of rot. He prepared himself to die, and wished he could have done so knowing Rose was okay.

His vision was getting fuzzy, tunneling into blackness. The last thing he saw was the shadow reaching for him, then all was dark.

CHAPTER TWENTY-EIGHT

The dead had noticed me. They reached out as my father dragged me past, their cold hands feather-light as they brushed my face, my hair, the flesh of my throat. What they wanted, I couldn't tell, but my father's goal was frighteningly clear. I was going through the door, the passage to the other side, one way or another.

I fought against him, scrabbling for purchase on the earthen floor, clawing at the rotted flesh of his arm, but he wasn't letting go. The dead moved aside for us to pass, and I saw with stark clarity what awaited me over there.

Oceans of the dead. As far as I could see, an endless, teeming stream of ghosts, pressing forward, reaching, wanting. What would happen to me if I passed through the veil without physically dying first? Would I enter that place as a living person, a beacon in the land of the dead? Or would the simple act of crossing over the threshold kill me? And which would be worse?

A voice, stronger than the rest, penetrated the chaos. It was Bella

Summers, standing with the legions of the dead in that cold cellar.

Let them take you over, Rose. This is the time—let them do their work.

I became aware, then, of the insistent draw of the Whispers. They were passengers no more, pushing to the forefront of my thoughts, wanting control. It was terrifying, like standing on the edge of a precipice, and being asked to close your eyes and fall. But if I didn't, Paul Summers would get what he wanted.

I closed my eyes and fell.

What happened next, I saw through a thousand eyes at once.

My father must have felt the change. He let me go and turned to face me—face the Whispers—with fear in his dead eyes. It filled me with heady pleasure, seeing that. I settled back into a dark corner of my mind to watch.

I could see them, the Whispers. They were in me, they were all around me, and they were everywhere at once. They were a thousand voices all together. Old, older than the earth, with such power at their disposal. Their noise began, blending and rising quickly. Dark bodies rushed the air, sharp claws and teeth. They came for my father.

Paul Summers put his hands where his ears used to be, a futile attempt to shut them out. But the Whispers would not be denied. He lifted his arms against them, trying to fight them off as they darted at his face, taking little nips of his desiccated flesh. He hadn't felt a thing when I'd clawed at him, but he felt the Whispers—he was screaming.

There was a crack of thunder, impossibly loud, and the surrounding dead began to back away from the gap. I looked through my eyes, and the eyes of the Whispers, and I saw that another door had opened, far on the horizon of the other side. The ghosts turned away, afraid to look into the evil light that shone there, but I was fascinated. With the Whispers inside me, I understood that I was seeing hell—their hell, from whence they had sprung in a time unrecorded and unremembered, in dark and heat and pressure. It was where they'd been trapped, cut off from humanity until Bella Summers sought their aid.

My father saw it too, and understood. His screams of pain were nothing compared to the animal roar of pure terror he emitted now, knowing where he was bound. He tried to run. Tried to shove me aside, to pass through the hordes of spirits that had stopped there in the cellar, but they would not move, and he could not pass.

They picked him up, the Whispers did. Vengeful winged creatures now, they plucked him up effortlessly, and off he went toward the gap, toward the hell on the horizon.

He screamed my name at the last, no doubt begging for mercy.

I watched, and I smiled.

* * *

I had no memory of getting outside. Though the whole house was now engulfed,   I hadn't sustained any further fire damage. I was standing in back, waiting to see what else might follow me out, but there was nothing.

Paul Summers was well and truly gone, I was sure of that. If the balance had been restored, then I supposed all the other things that had been crossing over might have gone home too. I hoped so, but it caused me a pang when I thought of Andy, and of Aaron. With Andy at least, I'd been given a gift. Now that I knew he'd been with me all along, that he'd never stopped looking out for me, it was like I'd been given back part of what I'd lost.

"Mom!"

I turned away from the fire and smiled so hard it hurt my scorched face. Lily and Tommy were pelting across the dry grass, Tommy's chubby legs working overtime to keep up. They nearly knocked me over, but I caught myself and hugged them both to me, breathing them in. Trying not to think of how sure I'd been, only an hour ago, that I'd never see my kids again.

"You're okay, both of you? Tommy, you're all right?" I knelt to look in my son's bright green eyes. He stared back at me solemnly, searching my face, his little brow wrinkled.

"Is anybody hurt?"

Lily stepped back and shook her head, pushing her crooked glasses up her nose with the back of one dirty hand. "We're okay, Mom. We just stink like smoke. Tommy woke up when we were in the cellar, and then Daddy got us out of the fire."

"Where's Dad, Lily?"

"He went back in the window—he went to look for you. Didn't he find you? I thought he got you out, too."

I stood and turned back to the burning house, staring hopelessly at the flames that had by now claimed the entire house. There was no chance that anyone left inside would make it back out. "Damn it, Sam," I said softly. "You never do listen."

"You know, you're a hard woman to please, Rose McFarland."

"*Daddy!*"

I turned and there stood Sam, smiling his crooked smile, the kids clinging to his legs. He was soot-stained and red-faced from the fire, missing his shirt, the ends of his hair crispy and his forearms cut to shit. I thought he'd never looked better, and I told him so when he leaned in to kiss me.

He traced his thumb lightly down the scar on my neck and kissed me again. "You've got weird taste, Rose."

"You're one to talk, McFarland."

"Where were you, Rose? I couldn't find you in there."

"The cellar." I couldn't stop a shudder running through my body. Sam put his arms around me. "Why'd you go back in, Sam? I told you not to. What if you hadn't made it out?"

"Dumb question, Rose. I went in after you once the kids were safe." He took my face in his hands and looked down at me. "I'm never leaving you alone again. No more of this Lone Ranger shit, babe."

I smiled up at him. "All right Tonto, have it your way."

"Did you do it? Did you—are they gone? Charlie and your dad? The ghosts?"

"Charlie and Dad, yes. At least I think Charlie—I closed the door and sent Paul back. I didn't see Charlie."

Sam grimaced. "I did. He just about had me—then he was gone."

"Jesus, Sam, I'm so fucking sorry. I never wanted this shit to come so close to you, or them." I nodded at Lily and Tommy, sitting cross-legged in the grass together several feet away, watching the fire with big eyes.

"It's not your fault. It never was. You need to quit carrying this burden, okay? Whatever comes, we're going to face it as a family." He

306

took a breath, dropped his hands to gather mine. "Can you forgive me, Rose?"

"For what?"

"For what I said to you, in the hospital. For what I did, sending you away. You were right, Charlie Akers was there all along. You weren't crazy, and what I said to you…"

Though the memory of his words still stung, I pushed them away. "I held a gun on our child, Sam. You did the right thing. Paul…my father, he wanted me to doubt myself, to hate myself. What better way than to make me hurt my son? How were you supposed to react?"

"But it wasn't your fault, babe, and I made it sound like—I didn't mean it, what I said. I've always known you were a good mother, a good person."

I smiled tremulously. "If anyone in this world can understand a person losing their temper, I'd say it's me."

He was still looking at me, searching my face and eyes the same way Tommy had. "What about the Whispers, Rose? Are they gone?"

"I think so, Sam. I think I did what I was supposed to, and restored the balance. They're back where they belong." Even as I said it, I wondered. I had never felt the Whispers leave me. What if they were still there, crouching, waiting to take control again?

There was a huge cracking noise, and we looked just in time to see the house cave in on itself in a shower of sparks and glowing embers. Lily and Tommy cheered, clapping their hands and yelling. "Take that, creepy crawlers!"

The early morning dew kept the fire from spreading any further, so we stood and watched it for a while. The county fire department this far out was volunteer, and there wasn't much for them to do anyway. I wanted to see the place gone, see the last traces of the Summers family swallowed and forgotten.

And though I didn't say so to Sam, I wanted to make sure nothing got out.

EPILOGUE

I sat on the steps of the broad wooden porch, huddled in a thick gray cardigan against the early morning chill that told me fall was finally coming. I looked out at William's acres, at the trees just starting to turn, watching for a car.

There was a coffee cup next to me, but I'd let it go cold, too nervous to put anything in my stomach. I wondered if I was doing the right thing. It was too late now, in any case. I'd set things in motion.

My heartbeat kicked up a notch when I heard gravel crunching down the drive as someone turned in from the highway. I relaxed when a black pickup truck bounced into view. It stopped a few feet away, and I stood as Luke eased himself out. I knew better than to offer any help, so I just watched while he limped up the drive, leaning heavily on a dark walnut cane William had carved for him from his hospital bed. The two of them had spent much of their recuperation time together, and were now fast friends.

Luke was moving slowly, but I was glad to see his skin returning to a healthy ruddy shade instead of the sickly gray it had been. His recovery had been a slow process, but he was much happier now that he could get around on his own. He hated being dependent on anyone, a sentiment I understood.

That Luke was living and breathing at all was a miracle beyond my understanding. When I'd said goodbye outside the farmhouse, I was afraid I'd never see him again. Though Zack's blade had missed his lung, Luke had been losing blood fast, too fast to last until help arrived. We only spoke of it once. While he was recovering in the hospital, I came to see him.

He'd smiled when I came through the door, pushing himself up on his pillows, his face sallow and his breath labored. "Rose McFarland, as I live and breathe. I was starting to think you'd forgotten all about me."

I smiled back and brushed tears away with the back of my hand. "I was here before, but all you would do was lie there, so I got bored and left."

He chuckled at that and took my hand in his. I clutched it and looked at him. "I'm sorry, Luke. I'm so fucking sorry that I didn't believe you."

Luke ran a thumb across my cheek. "You stop that, Rose. Neal lied to you, and he manipulated all of us. Granted, it was a ditzy move, trusting him over me, but you're a natural blonde, after all. I've grown to expect it out of you."

He told me about killing Neal, about Neal's instructions to ensure I didn't make it out of the house alive. He told me he'd been sure he was dying.

"I don't know what it was, Rose, but I think—when you touched me, looked at the wound and then sat with me, I felt better. I think you healed me somehow."

I shook my head, started to speak, but he put a hand up.

"I know what you're gonna say, but Rose, it ain't just me. The surgeon, he didn't get it either. He said the wound was sealed right up to the edges of the blade, all the way around. He said that was what saved me—it didn't let any air in, so the lung didn't collapse." He reached up to untie the top of his hospital gown and showed me the bandage. "Lookit here. See how small this is? And the edges are all smooth and everything. I think you did that."

I looked down so I wouldn't have to meet his gaze. "Put your clothes back on, Harris. You're teasing the nurses."

He grinned and complied, but reached for my hand when he was done. "It's not so crazy, is it? Not after everything else that happened."

I shook my head. "I'm not a healer, Luke. I'm a killer."

"What's to stop you from being both?" he countered, and I didn't have an answer.

If Luke's healing had been my doing, I'd left it incomplete. He still had a long road to recovery, and it was likely he'd never be back to full strength. He'd taken early retirement from the security company and begun drawing from his sheriff's office pension. He'd sold the house his dad had left him and planned to do something he never had in all his years—travel.

When he got close enough, he pulled me in for a tight hug and a kiss on my cheek, one that was almost, but not completely, platonic. He stood back and smiled, one hand held out to the side. "Well?"

"You're looking good, Luke—you're getting around pretty well with that thing." I nodded to the cane and he grimaced.

"It's the only thing that's ever made me feel as old as I really am. Can't wait to ditch it."

"You'd better at least take it with you. You're bound to get tired driving all day."

"Oh, I'll bring it. But I'm tossing it back in the truck at the first sign of a good-looking woman."

I grinned. "Fair enough." I looked back at his truck. "So you're all packed up?"

"Yep. Ready to hit the road. Couldn't leave without seeing you, though, and I wanted to wish you luck. Today's the day, right?"

My stomach did another flip, and I looked back down the drive.

"Want me to wait with you?"

I smiled. "Actually, that would be great. Keep me from worrying myself to death. I'll get you some coffee."

I poked my head into Lily's new bedroom on my way to the kitchen, hearing a low-voiced squabble between her and Tommy. They were in the middle of the floor with markers and poster board, Tommy patiently coloring at Lily's precise instruction.

Shades of Sam in his daughter, I thought with a smile, and left them to it.

Luke had eased himself down on the steps by the time I got back. He asked me about the renovations we'd been working on now that we'd moved out here to Millington, and I made him laugh with a few stories about learning to farm over the summer.

William was still recovering from his gunshot wound, and with regular physical therapy it didn't make sense for him to be so far out of town. He hadn't wanted the farm to be abandoned, so after a few weeks of Sam and me taking turns caring for the house and the dogs, William had asked us to take it over.

We'd fought him on it. I didn't want to take away what I'd always thought of as his solace, but he'd finally convinced us; eighty acres was simply getting to be too much for him to care for alone, and he liked the idea of Sam and me and the kids out there, making the most of it. Besides, he'd been staying with Joy in my place on Belvedere since getting out of the hospital, and I got the feeling he had a whole new source of happiness. I was waiting to see how Sam would react when he finally figured out his Mom was being courted by Aaron's father.

When we finally got back to Memphis on that endless morning back in June, we'd found Joy at William's hospital bed. She didn't have the slightest idea how she'd gotten there, or where she'd been in the interim. The last thing she remembered was waiting for the EMTs on her porch with Lily. She'd been unhurt and, once she knew the four of us were safe, completely placid. She told us about shooting Cora with no small satisfaction.

Not every ending had been happy. There'd been no miraculous healing for Zack Dayton—he'd stayed dead, with my bullets in his body. I'd expected to face consequences for that, and planned to make sure Anna Dayton never heard the truth. It was hard enough to lose her husband without knowing that he'd lost his mind in the last days of his life, that he'd been shot while trying to kill his friends. I still didn't understand what had happened to Zack. Had Paul Summers promised to give him his brother back? Had they showed him a twisted version of Matt to coerce him, like they'd tried with me and Andy? Had Zack been somehow possessed or controlled by Paul or Charlie, the same way I had been by the Whispers? I didn't think I'd ever know.

Luke had taken care of the legal ramifications by throwing the blame for Zack's death on Evan Neal. Neal already had a spotty record and a history of emotional instability. It hadn't taxed Luke's ingenuity too much to make Neal the all-around bad guy, and Zack a hero who'd paid with his life. Both of their bodies ended up burned too badly for anyone to question Luke's version of events, and he'd been the only one there. How those bodies had ended up in the fire was a question that seemed destined to remain unanswered.

Ethan Neal had finally woken from his coma right around the time Paul Summers was meeting his second, and hopefully final, end. Neal's son had no memory of his illness, or the events leading up to it. Luke told me Ethan had gone to live with his maternal grandmother, and I tried to be okay with it. I tried to remember that the Whispers weren't my responsibility, that I hadn't created Charlie Akers or my father, or set any of these events in motion. Guilt is a Southern skill, though; we've got it down to a fine art.

For myself, life was getting better all the time. Sam and I had remarried at the end of August in a courthouse ceremony with a minimum of fuss. My fire-drenched nightmares had receded, and nothing crept around the corners of the happy farmhouse in Millington. We'd gotten up the nerve to open up Sam's place on McLean, and even ventured into the cellar, but the house was empty of whatever had gotten hold of it. Tommy's bedroom was the only casualty, and Sam's insurance had covered the damage. He'd put the house on the market as soon as the repairs were finished, and already gotten several nibbles. It looked like it would go fast.

I kept a careful eye on Tommy, but for now, there was no more talk of Whispers or seeing gray people. Sometimes he watched dark corners in a way that reminded me unhappily of my own childhood, but if he was seeing something there, he wasn't saying. It bothered me that I didn't see what he did—if anything, I'd thought I would see more after letting the Whispers in. I wondered, too, if they were really gone. Sometimes Tommy looked at me in a troubling way, and even though I didn't sense them still inside me, every once in a while I felt a tremor. Sam promised to help me keep watch, both on Tommy and on myself, and I felt better knowing I wasn't alone, no matter what the future brought.

The sound of tires crunching on gravel told me the future had arrived, and I stood, trying to calm the butterflies in my stomach.

Luke struggled to his feet and put an arm around me, dropped a quick kiss on my cheek and said, "You'll be fine, McFarland. You're doing the right thing." He let me go and stepped away before the car came into sight.

"Kids," I hollered. "They're here, guys."

There was a thundering of feet—how on earth did two skinny little kids sound like a herd of stampeding bison, anyway?—and Lily and Tommy spilled out onto the front porch, a hand-lettered welcome sign held crookedly between them. They were grinning and hopping, and I hugged and kissed them both.

The little VW Jetta bumped into view and pulled in next to Luke's truck. Sam unfolded his long legs from the front seat and shot me a smile before heading around to the back. A short, pretty woman with dark red hair, stylish glasses, and a sweet smile climbed out of the driver's seat and gave me a wave.

I hurried down the drive to give the social worker a hug. She'd walked me through the entire adoption process, and we'd spent countless hours together over the past months. "Hey, Carla. Thanks a million for bringing them all the way out here."

She returned my embrace, stood back, and smiled again. "This is a good thing you're doing, Rose. Really. The best possible outcome for them, I'm sure of it."

My stomach doing backflips again, all I could do was give a nervous nod before following her to the back seat. She opened the door, and a little face looked up at me gravely from under shaggy blonde hair.

"Hi there, Abby," I said to Charlie Akers' daughter, kneeling down to work on getting her out of the car seat. I looked across to see that

Sam had already gotten Abby's brother Daniel out and was holding him on one hip, pointing out some of the farm sights to the little boy.

Abby came willingly enough, molding her little body to mine as I lifted her out of the car and Carla went around to the trunk for their tiny backpacks.

Sam and I smiled at each other across the roof of the car, then carried the newest members of our family up to the porch, where Lily was working herself into a fit of excitement.

"Hi, guys," she burst out as we climbed the steps. "We're so psyched you're here. You want to see your room? Or meet the dogs? Or you want a snack?"

I wondered if her jubilance would make the two quiet toddlers shy away, but they smiled and began to babble at their new sister, squirming to get down. We set them on the porch and they followed Lily and Tommy inside, headed for the kitchen.

"Don't let the dogs out until we get in there," yelled Sam, eliciting no response. He turned to me. "I'd better go after them."

I wrapped him in a quick, fierce hug. "Thank you, Sam. Just—thank you."

He kissed me. "You owe me, McFarland, and I'll be collecting later tonight."

Sam turned to shake Luke's hand before following the quartet inside. "No, Lily, don't pull that—"

A loud crash from inside made Luke, Carla, and I cringe, then burst out laughing.

"This is your new life, McFarland," said Luke, shaking his curly head. "I'll leave you to it before someone ropes me into babysitting."

I hugged him. "You're not getting off that easily, Harris. We know you'll be back for visits, and we'll plan our escapes accordingly."

He smiled, leaned down and kissed the side of my mouth, crushing me close. I let him do it because I knew he was saying goodbye—not to me, not for good. Just to us, to the idea of us, and I was glad. I wanted happiness for my best friend. I waved goodbye as he backed out of the driveway, and hoped the next time I saw him, there would be a good woman on his arm.

Carla pushed her glasses up her nose and made distressed sounds as she looked through the screen door. Sam could be heard trying to corral the kids, then there was another crash and a cacophony of barking as the three farm dogs made their escape.

"Oh dear," said Carla, looking at me. "I do hope it won't always be like this—I don't want you to regret taking them in."

I could have told her a lot of things—that these were my brother's kids, and that I'd helped make them orphans. That there was a good likelihood one or both of them could end up with the same visions Tommy and I had, and if so, I was their best chance for a normal childhood. That I wanted all of us to have the kind of family life I'd never had as a kid.

Instead I hugged my friend again, took the suitcases from her, and told her I'd be fine. Then I walked into my new home, following my husband into the fray, ready for whatever came next.

Laurel Hightower grew up in Kentucky, attending college
in California and Tennessee before returning home to horse
country, where she lives with her husband, son, and two rescue
animals. She works as a paralegal in a mid-sized firm, wrangling
litigators by day and writing at night. A bourbon and beer girl,
she's a fan of horror movies and true life ghost stories.
Whispers in the Dark is her first novel.

CPSIA information can be obtained
at www.ICGtesting.com
Printed in the USA
BVHW081421010719
552377BV00005B/219/P